Praise for th

**Miss Julia Rocks the Cradle**
"Charming [and] engrossing."                                          *ge*

**Miss Julia Renews Her Vows**
"Fans will have a ball."
—*Publishers Weekly*

**Miss Julia Delivers the Goods**
"A lighthearted page-turner to slip into the beach bag or to carry with us to a lawn chair in the garden when the sun is buzzing away high in the sky. . . Just grab this and devour it."                    —*Charleston City Paper*

"It's still early yet for beach reading, but a near-perfect candidate has already arrived. . . . Short of a return to Mayberry, Ross's version of small-town Tar Heels is hard to beat."                —*Wilmington Star News*

"Those who prefer a leisurely pace, a touch of screwball comedy, and gentle puzzles in their mysteries will enjoy this paean to small-town nosiness and steadfast loyalties."                        —*Publishers Weekly*

**Miss Julia Paints the Town**
"A fun confection where Miss Julia, in letting go of some of her own hidebound ideas and social prejudices, learns that her worst enemy may well be the guy she helped elect . . . and her best ally may be [one] she's always thought beneath her contempt. Yes, Miss Julia is back, and I, for one, am one happy camper."                                   —J. A. Jance

**Miss Julia Strikes Back**
"Fans will enjoy the change of pace and appreciate all the familiar elements that have made the series so popular."              —*Booklist*

**Miss Julia Stands Her Ground**
"Funny, feisty, frothy."                            —*Lexington Herald-Leader*

**Miss Julia's School of Beauty**
"It is impossible not to like irrepressible, perfectly proper Miss Julia."
—*The Roanoke Times*

**Miss Julia Meets Her Match**
"Funny and endearing . . . a merry romp that ends too soon."
—*The Dallas Morning News*

### Miss Julia Hits the Road

"Ann B. Ross and Miss Julia are fast becoming Southern classics. Readers eager for entertainment should tuck in their skirts, strap on a helmet, and hit the road with them."  —*Winston-Salem Journal*

### Miss Julia Throws a Wedding

"Good fun . . . lively entertainment perfectly suited for anyone who can relate to the thoroughgoing effort involved in keeping up appearances in such thoroughly tacky times." —*The State* (Columbia, South Carolina)

### Miss Julia Takes Over

"Imagine Aunt Bee from the *Andy Griffith Show* with a lot more backbone and confidence, and drop her smack in the middle of a humorous, rollicking plot akin to that of the movie *Smokey and the Bandit* and you have the tone and pace of Ross's entertaining second novel."  —*Publishers Weekly*

### Miss Julia Speaks Her Mind

"I absolutely loved this book! What a joy to read! Miss Julia is one of the most delightful characters to come along in years. Ann B. Ross has created what is sure to become a classic Southern comic novel. Hooray for *Miss Julia*, I could not have liked it more."  —Fannie Flagg

"In the tradition of Clyde Edgerton's Mattie Riggsbee or that quirky passenger Jessica Tandy brought to life in *Driving Miss Daisy*, Ann Ross has created another older Southern heroine in Julia Springer, who is—as Southerners say—outspoken, but by whom? A late-blooming feminist, Miss Julia is no shrinking violet in this comic plot that tweaks stuffy husbands, manipulative small-town neighbors, snoopy preachers, and general human greed, but ends by endorsing the love and vitality that energize Miss Julia's sharp tongue and warm heart."  —Doris Betts, author of *The Sharp Teeth of Love*

PENGUIN BOOKS

# MISS JULIA ROCKS THE CRADLE

Ann B. Ross holds a doctorate in English from the University of North Carolina at Chapel Hill and has taught literature at the University of North Carolina at Asheville. She is the author of the popular Miss Julia series and lives in Hendersonville, North Carolina.

# Miss Julia Rocks the Cradle

## ANN B. ROSS

PENGUIN BOOKS

PENGUIN BOOKS

Published by the Penguin Group
Penguin Group (USA) Inc., 375 Hudson Street, New York, New York 10014, U.S.A.
Penguin Group (Canada), 90 Eglinton Avenue East, Suite 700, Toronto,
Ontario, Canada M4P 2Y3 (a division of Pearson Penguin Canada Inc.)
Penguin Books Ltd, 80 Strand, London WC2R 0RL, England
Penguin Ireland, 25 St. Stephen's Green, Dublin 2, Ireland (a division of Penguin Books Ltd)
Penguin Books Australia Ltd, 250 Camberwell Road, Camberwell,
Victoria 3124, Australia (a division of Pearson Australia Group Pty Ltd)
Penguin Books India Pvt Ltd, 11 Community Centre,
Panchsheel Park, New Delhi – 110 017, India
Penguin Group (NZ), 67 Apollo Drive, Rosedale, Auckland 0632,
New Zealand (a division of Pearson New Zealand Ltd)
Penguin Books (South Africa) (Pty) Ltd, 24 Sturdee Avenue,
Rosebank, Johannesburg 2196, South Africa

Penguin Books Ltd, Registered Offices: 80 Strand, London WC2R 0RL, England

First published in the United States of America by Viking Penguin,
a member of Penguin Group (USA) Inc. 2011
Published in Penguin Books 2012

1  3  5  7  9  10  8  6  4  2

Copyright © Ann B. Ross, 2011
All rights reserved

Publisher's Note: This is a work of fiction. Names, characters, places, and incidents
either are the product of the author's imagination or are used fictitiously, and any
resemblance to actual persons, living or dead, business establishments, events,
or locales is entirely coincidental.

THE LIBRARY OF CONGRESS HAS CATALOGED THE HARDCOVER EDITION AS FOLLOWS:
Ross, Ann B.
Miss Julia rocks the cradle / Ann B. Ross.
p.  m.
ISBN 978-0-670-02255-7 (hc.)
ISBN 978-0-14-312043-8 (pbk.)
1. Springer, Julia (Fictitious character)—Fiction.
2. City and town life—North Carolina—Fiction.    I. Title.
PS3568.O84198M5696 2011
813'.54—dc22        2010048909

Printed in the United States of America
Set in Fairfield LH
Designed by Alissa Amell

Except in the United States of America, this book is sold subject to the condition
that it shall not, by way of trade or otherwise, be lent, resold, hired out, or otherwise
circulated without the publisher's prior consent in any form of binding or cover other
than that in which it is published and without a similar condition including
this condition being imposed on the subsequent purchaser.

The scanning, uploading, and distribution of this book via the Internet or via any other means
without the permission of the publisher is illegal and punishable by law. Please purchase only
authorized electronic editions and do not participate in or encourage electronic piracy
of copyrightable materials. Your support of the author's rights is appreciated.

ALWAYS LEARNING                                                    PEARSON

*This one is for all those who talk about, laugh with, share, recommend, buy, borrow, and read the Miss Julia books.*

Miss Julia Rocks the Cradle

# Chapter 1

*"Miss Julia, Miss Julia!"* The sound of Lloyd's voice bounced from one end of the house to the other as the back door slammed closed with a crash.

His feet pounded through the rooms downstairs, and with a lurch of my heart, I quickly threw aside my Christmas and New Year's thank-you notes for all the parties, dinners, and fruitcakes that had come our way, and hurried out on the landing.

Leaning over the railing, I called, "Up here, Lloyd! What's the matter?"

He raced up the stairs and came to a sudden stop, his tennie shoes screeching on the waxed floor. Breathing fast and hard, his face pale and his hair flying around his head, he caught his breath, gasping out, "Guess what just happened."

"I have no idea. Calm down, now, and tell me."

"Yes'm, I'm trying to." He took a deep breath, his eyes still big and wild looking. "You won't believe it, but it's all over school. Everybody's talking about it." He leaned closer and in a hoarse voice said, "They found a body in Miss Petty's outhouse."

"A *dead* one?"

"Yes, ma'am. Dead as a doornail."

"In her *outhouse*? I didn't know anybody had outhouses these days."

"Well, I guess it was more like a toolshed or something. Maybe an out*building,* like that. Anyway, we were in our social studies class—that's what Miss Petty teaches—and she was asking us questions about General Custer at Little Bighorn, and Mr. Dement came and got her. He didn't say why, just told us to keep doing our work and stay in our seats until the bell rang, but Billy Hedley looked out the window and saw some cops putting Miss Petty in their car." He stopped and patted his chest, still struggling to control his breathing.

"Come sit down," I said, leading him back into the bedroom where I'd been trying to recover from the holidays and prepare for the advent of his mother's twin babies. "Now get yourself together and tell the rest of it."

"Well," he started again, "when school let out, everybody kinda hung around, trying to find out what was going on. And Joyce McIntyre had been in Mr. Dement's office—she gets sent to the principal's office every day, seems like—and she heard it all. These two deputies showed up, asking for Miss Petty, and Mr. Dement made his secretary take Joyce out in the hall, but not before she heard about that dead body. But nobody knows who it is or how it got there or anything, except we're all afraid that Miss Petty knows something. I mean," Lloyd said, looking at me with eyes wide with wonder, "why would they come get her? What if she put it there?"

"Oh, I wouldn't think so. There're a lot of reasons a body might be found in somebody's toolshed, like, well, I guess a vagrant could just curl up and die. We've had some cold nights lately. So, see, it doesn't necessarily mean someone's at fault. The deputies could've come to get your teacher just to ask questions and, of course, to tell her what they'd found. She may know nothing about it."

"I hope she doesn't. She's a good teacher—not my favorite, but if you have to take social studies, which we do, then she's all right. Except when she yells. Then she's mean."

"She yells? Why?" I asked, thinking how unattractive it was

for a teacher to yell at children, and also thinking that the boy needed a little distraction.

"Oh, when somebody doesn't have their homework or when people talk in class or when you get snapped with a rubber band and you can't help but yell yourself. Like that."

"Well, under those circumstances, maybe she can't help raising her voice. But," I mused, unable to distract myself, "I wonder who it was who met his end in her toolshed?"

"Me too. Actually, though," he went on, "we don't even know if it's a man or a woman. Could be either one, I guess. Anyway, I was wondering if you'd heard anything."

"Not a word. It's been quiet all afternoon, what with Lillian out grocery shopping and Mr. Pickens taking your mother to Asheville for her checkup."

"Well, I sure would like to know what's going on," Lloyd said, frowning. "Maybe something'll be on the news tonight or in the paper tomorrow." He thought it over for a few seconds, then went on. "You reckon you could call Mr. Jones and ask him?"

"Who? You mean, Thurlow Jones?"

"Yes'm, Miss Petty lives right behind him on that street that parallels his. I bet he'd know something."

I did a little thinking it over myself. "I expect he would, Lloyd. He seems to know everything that goes on in this town. But he can be, well, a little on the eccentric side, so I hesitate to get mixed up with him again. Let's wait a while and see if Sam knows anything when he gets home. And Lillian might've heard something at the grocery store."

"Okay," he said, nodding judiciously. "That'd probably be better. Mr. Jones kinda scares me too."

~⟞⟝~

After assuring Lloyd that the sheriff's deputies would have the matter well in hand, I encouraged him to turn his mind to his homework until we heard more. But I couldn't turn *my* mind to anything else, and instead of finishing my thank-you notes, I worried at it, wondering who in the world could be in a teacher's toolshed, deader than a doornail, and hardly six blocks from my own toolshed.

Hearing Lillian come in downstairs, I hurried out to see if she'd heard anything and met Lloyd on the stairs, apparently on the same mission.

"I've been texting everybody I know," he confided, a frown of worry on his forehead, "and nobody knows anything. It beats all I ever heard."

"Now, Lloyd, don't get too worked up over this. It may be that the body hasn't been identified yet. But let's see what the word is from the grocery aisles."

To our surprise, there was none, for Lillian was as astounded as I had been to hear the news. She stopped putting away groceries when Lloyd told the tale of what had happened at school.

"Somebody dead in somebody's backyard?" she asked, her eyes about as big as Lloyd's.

"Well," Lloyd said, "not right out in the yard. What we heard was that it was found in the teacher's toolshed or her garage or something."

Then he looked at her, and Lillian looked at him, the same thought seeming to flash between them. "Lemme get my broom," she said, hurrying to the pantry as Lloyd headed for the back door.

"Wait a minute," I said. "Where're you going?"

Lillian hoisted the broom on her shoulder and marched out behind Lloyd. "We gonna see they any dead bodies in *our* toolshed."

# Chapter 2

Well, I thought, let them look. I couldn't imagine finding another dead body so close to the first one, but then, I hadn't been able to imagine finding one anywhere at all.

In spite of what I'd told Lloyd, I was sorely tempted to call Thurlow Jones to see what he knew. He was sure to have some information, as avidly interested as he was in everything that went on in town. And living so close to the scene, he would know what was known, although that could be precious little at this point. On the other hand, ignorance of the facts wouldn't stop Thurlow from saying whatever came into his head. The man seemed to live for stirring things up, and the more fat he could throw onto the fire, the better he liked it.

But to get mixed up with Thurlow again? I shuddered at the thought. I'd had my share of run-ins with him in the past, and I'd always ended up feeling he'd had the best of me every time. For one thing, he didn't care what he said, which put me at a great disadvantage because I couldn't bring myself to respond in kind. Any woman who wanted her conduct to be above reproach could never go tit for tat with Thurlow Jones because he could make more outrageous statements than anybody I'd ever known. He took inordinate pleasure in being offensive to a lady's sense of decency, to say nothing of his attempts to put his hands on her person. You would think that anyone as well-heeled as Thurlow would also have at least a modicum of culture and good taste. I mean, he could afford to learn some social skills even if he hadn't been born with them.

No, I told myself, I'd leave Thurlow to those who could put up with him, because I certainly wasn't among them. Besides, I had no business and very little interest in meddling in something that had nothing to do with me or mine.

In fact, I had promised Sam—not that he had demanded a promise, I'd offered it freely—to stick to my own knitting and not get involved with the problems of everybody else. And to tell you the truth, I was feeling a bit virtuous about it too. There was enough going on in my own household to keep my mind and my hands fully occupied.

First and foremost was the imminent arrival of the twin Pickens babies, an occurrence rife with anxiety, anticipation, and one headache after another. As LuAnne Conover, my long-standing friend, said to me right after she learned of the coming event, "You're getting a little more than you bargained for, aren't you, Julia? In the first place, Hazel Marie had some nerve throwing herself on your mercy after what she did with Wesley Lloyd Springer. And now this. I can't imagine why she'd get herself in such a fix as to have *twins*. I hate to say this because I like Hazel Marie, I really do, but that tells you what she's been doing, and a lot of it too."

I put LuAnne straight on that little matter in a hurry. I knew for a fact that Hazel Marie hadn't planned on one baby, much less two. And LuAnne should've known that I would not abide any criticism of Hazel Marie, in spite of her having shown up at my house with my own husband's little son in tow. But all that was in the past and behind me, helped considerably by the fact that Wesley Lloyd Springer was out of the picture and in his grave.

But Hazel Marie was not a young thing, and I didn't know how she'd withstand all that would be asked of her in the coming weeks. Even now she could hardly waddle around the house, needing to stop and catch her breath every so often and being unable to bend over even to put on her step-ins. And that doctor who specializes in risky situations told her she needed exercise, but in the same breath told her to stay off her feet as much as possible. Now I ask you, how's she supposed to manage both?

And another thing that preyed on my mind was not knowing exactly when to expect those babies. On the basis of that ill-advised trip Hazel Marie had taken with Mr. Pickens to San Francisco in the early summer, I'd figured sometime in February would be about right. But from the way she was looking, she couldn't possibly last that long. And every time I asked her when they were due, she seemed reluctant to give me a straight answer. "Well, you know," she'd say, "twins usually come early."

Well, it depends on just how early we're talking about, doesn't it? Maybe things had been going on before the San Francisco trip, and maybe I wouldn't be all that surprised if they had. I'd put all that behind me, though, because Hazel Marie and Mr. Pickens were married in plenty of time for the twins' birth, if not for their conception—whenever it had occurred.

And, always, there was the little niggling worry that Mr. Pickens would lapse into his previous pattern of marrying and divorcing one wife after another. He did not have a good track record as far as staying tied to one woman was concerned. So far, though, I had to admit that he was performing more than adequately in his role of solicitous husband and expectant father. Of course he was aware that I had my eye on him and knew that he'd do well to take his responsibilities seriously. He knew it because I'd told him often enough.

And then, here we were only a few days into the new year with all of us trying to recover, get the house straightened again, and deal with the fact that the anticipation of the holidays had been greater, as usual, than the realization. And also trying to watch

Hazel Marie like a hawk to be sure she didn't do too much, and making sure that Lloyd wasn't feeling left out, what with everybody so wrapped up in what was coming instead of what was already here, namely him. He'd been an only for all of his twelve years and the center of his mother's attention, as well as the center of mine, in spite of his striking resemblance to Wesley Lloyd, which I kept hoping he'd sooner or later outgrow.

And then there was Sam, my darling second and last husband. It had occurred to me that he might feel that he was being pushed out of house and home, especially because he had every reason to expect some peace and quiet at this time in our lives. I do think that a woman's second husband needs special care and reassurance, especially when he's living in a first husband's house and not only in the company of said husband's widow, but the man's former mistress and son as well.

I stopped and thought again about what the ensuing years since Wesley Lloyd Springer's demise had wrought in my living arrangements. I had come from being a lone widow with only the daily help of Lillian to now having to step over and around Sam, Hazel Marie, Lloyd, Mr. Pickens, and soon two infants, plus Lillian and Latisha, her great-granddaughter, both of whom spent more time at my house than their own. And thank the Lord they did. I couldn't have handled all the comings and goings by myself.

My worst fear not so long ago had been that Hazel Marie would pick up and move off, taking Lloyd with her, to have those babies by herself. It was only Mr. Pickens coming to his senses long enough to marry her that had prevented that catastrophe. So far be it from me to complain about having so many under my roof—that's where I wanted them even if you could hardly stir us all with a stick.

Lillian had told me once that if I didn't have one thing to worry about, I'd look around until I found two more. She may have been right, because it's my nature to take on the burdens of those I care about. But I'd been trying to let the rest of the world take care of itself, and so far I'd been doing a fairly good job of it. Now, though, someone had died under unknown circumstances practically on my doorstep, and I wasn't sure exactly how I could manage to stay above the fray. I mean, I couldn't help but be *curious* about it.

Going to the kitchen window, I saw Sam, bundled up in his overcoat, come walking down the driveway. As usual whenever I saw him, my heart gave an extra thump, and I smiled. I saw him take notice of the open garage door and, making a detour around the car, walk toward it to see what was going on. Lillian and Lloyd met him and they stood talking a few minutes. Then, as Sam started toward the house, I quickly turned from the window, patted my hair, and stood by the door to greet him.

As soon as he came in, I reached for his coat and he reached for me. He smelled of cold air and a hint of lemony aftershave.

"Hello, sweetheart," he said. "You know what those two are doing out there?"

I laughed. "Yes, I do. Have they found anything?"

"Lots of spiderwebs and junk. I suggested they clean the place out while they're at it, but that didn't go over too well. Oh, and here, Julia," he said, reaching into his pocket. "You left your checkbook in the car. I saw it on the seat as I walked by."

"Well, my goodness, I hadn't even missed it." I flipped through the pages. "It's my household account. It must've slipped out of my pocketbook when I was rummaging for the Texaco card the other day.

"But sit down, Sam," I said, as I tucked the checkbook behind the telephone, then hung up his coat. "I'll pour us some coffee, and you can tell me what you've heard."

"Well, that's the thing," Sam said, pulling out a chair from the table and sitting down. "What they told me is news to me. I haven't heard a word, but then I've been holed up all day working on my book. I haven't talked to anybody."

Now that he was retired from the practice of law, Sam spent most days at his house—the one he'd lived in before we married—writing a legal history of Abbot County. It seemed to be taking him years to get it done because facts had to be meticulously checked and rechecked to avoid lawsuits for libel by all those lawyers he was writing about. Lawyers are so litigious, you know. I wasn't sure Sam would ever get it written, but it was all right with me if he didn't. He was enjoying the process, feeling creative and productive—and what would he find to do if he did finish it?

"Lloyd is certainly exercised over it," I said, putting down two cups of coffee and taking a seat. "But his teacher is involved, so I'm not surprised. It's a shame, though, that the deputies had to come to the school to get her. I expect that upset every child there, and the term's barely started."

"Hazel Marie and Pickens not back yet?" Sam asked, abruptly changing the subject. It was as if he had no interest in pursuing any speculations about the who, what, and how a dead body ended up in a teacher's toolshed, which suited me because I was determined to keep my mind on our own problems and not go looking for anybody else's.

"No, but they should be back any time now. I hope the doctor tells her when those babies are due. I declare, Sam, I need to be prepared. Their onset was such a surprise to me that I don't think I can take their sudden and unannounced arrival. I've heard young women who were expecting talk about their due dates, and they were quite specific. Such and such a date, down to the month and day, yet we've not heard a word from the doctor or from Hazel Marie. For all we know, she could keep on expecting for months to come."

Sam laughed. "Oh, I don't think she'll do that." He reached over and put his hand on mine. "We don't need to know a date. They're all prepared for whenever it is. We've got the crib up, and from the looks of things in their room, Hazel Marie has all the blankets, clothes, diapers, and so forth they're going to need. We're ready and they're ready, so let's just take it as it comes."

"I know, I know, and I will, since I have to. I just like to know what to expect."

We looked at each other and laughed. "We pretty much know what to expect, don't we?" I said, feeling a bit foolish, but loving the way the skin around his eyes crinkled when he laughed. "You know, Lloyd was so disappointed when we didn't have Christmas babies. I think he was convinced that Santa Claus would bring them."

"Julia, honey, here's a news flash for you. He doesn't believe in Santa Claus. He got over that years ago."

"Why, Sam, you know not. He always makes a list of what he wants Santa to bring him."

"Yes, and he gives it to you, doesn't he? He knows the pretense is important to you, so he keeps it up."

"My goodness," I said, "I guess that means he's growing up, and I'm not sure I like it. Well, he can just keep on doing it, even though Santa wasn't able to deliver this year. Lloyd had to make do with that Guitar Hero instead of two little babies."

⤳⁚⤶

Lillian came in then, along with a gust of cold air. She walked over to the pantry to put away the broom. "Well," she announced, "one thing for sure: they's no dead folks 'round here."

"That's a relief," Sam said, smiling.

"Miss Julia," Lillian said, closing the pantry door, "I 'bout forget to tell you. When I went to the grocery store, I got Lloyd some new shoelaces for his tennie pumps. What he got now is nothin' but knots, an' they so short he can't hardly tie a bow. They right over here on the counter."

"Oh good, I'm glad you thought of them. Thank you, but where is he, anyhow?" I asked, getting up to bring the coffeepot to the table. "He still in the garage?"

"No'm, he get on his bicycle to go ride around."

"Why, Lillian," I said, stopping in my tracks, "you know he'll go to his teacher's house, and no telling what he'll hear and see. Next thing you know, he'll be having bad dreams. Sam, let's go look for him."

"He'll be all right, Julia," Sam assured me. "He won't get within blocks of the place. They'll have crime-scene tape strung everywhere, and the cops'll be keeping people back. He'll be on his way home in a little while."

"Well, but what if that body isn't just dead, but killed? And what if whoever killed it is still around? I don't like him being out by himself. Besides, it'll be dark soon, and he needs to be home."

"Okay," Sam said, rising, "I'll go get him. And," he went on as he slipped into his coat, "maybe I'll find out a little more about what's going on while I'm at it."

Uh-huh, I thought to myself, and maybe you're a little more interested in what was in that toolshed than you've been letting on.

# Chapter 3

Sam had been gone barely ten minutes when Mr. Pickens and Hazel Marie arrived, both of them looking happy and expectant. Well, of course, Hazel Marie looked expectant, generally speaking, but I'm referring to the expressions on their faces.

"Won't be long now," Hazel Marie said, as Mr. Pickens took her coat and eased her into a chair.

"Well, thank the Lord," Lillian said. "You look like you 'bout to 'splode any minute."

Mr. Pickens laughed. "Let's hope the explosion holds off a little longer. Two more weeks and we'll have us some babies."

"Two weeks?" I asked, as a surge of excitement ran through me. "If it's that definite, we'd better call Etta Mae and put her on notice."

Etta Mae Wiggins, the home health care professional—if six weeks of night school makes a professional—had promised to tend to Hazel Marie and the babies for a few weeks after the birth, and her eagerness to be of help gave me peace of mind. I'd had no experience of my own, having had no children, and it had been so long since Lillian had had hers that I wasn't sure how up to date she was. Etta Mae, on the other hand, had several years' experience as a nurse behind her and had dealt with all kinds of health problems. Disregarding the fact that the health problems she normally dealt with were those of senior citizens,

I was confident that Etta Mae could handle a pair of newborns as easily as she managed querulous and hard-to-please old people. Babies would be a cinch for her.

Etta Mae was a highly capable young woman, and I should know because she managed one of those seedy trailer parks for me. The park had been one of my first husband's less desirable properties, but I'd kept it and made Etta Mae the manager. She'd been thrilled to have the position, because, bless her heart, she was always trying to better herself. She'd jumped right in, cleaning house and taking names. The place sparkled now, and the sheriff rarely had to be called.

"Up to this point," I went on, "that doctor's been mighty unsure of your due date. How did he figure it out now?"

"He might have to take them," Hazel Marie told me. "He'll induce labor and see how I do. If everything goes all right, he won't have to do a Caesarean section. But if it doesn't, I'll be right there in the hospital. So it's all set up—two weeks from today, which means I've got to get to Velma's for a pedicure."

"You're talking about an operation?" I asked, immediately concerned for fear that something was wrong. "Oh my, Hazel Marie, is that really necessary?"

"I doubt it. He just wants me in the hospital so he can supervise my labor. To tell the truth, though, I wish he'd go ahead and do it, but he wants the babies to get a little bit bigger."

"My word," I said, "I'm not sure you can stand them getting much bigger."

"Me either. I have to sleep propped up on three pillows as it is. But," she went on, her eyes sparkling, "I'm not complaining. This is the happiest time of my life, and I'm going to enjoy it if it kills me."

Mr. Pickens put his arm around her. "Well, we're not going to let that happen." He looked around, then said, "Where's Lloyd? He doing something after school?"

So of course that led into the retelling of what was the talk of the school and what would probably be the highlight of the school year.

"Sam went to get him," I said after finishing the telling. "But it's time both of them were back. I don't know what's keeping them." I got up and walked over to the window to see if they were coming.

Lillian turned from the sink, a look of apprehension on her face. "You reckon Mr. Sam can't find him?"

"Lillian!" I cried, looking at Hazel Marie with concern. She didn't need any sudden frights. "Don't say that. They're probably standing around listening to all the speculation. I'll just run down there and tell them it's suppertime."

As I went for my coat, Mr. Pickens said, "I'll go. It's too cold for you to be out."

And before I could insist, he was out the door. "Well, I guess if anybody can find anybody, he can." Then, wanting to reassure Hazel Marie, I said, "It's nice to have a private investigator at your beck and call, isn't it? I always feel comforted when Mr. Pickens is on the job."

"You think Lloyd's all right?" Hazel Marie asked, frowning. "I hope J.D. can find him."

"I'm sure he will. I expect every child in Lloyd's class and then some are gathered around that teacher's house. He's probably with a group of friends, standing around hoping to see something. And as for Sam, well, you know how he is. He starts talking to somebody and loses track of time. Let's not worry about them."

Easier said than done, of course, but I didn't want Hazel Marie marking those babies. Which, as you know, can happen when an expectant mother gets a sudden scare.

Lillian clunked a spoon against a pot, then quickly spun around. "Oh, Miss Julia, I forget to tell you somethin' else. That groc'ry man say your last check bounce back from the bank an' he want you to come in an' see about it."

"What?"

She started to repeat herself, but I interrupted. "I heard you—I just didn't understand. I haven't written a check to the grocery store. You put everything on a credit card and I pay Visa every month. How could he have a check of mine?"

"I don't know, but he do 'cause he wave it 'round in my face."

"That's ridiculous," I said. "Why, I haven't even been in that store since way before Christmas."

"Well, what you want me to tell him if he get after me again?"

"Tell him he can just hold his horses. The bank has obviously made a mistake, and all he has to do is run it through again. Besides, Ingles will hardly go broke over one measly little check that's not mine anyway."

Lillian frowned but didn't argue. She took a small glass of orange juice and a few crackers and set them before Hazel Marie. "You need a little snack," she said.

"Oh, Lillian," Hazel Marie said, smiling, "I'm so full, there's hardly any room for anything else."

"That's why I jus' give you a little bit. But it'll carry you till supper, when I don't 'spect you to eat much then. You been eatin' like a bird anyway—a little peck here an' a little peck there."

"I'll take it with me to the bedroom," Hazel Marie said, as she clumsily leveraged herself out of the chair. "I want to call Etta Mae and get these shoes off before my feet start swelling."

"You better put those feet up," I said, taking her arm and the orange juice and walking her through the back hall to the room she now shared with Mr. Pickens. "Maybe you can catch a little nap too."

After getting her settled with a movie magazine, I returned to the kitchen, intending to question Lillian further about that returned check. But the telephone rang before I could open my mouth. Because I was right beside the phone, I answered it and got a sudden gush of words from LuAnne Conover.

"Julia," she said, her breath catching in her throat. "What's going on down there? I just got home from running errands downtown and came back on Polk Street. I passed your house and started to stop, but I had some frozen food and decided I better not. But anyway, right down the street from you, there were all these cars and people standing around like something was happening, and I stopped to ask about it, and would you believe that a deputy came over and told me to move along? He said I was blocking traffic, but there were only two cars behind me and they were just as interested as I was. So what was it?"

"Well, LuAnne," I said, "I don't have the details, but Lloyd came home from school saying that they'd found a body in his teacher's toolshed."

"A *dead* one? I can't believe that. Who was it? Which teacher? I'll bet you Thurlow Jones is involved. All those cars and people were around his house, in his yard, and on the sidewalk. I've never trusted that man."

"Me either, but I doubt he had anything to do with it. The teacher's house backs up to his, and that's probably as close as anybody can get."

"Who's the teacher?" LuAnne asked, and I could just see her eyes squinch up as she asked it.

"A Miss Petty, but I don't know her."

"Yes, you do, if she's the one I'm thinking about. Her father owned that hardware store, the one right off Main Street? You remember it, I know you do. It was about the only one around here for the longest, but he had to go out of business when Walmart opened. People just stopped giving him their business. They were so thrilled to have a Walmart that they did their shopping there instead of supporting the local stores. Why, I even heard of families planning outings to Walmart like they'd plan a trip to the movies. Anyway, I think Jim Petty died not too long afterward. But what was the daughter's name? Let me think a minute. Well, it'll come to me. But Julia, how're you doing?"

"Oh, I'm all right. Just perking along as usual."

"But aren't you *worried*? I mean, they could've found that body in *your* backyard. You're practically next door."

"Why, LuAnne, we're six blocks away. I wouldn't call that next door."

"Well, it'd be too close for me. If I were you, I'd find out all the details and take steps. No telling what could happen."

Then after telling me to be sure to call her if I heard anything more, she remembered something else. "Wait, I forgot to tell you. Did you know the Methodists have a new preacher? Not the main one, but an assistant or youth minister or something."

"Oh, LuAnne, their bishop is always rotating someone in or out, so that's not news."

"Well, *this* one is," LuAnne almost whispered. "It's a *woman,* Julia, and I heard that half the congregation is up in arms about the way she looks."

"How does…?"

"I've got to go, Julia," LuAnne said, suddenly in a hurry. "Leonard is having a fit for me to drive him by Thurlow's to see what's going on. He's sitting out in the car, blowing that horn for me to come on. But I'll call Mildred to see what she knows. I'll call you back if I hear anything else." And she rang off to continue tracking the news.

"Well, Lillian," I said, replacing the receiver, "the phone lines have started humming, and no telling what tales will be spread before we get the truth of it. But I just can't get exercised over it. I've made a vow to Sam that I'll stay out of matters that don't concern me, and I intend to keep that vow."

Lillian cut her eyes at me. "Uh-huh, I b'lieve that when I see it."

"You can believe it, all right. We have our hands full already. Just think, Lillian, those babies will be here in two weeks!"

"Yes'm, but they's somebody dead not far off from here an' I can't help but feel a little skittish 'bout that, 'specially 'cause that somebody didn't die in his own bed."

"It is worrisome, I admit. It's like death striking at one place, while life begins at another. But that's the natural way, isn't it? And the world just keeps on going." .

I had to sit down and rest after that profound philosophical moment. And a good thing I did because Lillian wasn't through.

"Yessum, it do. But don't sound like to me that whoever dead down there got that way in a nat'ral way. Dyin' in a toolshed seem 'bout as *un*nat'ral as you can get."

"You have a point," I said, leaning over and beginning to drum my fingers on the table. "But my concern right now is the where-abouts of Lloyd, Sam, and Mr. Pickens. I declare, one after the other leaves and none of them have come back." I got up and went to the window again. "I mean, what can be keeping them? They know we're sitting here waiting for them, and they're lingering and lingering. Besides, I need to ask Sam about that check. He'll know what to do about it. Lillian," I said, making a quick deci-sion, "don't say anything to Hazel Marie, but I can't stand this any longer."

"Yes'm, I been wond'rin' when you gonna do somethin', even though you promised Mr. Sam you gonna stop doin' it."

I gave her a quick smile and went to get my coat. "I only prom-ised to stop interfering in other people's affairs. I didn't say one word about staying out of the troubles of our own family. And come to think of it," I said, stopping to think of it, "that has always been the case." I slipped on my coat and headed for the door. "This may be just such another situation that calls for a little well-meant looking into."

# Chapter 4

Mr. Pickens had been right—it was cold. As the short winter day headed toward night, I put my head down against the wind and almost changed my mind about walking. Instead, I pulled the scarf from around my coat collar and wrapped it around my head.

As I headed down the sidewalk, I met small groups of people, most of them bundled up in scarves, hats, and gloves, coming and going along the sidewalks, some getting into parked cars as if the sightseeing tour were over, and others hurrying toward warm houses. I walked briskly through pools of light from the streetlamps, moving in and out of the areas of the late afternoon darkness, speaking but mostly just nodding to the people I passed. Some wanted to stop and talk, but I had neither the time nor the inclination for chitchat.

Squinting my eyes against the cold, I scanned those I passed for a glimpse of the ones I was looking for, hoping to meet them as they headed home. As I got closer to Thurlow's house, I saw cars lined up on each side of the street. Up ahead at the intersection that led to Thurlow Jones's house, there was a patrol car parked crosswise to the street. Some distance away, red and blue strobing lights reflected off the surrounding houses and the low-lying clouds, indicating the presence of emergency vehicles.

Stopping at the corner, I looked farther down Polk Street and saw patrol cars blocking several intersections. So it was a good thing I had not driven the car—I would've been on foot anyway.

Turning onto Thurlow's side street, I kept a sharp eye out for any of the three I was looking for, pausing just long enough to ask the people I passed if they'd seen Sam or Lloyd. I didn't ask about Mr. Pickens because few people in town knew him by sight.

Gradually, I began to realize that I knew few of the people coming from the scene of the crime. The word seemed to have gotten out—probably by way of schoolchildren getting home with the news—and folks from all over had come to bear witness or just to see what they could see. I couldn't imagine the attraction that would draw people from warm homes on a cold evening right at suppertime to stand around and watch a body being removed. It would take a great deal more than that to get me out, as, in fact, it had.

Then I saw part of the attraction. A large group of people was standing around a van that was double-parked by a patrol car. Thick black cables from the van snaked down the street. WLOS, Channel 13—or Channel 3 if you had cable—had their roving reporters on-site. I knew what we'd see on the news that evening: a pretty blonde right out of college speaking in a childish but awed voice giving a report that would tell nothing more than what we already knew, then filling the time interviewing the spectators, who would express both excitement and fear. In other words, no news at all.

Sidestepping a stroller pushed by a woman who should've known better than to bring a baby to such a place, I almost bumped into Ralph Peterson, the salesman from Abbotsville Motors.

"Oh, Ralph, excuse me. I almost ran into you."

"Why, good evening, Miss Julia. What brings you out this time of a day?"

"Possibly the same thing that brought you out," I said with some asperity. "Actually, though, I'm looking for Sam and Lloyd. Have you seen them?"

"Yes, ma'am, I b'lieve I did get a glimpse of 'em. Mr. Sam was talking to ole Thurlow on the other side of his yard a little while ago. Right down there a ways," he said, pointing in the direction of Thurlow's house. "I think maybe the boy might've been with him."

"Well, thank you, I'll track them down from here," I said, moving on past him. "It's past time for decent people to be home where they belong."

When I got to the middle of Thurlow's block, right across from his house, I realized the crowds had thinned out. I would've thought that would be where the most onlookers would be, but apparently the deputies had contained the area to only those who lived on the block. If so, they'd missed me and I intended to keep it that way. I scanned Thurlow's large front yard, but could see hardly anything for all the overgrown shrubs and trees. His was the most unkempt yard in town, and he was forever being given citations for it. A couple of weeks after receiving one, he'd hire the cheapest pickup truck driver with a John Deere mower to cut the grass and trim the branches over the sidewalk. That happened about once a summer; then he'd let it all grow back until the next time the town had had enough of it. In other words, he did as little as he could get away with, and the town let him. His yard, as well as his house, inside and out, was a shame and a disgrace. And it wasn't a matter of the wherewithal to keep things up. Thurlow Jones was loaded, most likely because he rarely spent any of it. I recalled the time a new member of the garden club, one who'd just retired from up north, proposed that the club take on Thurlow's yard as our yearly beautification project so we could "help that poor, pitiful man who's just *existing* in such a shambles." Mildred Allen nearly fell out of her chair laughing.

I didn't see Sam, and I didn't see Lloyd or Mr. Pickens, and it was getting darker. I didn't know where to look next, because I certainly didn't want to look in the next block where Miss Petty's house was—first, because I didn't think the deputies would let me get that far, and second, I didn't want to see any of the gruesome details, LuAnne Conover notwithstanding.

Then a brilliant light suddenly turned on across the street at the end of Thurlow's front walk. A television camera on the shoulder of a heavyset man was filming two figures—one was Thurlow and the other, a slip of a girl holding a microphone.

Thurlow had not improved one iota since the last time I'd seen him. I declare, you'd think if he was going to be on television, he'd have cleaned himself up, but he was his usual unkempt self, made even more so in the glare of the camera lights. I watched as he made the most of his time in the spotlight, waving his arms and talking, then leaning in close to the girl interviewer. I just shook my head at his antics, dreading having to deal with him.

But I took a deep breath and stepped off the sidewalk onto the empty street and walked toward the small group of neighbors waiting their turn to be on television. I stopped on the edge of the group as the interview drew to a close and peered at Thurlow, hoping for some indication that he'd mended his ways. As far as I could tell, he hadn't.

He was a wiry man, short enough for me to look at him eye to eye, something I tried to avoid because devilment was always glittering behind his glasses. His hair was mussed up, probably from snatching off his hat so the camera could get a close-up of his face. His clothes hung on him and were, no doubt, stained and dirty, as they usually were. When he turned his head, I could see in the glare of the light the white stubble on his face. I'd once heard him say he shaved twice a week whether he needed to or not, and it was obvious that he was holding to his schedule. His shirttail was only partially tucked into his trousers, and over it he wore a stained canvas coat that had seen better days a long time ago.

Hating to get mixed up with Thurlow again—the man had no shame—I nonetheless circled the small crowd of sightseers and stood right outside the pool of light, waiting to ask him about Sam and Lloyd. I positioned myself so that Thurlow could see me just as the interviewer turned toward the camera, stumbled through a wrap-up, then, with a much more assured delivery, said, "This is Mandy Wright, Channel 13–WLOS *Nightly News,* reporting from Abbotsville. Back to you, Darleen."

The camera light went off, leaving me practically blind in the dark. But I dodged the shoulder-held camera as the man swung around to leave and pursued Thurlow as he turned toward his house.

"Mr. Jones," I called. "Thurlow, wait a minute, please."

He turned, looked me up and down, then said, "Why, if it's not Lady Springer. Oh, pardon me all to hell, it's Madam Murdoch now, ain't it?"

"Watch your language, Thurlow. I'm of no mind to put up with your foolishness. I wanted to ask if you've seen Sam."

Thurlow's eyebrows went up and his gold-rimmed glasses slid farther down his nose. A pleased smile deepened the wrinkles on his face. "Ha! Lost him, have you? I coulda told you it wouldn't last, and now you know."

"Oh for goodness sakes, Thurlow. Use some sense. I haven't lost him, I'm just looking for him. It's suppertime. And Lloyd needs to be home. Ralph said they were talking to you, so do you know where they went?"

Thurlow's eyes glittered as he thought of an answer. "Well, I tell you," he said after some consideration, "I've seen so many people tonight that I'll have to think who all they were. Why don't you come on in the house and get warm?"

I took a step back. No way in this world would I be enticed into his house again, much less go in alone. Why, the last time I was there, the man put his hand on my person and *pinched.* And he even did it in full view of Lillian.

"You don't need to think about it," I said. "You either saw them or you didn't, so which is it? And I don't have time to visit with you. That boy needs to be home."

He poked his head toward me and said, "You don't want to hear about the body they found? Everybody else does. Where's your curiosity, Madam Murdoch? I can give you the lowdown, but it's cold as an Eskimo's you-know-what. Come on in, and I'll tell you everything I know. And," he said with a wicked grin, "I know everything you'd like to know."

I stepped back again, first from his leering face, and second from the vile suggestion I had no doubt he was making. But that was his way, always looking to embarrass and humiliate a lady. I'd occasionally wondered what he'd do if someone ever took him up on it, but—and you can count on this—that someone would never be me.

"Keep your mind on what I'm asking you," I said, "because I don't want to know anything else. I haven't the slightest interest in delving into the death of some stranger who had the misfortune to end up next door to you. Now, please give me a straight answer. Did you see where Sam and Lloyd went?"

"Well," he said, heaving an exaggerated sigh of defeat, "you are one captious woman and hard to please to boot. But if I was you, I'd head on home. That's where they were going. Unless, of course, they're sending out a search party for you by now. If women stayed home like they're supposed to, they wouldn't be runnin' around after dark, worryin' people half to death."

That just flew all over me. I drew myself up and said, "You're a fine one to talk. Worrying people half to death is all you do, and you take pleasure in doing it too. I should've known I wouldn't get a straight answer out of you."

And off I went, leaving him laughing behind me in the dark. I'd gotten halfway across the street when I heard him say, "Come on back anytime Murdoch goes missin' again."

# Chapter 5

It was a relief to get out of the cold night air and walk into the warm kitchen, and a much greater relief to find Sam, Lloyd, and Mr. Pickens there waiting for me.

Sam met me at the door, a look of concern on his face. "I was about to go looking for you. Come on in here and get warm."

"Well, I'm glad you didn't," I said, taking off my coat. "It's been one after the other going out to look for somebody, then getting lost themselves. I don't know how I missed you, but, of course, I got mixed up with Thurlow because Ralph Peterson said he'd seen you talking to him. I could've gone all day without that little run-in."

Lloyd immediately perked up. "What did he say about that dead body, Miss Julia?"

"Not one thing, because I wasn't interested in hearing it. He tried to get me to go inside with him where, he said, he'd tell me everything I wanted to know. But all I wanted was to find you and get you home."

Mr. Pickens, who, strangely enough, was stirring something on the stove, laughed. "Good thing you didn't go in, Miss Julia. Sam might've had to shoot him."

Now what do you say to a comment like that? I rolled my eyes and pretended I hadn't heard him.

Finally catching my breath, relieved that they all were home where they were supposed to be, I realized that the kitchen table was set, Lloyd was putting rolls in a basket, Mr. Pickens was dipping up vegetables, and Sam was slicing a pot roast.

"Where's Lillian?" I asked.

"We sent her on home," Sam said. "We didn't know how long you'd be, and it's getting late. Besides, we have three good cooks here who can handle putting a meal on the table."

"Uh-huh," I said, smiling, "after it's all cooked, I guess so. Well, then, where's Hazel Marie? She still resting?"

Mr. Pickens glanced up. "I'm taking a plate to her. She's propped up on the bed because her back's hurting."

That stopped me. "Her *back's* hurting? Why, Mr. Pickens, that's an early sign."

His face went white, and he dropped both spoon and potato into the roasting pan. The resulting splash sprinkled the front of his shirt, but he didn't notice.

He ran for the bedroom with me close behind. We burst into the bedroom to find Hazel Marie sitting almost upright on the bed, three or four pillows behind her back, leafing through another movie magazine.

She looked up and smiled. "Hey, J.D., hey, Miss Julia. Did y'all know that Brad and Angelina may be breaking up? They're having a real hard time."

Mr. Pickens wasn't interested. "How's your back? You want me to call the doctor?"

"It could be a sign, Hazel Marie," I said, looking her over for any other indications. "That's how Marilee Cooper knew her last baby was coming."

Hazel Marie frowned, thinking about it. "I think I'm all right. It only hurts when I stand for a while or sit in a straight chair. As long as I stay propped up like this, it feels fine."

"Maybe I better call the doctor," Mr. Pickens said, clearly unconvinced.

She laughed and took his hand. "Don't do that. I'm really all right. Now go on and eat your supper. I'll let you know if anything changes."

"Well," I said, relieved, "if you can laugh, you're not in labor. From what I've heard, it's not exactly a laughing matter. Come on, Mr. Pickens, and get your supper. Then you can come back in and watch her."

That seemed to reassure him, but he was reluctant to leave her. As we walked through the back hall to the kitchen, he stopped, brushed his hand through his hair, and said, "I don't know what to do. The doctor doesn't want her to go into labor. He wants to start it in the hospital so he can monitor her. And you know it'll take a good thirty minutes to get to Asheville, so if she has the least twinge, we need to leave."

This was a time when I wished I'd had the labor experience myself, so I'd know whereof I spoke. But I hadn't, and that was all there was to it. I had to rely on what I'd picked up over the years at the garden club and the book club, and occasionally at the Lila Mae Harding Sunday school class. Oh, and a few tidbits from Lillian as well.

"I think we can rely on her mood, Mr. Pickens," I told him with a great deal more assurance than I was feeling. "As long as she's more interested in movie-star doings than in what's happening inside, I think she's okay. But if she gets a sort of inward look on her face, like she's listening to something or feeling something different going on, that's when you better heat up the car."

He nodded, a frown of worry still on his face. "I'm glad you're here, Miss Julia. I've never gone through this before."

Well, neither had I, so I figured it was time for some help. "Maybe we should see if Etta Mae Wiggins can come before the babies do. Two weeks isn't too early for her to be in the house and on call. And, surely, she'd recognize labor signs before we would."

At least, I hoped so, for as far as I knew, Etta Mae had not had any firsthand experience either.

"I'll call her first thing in the morning," Mr. Pickens said with a noticeably relieved look at the thought of having a trained observer on hand. "From the way the doctor talked, we wouldn't have to worry about this. He said that waiting two more weeks wouldn't be a problem." He rubbed his face, then ran a hand through his thick hair. "That's why I went ahead and took a job in Raleigh. I'm supposed to leave tomorrow and be gone about five days. But now I don't know whether to go or stay."

We stood in the dim back hall, light from the kitchen allowing me to see the worry on his face. I knew that Mr. Pickens was deeply concerned about providing for his ready-made family, even though that family had brought enough assets with it to cover everybody's expenses with a good deal left over. One of the things I admired most about Mr. Pickens was his determination not to live on Lloyd's inheritance. A lot of men would've, you know. So he needed to work, or felt that he did, which was about the same thing in my opinion.

"Why don't we do this," I said. "Let's talk to Etta Mae, and if she thinks Hazel Marie will last five more days, then you go on and do your job. I think having her look in on Hazel Marie would ease your mind. And think of this: you can be home from Raleigh in five hours."

"If she goes into labor," he said with the hint of a rueful smile, "four."

～

We all sat around the table after finishing the meal that Lillian had left. Lloyd and Mr. Pickens kept glancing toward the bedroom, apparently expecting something to happen any minute. But I had earlier tiptoed back there as they began to clear the table, and Hazel Marie was sound asleep, magazines spread out across the bed. I was fairly confident that we'd have no labor alarms any time soon.

"Miss Julia," Lloyd said as he ate the last bite of apple pie, "I can't believe that Mr. Jones didn't tell you anything. I bet he knows all about it."

"Lloyd," I said, and quite firmly too, "I didn't ask him because I don't want to get mixed up in other people's problems. It's so much like meddling, don't you think? Besides, it'll be in the paper tomorrow."

Sam smiled at him, understanding the boy's fascination. "I don't think Thurlow knows any more than anybody else, Lloyd. He pretends he does, but his backyard and Miss Petty's backyard are both large. I doubt he saw or heard anything until the sheriff's deputies showed up."

"Well, then," I said, suddenly struck with a basic question, "just who found that body? Deputies don't normally do routine checks of garages and toolsheds, do they? And we know it wasn't Miss Petty herself, who was the only person with reason to go into her own shed, because they had to get her out of school to tell her about it."

"Good question," Mr. Pickens said. "And here's the answer straight from one of the deputies. Seems a water line broke sometime over the weekend and water spewed out on the street, freezing as it went. It was making pretty much of a skating rink out there. Anyway, that line connected to one that goes to the Petty house and a crew from the water department went out early this morning to fix it. They were working in the yard and one of the crew went in the shed to get out of the wind to have a smoke and found more than he bargained for. Of course, though," he glanced at me from under those black brows, a glint of mischief in his eyes, "I'm with Miss Julia. I don't meddle in other people's business either."

"And rightly so," I said with a firm nod of my head, and wondering who I knew at the water department. "Although you'd get paid for it if you did. Still, it's natural to be a little curious. After all, it's happening to a neighbor, and we're supposed to love our neighbors as ourselves and do for them as we would have them do for us. In fact, I'll ask Lillian to make a casserole for Miss Petty tomorrow and take it to her. That's not meddling. That's being neighborly."

"And," Mr. Pickens said, those black eyes sparkling, "if she just happens to want to talk about it, you'll be right there to listen."

"Yes, and we're supposed to bear one another's burdens, so of course I'll listen. Drink your milk, Lloyd."

"Yes, ma'am," he said, picking up his glass. "But I think I better not go to school tomorrow so I can go with you. Miss Petty might need some yard work or something, and we're supposed to help the needy."

Sam laughed. "Nice try, Lloyd, but I expect you'll find out more in school than picking up limbs in Miss Petty's yard."

"And," I said, "I want you to come straight home from school tomorrow. No standing around listening to rumors, and certainly no going over to Miss Petty's house or to Thurlow's."

"No, ma'am, I won't. I mean, I'll come straight home, and I won't go anywhere else. But I bet Miss Petty won't be at school, and that means we'll have a substitute." Lloyd rolled his eyes in mock despair. "I might as well stay home for all the learning I'll get."

"Another good one," Sam said, amusement in his voice. "But you go on to school, then hurry home to tell us everything you've heard. I have a feeling that you're going to be the one to keep us up to date."

"Don't encourage him, Sam," I said. "He doesn't need to have dead bodies on his mind. He'll end up having nightmares. Besides, Lloyd," I went on, turning to him, "you'll be better off putting your mind on the Little Bighorn, as Miss Petty wants you to."

"Well," he said, his eyes sparkling, "looks like that'd give me nightmares too, 'cause that place was just about covered with dead bodies."

# Chapter 6

The next morning, right after breakfast, I realized that Sam was dithering around the bedroom instead of immediately heading out for the office at his house, as he usually did.

"What's bothering you, Sam?" I asked. "You keep going downstairs and coming back up again."

"I'm trying to decide whether I want to go to Raleigh with Pickens."

"Why in the world would you want to?"

"Well, the family of a deceased judge just released his personal papers, and those papers throw a different light on a number of cases that I've already written about. I may have to rewrite a few chapters, but before I do, I want to go through the archives in Raleigh to make sure."

"Oh, Sam," I said, already thinking of how empty the house would be without him. "Five days are an awfully long time to be gone. I'll miss you, but on the other hand, it would save you from making the trip later on by yourself. You might as well go now if you're going to have to go sometime. At least you won't be doing all the driving."

"I guess I will, then," Sam said, pulling out some shirts to pack. "I'll get a rental car once I'm down there so Pickens can do his business and I can do mine—if it suits him for me to go with him."

It suited Mr. Pickens fine to have a companion on his road trip, although Sam almost backed out when he learned that Mr. Pickens planned to stay at a Motel 6.

By the time the travel plans were made, Hazel Marie had eaten a huge breakfast and was humming around the kitchen helping Lillian clean up with no indication of an early delivery. Mr. Pickens had already called Etta Mae, and had done it so early that she'd still been in bed. From the sound of his end of the conversation, she woke up fast. She promised to drop by later in the day to see if she should move in with us. Acting on her reassurances and Hazel Marie's contented state, he began to pack for his Raleigh trip, although he kept stopping to wonder if he'd made the right decision.

Lillian reassured him too. "She don't look like she in labor to me, Mr. Pickens. I can always tell when it's comin' on, and I don't see it comin' any time soon. 'Sides, she worryin' more 'bout her toenails than anything else."

With that, Sam and Mr. Pickens finally got in the car and left. I think by that time they were glad to be on their way because they were probably tired of hearing me tell them to be careful.

~

Hazel Marie had come to the table that morning looking happy and unconcerned with intimations of an impending confinement. She had her mind set on those babies' making their appearance two weeks later, one way or another.

Lloyd had left for school, eager to catch up with the latest news, promising to call me at lunchtime if he heard anything interesting. Because we'd learned nothing we didn't already know from the paper or the television news, I figured the authorities knew no more than we did. If the body had been that of a vagrant, it could be days or weeks before it would be identified.

But just as I folded the paper and put it aside, the pastor's wife,

Emma Sue Ledbetter, called. She was having one of her do-good spasms, which always meant roping in everybody else to help her.

"Julia," she began, "we really have to do something about the homeless in this town. That poor person died all alone in the cold and the dark, and that should shame every one of us. I've talked with a number of people this morning, and we've decided to do it right away, maybe next week, just as soon as we can get the word out. Now, I know you'll want to join us, so be thinking who you can get to sponsor you."

"Sponsor me for what?"

"Why, for the Homeless Walk, Julia. You get people to pledge so much for however long or far you plan to walk."

"Emma Sue," I said, just done in by another one of her enthusiasms, "I don't plan to do any walking. It's winter out there if you haven't noticed, and I'm not about to walk around in it."

"But, Julia, think of all those poor people who don't have a warm house like you have. We have to do something to help them, and walking a mile or two would be easy enough to do. I thought we could walk up one side of Main Street and down the other, then round and round as long as anybody wants to. I know the *Abbotsville Times* will publicize it for us. We can gather on Main Street to start our walk, and our picture will be in the paper."

"Listen, Emma Sue, I appreciate your thinking that I have the strength and stamina to go on a sidewalk merry-go-round, but I don't. And here's another thing: we don't need another cause to expect people to support. I mean, have you noticed the economic news lately? It'd just be another bright idea that sooner or later would be turned over to the taxpayers." I took a deep breath and went right on, knowing that my hardened heart would bring her to tears at any minute. "And think of this, there are plenty of homeless shelters in town already, and the last I heard, all of them need help. There's the Salvation Army with that huge building full of beds on Pine Street, and the Interfaith Mission and the

Community Action thing, and a rescue mission down by the bus station. And every church in the county has an emergency fund for needy people, and some of them serve meals and provide beds for whoever needs them. I'd much rather donate to one of them than start something new that would have to depend on how long my feet hold out."

"Oh, Julia," Emma Sue said with a catch in her voice, "you sound so coldhearted and I know you're not. If you'd just think of that poor soul who froze to death practically next door to you, I know you'd feel the need to do something."

"Who said he froze to death? It's been cold but not frigid. And how do you know it was a he?"

"Well, I just assumed it was a man, and the weather has been bad. How else would he have died?"

"A lot of ways. For all we know, he—if it was a he—could've been inebriated and thought he was in his own bed. I think the least you should do, Emma Sue, is wait till we know more about what actually happened. We'd look awfully foolish organizing a homeless walk for somebody who had a home just as warm as yours and mine, and just hadn't been able to find it. Besides, we're due for snow this time of year, do you really want a bunch of women floundering around in it? Think about broken limbs and hips and chapped lips and I-don't-know-what-all."

"But, Julia, we should strike while the iron is hot. You know, while it's on everybody's mind—that's when people are most willing to give from the heart. Every fund-raiser knows that, and besides, the weatherman says no snow any time soon."

"Well, that's something you can really count on," I said with a touch of sarcasm I didn't think she'd catch.

"Well," Emma Sue said right back at me, "all I can say is you ought to be glad I'm not organizing a *run*. I just don't understand why you don't want to support such a wonderful cause."

"I've told you why, Emma Sue," I said, becoming exasperated

because she wouldn't turn it loose. "But let me put it this way: if you're determined to go through with this, I will make a donation, but I will not walk and I will not sponsor anybody to walk for me. If they want to get out in the cold and stroll around, more power to them, but I'm not going to pay them to do it."

"Oh, Julia, you don't understand the whole concept." Emma Sue was crying by this time, but it wasn't dampening her commitment to the cause. "If everybody felt the way you do, the homeless would never have a roof over their heads."

"If everybody felt the way I do, they'd send a check and be done with it. So if anybody wants to walk, they can sponsor themselves."

I had to listen to a few more "Oh, Julia's" and her unsuccessful attempts to stifle her sobs, but I did not relent. When I was finally able to end the call, I stood there for a minute wondering at my state of mind. I was already a fairly cheerful contributor to all kinds of requests from the church and from the community. No one, I assured myself, can contribute to every cause that can be dreamed up, and Emma Sue was a first-class dreamer of causes.

"Lillian," I said as I went to the kitchen for a little solace from the twinges of guilt I was feeling, "that was Emma Sue Ledbetter on the phone, wanting me to take a walk in this weather. I told her no, and now I feel bad about it."

"What she want you to take a walk for?"

"To raise money, because she thinks I'm made of money. Every time I turn around, she's after me for a donation for some cause or another."

"How you s'posed to raise money takin' a walk?"

"Well, that's the question, isn't it?" I sat down at the table, going over in my mind what I should've said to Emma Sue. "It's complicated, Lillian, and I don't half understand it myself. But what I should've told her was that I'd be happy to sponser somebody to walk around for an hour or two, but I'd have to take it out of my pledge to the church. That might've put a different light on it for her."

"Uh-huh, you talk big, but I know you gen'rous when it come down to it."

"Thank you, Lillian. I needed that." I sighed, then stood up to find something to do. "Where's Hazel Marie?"

"She in there goin' through all her baby things, seein' if she missin' anything. But, Law, Miss Julia, if she buy much else, that room won't hold it all. Mr. Pickens 'bout be crowded out now."

"A good thing he went on to Raleigh then." I laughed, thinking of how he had been torn between his job and his wife that morning. "I tell you, Lillian, he is displaying all the concern I could hope for but was afraid I wouldn't see. It does my heart good to see him all worried and anxious about Hazel Marie. He hasn't, in the past, shown himself to be particularly uxorious."

Lillian turned and frowned at me. "I don't know 'bout that, but he bein' a good husband. You can tell jus' by lookin' at Miss Hazel Marie—she happy as a lark."

"She certainly is. I just hope it continues. And so is Lloyd, if he can ever turn his mind off that body they found down the street. It's not healthy, Lillian, for him to dwell on such things like he's doing. I'm hoping Etta Mae can distract him, entertain him, keep him occupied, or whatever, when she gets here." I started out of the room. "And that reminds me, I'm going upstairs to check on the sunroom. If she thinks she should move in now, I want to be sure it's ready for her."

"I already make sure," Lillian said. "But you go on if you need something to do."

I was halfway out of the kitchen when something else occurred to me. "Lillian," I said, turning back, "tell me again about that grocery store check. I don't understand it, because I looked in my checkbook and I haven't written any checks to that store."

"No'm, I didn't think so, 'cause you don't buy no groc'ries."

"I meant to mention it to Sam and completely forgot about it. So I guess I better look into it. Did you see how much it was for? Was my name on it?"

"No'm, I don't see nothin'. He jus' wave it around an' say he gonna run it through one more time an' he 'spectin' funds in there to cover it. Else he have to turn it over to somebody doin' the collectin'."

"Well, for goodness sakes, we've done enough business with that store not to be threatened with a collection agency, especially over something that's obviously an error. I'll call the bank and get it straightened out." I continued my exit from the kitchen, murmuring to myself. "Just one more thing on top of everything else."

# Chapter 7

Having second thoughts as I climbed the stairs, I decided to go to the bank in person and show them in black and white where they were wrong. I retrieved my household checkbook from the desk where I'd put it after Sam had brought it in, stuck it in my pocketbook and, after a moment's hesitation, put in my money market checkbook as well. It wouldn't hurt to remind whomever I spoke with that I was able to cover any amount written for a bag of groceries, as well as show how my various accounts added to the bank's bottom line.

I told Lillian where I was going, asked her to keep an eye on Hazel Marie, and braved the bitter cold as I drove to the bank. Taking note of the lowering clouds, I finally found a parking place, thinking also of Sam and Mr. Pickens on the highway and hoping that they were having good weather.

Bitsy Simpson, whose first name did not inspire a great deal of confidence (nor did her long flowing hair and tight sweater), was the bank officer whose cubicle I was ushered into after I'd stated my business. She was pleasant enough, as well she should've been because I'd known her for most of her life. I'd barely sat down in front of her desk before she immediately confirmed my worst fears.

"That's right, Mrs. Murdoch," she said with unnerving complacency. "That check to Ingles did bounce and this morning two more have gone back out due to insufficient funds."

"*Two more!* But there *are* sufficient funds in this account," I said, waving the checkbook. "Just look at this and tell me why you're bouncing checks all over town, and doing it without notifying me."

"We don't do personal notifications anymore," she said with a condescending smile. "Everything's computerized these days, so checks are returned automatically. We expect our customers to keep up with the checks they write."

"I *do* keep up with my checks. Why do you think I'm here? Now, Bitsy, you just look at the register in this checkbook and you'll see that you have undoubtedly attributed somebody else's checks to my account." I handed her my checkbook, the bottom line of which revealed more than sufficient funds to cover several months of groceries. I watched as she looked back and forth from the register to the computer screen.

"Hm," she said, then clicked her keyboard and stared at the screen. "You must've forgotten to enter the check to Ingles and this one to the Sav-Mor drugstore. Then here's one to Jiffy Lube you weren't able to cover."

"*Jiffy Lube? Sav-Mor?* What are you talking about? I don't even know where those establishments are. I certainly haven't written checks to them."

"Oh," she said, peering closely at the screen, "here's your problem. On January the fourth, you wrote a check for thirty-five hundred dollars to cash, which was just barely covered. Nothing else cleared after that. You must've forgotten to enter it."

"*Thiry-five hundred!*" I popped straight up out of my chair and stood there, clutching my pocketbook. "To *cash*? I'll have you know, young lady, that a mistake has been made and I am not the one who made it. Look at that register and you'll see that the last check I wrote, which was for the electric bill, was number

4991, and the next check, just waiting to be written to Maxwell's Dry Cleaners, is number 4992, and it's right here. I never forget to enter *any* checks I write, much less one for that amount of money."

"Well, I don't know what to tell you, Julia," Bitsy said, addressing me with an unwonted familiarity, as many bank tellers felt free to do. "This account is empty and is, in fact, in the red. Perhaps you can make a deposit or transfer some funds from another account."

"No," I said, trembling from anger or anxiety or simply from my inability to get through to her. "I'll not put another cent into an account that is leaking funds from somewhere. What good is it to put money in when you're letting it fall out the back door?"

Bitsy leaned back in her chair and coolly considered me. "I have a suggestion, Julia, which I hope you won't take the wrong way. We all reach a certain point in our lives when we could use some help. Perhaps there's someone in your family who could manage your funds for you. It's a simple matter to give your power of attorney to a responsible relative. My advice would be to consult an attorney so you won't have this problem again."

I snatched the checkbook from her hand and marched myself to the door. "And my advice to you would be to find out why that computer you think so much of is making such egregious mistakes. As for me, I will certainly consult my attorney, but not because I've lost my ability to add and subtract." I lifted my head and sailed down the hall, my nerves so frayed I could hardly stand it.

⌁⦂⌐

But consulting my attorney had to wait because Binkie Enloe Bates, my attorney of record, was in court for the entire day and possibly for the rest of the week.

"Wouldn't that just frost you?" I mumbled to myself as I drove home, shaking from the cold. "Binkie's in court and Sam's tooling down the highway, while my financial reputation is being absolutely shredded."

What was I to do with both lawyers unavailable? For it was Sam and Binkie who took care of Wesley Lloyd Springer's estate, which had been left jointly to Lloyd and me. Well, not exactly left jointly, because Wesley Lloyd had intended to leave it all to Lloyd, and would have if the state hadn't stepped in with a reminder of something called widow's rights, meaning half the estate came to me, Wesley Lloyd's intentions notwithstanding.

Fuming and fussing at being unable to immediately clear up the matter of bouncing checks, I began telling Lillian about it as soon as I walked in the door.

"What's the use of having two lawyers when neither is around when you need them?" I complained, plopping my pocketbook on the table. "And I tell you, Lillian, I am torn up over Bitsy Simpson. That little snip as good as said that I'm too far over the hill to manage my own finances. I should speak to her mother about her, and I would if her mother wasn't in a nursing home."

But before I could continue, Etta Mae Wiggins came breezing in, and not wanting to share my banking problems with her, I put them aside and turned my mind to Hazel Marie's situation.

Etta Mae was her usual happy little self, pleased to be called on to help. She was dressed in a light blue pantsuitlike outfit that did little for her. She'd once told me that she didn't like wearing what she called scrubs, but with the kind of work she did with incontinent and bedridden patients, they saved her good clothes. And I supposed the outfits created a more professional look than her usual jeans and pointy-toed boots.

"Hi, Miss Julia, Lillian," she said, her face reddened by the brisk weather. She put down her heavy tote bag and slid off her padded coat. "How's the little mother this morning?"

"We think she's fine," I said, "but we'd love some reassurance. It was Mr. Pickens who got all concerned and upset thinking she was going into labor, which, I've been told, her doctor doesn't want her to do."

"That's right. Not if he wants to monitor her in case she needs a section. At her age he's being extra careful. But don't tell her I said that." Etta Mae sounded knowledgeable, but I kept thinking about that technical school course she'd taken and wasn't all that comforted. Still, she knew her limitations and was always trying to better herself one way or another, which I admired and commended her for.

"Well, let's go take a look," Etta Mae said, sounding like Dr. Hargrove at his breezy best.

I led her through the back hall to Hazel Marie's room, with Lillian following us. We found her sitting on the foot of the bed, folding the tiny shirts and leggings and blankets and this, that, and the other that make up layettes for twin babies. She looked up as we filed in, pleasure lighting her face.

"Etta Mae!" she cried. "I'm so glad to see you." Then she stopped and frowned. "Is anything wrong? I thought you'd be working."

"I am, but I had some time between shut-ins, and your husband is so worried about you, I thought I'd drop by."

"J.D. called you?"

"Yeah," Etta Mae said, and laughed. "About five o'clock this morning. Woke me out of a sound sleep."

"Oh, I'm sorry. I didn't know he was doing that. But I'm fine, Etta Mae, just a little indigestion now and then, but no wonder. Just look at me! I'm as big as a house."

By this time, we'd all found a place to sit, although Etta Mae had to move a stack of baby things to make a place on the bed beside Hazel Marie. There was hardly room to turn around for all the accessories that two babies seemed to require. There was a crib—and thank goodness, only one because Hazel Marie had read that twins should be kept together for the first few weeks—and a changing table and a huge laundry hamper and a large upholstered rocking chair with a matching ottoman and another chest of drawers besides the one already in the room. Opened gift boxes were stacked in the corners, their contents waiting to be used or put away. They'd come from the baby shower that LuAnne had hosted before Christmas, and every time I saw them I cringed a little, always uncomfortable about social events that required the bringing of gifts.

"Oh, look at this," Etta Mae said, spreading a tiny yellow garment on her knees. "It's the cutest thing. Just look at all the smocking."

Hazel Marie beamed with pleasure as she held up another garment just like it. "I love it too. And of course I have two of them. Two of everything, actually."

"Yellow is a good choice," I said. "It'll suit either boys or girls, or one of each."

Etta Mae asked, "You still don't know what you're having?"

Hazel Marie shook her head. "No, sometimes I think I want to know, but we decided we wanted to be surprised. The doctor thinks he knows what one of them is."

Lillian started laughing, then Etta Mae did too.

"You know what that means, don't you?" Etta Mae said.

"I don't," I said.

"It mean," Lillian said, still laughing, "that one of 'em have something extra, something he can see."

"Oh," I said, finally getting it and trying not to be embarrassed at what came to mind.

"Well," Hazel Marie said, "it's hard to tell one thing from another on those sonograms—I don't care what he says. So I'm not counting any chickens before they're hatched."

Lillian looked her over, then with a sage nod of her head said, "They's at least one girl in there 'cause you carryin' 'em so low."

"Well, of course she's carrying them low," I said, discounting another old wives' tale. "With that heavy a load, she can't do anything else. She's sagging, Lillian."

Hazel Marie laughed, then put her hand on the small of her back, stretching to ease the cramped muscles. "I've got to get up from here," she said. "Maybe walk around a little. Everything's so crowded up inside that I can hardly breathe sometimes."

Etta Mae helped her to her feet. "Let's walk to the kitchen and see if that helps."

Lillian was out the door before the rest of us. "She need a little snack too."

Hazel Marie whispered to me as I took her arm. "Bless her heart, Lillian's going to snack me to death."

Etta Mae got Hazel Marie settled at the table, while I brought over the coffeepot and Lillian fixed her a cup of spiced tea because she was off coffee for the duration.

After putting a plate of cookies on the table, Lillian asked, "Anybody heard anything more 'bout that dead body they found?"

"Just what was in the paper this morning," I said, hoping to move the conversation on to other topics. "That seems to be the extent of what anybody knows."

"Well, let me tell you what I heard," Etta Mae said, perking right up. "When I stopped at McDonald's for a biscuit, there was a bunch of construction workers talking about it—some of them were volunteer firemen, so they knew. They said it was definitely a man, and he'd been dead for at least a couple of days. And he was wearing a real nice overcoat and a suit under that. They said everything was dirty and stained, but you could tell that his clothes were better than you'd expect on a hobo or something."

"That may not mean anything," I said. "People occasionally donate some very good things when they've outgrown them or gotten tired of them. I heard Maureen Langley say one time that she'd taken an armful of Carlisle outfits to the Salvation Army, and Louise Murphy heard about it and went right down there and bought them for herself. So I'm not sure that the quality of his clothes tells us anything."

"Just that he had good taste," Hazel Marie said. She took a sip of tea, then said, "I'd sure like to know how he ended up in Miss Petty's toolshed."

"Me too," Lillian said. "You reckon he a friend of hers?"

"I hope not," Etta Mae said, laughing. "I'd hate to be her friend if that's her guest room."

Even though I'd been determined not to be drawn into other people's problems, I couldn't help being interested in the conversation. For one thing, it distracted me from stewing over the bank's mistake and how I could make them admit to it. "Do any of you know Miss Petty? LuAnne told me that her father used to own that hardware store downtown that closed a few years ago, but that's all I know about her."

"Oh, she's real nice," Hazel Marie said. "I met her on Parents' Night at the school back in the fall. She was kinda quiet and mousy looking, though I hate to criticize. I remember thinking that she'd look so much better if she'd take a few pains with her hair and put on some makeup."

"Maybe you ought to offer to do a makeover for her," Etta Mae suggested. "You're real good at that."

Hazel Marie laughed. "I expect she has more on her mind than a makeover right now. She must be scared to death knowing that somebody died in her backyard. And she lives alone, doesn't she?"

I thought about it for a minute. "She must. I know her father's gone, and I believe her mother died years ago. She must've inherited the house, because LuAnne said that's where her folks lived before they passed. I don't know about any brothers or sisters. And I guess with her name still being Petty, she never married."

"Speaking of names," Etta Mae said, her eyes bright with a

sudden thought, "if that man had on a decent suit, wouldn't he have had a billfold or something? I mean, some kind of identification on him?"

"You would think so," I said, realizing that Etta Mae had asked an astute question, taking us right back to that dead body. "Yet the paper said he was unidentified."

"Hm," she said. "Maybe they know who he is but just haven't released the name. They do that, you know, so they can notify the family first."

"Then all we have to do," Lillian chimed in, "is ride around till we see who got a black wreath on they door."

"Well," Hazel Marie said, as if she hadn't heard the intervening comments. "All I know is that Miss Petty had nice things to say about Lloyd—what a good student he is and how polite he is—so she must be a nice person."

"Except," I said, "when she yells at the students in class. At least that's what Lloyd told me, but it sounded as if she has reason to yell at times. Still, that means she's not quite as quiet and mousy as she looks."

Lillian said, "I'm waitin' on Lloyd to get home. I bet he gonna know all they is to know."

"I bet he will!" I said, as we all laughed. "That school will be rife with rumors and speculations and wrongheaded theories. I just don't want him to get too wrapped up in what's going on."

Hazel Marie hunched her shoulders as a shiver ran across them. "What if that man was *murdered*?"

"That's what I'm won'drin'," Lillian said as she reached for a cookie. "An' that's what everybody gonna think with him layin' out there with rakes and shovels in the dead of winter."

"Oh my," Etta Mae said, her eyes big, "you think that's what happened? Who could've done it? And just imagine Miss Petty sleeping right across the yard while somebody was killing him. I'd never get to sleep again."

"Now listen, you three," I said, and right sharply too. "There is no reason to think that or even to mention it. Hazel Marie, you're supposed to be thinking pleasant thoughts and keeping your mind off distressing subjects."

"I know," she said, nodding agreement. "But it's so interesting and just scary enough to make you *want* to think about it. I'm just glad it didn't happen any closer than it did." She nibbled on a cookie, then said, "What I'd like to know is this: Did Miss Petty know him? I mean, he could've been visiting her, then he could've left and had a heart attack or something in her yard and tried to crawl back but could only get as far as the toolshed before giving up the ghost."

"Oh, Law," Lillian said, raising both hands in the air, "don't be talkin' 'bout no ghost!"

"That's enough speculation," I said, standing up and taking my cup and saucer to the sink. "Lloyd won't be the only one having bad dreams. Hazel Marie, clear your mind and think about something warm and fuzzy."

She closed her eyes and smiled. "J.D.," she said dreamily.

"Oh for goodness sakes," I said, but I had to laugh with the others.

"Well," Etta Mae said, picking up her coffee cup as she stood, "I can't top that, so I better be going. Hazel Marie, you're doing fine, but if you need me, just call me on my cell. Miss Julia," she went on as she turned to me, "it looks like the doctor's right and it'll still be a while before anything happens. But everything's arranged with my boss so I can be here whenever you call." She leaned in close to me and whispered, "I don't know how you managed it, but whatever arrangement you made has Lurline riding high. Otherwise, she'd never let me off."

If Etta Mae's employer heard that my checks were being returned for insufficient funds, she might not be riding quite so high. I might be forced to pay her with a cashier's check or with, heaven help us, cash on the barrelhead.

Slipping on her coat, Etta Mae picked up her bag, speaking to Hazel Marie as she headed for the door. "Tell J.D. that I don't think I need to move in quite yet. Don't want to wear out my welcome too soon."

# Chapter 8

It was a quiet, easy day after Etta Mae left, although there was an underlying tension along my nerves that made me feel as if we were living in the calm before the storm, in spite of Etta Mae's reassurances. Until those babies had safely arrived and the bank had my account straightened out, I knew I was in for unremitting anxiety. It didn't help that Sam was gone. I was so accustomed by now to his sane and steady approach to whatever happened that without him I felt uneasy and at loose ends.

But the day wore on, as days usually do, with the temperature dropping so that almost as soon as the furnace clicked off, it clicked back on again. I kept busy, finishing up my thank-you notes and going over the figures in my check register again, which I confirmed were absolutely correct. Hazel Marie stayed in her room most of the day, making sure her suitcase was packed in case she had to make a hurried trip to the hospital. Lillian entertained herself by listening to gospel music on the radio while preparing the evening meal.

A little after noon I walked back to Hazel Marie's room to check on her and, looking in the open door, saw her stretched out on the upholstered rocking chair, her feet on the ottoman and a pillow behind the small of her back.

I tiptoed in and spread a cashmere throw over her. Even with the furnace going full blast, there was still a chill in the air. She blinked and raised her head.

"Sorry, Hazel Marie," I whispered. "Just covering you up. Go on back to sleep."

"I wasn't asleep," she said, yawning. "Just resting my eyes." She smiled and put her head back down.

"Are you feeling all right?"

"I think so. A few little contractions now and then, but the doctor said that's normal at this stage and not to worry about them unless they started coming regularlike."

Immediately concerned, I asked, "Well, are they?"

"No, just every now and then, enough to make me not want to do anything but lie around." She laughed. "So that's what I'm doing."

"Good. You need all the rest you can get. There'll be none for the weary when those little ones get here. You think you could eat some lunch? It's getting so late, I'm surprised Lillian hasn't brought you any."

"I guess so, though I'm not really hungry." She laughed again and held out her hand. "If you'll help me out of this chair, I'll try to get up. I need to move around a little."

When we got to the kitchen, Lillian looked up and said, "'Bout time you ready to eat. I looked in on you a while ago, but I jus' let sleepin' dogs lie. Set on down now an' I'll put something on the table."

We did and she did, and it was almost like old times, although the times weren't that old. But not so long ago there had been no Sam or Mr. Pickens in the house, and with Lloyd in school most of the day, there had been only the three of us.

Lillian sat down with us, propped her arms on the table, and looked squint eyed at Hazel Marie, then turned to me. "I don't want to worry y'all none, but the radio say we might be in for snow tonight."

"Oh my," I said, dropping my fork. "Hazel Marie, maybe you should go on to the hospital."

"I don't think so," she said, shaking her head. "I'm not anywhere close to needing to do that. They'd just send me right back home again. Besides, even if it does snow, it'll likely be melted by tomorrow."

"That's true," I said, recalling the numerous snows we'd had in the past that did little more than cause a run on bread and milk at the grocery stores.

As if reading my mind, Lillian heaved herself out of her chair, saying, "I better get to the grocery store sometime today. Everything be gone if I don't."

Feeling some anxiety in case the Ingles manager accosted her again, I said, "Why, Lillian, you just went yesterday, didn't you?"

"Yes'm, I did, but no tellin' when I get to go again. Y'all think of anything we need?"

"Some of those seedless green grapes would be nice," Hazel Marie said. "I've had them on my mind all day."

"I get some then. Miss Julia, anything you want?"

"I can't think of anything right offhand," I said. "Well, maybe something we can eat cold if the power goes off." Then, at the thought of cold food and a cold house, I had to get up and walk around, spouting emergency plans as I walked. "Hazel Marie, are you sure you'll be all right if the power goes out? I better get Lloyd to put some more wood on the back porch. We can all sleep in the living room by the fireplace if we have to. Why in the world didn't I get a generator before this? By now, every generator in the county will be sold. Lillian, why don't you and Latisha spend the night?"

"Miss Julia," Hazel Marie said, laughing. "It's not going to get that bad. It'll just be a flurry or two—if we get that much."

Lillian nodded in agreement. "That's what the weatherman say. He say we dodging the bullet, 'cause they's a big storm gonna pass us by. But I'm gonna go on to the store when it time to pick up Latisha, jus' in case he get it wrong, which everybody know wouldn't be the first time."

As Lillian cleared the table, Hazel Marie declared herself ready to change positions. "If I sit too long in one place," she said as she managed to get to her feet, "my back starts aching."

And no wonder, I thought, the poor woman was so front heavy that she'd become swaybacked to counterbalance the load.

So with one busy and the other lying down, I went to the living room, lit the fire that was already laid, and sat down to enjoy the warmth and the look of the flames as I continued to worry about the weather. Getting up now and then to look out the window, I saw no snowflakes as yet and hoped that they would indeed pass us by. Even though the sky was overcast, it seemed no more threatening than the usual January day. The wind, however, was picking up and I saw trees whipping back and forth and power lines swaying in the gusts.

I declare, the weight of decision making—when or if Hazel Marie should go to the hospital—hung over me, and I wished to my soul that Sam hadn't gone halfway across the state. Even Mr. Pickens would do in his place—anyone who would relieve me of the responsibility for Hazel Marie's departure time.

When the phone rang, I nearly jumped out of my chair, the noise was so loud in the silent house. Hurrying to answer it before it disturbed Hazel Marie, I was so surprised at who was on the line that I had to sit down again.

"Madam Murdoch, this is Thurlow Jones. Remember me?" he asked, as if I could ever forget. I had immediately recognized his voice, although his usual taunting and mocking tone was missing. "Can you talk?"

"Of course I can talk. What can I do for you?"

"I wanta know what you've heard about that body they found."

"Why, I haven't heard any more than what everybody seems to

know: it was an unidentified man dressed in nice but soiled clothing. Somebody from the water department found it and called the sheriff. The body's been sent to Winston-Salem for autopsy, according to the paper, and that's the extent of my knowledge. Why are you asking me?"

"Because you're close to that Sergeant Bates and because a private investigator lives in your house. At least he did the last I heard. That's why."

"I doubt that either of them knows any more than the rest of us, and they wouldn't share it with me if they did. In fact, Thurlow, everybody thinks you know more than anybody, seeing that it happened practically in your yard."

"Well, they're wrong," he snapped, sounding more like himself. "I figured you'd know what's being said, whether it's true or not. And most likely it wouldn't be, the way you women like to gossip."

"I'll have you know that I do not gossip, and I resent the implication."

"Oh, don't get on your high horse, Madam. I didn't mean you'd pass it on, just that you might've heard something."

"Yes, and you figured I'd pass it along to you, didn't you? Then you'd have every right to call me a gossip."

He sighed dramatically. "You are the most contentious woman I know. I can't ask a simple question without you getting your back up. I'm just concerned about Laverne Petty and what folks're saying about her. She's my neighbor, you know."

"Well," I said, calming down at this indication that he had some normal feelings. "I'm concerned about her too. She's one of Lloyd's teachers and he was in her class when the deputies came to get her. That seems to prove she didn't know anything about it, much less have anything to do with it. But you're so near, Thurlow, did you hear or see anything that night?"

"Nope, not a thing. I sleep upstairs at the front of the house.

But I don't want people spreading rumors about Laverne. She's a nice lady who goes about her business without bothering anybody, and if it so happens that she has a few visitors now and then, well, it's her business and nobody else's."

"Visitors?"

"See, now there you go jumping to conclusions. Typical woman is all I can say."

Talk about contentious, I couldn't believe him. "This conversation is over, Thurlow. Call the sheriff's department if you want to know anything else. I'm hanging up." And I did, fuming so much I could hardly see straight.

I couldn't sit still after that, for the more I thought of Thurlow's sly insinuation about Miss Petty's morals, the more outraged I got. Why, if whispers like that got around, the woman could lose her job. The school board would have her out before she turned around good. Something had to be done to nip this in the bud.

Sticking my head into the kitchen where Lillian was, I said, "I'm going over to Mildred's for a few minutes."

"You better bundle up then," she said.

After buttoning my coat and placing a screen in front of the fire, I sailed out the front door, intent on enlisting Mildred's aid in curtailing Thurlow. I almost ran right into two deputies, one of whom had a finger pointed to ring the doorbell.

"Why, good afternoon," I said, quickly regaining my composure as I looked up at the two markedly similiar deputies. Both were big men, made even more so by the padded jackets they wore. Both had blond crewcuts and both wore solemn expressions on their wind-reddened faces. "What can I do for you? Is anything wrong?"

"Julia S. Murdoch?" one of them asked.

"Yes." I nodded, then with a gasp asked, "Has there been an accident?" Visions of Sam lying broken on the side of a highway flashed through my mind. "Or Lloyd? Has something happened to him?"

The taller by maybe an inch edged forward and with a stern look said, "We have no information on any accidents, ma'am. We're here to escort you to the station."

He took my arm as politely as Sam would've done and urged me down the steps. It was then that I saw the patrol car parked at the curb, with doors open and motor running, wasting gas as they wasted my time.

"Well, wait," I protested, as I was gently propelled to the car. "What's this about? Why do I have to go to the station? I need to call my husband, my lawyer, somebody. Just wait a minute now."

"Ma'am, we'd like you to come down for questioning. You can make a call when we get there."

"*Questioning?* What about?" I almost stumbled and would have without his firm hand on my arm. Looking over my shoulder at the house, I tried to call Lillian, but could only manage to pitifully whisper her name.

Stunned and confused, I quickly found myself in the backseat of an official car that had a reinforced mesh screen between me and my abductors and no handles on any of the doors.

Reviving somewhat as the driver made a screeching U-turn on Polk Street, I leaned up and knocked on the screen. "Young man," I called, "I can answer your questions in the privacy of my home, so stop this car this instant. I want you to call Sergeant Coleman Bates right now. Or Lieutenant Peavey, either one. They'll tell you you're making a mistake."

I could've been talking to the wind for all the notice they took. They didn't even have the courtesy to give me a glance, which proved how ill bred and poorly raised they'd been. Defeated, I slumped back in the corner of the seat, which was rank with sweat and other unsavory odors, hoping with all my heart that no one would see me being taken in like a common criminal.

# Chapter 9

I stormed back into the house and stomped through the rooms until I found Lillian cleaning the downstairs powder room. Fuming and outraged, I recounted to her an experience that no person of my standing should ever have to endure.

"And would you believe," I ranted, torn between shame and mind-ripping anger, "they questioned me about checks I didn't write, showed me what appeared to be my signature but wasn't, and wouldn't listen to a word I said. And they *fingerprinted me*! Then they took my picture, Lillian, and I'll probably be tacked up on every post office wall in the country. Oh," I said, my knees wobbling as I leaned against the vanity cabinet, "I have never in my life been so humiliated. It was that bank that turned me in, and believe me, they're going to be sorry."

"Now jus' calm yo'self down," Lillian said, taking my arm and guiding me out of the powder room. "Jus' wait till Miss Binkie get ahold of 'em. They know not to mess with you then."

"Binkie's in court," I said, wringing my hands and trying not to cry. "And Sam's gone and Coleman was unavailable, whatever that means. They took me to *detention*, Lillian, as if I were in grammar school! They made me stand in front of a magistrate and I *knew* him. I could've gone through the floor, because he just looked at me over his glasses and shook his head." I stopped and pressed a Kleenex to my nose. "And he made me promise to

appear in court next month, but, Lillian, I had my fingers crossed."
I looked up at her as the anger surged through me again. "Because
I am not going to court! I'm not the one who committed check
fraud. Somebody else is committing it on *me*. But nobody would
listen to me, and now I have a criminal record, and I'm probably
going to jail, and I'll never in my life live it down."

"Come on," Lillian said, urging me along. "I'm gonna set you
by the fire and bring you some spiced tea and let you calm yo'self
down. Nobody gonna be puttin' you in jail—I don't care what
kinda record you got." With an arm around my shoulders, Lillian
walked me to the living room. "How you get outta there, anyway,
without Mr. Sam or Miss Binkie?"

"If it hadn't been for Lieutenant Peavey, I'd probably still
be there, rotting away in a cell somewhere." I collapsed in the
wing chair beside the fireplace, so overcome with misery that I
wanted to curl up in a closet somewhere. "He spoke up for me,
and, Lillian, it just humbled me because I don't even *like* him."

"Yessum, he something, that man. Now I got to get on to the
store and pick up Latisha, so you jus' put yo' head back and rest
awhile. This get straightened out—see if it don't." She put a throw
over my lap and left me to come to terms with my new criminal
status. I immediately went to sleep, which as I later learned from
Mr. Pickens, was a sure sign of a guilty conscience.

❧

"*Miss Julia! Miss Julia!*" Lloyd's voice resounded throughout the
house as the back door slammed closed with a crash. "Guess what
I heard!"

Determined to keep my legal problems to myself, I sprang
from my chair to quiet him, meeting him as he burst through the
swinging door into the dining room. "Shh, Lloyd. Your mother's
resting."

He hunched his shoulders and squinched up his face in an

attempt to undo his boisterous entrance. "Oh, sorry," he whispered, as he slipped off his heavy coat. Static electricity crackled through his hair as he pulled off his knit cap.

"Come on in by the fire," I said. "You're about half frozen."

He tiptoed behind me to the chairs beside the fire, but didn't take a seat. He hung on my chair, his eyes big with the latest news.

"Now what did you hear?" I asked, smiling at him.

"You'll never guess," he said, leaning forward and trying to hold his voice down, "but that body they found was somebody who used to live here. It's all over school, but nobody knows who it was."

"Somebody who used to live here?" I repeated. "That could cover a lot of ground, Lloyd. People come and go all the time. I'm not sure that's much help."

"Yes'm, but everybody's saying it was somebody who was real *rich*. That oughta narrow it down. I bet we could figure it out if we give it a little thought." He pulled a footstool closer and sat beside me. "You probably even knew him, Miss Julia. It could be anybody who had a lot of money and used to live here but doesn't anymore. I can't come up with a soul, but I bet you could if you put your mind to it."

I gazed down at the avid look on his face and, still stung by Thurlow's accusation, recognized the danger the boy was in. And recognized, also, the part that I, all unwittingly, may have played in whetting his interest in rumors, hearsay, and—I admit it—gossip.

"Lloyd," I said, wondering how I could best phrase my warning, "it's perfectly natural—and commendable—to be interested in the things that happen in our neighborhood. We all are, but we mustn't let ourselves get carried away. We have to put this unfortunate occurrence in the proper perspective. Moderation is what we should aim for."

"Yes'm, I understand and I'm moderating as best I can. But, Miss Julia, it's not every day that a dead body turns up in your own teacher's backyard. I can't help but wonder who it was and how it got there."

"Well, yes, I suppose so. But you do have to be careful how you express that wonder. You can be interested but not obsessed, and it's all right to listen but it's not all right to pass along what you hear."

"Oh," he said, frowning and leaning back. "You mean I can't tell you or Mama or Lillian or Mr. Sam, or even J.D., what I hear?"

"No, no. I wouldn't go that far. Of course it's perfectly all right to tell us anything you want to. I'm just saying that we all have to be careful about becoming known as gossips. As long as we keep it in the family, we're all right."

"That's what I'm doing, 'cause I haven't told another living soul, not even at school."

"Well, good," I said, pleased that the boy was able to take correction with such ease.

"Yes'm," he went on earnestly, "and I wasn't even going to say anything to Miss Petty because I thought it might upset her, even if I just said, 'I'm sorry for your troubles.' But I didn't get the chance to not say anything because she wasn't there. We had a substitute like I thought we would."

"Oh dear," I said, thinking of that lonely woman who was now the focus of so much talk. "I hope she has friends to help her through this time. It must be so unsettling for her. I take it she lives alone, but she must have friends among the other teachers. Most likely they'll gather around for support. I expect she has a special friend, maybe one from school, don't you think?"

He shrugged his shoulders. "Beats me. I just see her during fourth period and sometimes at lunch, but that's all I know. Why? You think she has a boyfriend or something?"

"Goodness, I don't know. I'm just concerned about her well-being, living alone as she does and all this happening so close by. Your mother, though, speaks quite highly of her after their meeting at Parents' Night."

"I can try to find out if you want me to. I bet Joyce McIntyre would know. She hears everything when she gets sent to the principal's office."

"They're not likely to speak of a teacher's boyfriend in the principal's office, so I doubt your friend would know anything."

"You'd be surprised, Miss Julia. Joyce knows lots of things, or pretends she does, one."

"Well, don't ask her. That's the way rumors get started. Someone asks a simple question out of real concern for another person, and next thing you know, it becomes a statement of fact. No, Lloyd," I said, speaking to myself as much as to him, "let's not ask any questions or volunteer any information we might have. In that way, we won't be responsible for starting something that might not be true. Just let little Miss Joyce McIntyre alone."

He nodded gravely in agreement. "I know what you mean. You should've heard what she said about Mr. Dement one time, and I know that wasn't true. But a lot of kids still believe he cuts his grass in his boxers."

Hearing a car turn into the driveway, I said, "That must be Lillian. Run help her bring in the groceries, Lloyd, and I'll be there in a minute to help put them away."

He immediately stood up, ready to go. "Can I tell her about him being rich and how he used to live here? She might know who it was."

"Yes, you can tell her." I stood too and reached for the poker to shift the logs on the fire. But what I really needed was a minute or two to think. For one thing, my nerves were still frayed from my run-in with the Abbot County Sheriff's Department, and they'd stay that way until I could prove I was a victim, not a perpetrator.

And now, after cautioning Lloyd about how easily a person

could start a rumor, sometimes by throwing out only a suggestion that quickly became accepted as settled fact, it occurred to me that I might have become a victim again in a different case.

I thought back to my conversation with Thurlow Jones. His professed reason for calling was concern for what people were saying about Miss Petty. But what if his real purpose was to plant the image in my mind of her having questionable visitors? And if so, he'd certainly succeeded because I had immediately asked Lloyd about her friends.

I was ashamed to realize that behind my question had been an attempt to find out who her friends were, specifically her male friends, in case the body in the toolshed turned out to be one of them.

I thought I'd been subtle enough not to plant any images in the boy's mind, but I couldn't be sure. Thurlow had certainly managed to pique my imagination easily enough—it made my blood boil to recall how easily he'd snagged me. *"Visitors?"* I'd asked, immediately thinking of men slipping in and out of her house at all hours of the day and night, with not one iota of proof, fact, or evidence of any such thing occurring.

Oh, that devious old fox! He was trying to use me—*me,* the least likely person in town to spread gossip—to besmirch Miss Petty's reputation and put suspicion on her.

Well, we'd just see about that, I thought, giving the bottom log a vicious poke.

Except, why would he do that? Leaning against the mantel and gazing into the fire, I tried to figure out why Thurlow would want to make Miss Petty the subject of talk. His stated aim had been to deflect gossip from her, but plainly he had done the opposite.

Or was I the one at fault? Had Thurlow chosen to call me because he'd known that I would let one little word—*visitors*—expand into an entire mental scene of shadowy figures in a teacher's secret life? What if he'd called LuAnne Conover instead? What would she have made of that word?

Well, I didn't need to ask. LuAnne would've immediately thought the same as I had. The only difference would've been that she'd begin phoning around to pass the word that Miss Petty had secret admirers calling after dark. In other words, it would've not only spread, it would've grown.

Not with me, though. I determined to say nothing more about Miss Petty's visitors, if there'd even been any. So if Thurlow had some hidden agenda to damage Miss Petty's reputation, I intended to stop it in its tracks. His crafty plan to use me to spread gossip had just come to a screeching halt.

As I headed toward the kitchen to help Lillian, I heard Hazel Marie's phone ring. Just as she answered it, my phone rang with Sam on the line.

"Hey, honey," he said. "We're here safe and sound, all checked in and about to go out to eat. How're things there?"

"Oh, Sam, I'm so glad to hear from you." I gripped the phone tightly, wanting to plead for him to come home and get me out of the mess I was in. But I refrained, assuring myself that the bank would surely admit its mistake eventually, at which time I intended to move my business. So not wanting to disrupt Sam's trip, I fell back on an inane question. "How's the weather in Raleigh?"

"Cloudy and threatening, but the weather reports say it'll pass south of us. How's Hazel Marie? Pickens is in his room calling her now."

"Well, that's the question, Sam. She says she's fine, but I'm worried about the roads if it snows. I'd like to get her in the hospital where people who know what they're doing can make the decisions. I wish you both were back here."

He laughed. "We might be back before you know it. If Pickens doesn't like the way she sounds, I wouldn't be surprised if we don't make a return trip tonight."

We chatted a few more minutes with Sam reassuring me that any snow we were likely to get would soon melt. "But don't you be driving in it," he cautioned. "If you have to get out, call an ambulance or the emergency crews. But it's unlikely, Julia. Remember, Hazel Marie just saw the doctor and he said she has a couple more weeks, and she'll have to be induced even then."

That was true and his reminder relieved me. After a few minutes of a little more intimate talk, I hung up to proceed to the kitchen, my spirits low and my feet dragging with the heavy load I was bearing.

# Chapter 10

"Goodness, Lillian, you must've bought out the store," I said as I entered the kitchen and saw the array of sacks and bags on the counter.

"Have to get it while the gettin's good," she said, beginning to unload the sacks. "Ev'rybody an' his brother was in there, pushin' them carts all around an' just about runnin' over people."

Latisha came in carrying a bag of oranges, her little pink book bag on her shoulder and the earflaps of her stocking hat dangling around her face. "Hey, Miss Lady," she said in her high piercing voice, "Great-Granny got me an' Lloyd workin' up a sweat, 'cept it too cold to do much sweatin'. Where you want me to put these oranges?"

Lillian pointed to the table. "Take 'em out of the bag an' put 'em in that bowl over there. An' don't fall climbin' up on a chair."

Lloyd came in then with two sacks of groceries, closing the door behind him. "That's it," he said, making room for them on the counter. "Boy, it's cold out there."

"It shore is," Latisha said, as she carefully arranged oranges in the bowl. "Why, not too long ago I saw some of them little sparkly specks dancin' in the air. That means it's real bad out there."

Lloyd grinned at her. "They were ice crystals, Latisha—little drops that froze before hitting the ground."

"Well, I tell you one thing," Lillian announced, "they keep on dancin' out there an' some of 'em gonna pile up on the ground. They's big black clouds halfway 'cross the sky, an' that mean bad weather a-comin', I don't care what that weatherman say. All you got to do is look at the empty shelves in the grocery store to know people's stockin' up."

"I done fixed these oranges, Great-Granny," Latisha said. "What's next?"

"I know," Lloyd said. "We didn't bring in your overnight bags. Let's go get 'em."

"All I got's a grocery sack with my gown an' toothbrush in it," Latisha said, following him out the door. "But Great-Granny's got a suit satchel 'cause her clothes is bigger than mine."

"Lloyd," I called, hurrying to the door after him. "Would you get a few armloads of wood from the woodpile and put them here on the porch? Just in case?"

I turned back to the counter to begin unloading a bag filled with canned fruits and vegetables. "We can't let them stay out too long, Lillian."

But the children didn't linger. Shivering with the cold, they hurried in with Latisha's grocery sack and Lillian's suit satchel.

"All done," Lloyd said, removing his gloves. "I hate to tell y'all this, but it's sleeting out there. Latisha nearly slid off the steps."

"Oh my goodness," I said, looking out the window to confirm his announcement. "Lillian, just listen to it. And look, there's already a glaze on the bushes. It's really coming down. It'll be power lines next." Turning around, I went on, "Lloyd, you and Latisha look around the house and find as many flashlights as you can. There're a couple in the pantry, but be sure to check the batteries. There's one in your room and one in Sam's bedside table, but leave that one in case I need it. Oh, and candles. Bring all the candlesticks you see and put them here on the counter where we can find them."

Lillian said, "Y'all can put one of them flashlights by my bed so I don't fall down no stairs if I have to get up."

"Come on, Latisha," Lloyd said. "It'll be like pioneer days, except," he paused and grinned at me, "except it'll probably be sixty degrees tomorrow. When we get through, I'll help you with your homework, then we'll play a video game."

"I don't need to do no homework," Latisha said, following him out of the kitchen. "It gonna ice up all over the place an' they won't be no school tomorrow."

As the door closed behind them, I turned to Lillian. "What do you think? Is it going to get bad?"

"Law, I don't know, Miss Julia," she said, but she looked plenty worried about it. "I listen to the weatherman in the car, an' he still sayin' it gonna miss us. But the signs is all out there, an' 'sides that, I been smellin' snow all day."

"You *smelled* it?"

"Yes'm, plain as day." She nodded wisely. "It in the air, an' it might miss us like they say, but it gonna be a close miss."

"Well, I don't know what to do. If Hazel Marie goes into labor and we're iced or snowed in, we'd be in real trouble. Maybe we ought to just take her on to the hospital."

Lillian cocked her head to the side, her eyes roaming around the room as she considered the situation. "Well, first off," she said as if she'd come to a conclusion, "Miss Hazel Marie don't wanta go, though I guess if you tell her to get in the car, she would— but she not be happy about it. An' second off, even if we do get snow, it might not be more'n a inch or two, an' they scrape the roads pretty quick. We wouldn't be snowed in long. An' third off, if she was to have to go, you could call Coleman an' he get all his deputy friends an' highway patrolmans to get us to the hospital." She stopped to do a little more considering. "An' fourth off, why don't you call Miss Etta Mae an' let her do the decidin'?"

"That's exactly what I was thinking! I'll ask her to come spend the night, then we'll see what the morning brings."

I reached Etta Mae on her cell phone and learned that not only was she in her car, she was on the outskirts of Abbotsville.

"I'm glad you called, Miss Julia," she said. "It's getting pretty slick out here, and I was just wondering if I could make it to Delmont. You're nearer than my single-wide, so I'll head your way. How's Hazel Marie?"

"She's fine, but I'm not. This weather's making me antsy, and I'd feel a whole lot better if you were here with us. But be careful, Etta Mae, don't have a wreck on those slippery streets."

"I've got snow tires, so I'll be all right," she said and went on to assure me that she was accustomed to driving on county roads covered with ice and snow. "Of course," she added with a nervous giggle, "when it's bad, I get to take the boss's 4Runner. That's the only time Lurline let's anybody touch it."

After hanging up the phone, I looked up to see Hazel Marie wandering into the kitchen.

"Has anybody looked out the window?" she asked, a dreamy smile on her face. "It is just beautiful out there. It looks like a Christmas card with the sleet falling in the light of the streetlamps and covering the bushes."

A gust of wind rattled the windows and we heard the ping of sleet hitting the panes. "Just listen to that," she said. "I'm glad J.D. and Sam are safely in Raleigh."

"I am too," I said. "Nobody should be driving on a night like this." Except, I added to myself, Etta Mae, who I hoped would make it.

And it wasn't long before she did, running in along with a blast of cold air, laughing and holding on to the door frame to keep from falling.

"Etta Mae!" Hazel Marie cried. "What're you doing here?"

"Looking for a safe harbor in the storm," Etta Mae said, as she set the black valise that held the tools of her trade on the floor and began pulling off gloves and coat. "Hey, Miss Julia, Lillian. Boy, I almost didn't make it, and if I'd tried to get to Delmont I'd probably be sitting in a ditch right about now. And, uh, Miss Julia, I'm real sorry, but I sideswiped one of your boxwoods when I turned into the driveway. The back end of the car just slid right into it. I'll pay for it, though."

"You'll do no such thing," I said, taking the heavy coat she was about to hang over a chair. "You're doing us a great favor by being here. If we lose power, we can all huddle up and keep warm."

"It's not going to get that bad," Hazel Marie said with unnerving confidence. "J.D. said it's clear as a bell in Raleigh, so this will soon blow over."

I glanced sharply at her, but held my peace even though that hadn't been what Sam had told me. But of course Mr. Pickens hadn't wanted to worry her, so I didn't correct the weather report he'd given.

📜⚬📜

After a body-warming meal of corn bread and beef stew with every vegetable known to man in it, we sat around the fireplace in the living room and talked about everything except what was heavy on our minds: Hazel Marie's condition and the weather.

As for me, I mostly listened, having even more on my mind, what with being burdened by Thurlow's selecting me as the town gossip, to say nothing of having an arrest record and a court date hanging over my head, none of which I wanted to talk about.

Hazel Marie, however, seemed lighthearted and content, laughing as she played Old Maid with Etta Mae, Lloyd, and Latisha. Occasionally, though, I saw her hand rub the small of her back as if it bothered her.

Later in the night, after I'd banked the fire and been asleep for some time, I heard the shrill whisper of a voice right in my face.

My eyes sprang open, then just as quickly closed in the glare of a bright light. Latisha was standing by my bed, her head practically in my face as she aimed a flashlight at me.

"Miss Lady," she whispered, "that sleet's not comin' down no more."

"What? Oh, Latisha, well, honey, that's good, but move that flashlight out of my eyes. Thank you for the report, but you better run on back to bed."

"Yes'm, but I looked out an' that snow's a-comin' down like sixty."

"What?" I said again and began to get out of bed. Reaching over to turn on the lamp, I felt a heavy cold seep inside my flannel gown. It got even colder when the lamp didn't come on.

"Oh my goodness, the power's off." I grabbed my robe and stuck my feet in bedroom shoes, worried immediately about Hazel Marie.

"Yes'm," Latisha said. "I 'spect it is, but it's real light, anyway."

And it was, as soon as I opened the draperies. The snow that was falling and had already fallen lit up the inside of the house, and we had no trouble going down the stairs. Even so, I was glad to have Sam's flashlight in hand.

"Let's go build up the fire, Latisha," I said, "and get you wrapped up. We'll let the others sleep as long as they can. At least they'll be warm in bed."

We crept into the living room, where I was thankful to see a few embers still glowing in the fireplace. I piled on the wood, then began lighting candles, putting them safely away from the edge of tables or curtains. Latisha curled up on the sofa with a throw wrapped around her.

I sat in my Victorian chair as close to the fireplace as I could get, listening with apprehension to the wind buffeting the house and rattling the windows. The house was rapidly chilling down, and I wished to my soul that we had taken Hazel Marie to the hospital. At least there'd be generators there.

"Why'd you wake up, Latisha?" I asked.

"I had to go to the bathroom, but it was so dark I almost didn't make it."

I smiled, then with a jerk, I came straight up out of my chair as a bone-chilling wail emanated from the back of the house. "Hazel Marie!"

I nearly broke my neck getting to her room, the beam from the flashlight in my hand jumping from wall to floor and back again until I finally reached her door and aimed it at Hazel Marie. She was standing in the middle of the room, the hem of her nightgown clutched in her hands and a look of distress on her face.

"Oh, Miss Julia," she moaned, "I think I've ruined your rug."

In the beam of the flashlight, I saw her bare feet standing in a large wet spot that had darkened the colors of my Oriental.

# Chapter 11

"Oh, Lord, don't worry about that," I cried, running to her. "Get in the bed, Hazel Marie. Lie down. Are you in labor? I'll call somebody." Grabbing her by the shoulders, I led her back to the bed. "Lie down and be real still."

"I, uh, don't think I can," she said. "So much pressure." She lowered herself gingerly on the side of the bed, groaning with each breath.

"Is them babies comin'?" Latisha asked. I swung the flashlight around to see her, wrapped in the throw and standing in the doorway taking it all in. Her eyes shone in the light.

"Latisha," I said, trying to steady my voice, "get your flashlight and run upstairs. Wake up your great-granny and Miss Etta Mae. Tell them I need them down here, but don't wake up Lloyd. Then I want you to get back in bed and stay there."

"Well, I wanta see them babies."

"There are no babies here and there won't be. We're going to the hospital. Now run on as fast as you can." I turned her around and sent her on her way, then went back to Hazel Marie. She was sitting on the side of the bed, her hands clasping her spraddled knees, an inward look on her face.

"Hazel Marie, get your coat and shoes on. I'll heat up the car. Hurry now, and I'll be right back." I left my flashlight for her, then ran to the kitchen, bouncing off a couple of walls in the dark, grabbed another flashlight and clicked it on. Slinging a coat around my shoulders, I snatched up the car keys and flung open the back door. And stood there, my mouth gaping open. It looked as if a solid white wall had come down between me and the yard. In the beam of the light, I saw thick snow, not falling, but blowing crosswise with the wind howling like a freight train. I stopped in wonder, having never seen the like before. But this was no time for hesitation. I crossed the small back porch, pushed open the screen door with some effort, and plunged outside, sinking shin deep into snow. The wind whipped around me, throwing up snow and blowing it until I couldn't see anything but more of it. I couldn't see the cars; I couldn't see the garage; I couldn't even see the house behind me. Everything—ground and air—was wrapped in swirling snow with the wind lashing at me so that I could hardly stand upright. The word *blizzard* flashed through my mind as I jiggled around in the snow, stepping on my gown and almost upending myself.

But blizzard or not, I was not going to be stopped on my appointed rounds. I took a step toward where I knew the car to be, then stopped again as a loud crack scared the daylights out of me. A swishing, crashing noise followed the crack and I saw the large oak on the edge of Mildred Allen's yard flash through the snow and land across my driveway, limbs covering the back of my car and Etta Mae's as well.

Blocked in! Frenzied with fear and stiff with cold, I sloshed back through the snow and felt around until I found the screen door. I lunged for it and held on for dear life. Pulling myself out of the snowdrift, I left my bedroom slippers behind. Half frozen, with my feet like blocks of ice and the hems of my gown and robe wet with clinging snow, I stumbled back inside.

I closed the door, knowing we couldn't get to the local hospital, much less to Asheville. We couldn't even get to the car sitting right out there in the driveway, which wouldn't do us any good anyway because the car wouldn't be going anywhere until a few snow shovels and a power saw uncovered it.

With shaking hands, I snatched up the telephone, heard no dial tone, and ran back to Hazel Marie's room, thinking *cell phone, cell phone.* "Hazel Marie, where's your cell phone?"

She hadn't moved from the bed while I'd been gone, except now she was rocking back and forth, moaning with each rock. "On the, uh, the dresser."

Finding it, I dialed 911, waited an interminable time before hearing, "911, what is your emergency?"

"We're having a baby! *Two* of them! We need help—please send some help! Hurry!"

"Calm down, ma'am. What is your location?"

I told her, then pled for an ambulance and a doctor.

"All our crews are out on emergency runs, ma'am. Can you get her to the hospital?"

"No! That's why I'm calling you. We can't get the car out. It's snowing over here and trees are falling!"

"Yes, ma'am, I understand. We have some volunteers in four-wheel-drive vehicles, so somebody'll be there as soon as possible."

"But we need help now! What am I going to do? I've never had a baby or delivered a baby and—oh, Lord, Hazel Marie! What're you doing?"

Hazel Marie had fallen back on the bed, her knees raised as she groaned deep in her throat with a sound that sent a cold shiver down my spine.

"Ma'am? Ma'am?" the dispatcher said with a little more urgency than she'd heretofore exhibited. "Is she crowning?"

"Is she *what*?" I gripped the phone hard enough to crush it, trying to understand the question.

"Crowning. Is she crowning?"

"I don't know what she's doing," I wailed. I glanced at the bed.

"Hazel Marie, are you crowning?" Then to the dispatcher, "She can't talk. Please, please send some help."

Hearing another awful groan from Hazel Marie, I dropped the phone, thinking *thank goodness for Etta Mae.* If push came to shove, which it was fast becoming, she'd know what to do.

About that time she and Lillian, with bathrobes flapping, ran into the room, both of them exclaiming, "What's happening?" "What's going on?" "Is she in labor?" They hurried to Hazel Marie, took one look at her, and stopped cold.

"What're we going to do?" I asked, as tremors ran from my head to my feet. "All the emergency crews are busy and a tree is down. I can't get the car out—I can't even get *to* the car, and the power's off and we're going to freeze to death!"

"No, we're not," Etta Mae said, putting her arm around Hazel Marie's shoulders and helping her up. "Build up the fire, Miss Julia, and get some blankets and pillows. Hold on to me, Hazel Marie. We're going to the living room. Miss Lillian, spread out some newspapers on the floor. Put down some plastic trash bags too."

As Etta Mae walked Hazel Marie toward the living room, she had to stop twice as Hazel Marie bent over with deep groans. "I think it's coming," she panted. "I think it's coming!"

I ran ahead and moved the coffee table and the fireside chairs back, while Lillian spread newspapers and plastic bags on the living room floor. Then she ran to Hazel Marie and with Etta Mae's assistance managed to lay her down in front of the fire. I threw a blanket over Hazel Marie's shoulders and put a pillow under her head. Then I ran around closing all the doors to keep the heat in the room and to prevent any noise from drifting upstairs.

"Oh, Lord," Etta Mae said after a quick look. "It's coming! What do we do?" Her face was as white as a sheet.

"Don't you know?" I asked, my voice rising up the scale as I realized that my backup plan was turning out to be as futile as the original.

"I've read about it, but I've never done it," she said. "Old folks don't have babies."

Hazel Marie interrupted with a bone-grinding, bearing-down groan that even I knew presaged some kind of expulsion.

Lillian got down on her knees beside one of Hazel Marie's, took a look, and said, "Warm one of them blankets, Miss Julia, an' be ready for this baby. It comin' real soon."

I went to the fireplace to warm a blanket, which put me at Hazel Marie's feet—right in the line of sight. But I didn't look. My stomach was knotted up enough without actually *seeing* anything.

Lillian put her hand on Hazel Marie's abdomen. "Here come another big ole cramp. Now, Miss Hazel Marie, don't you worry none. It be a fac' that when babies come on they own like this, they don't have no problems."

Lillian worked around Hazel Marie, humming softly to calm her, then said, "One more, little mama, an' we have us a baby."

"Ah-h-h," Hazel Marie said, her neck extended and her hands scrabbling on the plastic beneath her. With a sudden gush, a tiny, wet baby slid out onto the warm blanket that I'd put in place. I thought I'd faint dead away.

"Gimme something!" Lillian said, then took the hem of her robe and wiped the baby's face. She held it up by its heels and gently patted its back until it emitted a quavery cry.

Hazel Marie lifted her head. "Is it here? Is it all right? Let me see, let me see."

"We gonna give her to you. Jus' wait a minute—this fine girl gonna have her mama in a minute. Law me, jus' look at that head of hair."

I took a look and was amazed at the thatch of black hair on that infant's head. Was that normal? I didn't know, but one thing was for sure: Mr. Pickens had made his mark.

"Miss Julia," Lillian said, turning to me, "we need us some string and some scissors, quick as you can."

*String and scissors, string and scissors.* I ran to the kitchen, my bare feet slapping on the floor. My mind was going ninety miles an hour while my heart fluttered in my chest as I tried to think what I could find. "Scissors, scissors," I said to myself, pulling open a drawer.

I grabbed Lillian's kitchen shears, then stopped. String? What kind of string? Sewing thread? My sewing box was upstairs, and the rough twine in the pantry wouldn't do.

Lloyd's shoelaces! There they were on the counter, still in their wrapper. I snatched them up and ran back to the living room, the wet hem of my gown flopping around my ankles.

"Perfect!" Etta Mae said, as I handed them to her. She knelt down, tore off the wrapper, then looked at Lillian. "What do I do with it?"

"Tie it on real tight here and here," Lillian said, pointing, but I didn't look to see where.

"Now cut it right about here," Lillian said, guiding the kitchen shears, as Etta Mae did the snipping. Lillian whispered a few more words of instruction, then she wrapped the baby in the warm blanket and laid it in Hazel Marie's arms.

There is nothing in this world more beautiful than a mother's face as she holds her newborn. I could've cried, as she was doing, with relief, until I remembered that we had another one to go. Or rather, to come.

# Chapter 12

By this time I was shaking all over, my hands trembling and my heart racing. Yet a swelling relief flooded my soul—we'd delivered a baby with no trouble at all. I sank down in a chair, unable to stand a minute longer. You'd think I'd had that baby myself.

Lillian and Etta Mae were sitting back on the floor, resting as Hazel Marie crooned to her new little girl.

"What're we waiting for?" I asked. "Can't we do something and get this over with? Or maybe," I went on brightly, "it'll wait till some help gets here."

"No'm," Lillian said with her hand on Hazel Marie, "'less they comin' in the door right now, 'cause she crankin' up again."

And she was, her face getting that intense look on it and a low moan coming from her throat.

"Miss Julia," Lillian said as she hunched over Hazel Marie's nether parts, "take that baby an' hold it while this one's a-comin'."

Never in my life had I held a newborn and I didn't know how to hold it or what to do with it. But Hazel Marie was now concentrating on the next one, so I had to take up the little bundle whether I knew what I was doing or not.

Easing stiffly onto a chair, I cradled the baby in my arms, so fearful of doing some irreparable damage that would maim it for life. I could feel it move inside the blanket, although there was more blanket than baby, and I was afraid the baby would slide right out of my arms. Then it starting mewling, sounding like a kitten. "Is this one all right?" I asked, holding it away from me. "It's about to cry."

Lillian didn't even look up from her ministrations. "Hold it close, Miss Julia, so it hear yo' heart beatin' an' it be all right."

Well, they Lord, I thought, is that all it takes? I cradled the baby a little closer, not wanting to crush it, and felt it nestle in.

Hazel Marie was panting by this time, her arms outstretched with fingers clutching at the plastic. Poor thing, she was going through it all again, and my stomach cramped up along with hers. It was almost more than I could take, but I didn't dare stand up and try to walk with a baby in my arms. So I sat there and watched and listened as Hazel Marie labored and sweated and moaned and bit her lip and struggled to bring another infant into the world.

"You can scream if you want to, Hazel Marie," Etta Mae said. "It's all right."

"No," she gasped. "Lloyd might hear."

And right then I realized again how much depth there was to Hazel Marie, in spite of her affinity for heavy makeup, short skirts, and sky-high heels. She had an inner strength that was seeing her through this ordeal as it had a few other trials and tribulations along the way. Of all the occasions in the world when a woman has license to scream and yell her head off, this was it. Yet she was concerned about disturbing her son.

I wondered if she was giving Mr. Pickens a thought, and if she was, if she still figured he was worth what she was going through. He was undoubtedly piled up in bed at a Motel 6, snoring away without a care in the world, while Hazel Marie was here paying the price. Although there'd been times in my life when I'd regretted having no children, what I was witnessing made me glad I was past my prime and in no danger of paying that particular price.

Suddenly with another gush and a muted cry from Hazel

Marie, Lillian said, "I got it, I got it. Hold on now, we jus' about done."

I could see her wiping another little naked black-haired baby, patting its back, then beginning to wrap it in the throw that Etta Mae had warmed. "You better cry now," Lillian said, quickly unwrapping it and dangling it upside down. "Lemme hear you cry," she urged as she gave it a right smart slap on the back.

The baby gasped, then let out a quavering wail, its little arms waving in the air and its body trembling all over.

"Is it all right?" Hazel Marie cried, craning her head to see what was going on. "Is it breathing?"

"It breathin', all right," Lillian said, smiling, as the baby took a deep breath and let us know in no uncertain terms that it had emerged unscathed. "An' this one got a real set of lungs on it. Jus' listen to it. You got another fine girl, an' Mr. Pickens gonna be struttin' 'round here so bad that none of us be able to stand him." She and Etta Mae went through the string and scissors procedure again, then Lillian wrapped the infant snugly and laid it in Hazel Marie's arms.

I leaned back in my chair and closed my eyes, utterly overcome with what we'd accomplished. Two babies delivered alive and well in the midst of a ferocious storm. It was more than I could take in, but it was over and as far as I could tell, no harm done at all. This would be something to talk about at the next book club.

I sat up and asked, "Can we get her on the sofa now and wrap her up?"

"No'm, not yet," Lillian said, her hand kneading Hazel Marie's abdomen. "Miss Etta Mae, we gonna need a pan of some kind. Run get that Dutch oven outta the kitchen."

I was stunned. "Don't tell me there's a third one in there!"

"No'm, we jus' got to finish up here," Lillian said.

Etta Mae returned with the Dutch oven, and she and Lillian bent over Hazel Marie again, delivering something else that I didn't see and didn't care to see. The baby stirred in my arms and one little arm flailed out of the blanket as it started kicking. I patted it and began rocking back and forth, hoping it would calm down.

Etta Mae took the other baby from Hazel Marie so Lillian could turn her and clean her up. That was another thing I couldn't watch. I declare, you might as well hang up your modesty the minute you find yourself with child.

Lillian warmed another blanket and spread it on the sofa. Then she helped Hazel Marie into it and wrapped her up. After putting a pillow behind her head, Lillian said, "Le's give them babies to her now an' they all get some rest."

Etta Mae and I laid a baby in each of Hazel Marie's arms. Her face glowed as she held them close. "You're sure they're all right?" she asked, then laughed. "I need to count their fingers and toes, but I don't have a free hand to do it."

Hearing a rumbling, grinding noise outside and seeing the flash of lights and the sound of motors, I hurried to a front window. "Well, would you look at that. They're finally here."

The snowplow went on past and was soon lost to sight in the falling snow, but two oversized pickups had stopped in the middle of the street. Four dark, bundled-up figures disembarked from the trucks, leaving headlights on and motors running, as they struggled through the snow toward our door, the strong beams of their flashlights lighting up the yard. I could see huge oak branches stretching across the driveway and covering our cars.

Opening the door, I barely recognized Sergeant Coleman Bates in a heavy coat and a knit cap that covered his face. He and the others stomped their feet, then came in. I quickly closed the door to keep what heat we had inside.

"Hey, Miss Julia," Coleman said. "Hear you need some help."

"I should say we do, or at least we did. Just look what's happened." I motioned toward Hazel Marie and her armful with some pride at what we'd accomplished.

Hazel Marie beamed at Coleman. "Look, Coleman. Two little girls."

"Beautiful," he said, but he wasn't really looking. "We're going to get you to the hospital now. Miss Lillian, we'll need a few more blankets, please, ma'am."

"But, the ambulance…?" I started, knowing there was no ambulance out there.

"All we have are four-wheel-drive double-cab vehicles, Miss Julia," Coleman explained. "Only way we can get around. Douglas, you take one baby and, Len, you take the other one. Wrap 'em up good and don't fall. Hazel Marie, I'm gonna carry you to the truck." He leaned down and picked her up as if she were as light as a feather, which she probably was after such a sudden loss of weight. Lillian wrapped another blanket around her as Coleman nodded to the fourth man. "Chris, beat a path for us and get the back doors open."

"Oh, Lord," I said, "don't anybody drop anybody."

Etta Mae suddenly appeared beside me, pulling on her coat and stepping into her boots. "I'm going with them."

"Oh good. Call us on Hazel Marie's cell phone and let us know when you get settled. We'll be over as soon as we can get out."

"I'll come get you when I get off," Coleman said. "Around eight, unless we're still shorthanded."

As Coleman turned sideways to get Hazel Marie through the door, I saw the lines of fatigue on her face and wanted to comfort her. "You were wonderful, Hazel Marie," I said. "I'm so proud of you."

She managed a tired smile. "Call J.D. for me," she said, as Lillian reached out and pulled the blanket over her head.

Lillian and I watched as the laden troop slogged through the drifts to the trucks. The two men with the babies got into the backseat of one truck, and Coleman lifted Hazel Marie into the backseat of the other one, with Etta Mae following her. Then

Coleman and the fourth man got behind the wheels, put the powerful engines into gear, and slowly edged away down the street.

"Well, Lillian," I said, as we closed the door, "we've done a night's work, haven't we?" Then, as we both went to stand in front of the fire, I reconsidered. "No, *you*'ve done a night's work. Oh, Lillian," I said, leaning my head against her shoulder, "what would we have done without you?"

# Chapter 13

Lillian patted my back. "Ever'body do a good job tonight," she said. Then with a shuddering breath which made me realize the strain she'd been under, she looked around. "We better get this room cleaned up. Them chil'ren be up 'fore long."

"What time is it, anyway?"

"No tellin'. All the clocks is stopped down here, but it late. Or maybe real early. An' you know what, Miss Julia? We didn't see what time them babies come."

"I didn't even think of it," I said, wondering at my lapse. "I'll run upstairs and get my watch." Then, feeling the cold even more, I said, "and get some warm clothes on too. My feet are about frozen with this wet gown clinging to them."

"You go on then," Lillian said as she swept up an armful of newspapers from the floor. "I got to get this pan outta sight 'fore Lloyd and Latisha get up."

I took a flashlight and headed out of the room, thinking that the second thing I was going to do as soon as I could get the car out was to buy another Dutch oven for the kitchen.

It was too cold to dress in my bedroom, so I got the warmest clothes I could find, plus a heavy coat and shoes, and went downstairs to put them on by the fire. I declare, I didn't think my feet would ever be warm again.

When Lillian and I had the furniture back in place, you could hardly tell that my living room had doubled as a delivery room except for the pile of blankets and stack of unused towels that we hadn't bothered to put away.

"Oh, Lillian," I said, a sudden thought coming to me. "Were we supposed to boil water?"

"What for?"

"I don't know. Maybe to wash our hands, but we didn't do that either."

"We do the best we can, 'cause that's all we could do. No time for nothin' else. What time you got, anyway?"

Looking at my watch, I said, "Almost five-thirty. You want to take a guess at when those babies were born? The birth certificates may ask for it."

"I say 'bout a hour ago, don't you?" Lillian stopped and gave the matter some thought. "Le's us say the first one come 'bout four-thirty, an' the other one, 'bout four-forty. That sound right to you?"

"I think it was a little before that. What about the first one at four-twelve and the next one at four-twenty-two? That sounds more precise."

"That's fine with me, but you better be callin' Mr. Pickens 'fore it get too much later."

"Oh my, yes, but that means I've got to go into Hazel Marie's cold room and look for her cell phone. And you need to get some clothes on too."

Each taking a flashlight and braving the cold again, we went our separate ways. Going into Hazel Marie's room, I swept the area with the flashlight beam and couldn't see the cell phone anywhere. I knew I'd talked to the emergency dispatcher on it, but I couldn't remember what I'd done with it after that. I might've still been searching if it hadn't started ringing.

Snatching it up from under the bed where I must've flung it, I answered it.

"Miss Julia? It's me, Etta Mae."

"Is everybody all right?" I asked, gripping the phone. "How're the babies? How's Hazel Marie? Is the doctor there?"

"Not *her* doctor. He's in Asheville. But some other doctor who was already here checked out the babies and her too. Then he decided—now don't get upset because I'm not a bit surprised—that she needed a little repair work. He's doing that now. But they've called Dr. Hargrove, who'll get here as soon as emergency workers pick him up. He can't get out on his own. I tell you, it's slick out there." She paused to take a breath. "How're y'all doing?"

"We're all right," I said, walking back into the living room where there was a modicum of heat. "Candles have about burned down, so I'll have to search for some more. And I still haven't called Mr. Pickens."

She laughed. "You better get on that pretty quick. She was asking about him before they took her to the operating room."

"Operating room! What're they doing to her?"

"Just a little nip and tuck," Etta Mae said. "She'll be back in her room within the hour, so I wouldn't even mention it to J.D."

"I was just about to call him. But, listen, Etta Mae, Coleman said he'd come pick us up when he gets off duty and take us over there. You want me to bring you some clothes?"

"Yes, ma'am, I sure do. I'm still wearing my coat 'cause this ole bathrobe is so tatty looking. Everything I need is laid out on the chair in the sunroom, if you don't mind bringing it all. Oh, and Hazel Marie wants her makeup case."

After a few more reassurances from her that Hazel Marie was fine and after she'd given me a rundown on the babies' weights and measurements, we hung up so I could call Mr. Pickens.

But just as I started to punch in his cell phone number, the door to the hall slid open.

"Has them babies got here yet?" Latisha stood there, bleary-eyed and yawning.

I opened my mouth to announce their arrival, then thought better of it. "Run wake up Lloyd, Latisha, and both of you bring down your warmest clothes. I'll tell you all about it when you get back."

Her face lit up and she turned to dash upstairs. I walked over and closed the door she'd left open, trying to retain what little heat the fireplace was putting out.

Then I called Mr. Pickens.

He answered in a deep sleep-laden voice. "Yeah?"

"Mr. Pickens, this is Julia Murdoch. I'm calling to tell you that your babies have arrived. Everybody's fine and they're all over at the hospital, being well taken care of." Then hearing a beep on the line, I asked, "What's that?"

"What's that?" he repeated.

"I said," I said, "your babies are here. Two little girls, one weighing four pounds, six ounces, and the other, five pounds even. Hazel Marie's asking for you, but I'm not sure you can get here. We're snowed in—power lines and trees are down, and not even the emergency services could get to us. Coleman had to bring in four-wheel-drive pickups to get her and the babies to the hospital." I heard another beep and decided to watch what I said in case our conversation was being recorded.

But the next beep was drowned out by the swish of covers as he sprang out of bed. "What'd you say?"

So I told him again and he could hardly take it in, kept asking the same thing over and over. "In the living room? You mean, *your* living room? Who delivered them? Is she all right?"

Finally I got tired of it and said, "Mr. Pickens, I've already told you all I know. Now, you should check the interstates before you start for home. You may not be able to make it up the mountain."

"Oh, I'll make it. Soon as I wake Sam, we'll be on the road."

"Well, you be careful and don't have an accident. I tell you, after last night I don't need another thing to have to deal with."

Just as we hung up, Lillian came in bearing a tray filled with cereals, bowls, a carton of milk, cups, and a saucepan. "I'm gonna see can I heat this water up over the fire and we'll have us some instant coffee."

Instant coffee was not normally my cup of tea, but right then it would certainly hit the spot. Lillian, fully dressed—in fact, more than fully dressed with heavy stockings and socks over those, plus two sweaters over her dress—drew up a footstool and stoked up the fire.

We heard the clumping of feet on the stairs and Lloyd and Latisha bounded into the room. Lloyd's hair was standing on end and his eyes were huge and wild looking.

"Where's Mama?" he asked, shivering in his flannel pajamas. "Latisha said the babies came."

"They did," I said, reaching for him. "And they're all at the hospital. You have two baby sisters, Lloyd. And we can thank Lillian for their safe arrival."

"You mean . . . ?" His head swiveled from one to the other of us, although I didn't know how he saw either one because his glasses were askew on his face. "You mean they came here, *right here,* and *nobody woke me up?*"

"Your mother didn't want to disturb you, honey," I said, attempting to soothe his hurt feelings. "And, besides, giving birth is woman's work, always has been, always will be." Of course, that pronouncement didn't take into account all the male obstetricians around, but Lloyd didn't notice and I didn't add a disclaimer.

"Well, that just frosts me good," he said, shivering from cold or excitement, or maybe both. "Looks like somebody could've called me. I could've helped, couldn't I? I mean, they're *my* little sisters, aren't they?"

"I knowed they was comin'," Latisha chimed in. "But I got sent back to bed, so I didn't get to see a thing."

"Look now," I said, trying to reassure the boy, "Coleman will be here in a little while to take you and me to the hospital. We'll visit with your mother and see the babies and hopefully get warm. So you run and get your warmest clothes, both of you, and get dressed here by the fire."

"I wanta go too," Latisha said. "I jus' got to see them babies."

Lillian, who was heating milk over the fire for hot chocolate, turned to her. "You not goin', little girl. Them babies is Lloyd's sisters, so he gets to see 'em first. 'Sides, I need you here with me. We may have to bundle up and keep each other warm."

Hazel Marie's cell phone rang then and I hurriedly removed it from my pocket. Glancing at the display, I saw that the charge was low, and no wonder, because it'd been under the bed most of the night. It had been warning me, I realized, by beeping its head off and was still at it. Hoping it would last a few more minutes, I answered it to hear Mr. Pickens.

"How is everybody?" he asked without any kind of greeting.

"Cold," I responded.

"I mean, how's Hazel Marie?"

"She must be doing fine. She's asking for her makeup case. Coleman is coming to get Lloyd and me in a little while, so I'll be able to tell you more when I can recharge this phone. So talk fast."

"We're just past Greensboro, so we'll be there in a couple of hours. Maybe three."

"Don't count on it, Mr. Pickens. If the highway is anything like Polk Street, you're going to have trouble getting up the mountain. If the highway patrol even lets you try."

"Is it that bad?"

I cut off the sharp retort that was on the tip of my tongue and said instead, "Under ordinary circumstances, Mr. Pickens, we would not have had a home delivery. So, yes, it is that bad and we're about to freeze to death."

"Did you check Sam's house? The power may be on there."

"Why, Mr. Pickens, I didn't even think of that. Of course, we have had a busy night and Hazel Marie was in no condition to walk four blocks in a foot of snow, and there is a tree down across the driveway, covering my car and Etta Mae's, and power lines are down, flipping and snapping in the streets, but I've really been slack for not looking into that possibility."

There was silence on the line and I worried that the phone had given out. Then he said, "Okay. We'll get a generator as soon as we get back."

"What a good idea," I said, warming to him again. "Except, I expect everybody in the county has already had the same one."

"Figures," he said in that snippy way of his. "Maybe Sam can find one. Just tell Hazel Marie I'm on my way."

"Speaking of Sam, may I speak to him?" But the phone went dead and that was the end of that.

Lloyd and Latisha came in, bearing armloads of clothes, their teeth chattering as they hurried to the fire.

"Boy," Lloyd said, "this house is freezing."

"That's why we got all the faucets dripping," Lillian said. "Next thing you know, water pipes be bustin' all over the place. Y'all wrap a blanket 'round yourselves and drink this hot chocolate while it hot."

Latisha took her cup, eyed it carefully, then said, "I sure wish we had some mushmellers to go in here."

As Lillian started to tell her to be thankful for what she had, Lloyd got tickled and almost spilled his cup. "Well," he was finally able to get out, "I wouldn't mind having some mushmellers either." And that set them both laughing.

After Lillian got the hang of toasting bread over an open flame without setting it on fire, we had the semblance of a breakfast.

"Time for you both to get dressed," I said, after my second cup of lukewarm instant coffee. "It's getting light outside and Coleman will be here before long. We can't keep him waiting, Lloyd, so hurry and get your clothes on."

"You mean, right here in front of *every*body?" The boy was shocked at the thought.

"No, you and Latisha can each get behind a chair. Nobody will look, I assure you."

While they did that, I went to the window and opened the draperies. The sun was up in a clear sky, shining as if a storm had never ravaged the landscape. But the evidence was there in the damage left behind. Still, it was a scenic view with snow covering the boxwoods, the walk, the street, and the church across the street. In fact, it was beautiful if you didn't have to go out in it and if you could admire it from inside a warm house, neither of which applied to me. All I could do was wish I were gazing at a Hallmark card instead of the real thing.

"One good thing," I said, turning back to Lillian. "Looks like the snow has stopped and the wind's died down. Maybe the storm's passed on by."

"Le's us hope," she said, as she buttoned Latisha's sweater. "I already had enough of it."

Lloyd turned himself around to warm his back as he stood by the fireplace. "Me too," he said. "The worst thing about a fireplace is that you burn up on one side and freeze to death on the other. You never can get warm all over."

Lillian rose from her chair and wrapped a blanket around Latisha and placed another one across Lloyd's shoulders. "That's the way people used to live all the time. Now you chil'ren stay close to the fire and not be runnin' all over the house."

Wishing I didn't have to run all over the house, I nonetheless left on my rounds to gather Etta Mae's clothes and Hazel Marie's suitcase, long packed for the expected trip to the hospital, as well as her makeup case. If that was left behind, somebody would be trekking back to the house on a pair of snowshoes.

# Chapter 14

Hearing the growl of a heavy motor and the crunching of ice as I brought the plunder into the living room, I glanced out the window.

"Coleman's here, Lloyd. He's a little early, so get yourself ready. Bundle up—coat, cap, gloves, everything. You have your boots on?"

"Yes'm, I do, but you better get yours on too."

I already had my coat on but sat down and pulled on a pair of galoshes that were so old the snaps no longer worked. They barely covered my shoes, which meant that I was going to have another case of frozen feet as they flapped around my ankles.

Coleman came in looking bone tired and half frozen, but he got Lloyd and the suitcases loaded into his truck, while I lingered at the door listening to Lillian tell me not to fall and break something. It was the first time I'd gotten a good look at the tree that had fallen during the night, seeing that it wasn't the actual tree but a huge limb that had broken off. Still, it covered my car and Etta Mae's, and would take a chain saw to remove. But the day was clear with no sign of the heavy clouds that had brought so much snow the night before.

Coleman crunched back through the snow to the porch where I waited. "Hop up on my back, Miss Julia. I'll carry you to the truck."

"I certainly will not," I said, picturing what I'd look like with arms and legs clamped around his back. "Just let me hold on to your arm and I'll get there under my own steam."

He laughed. "Let's do better than that." He lifted me off the porch, then with an arm around my shoulders walked me safely to the truck, which, thank the Lord, was warm.

It was a slow ride to the hospital over streets that had been scraped of snow but left with a layer of ice. Tree limbs, heavy with ice, hung over the streets, and power lines drooped low over the sidewalks. Broken limbs littered the yards.

"How long do you think we'll be without power?" I asked as Coleman gave his full attention to his driving. Lloyd hung over the front seat, breathing excitedly through his mouth.

"Couple of days," Coleman said. "Maybe more. Almost the whole county is out, except for spots here and there. Binkie says ours is still on, but who knows for how long. Duke Power has crews working, and they're calling others in, but it'll be a while before everybody's back on line."

"Well," I said, glancing at the tired lines around his eyes, "I know you've been out all night rescuing people, and thank goodness you were or we'd've been up a creek. And I know you need to go to bed, but do you think Sam's house might have power?"

He didn't answer for a few seconds as he maneuvered a tricky curve into the hospital parking lot. "Depends on what grid his house is on. The linemen are already getting Main Street up and running, so his may come in on that. Yours too, for that matter. Still, it's worth looking into. Want me to go by and see?"

"Oh, Coleman, would you?" I rummaged in my pocketbook and brought out a set of Sam's keys. "I just happen to have these with me. If his heat is on, would you let Lillian know so she and Latisha can go over there?"

"If it's on, I'll get them there."

I could only murmur, "Thank you." I hated asking another thing of him—he needed to be in bed.

As Coleman aimed for the emergency entrance, which had been thoroughly scraped and salted, Lloyd, who'd been unnaturally quiet, said, "I can hardly believe I've got two sisters, can you, Miss Julia?"

Before I could answer, Coleman said, "You're in for a treat, Lloyd. There's nothing like a little baby girl, and you have two of them. I call Gracie my Everything Girl, and you'll feel that way about your sisters. You might've wanted a little brother or two, but believe me, girls will steal your heart."

"Well, I don't know," he said. "I guess I was kinda counting on at least one little brother, but I'm trying to be content in whatsoever state I find myself."

I glanced sharply at him. "Who's been teaching your Sunday school class?"

"Mrs. Ledbetter."

*Uh-huh,* I thought. "Well," I said aloud, "far be it from me to contradict her, but consider this: if everybody remained content in whatsoever state they found themselves, nothing would ever get discovered, invented, completed, improved, or done. There's more to knowing Bible verses, Lloyd, than simply being able to repeat them." I gathered my pocketbook as Coleman, a smile lurking at the corners of his mouth, pulled to a stop beside the emergency entrance. "You have to rightly discern the word of truth. Thank you so much, Coleman. Would you like to come in and see the babies?"

"No'm, I better get on. I'll get the suitcases inside for you if you and Lloyd can manage after that. Then I'll check on Sam's house and Lillian."

I opened the door and considered the long slide to the ground. "You've been a wonderful help, Coleman. We'd still be stranded at home if not for you."

"I'm just glad you didn't try to get out on your own. There were more than a hundred wrecks in the county last night, and by this time I'm feeling like a regular Saint Bernard." He grinned, then hurried to my side of the truck just in time to save me from an embarrassing fall as my feet slid out from under me.

～:～

Having received directions to Hazel Marie's room, Lloyd and I rode the elevator to the maternity floor, our hands and arms laden with suitcase, makeup case, and a grocery sack of Etta Mae's clothes. Lloyd was having a hard time half carrying and half sliding his mother's suitcase along. It had been packed and ready for weeks, and from the weight of the thing, she'd prepared for a lengthy hospital stay.

I tapped on her door, then pushed it open. She was asleep and so was Etta Mae, who was curled up in a large upholstered chair over in the corner.

Before I could stop him, Lloyd ran to the bed. "Mama?" he whispered.

She came awake immediately and clasped him in a loving hug. He had about outgrown such affectionate maternal displays and usually slithered away from them. But not this morning. He not only endured, he hugged her back.

"Have you seen your sisters?" Hazel Marie asked.

"No, we came straight here. But, Mama, I didn't know a thing until Latisha woke me up this morning. I sure wish I'd been there when they came."

"Well, you were," Hazel Marie said. "You were upstairs, right over our heads. And, Lloyd, they came so fast that nobody had time to do anything else. But I was thinking about you the whole time."

Etta Mae stirred in the chair and came awake with a wide, uncovered yawn. "Hey, Miss Julia. Man, I'm glad to see you and my clothes." She laughed. "I'm not used to running around in my pajamas half the day. Hey, Lloyd. Let me get dressed, and I'll take you to the nursery to see the babies."

I gave her the grocery sack and she went into the bathroom to get dressed. "Hazel Marie," I said, walking to the foot of the bed, "I brought your makeup case."

"Oh good. I don't feel right without my face on. Did you talk to J.D.? What did he say?"

"He said he'd be here sometime this morning, but I tell you, Hazel Marie, the roads are bad and it wouldn't surprise me if it's later than that. I'd worry about his driving if Sam wasn't with him. He won't let Mr. Pickens take any chances. But tell me," I went on, "how're you feeling this morning?"

"Sorta like my granddaddy used to say: like I've been rode hard and put up wet." She smiled, lighting up her pale face. "But oh so happy that they're here and everything's all right. I just wish J.D. had been home."

"Well, Mama," Lloyd said, "Miss Julia said that having babies is woman's work, so you pro'bly would've let him sleep through it too."

Hazel Marie reached up and stroked the side of his face. "I probably would've."

But I knew better. If Mr. Pickens had been there, he'd have been in the thick of it, getting in the way, insisting on driving her to the hospital—tree blocking the drive or not—giving orders without knowing a thing about what was taking place, and generally making a nuisance of himself.

On second thought, however, it struck me that contrary to his usual take-charge manner, he might've been reduced to a quivering mass of nerves, completely unable to face up to the consequences of his actions. It would've been interesting to have seen his reaction to a home delivery, but I hoped to high heaven that Hazel Marie had had her last one because, interesting or not, I could do without seeing what he would do.

Etta Mae dashed out of the bathroom, fully clothed, including her pointy-toed boots. "Thanks so much, Miss Julia, for bringing my toothbrush and comb. I'm feeling halfway human again." She turned to Lloyd. "Ready to see those babies?"

"*Yes, ma'am!* Come on, Miss Julia, let's go see 'em."

Etta Mae led us to the end of the hall, where she stopped at a wide window that was covered with blinds. She tapped on a door and asked if we could see the Pickens twins. Then the three of us stood before the covered window waiting for the curtain to go up. When it did, we saw a row of bassinets, each with a swaddled baby in it. The nurse pointed to the two right in front of us, but I declare, I had to take her word for it. I wouldn't have been able to pick them out from any of the others.

Lloyd gasped at the sight and pressed his face against the window. In an awed voice, he said, "They're so little."

After he'd steamed up the window, he turned to Etta Mae. "Why've they got those little caps on?"

"That's to keep them warm," she said.

"Oh." He gazed at the babies again until one of them yawned and the other screwed up its face. "Oh look! One's sleepy and one's about to cry. Is it all right?"

"They're both fine," Etta Mae assured him. "And if you watch long enough, you might see them smile in their sleep." She paused. "That means they have gas."

"My goodness," I murmured. But I was as awed as Lloyd was. I could hardly take in the presence of these two little ones in our lives. And all because Wesley Lloyd Springer, my first unlamented husband, hadn't been able to walk the walk as well as he'd talked the talk. Because he'd taken Hazel Marie to his adulterous bed, then left her and his son penniless, which brought them as a last resort to my door, I now had a life richer than any wealth he could have left. And he'd been no slouch when it came to amassing worldly goods.

It did my heart good to know that he'd be gnashing his teeth if he knew where and to whom his money had gone.

Actually, whenever I was able to take a cosmic view of things, I had to laugh at what Wesley Lloyd had unwittingly wrought in my life, even though I well knew that my welfare had been the last thing on his mind during his dalliance with Hazel Marie.

It just goes to show, as Emma Sue Ledbetter was known to say, that all things work together for good. I'd once made it my business to look up that verse and found that she often left off the last part of it. But that didn't matter, the last part of the verse assured me that I still qualified for having things work out for good, anyway.

# Chapter 15

By the time we got back to Hazel Marie's room, she had finished her beauty regimen and had her bed cranked up behind her back. She looked considerably better than she had the night before, but the circles were still under her eyes and tired lines marked her face. And no wonder. If I'd gone through what she had—and without a whiff of anesthesia, mind you—I'd have looked worse than the wreck of the *Hesperus*.

She stopped brushing her hair and held out a hand to Lloyd. "Did you see them, honey?"

"Yes'm, and I still can't believe it. One of 'em was fixing to cry and the other one was yawning."

Etta Mae stood behind Lloyd with her hands resting on his shoulders. "They were waking up and about to let us know they're hungry. The nurses will be bringing them in to your mother pretty soon."

"Well, but," Lloyd said, "how're we going to tell which one is which? They both looked alike to me."

My eyes got wide and something dropped in the pit of my stomach. Had we mixed them up to begin with? How in the world would we be able to tell one from the other?

Etta Mae laughed. "Lillian and I made sure we knew which was which, don't worry about that. By now, though, the nurses will have little pink bracelets on their arms. One will say Baby Girl Pickens One and the other will say Baby Girl Pickens Two."

"Well, that's a relief," Lloyd said, but it wasn't to me because I hadn't seen Lillian or Etta Mae do a thing to distinguish those babies. All I knew was that I had held the firstborn, then we'd given both to Hazel Marie while we waited for Coleman. And for the life of me, I couldn't remember which baby was which after that.

"I tell you what," Lloyd said to his mother. "When you pick out their names, we can put them on their bracelets. So I think you better do that as soon as you can."

"Well, I've been thinking about names," Hazel Marie said. "But I can't decide. For one thing, I really didn't expect to have to name two little girls. If one had been a boy, I was going to name it for J.D., and if it'd been two boys, the other would be for Mr. Sam."

My goodness, that pleased me enormously, as I knew it would Sam as well. Too bad that it was water over the dam now.

"And," Hazel Marie went on, "I'd about decided on Britney if only one had been a girl." She stopped and thought about it. "I guess I was counting on one of each, now that I think about it. They'd have been Jamie and Britney."

*Well, I declare,* I thought, so Mr. Pickens's first name was James. That was a good, strong name. I couldn't, however, say the same for Britney. I so wanted to caution Hazel Marie about choosing a name that would date the child. A name made popular by some flash in the pan quickly goes out of fashion, while the child remains burdened with it. What, I wanted to know, was wrong with good old-fashioned names like Mary or Alice or Elizabeth?

"Well, but, Mama," Lloyd said, "you've got to come up with another girl's name now."

"I know," she sighed, "and I love Lindsay too, but I'm afraid that's out."

"I should say so," Etta Mae chimed in. "And Britney too, for that matter. You wouldn't want to name those babies for two of the wildest girls in Hollywood, would you?"

"No, I guess not," Hazel Marie said, as I mentally thanked Etta Mae for saying what I was thinking. "Anyway, I'll wait for J.D. and see what he says."

"I thought you had to have names that rhyme," Lloyd said. "You know, like Loyce and Joyce, or Annie and Fannie or Frannie or something."

Hazel Marie smiled. "People don't do that so much anymore, honey. Besides, I can't think of any rhyming names I like."

Etta Mae said, "I used to know some twins named Carrol and Farrol. They were brothers."

I wanted to add my two cents' worth, but it hadn't been asked for, so I refrained. I couldn't imagine what names Mr. Pickens would think up. You could never tell with him, and with a last name like Pickens, I hoped he would carefully consider the aptness of whatever he chose.

"Knock, knock." A nurse pushed in through the door, holding a cocooned baby. "We have two hungry babies here."

Another nurse, carrying the other baby, followed her in, and Hazel Marie's face immediately lit up.

Lloyd and I backed away from the bed to give them room. I thought we'd be told to leave, but Hazel Marie began unwrapping one of the babies.

"Look, Lloyd," she said. "Come look at her little tiny feet. You want to hold her?"

Lloyd edged closer, but not too close, as the baby began to cry, its little arms and legs waving in the air.

"No'm, I'll wait," he said.

"Good thing too," the nurse said. "This little girl is hungry." She began to disrobe Hazel Marie as the other nurse propped up some pillows for the second baby.

I couldn't believe it. They were putting both babies to the breast at the same time, and right out in view of us all.

"Lloyd," I said, "let's you and me go to the snack shop. I could use some coffee right about now. You can hold them when we get back." And, I thought to myself, when the feeding spectacle is over. There are some scenes to which children just should not be exposed.

After asking Etta Mae to join us and being turned down in favor of staying to make sure the babies nursed properly, Lloyd and I left. I was just as glad to be out of the room, and more than glad that he was out of it. It was amazing to me, given my limited experience with newborns, that babies have to be guided and coaxed into nursing. The last straw for me had been when one of the nurses had shown Hazel Marie how to encourage the baby to *latch on*—a concept too graphic for me to take in.

Lord! I had to get out of there and get Lloyd out too.

After hot chocolate for Lloyd and coffee for me, along with toast for both of us, in the snack shop, we went back to the room. By that time I'd warmed up enough to come out of my coat, feeling guilty about Lillian and Latisha at the same time. Here we were in the warm hospital while they were shivering in that frigid house.

"I should've brought all the cell phones, Lloyd," I said as we stepped off the elevator. "We could've recharged them here."

"Yes'm," he agreed, but his mind was on something else. "You think the babies are still with Mama?"

"Probably," I said, nodding. "We haven't been gone that long. But now that I think of it, Lloyd, even if I'd brought the phones, it wouldn't have done us any good. We wouldn't be able to call them if all the phones were with us."

"Maybe they're at Mr. Sam's house getting warm."

"I hope so." But I feared not.

He pushed open the door to his mother's room and I walked in behind him. Hazel Marie had one baby on her shoulder, patting its back, while Etta Mae stood by the bed with the other one.

"Here they are," Etta Mae said. "Come sit down, Lloyd, so you can hold your sisters. They've had their breakfast and this one told me she wanted you."

Lloyd grinned as splotches of color tinged his cheeks. He went over and sat in the chair that had been Etta Mae's bed. "Is it all right for me to hold them?"

"Of course it is," Hazel Marie said. "Just crook both arms and Etta Mae will give them to you."

I bit my lip, wondering about the appropriateness, to say nothing of the safety, of such seeming carelessness. Oh, I knew Lloyd wouldn't drop them or hurt them in any way. It was just that I'd always thought you shouldn't handle newborn babies too much. Like puppies, you know. Why, I once knew a woman who'd had a baby, and she carried that infant around on a pillow for the longest time. It must've been sitting alone before she ever picked it up and held it without that pillow between her and it.

I've often wondered how that child turned out.

When Etta Mae stepped back, I could see Lloyd holding both babies, one in each arm. His face was beaming with pleasure and, I think, with embarrassment at being the center of attention.

"Get your camera, Etta Mae," Hazel Marie said, as she leaned over to watch her three children. "I have to have a picture of that."

Etta Mae got out her fancy phone and snapped away. "Just hold real still, Lloyd."

"Well, but they're wiggling," he said, frowning as one kicked out. "Are they all right?"

"They're fine," Hazel Marie said. "I think they know their big brother has them."

The nurses came in then to take the babies back to the nursery. They oohed and aahed at the sight, everybody thinking it was so cute, as they said, for big brother to be taking care of his sisters. But it was a relief to me to have those babies back in professional care. I think it was to Lloyd too, because he'd barely taken a deep breath the whole time he'd had them.

"You did real good, Lloyd," Etta Mae said. "There's only two things you have to watch out for with little babies. One is to always support their heads, because their neck muscles aren't strong enough yet. And the other thing to watch out for is the soft spot on their heads. The bones in their heads haven't grown together yet, so you have to be careful about that."

Lloyd's eyes grew big. "You mean they have *holes* in their heads? Where? I didn't see any."

Etta Mae started laughing as Hazel Marie began explaining newborn anatomy to Lloyd.

I pulled Etta Mae to the side, whispering, "Etta Mae, I'm worried to death that we mixed those babies up. Do you really know which one came first?"

"Yes, ma'am, I do. Lillian told me to tie a bow on the first one and a knot on the other."

"A bow and a knot? Where?" Thinking of hair ribbons for little girls, I went on, "And with what?"

"With Lloyd's shoelaces, Miss Julia, and if you think about it, you'll know where."

# Chapter 16

After the babies were gone, we all found chairs and sat around watching as Hazel Marie's eyes got heavier and heavier. Actually, I began to nod off myself, in spite of the hard chair I was sitting on. It had been a busy night with little sleep for anyone. If I'd had a car and if the streets had been passable, I would've gone home. If, that is, home had been as warm as the hospital.

As it was, Lloyd and I were stuck, which wouldn't have been so bad if I hadn't been worried about Lillian and Latisha. Still, I had no desire to spend the day watching Hazel Marie catch up on her sleep.

It was midafternoon before things began to change. Hazel Marie had been brought a lunch tray earlier than we normally ate, then the nurses appeared again with the babies. At that point, Lloyd, Etta Mae, and I went to the snack shop and had lunch ourselves. Then we all settled down again to doze in between assuring Hazel Marie that Mr. Pickens would soon put in an appearance.

Unless he and Sam were in a ditch somewhere after skidding off the road, but I didn't bring that up. Actually, though, I was as eager for them to get home as Hazel Marie was. It would be a relief to turn Sam loose on the bank and on that magistrate who wanted me in court. We'd just see who'd made a mistake then, and believe me, I was just outraged enough to bring a lawsuit against that bank for putting me in the untenable, not to say deeply embarrassing, position of having an arrest record. Sam could handle that too.

Just as I squirmed in my chair, reliving the humiliation, the door swung open and Mr. Pickens came flying in, almost stumbling over my feet, and headed across the room. He practically picked Hazel Marie up from the bed, burying his face in her neck. She clasped her arms around him, while I was mesmerized by the intensity of their greeting. At the same time, I looked around for Sam. I might not have greeted him with the same powerful display of emotion—it was in public, after all—but I would've been mightily relieved to see him.

"Honey," Mr. Pickens murmured. "Oh honey, I'm sorry I wasn't here. Are you all right?"

Hazel Marie disentangled herself and with a glowing face reached up to run her hand down his unshaven face. "I'm so glad you're here," she whispered. "I'm all right. I had the best doctor and the best nurses in the world."

Mr. Pickens straightened up and looked around. "I can't tell you how much I appreciate what you all did. Etta Mae, thank you for taking care of my girl."

"Not me," Etta Mae said brightly. "It was Lillian who did the honors. I think she must've been a midwife in another life."

"But you did a lot," Hazel Marie said. "And Miss Julia did too. She held the first baby while the second one was coming. Everybody was so good to me, J.D. And, of course, Coleman came with some other men and got us all to the hospital."

Mr. Pickens rubbed his face, making a scratching sound. "I have a lot of folks to thank, and, Lloyd, you're the first one," he said, turning to him. "Thank you for looking after your mother."

"Well, but I didn't do anything. I would've, though, if I'd known what was happening."

"You were there," Mr. Pickens said, "and that's enough for me."

He reached over and drew the boy close to him. "Have you seen your sisters?"

"Yes, sir, and held them too. They're awfully little."

Hazel Marie ran her hand up and down Mr. Pickens's arm, as if she needed to feel him. "Have you seen them?"

"Not yet," he said. "You come first. Always, you come first." And then to Lloyd, "Want to show me where they are?"

Lloyd's face lit up. "They're in the nursery. Come on and I'll take you."

Before the door swung behind them, Mr. Pickens stuck his head back in. "Almost forgot. Miss Julia, we found a generator, so you have power now. And Sam has Poochie Dunn and a helper cutting up the limb that fell on the cars."

"Oh my word," I said. "Poochie with a chain saw? Etta Mae, our cars might not survive."

Mr. Pickens laughed. "That's why Sam didn't come. He didn't want to leave him on his own. I'll run you all home soon as I get back."

❧ ❧ ❧

The glare on the snow hurt my eyes as Mr. Pickens drove Etta Mae, Lloyd, and me home. I declare, who would've thought that so much snow could have fallen in just a few hours the night before, then have the next day turn out as clear as a bell. But it was cold, bitterly cold. What lay on the ground would be with us for a while. The old folks say that when snow stays on the ground for any length of time, it's waiting for more.

I tell you, I don't think I could live where snowstorms were as common as weeds. I knew that what we'd just experienced would be laughable to folks who lived farther west or north of us. But we're unaccustomed to and unprepared for such shocks to our weather systems.

I closed my eyes against the glare and held tightly to the

armrest as the back end of Mr. Pickens's car slid on a curve, then straightened out as his big tires got traction.

"Be careful, Mr. Pickens." I couldn't help but caution him. We didn't need anybody else in the hospital.

He glanced at me, a smile on his mouth. "Didn't mean to scare you."

I didn't respond, still thinking of what we'd gone through the night before. If you want to know the truth, the storm hadn't been all that bad, now that it was over and done with. It would've been a mere inconvenience if, that is, we hadn't lost power and if Hazel Marie's babies hadn't chosen to emerge during the midst of it. That made it one of those storms of the century in my book.

As Mr. Pickens steered the car to a stop before my house and beside a mound of snow left by the snowplow, I heard the whine of a power saw. Sam was standing where my driveway was supposed to be, watching Poochie Dunn cut small limbs from the large one across the cars. Another man was stacking the cut pieces along the side.

"I wish Sam wouldn't stand so close," I said, as the grinding noise revved up and another limb fell. "Half the time Poochie doesn't watch what he's doing."

Mr. Pickens grinned. "Maybe not, but Sam was glad to see him. There'll be a bunch of people out today, trying to make a little money. Poochie's probably as good as any."

"Well, I hope so," I said, buttoning my coat. "Anyway, one good thing about living so close to town: we'll get power back when Main Street does. I expect there'll be people living farther out who'll be without it for days to come."

"I wouldn't doubt it," Mr. Pickens said. "Wait till I come around, Miss Julia, before you get out. It'll be slick."

I looked at Etta Mae and Lloyd in the cramped backseat. She was sound asleep, but Lloyd was eager for me to get out so he could climb over my seat.

"I can't wait to tell Lillian and Latisha about my sisters," he said. "And that I got to hold them."

I leaned back and patted Etta Mae's knee to wake her. "We're home, Etta Mae. But wait and let Mr. Pickens help you to the door. The walk hasn't been shoveled yet. Then I want you to go to bed."

She came awake yawning, glanced around and said, "I still feel bad about leaving Hazel Marie."

"You shouldn't. You didn't get any rest last night, so it's no wonder you're tired. Besides, Mr. Pickens is going back over there and he'll be with her all afternoon."

Mr. Pickens opened my door and offered his hand. I was glad to have it, for the street was like a skating rink. As we high-stepped it through the snow to the front door, Sam left his supervisory job and took over from Mr. Pickens.

He put his arm around me and steadied me as we slogged through the snow. "I'm so glad you're home, Sam," I said. "It's been a night to remember and one I wouldn't want to repeat."

"You're not likely to," Sam said, laughing. "Pickens wouldn't survive it."

"I don't know why not. By the time he knew anything, it was all over." When we stepped up on the porch, I stomped the snow off my galoshes and held the door for Etta Mae and Lloyd. "Sam," I said, lowering my voice, "I really need to talk to you. You're not going to believe what else happened yesterday."

"Okay, sweetheart, but I better stick with Poochie till he's through."

"Tell him to hurry. This is important."

Mr. Pickens waved, got in his car, and left to go back to the hospital.

"Oh my," I said, waving back. "I thought he'd come in and at least get himself shaved." Then turning again to Sam before going inside, I said, "Sam, please don't let Poochie do any damage. He's as likely to cut up a car instead of the tree."

"He's doing fine. Now you go on in and get warm. I'll be in soon, and I want a play-by-play account of last night."

He would get more than that by the time I was through telling him how I'd been treated. But what a relief it was to find the house warm and the lights and appliances working. The roar of the generator was little enough to put up with to have hot water. Longing for a bath, I quickly greeted Lillian, then started upstairs, leaving Lloyd excitedly telling Latisha and Lillian about holding his baby sisters.

"It's gonna be my turn next," Latisha said, her piercing voice following me upstairs. "Great-Granny say they have lots of hair, so the first thing I'm gonna do is put in some cornrows."

I laughed as I headed for our temporary bedroom, once Hazel Marie's, making tracks to a hot bath.

Lillian had a pot of coffee ready when I came downstairs, freshly washed and clothed. I'd been tempted to lie down for a while, as Etta Mae was doing, but decided I'd be better off with an early bedtime.

Sam came stomping in, his face red from the cold, just as Lillian and I sat down at the kitchen table with cups of hot coffee and a plate of cookies.

"Well, Julia," he said as he removed his coat, "your cars are now uncovered. I've got Poochie and his helper clearing the driveway and the walk. I don't think they can do any damage with shovels."

"I wouldn't be too sure about that," I said, smiling as I poured coffee for him. "Sit down and get warm, Sam. Lillian and I were just about to relive last night."

"I want to hear all about it," Sam said, pulling his chair up to the table. "Start at the beginning and tell me everything."

"Well, the first thing that happened was Latisha waking me with a flashlight in my face to tell me the power was out." Then with help from Lillian I started telling it, step by step, and the

further along I got, the more my heart expanded at how extraor-
-dinarily we had all performed, and the more I began leaving the
story to Lillian. It was her time to shine, and Sam was appropri-
ately impressed with the tale of her skill.

I sat and listened but desperately wanted to get Sam off alone
to put my case against the system into his hands. I could barely
contain myself, but Lillian deserved his full attention and my
time would come.

# Chapter 17

But not for a while, because Sam offered to take Lillian and Latisha to the hospital to see the babies, although I knew he was eager to see those infants too. My legal consultation with him would have to wait. Maybe it was just as well because the more I thought about it, the less eager I was for him to know he was married to a woman with a mug shot and a record.

Latisha, of course, was beside herself with excitement, and Lillian glowed with anticipation. Lloyd decided to go with them but assured me he'd come back when they did.

"It's fun to see the babies," he said in that solemn way of his, "but it sure gets boring watching Mama sleep."

As Lillian shrugged into her coat, she said, "I'm gonna try to get Mr. Pickens to come eat supper with us. He prob'ly not had a bite all day. Everything's in the oven, an' we'll eat soon as I get back."

"I'm gonna ask Miss Hazel Marie what she gonna name them babies," Latisha announced, as Lillian tied a hat on her head and handed her a pair of gloves. "Me and Lloyd been thinking up some good ones."

After they left, I settled down beside the fireplace, luxuriating in the warmth from it and the furnace. We never truly appreciate the common pleasures of life until we have to do without, and I determined to mend my ways accordingly.

Even though I was about to nod off as I stretched out in a wing chair, my feet on an ottoman, the ringing of the telephone was a pleasant surprise. The lines were working again, so we didn't have to depend on cell phones, which I'd not recharged, anyway.

"Julia," LuAnne Conover said when I answered, "do you have power?"

"We do now, but only because Sam found a generator. But oh, LuAnne, let me tell you what happened."

"Well, first," she said, talking right over me, "let me tell *you* what happened. You won't believe this, Julia, but guess who spent the night with who."

"Who?"

"That teacher, what's-her-name Petty, spent the night with *Thurlow Jones!*" LuAnne had to stop to get her breath as the words caught in her throat.

"Oh, that couldn't be true."

"Well, it could too. I just talked to Mildred and she heard it from Doris Allman, and Doris got it straight from the horse's mouth. She's close friends with the Walkers and you know they live right down the street from Thurlow, and Bob Walker went out early this morning to check on the neighbors and he saw Thurlow walking the Petty woman home through the snow in their backyards. And here's the thing, Julia, Bob said she still had on her gown! It was hanging below her coat, so it hadn't been just a brief visit."

"I don't know, LuAnne. It could've been nothing more than a neighbor helping a neighbor. This whole section lost power, and I expect Thurlow was simply looking after her. She lives alone, you know."

"I do know it, so she has no one she has to answer to. And I think it's awfully suspicious to be sneaking home at sunup. Bob said she was hanging on to Thurlow as if her life depended on it."

"It probably did," I said, recalling how I'd hung on to Coleman and Mr. Pickens and Sam, in turn, as they helped me slog through snowdrifts. "But I'll tell you, LuAnne, when you lose power in cold weather, any port in the storm will do. So maybe he had heat and she didn't. I can't think of another reason in the world why any woman would spend a night with Thurlow Jones. And, frankly, I'd have to be near freezing to do it."

"Well, me too," LuAnne said, then in a musing sort of way went on. "But still waters do run deep, and we don't know why that man was found dead in her toolshed or garage or wherever. In fact, we don't know anything about *her,* and I think that's strange. She's lived here all her life, except for college, I guess, and who knows her? I don't even know where she goes to church. *If* she goes. And if she doesn't, that would be a pretty come-off for a teacher of young children. We need to look into this, Julia. No telling what goes on in that little area of town. Everybody leaves Thurlow alone because you never know with him. And that leaves him free to do whatever he wants. But a *teacher?* We ought to find out what's going on."

"Well, you'll have to do that yourself, LuAnne. I have my hands full here." Then I went on to tell her what had happened the night before: how Lillian and Etta Mae had delivered Hazel Marie's twins in front of the fireplace with a storm raging outside and our cars blocked in and Sam and Mr. Pickens halfway across the state and how fortunate we'd been that Lillian had bought new shoelaces for Lloyd's tennis shoes.

"*Shoelaces?*" she asked. "What did shoelaces have to do with it?"

So I told her and her reaction was all I could've hoped. "I can't get over it, Julia," she said as she gradually realized how monumentous a task a home delivery had been. "You actually helped deliver those babies? On your living room *floor?* How in the world will you ever have a Circle meeting in there again? And serve *food?*"

"Oh, LuAnne, nobody'll think a thing about it. But listen, the whole thing was just remarkable, and Lillian was—well, I can't praise her enough. You know I'd never seen a delivery before. Not that I actually *looked*, but you know what I mean."

LuAnne was properly impressed with what had happened, and to tell the truth, so was I. The more I thought about it and talked about it, the more wonderful it seemed. But I tried not to think about the birthing episode in too much detail because every time I did, I'd think of all that could've gone wrong. Then my nerves would start twanging and my stomach would clutch up on me and I'd have to quickly think of something else.

So to turn my thoughts in another direction, I said, "LuAnne, I think we should give Miss Petty the benefit of the doubt and not assume that anything unsavory went on last night. You know what it's like to be in a cold, dark house with no idea when the power will be back on and a terrible storm bringing down trees all around you. I expect if she did go to Thurlow's, it was because she was frightened. Or it could be that he went over and insisted she come to his house—purely out of neighborly concern for her welfare."

I stopped and considered the possibility of Thurlow's having any neighborly concern for anybody and thought it unlikely because he'd never shown any signs of it before. Still, I couldn't discount the possibility that some empathy for the plight of Miss Petty alone in a freezing house had welled up in his stony heart. For one thing, he probably hadn't wanted another dead body showing up practically in his own yard.

"I think," I went on, "that without any further indication of wrongdoing, we ought to assume good motives on the part of both of them. And with all I have to contend with right now, I'm going to figure it's their business and not mine."

"Well, I'll tell you this," LuAnne said, "if I had a child in her class, I'd *make* it my business. I'd make it my business to find out exactly what went on last night and what might be continuing to go on. Lloyd is at just the right age to pick up on things like that and be mortally influenced. And with his mother having her hands full looking after those two babies, and at her age too, who's going to be looking after him? You, Julia, that's who. If I were you, I'd want to know what kind of life his teacher is leading."

"I guess if you put it that way..."

"What other way is there to put it? I'll let you know if I hear anything else, because I'll bet you anything there *is* something else. Thurlow's been without a woman for years and years, and you know that's not normal." LuAnne stopped momentarily, then clarified her statement. "Of course he's not normal anyway, but still. Maybe the reason he's been single so long is because Miss Petty's been on call next door."

"*LuAnne!* That's really jumping to conclusions and I just don't believe it. Oh, I wouldn't put it past *him,* but her? No, that's too much risk for a schoolteacher, well, for any woman who values her reputation. Nobody gets by with anything in this town, and you know it."

After we hung up, I thought of a dozen things I should've said to distract her from pursuing the ins and outs of Thurlow's personal life. To say nothing of pursuing whatever personal life Miss Petty had. But then I realized that there was no way LuAnne could do any pursuing at all, not without doing a stakeout with night-vision binoculars, which in the present weather conditions I doubted she'd be inclined to do.

So I leaned back in the chair, gazed at the fire, and congratulated myself that I was keeping the vow I'd made to Sam to stay out of other people's business. Besides, I had enough unsettled business of my own to keep me fully occupied.

But then I had to stop and rethink the whole situation. Did, or would, Miss Petty's escapade last night affect Lloyd?

Ridiculous, I told myself. The woman had had no lights or

heat and, frankly, I myself would not have hesitated to bang on Thurlow's door last night—if he'd lived next door—to get Hazel Marie into a warm place.

And LuAnne's implication that Miss Petty had been the reason that Thurlow was able to go so long without a woman in his life just tore me up. The idea, in the first place, that a man *has* to have a woman was one that I just could not accept. Thurlow was no teenager with raging hormones. He'd lived his whole life without a wife; why in the world would he suddenly feel a ravenous need for a substitute? Of course, as LuAnne said, Thurlow wasn't what you'd ordinarily call normal, so who knew what he'd feel? But Miss Petty was half his age and I couldn't imagine that she could do no better than to take up with a man who rarely washed, shaved, or changed his clothes.

No, I was going to stay out of it. It was none of my business, unless proof positive of Miss Petty's living a double life happened to emerge. Then I'd rethink my stance.

But one last thought occupied my mind as I heard Sam drive up, bringing Lillian, Latisha, and Lloyd home. There was no reason in the world why a person could not live, and live well, without a member of the opposite gender. There is such a thing as self-control, you know, although in my opinion, it's in remarkably short supply. I myself had had every intention of living alone after Wesley Lloyd Springer passed on. In fact, the single life had seemed devoutly to be desired after living so long with him, and I'd looked forward to it. That was, of course, before Sam came along and changed my mind and my life.

# Chapter 18

Hearing car doors and back doors slam, along with the rush of feet and the gabble of voices, I hurried to the kitchen, where Lillian, Latisha, Lloyd, and Sam were coming in. The first thing I noticed was Lillian's beatific smile, as she completely ignored the fact that Latisha was bouncing around her in a frenzy of excitement.

"Tell her, Great-Granny," Latisha was saying. "Tell her what they gonna do!"

Then I noticed the big smiles coming from Sam and Lloyd. Something was up, and I hoped I'd be as happy about it as they seemed to be. "Tell me what?" I asked.

Latisha bounced over to me. "They done named them babies, an' one of 'em is named for Great-Granny!"

"Why, my goodness," I said as I looked for confirmation from Lillian. Her face told me all I needed to know. "What an honor, Lillian! And well deserved, I must say."

"Well," Sam said, "the honors just keep on coming because the other one is named for you."

"Oh," I said, my hand going to my throat in dismay. If that was true, then that child would be Little Julia and I would be Big Julia for the rest of my life. I didn't want to be Big Julia, but how could I refuse? "That *is* an honor," I managed to say, although it was one I could have easily done without.

Lloyd had his coat off by this time, and in his excitement he'd let it drop to the floor. "Let me tell the rest of it," he said. "You're gonna love it, Miss Julia, 'cause J.D. made everything come out right. For a long time, Mama kept saying that she should've had triplets so she could use everybody's name, but J.D. said if that was the case, she should've had quadruplets 'cause he wanted to name one of 'em for her. But after a while, he came up with the solution and she's real happy about it."

Oh my word, I thought, she's used Britney and Lindsay after all. But I said, "I can't wait to hear."

"You're gonna love it," Lloyd said again. "See, here's what they decided. The first one is named Julia Marie for you and Mama, and the other one's named Lillian Mae for Lillian and Etta Mae. They got everybody in, just like they wanted to, 'cause J.D. said it took all four of you to get my sisters here."

"I'm overcome," I said, sinking into a chair. All I could think of was how I'd wanted those babies to have good old-fashioned names, but this was too much of a good thing.

"Yes," Lloyd went on, "and they're going to call them Julie and Lily Mae, you know, to keep from mixing everybody up."

*Julie!* I thought with even more dismay—the name that was the bane of my existence because so many people misread or misspelled my name and had to be corrected. Well, I thought, I'd have to get over that in a hurry. And I would, for having a little namesake, even though she'd be called by an aberration, was indeed an honor. At least there'd be no Big and Little Julias, and for that I was more than thankful.

By the time the evening meal was over and Sam and I had retired to our room, I was about ready to jump out of my skin. Not only was fatigue making me jittery, it'd been all I could do to keep from shouting, "They arrested me! Help me! Help me!" and disrupting everybody at the dinner table.

But, finally, I could cut loose as Sam closed the door to the hall and said, "Now, sweetheart, what did you want to talk about?"

"I was arrested yesterday," I said, as if it had been the most normal occurrence in the world. Unable to meet his eyes, I looked around Hazel Marie's pink room, which she'd been unable to use since she'd been ordered not to climb the stairs.

"What?"

"Two deputies came to the house, Sam," I said, as my composure broke. "And took me in for questioning. *For bouncing checks,* of all things! And they fingerprinted me and took my picture and made me appear before a magistrate!"

"Julia, honey," Sam said as he put his hands on my shoulders, "that wasn't exactly an arrest, but you don't need to be bouncing checks. If you need more money, Binkie can make it available. Just tell her what you want."

"But they weren't mine! I didn't write a single one of them. Just look, Sam," I said, waving my household checkbook, "the figures are absolutely accurate, because I reconcile this thing every month when the statement comes in. And how anybody could make copies of my checks, I don't know."

"Let me see," he said, taking it from me. "You haven't gotten this month's statement yet, have you?"

"No, but I've gone over every check I've written, double-checked my figures with a calculator, and I know I'm right. It's the bank that's messed up everything and they won't admit it. And, Sam, Bitsy said I'd written a check for thirty-five hundred dollars—to *cash,* if you please—and that was what wiped me out. And you know I did no such thing. I mean, I could've if I'd needed it, but I haven't needed it."

"All right. Let's think this through. How many checks have bounced?"

"One to Ingles, one to something called Sav-Mor, and one to Jiffy Lube, and no telling how many more will come bouncing in."

"What did your signature look like?"

"I didn't see it. Everything's on that computer, and Bitsy wouldn't show it to me. Oh me, I should've gone right to the grocery store and looked at that one, but he's run it back through by now, which means it'll bounce *again*!"

"Don't get upset, honey. It's obvious that somebody's forged your signature."

"That's what I think! But how did they get any checks to forge? They couldn't use counter checks, could they? They had to have mine."

Sam looked up from the checkbook and gazed off in the distance. "How long was this checkbook lying out there in the car?"

"Let me think," I said, thinking back. "At least three days, maybe four—ever since I stopped for gas last week. That's the only time I dumped everything out looking for my Texaco card. But, Sam, it *stayed* in the car, right where you found it. It hadn't been stolen, so we still don't know how somebody could have gotten any of my checks."

"Hm," Sam said, looking through the checkbook again. He noted the last check I'd written for the electric bill and saw that it was correctly entered in the register. Then he riffled through the remaining checks. "Here's your problem, sweetheart."

"Where?"

"Right here in the middle of the book. Looks like five checks are missing, right where you wouldn't notice."

"Wouldn't notice till they bounced! They just tore them out of the middle? Who would do such a thing? And when?" Then, with a sudden jolt to my system, I knew. "It had to've been at *night*! Oh, Sam, somebody's been sneaking around our house at night."

"Sure looks like it. And I'm wondering if it had anything to do with that body they found."

"Oh, don't say that! I'm in enough trouble with the law as it is."

"Okay, I'll go down early tomorrow and talk to somebody at the bank..."

"Not Bitsy. Find somebody who can do something besides tap a computer."

"Okay," he said, "then I'll talk to Lieutenant Peavey and..."

"Be nice to him, Sam. If it hadn't been for him, you'd be visiting me in jail."

"Anyway," Sam said with a grin, "I'll get it straightened out tomorrow."

I put my head against his chest. "You don't know how relieved I am. Nobody would listen to me, but you always do."

He hugged me, then looked down. "Something we need to think about, though. We know where four of those checks went, but there are five missing from your checkbook. One is still outstanding."

I dropped my head back against his chest. "I guess that means there'll be deputies on my porch again. This is a nightmare, Sam."

He hugged me tighter. "No, you're going to have sweet dreams tonight. Your personal lawyer's on the job now."

# Chapter 19

Knowing that I was now in good hands, I fell asleep as soon as my head hit the pillow and would've slept the night through if I hadn't heard Mr. Pickens and Etta Mae come in around eleven that night. I vaguely thought of rising to ask how Hazel Marie was doing, but all I did was turn over and go back to sleep, making up for what had been lost the night before.

The next morning dawned cold and windy with no sign of melting snow. That meant there'd be no school because the buses couldn't run on icy roads. And still no power, which meant putting up with the generator racket and using appliances one at a time. We let Lloyd and Latisha sleep in, but the rest of us gathered in the kitchen, where Lillian produced a prodigious number of pancakes.

Sam had just come in from a slippery walk to Main Street to pick up a newspaper because ours had not been delivered. He'd stomped snow off his boots, then left them on the porch as he came in in his stocking feet.

"Interesting news, Julia," he said, handing me the paper. "See what you make of it."

I passed Mr. Pickens the syrup, noticing as I did that Etta Mae perked up at the mention of news. She'd done little more than yawn between bites of pancake ever since she'd come to the table.

At the top of the front page, I read BODY IDENTIFIED and quickly scanned the article to see if I'd known the person found in Miss Petty's toolshed.

"Well, of all the teasing headlines!" I said, shaking the paper in frustration. "I've never seen the like."

"What is it?" Mr. Pickens asked.

Sam laughed and shook his head. "The authorities know, but they aren't telling."

"Just listen to this," I said as I skimmed the article for the pertinent sentences. "The body found Monday morning in the toolshed of a local teacher was formally identified yesterday, but the authorities aren't releasing the name until the next of kin have been notified. The *Abbotsville Times* reporter was able to learn that the individual had been a real estate broker, entrepreneur, investment counselor, and community leader well known, he says, in local circles." I looked at Sam. "Maybe Lloyd is right and we do know him. He sounds like somebody we ought to know."

Sam nodded. "Yeah, it does, but the word will get around soon enough." He grinned at me. "Maybe LuAnne will call and let you know."

"Well, I hope she does. Because now I'll worry with it all day, trying to figure out who it was. Whom do we know who's both a real estate broker and an investment counselor? I'm not sure I knew those two lines of work went together."

"Maybe he was one at one time," Etta Mae said, "then switched to the other at another time."

"Could be," Mr. Pickens said. "Entrepreneur usually means somebody who dabbles in a lot of things. You can also figure he wasn't a young man. If he'd done all that, I'd guess he was getting on up there."

"Could be most anybody," Sam said, pushing back his plate. "Every businessman, lawyer, or doctor pretty much has a finger or two in first one thing and another."

I folded the newspaper and put it away. "I don't know why they bother to print something when they don't know the first thing about it, or can't tell what they do know."

"Mr. Pickens," Lillian asked, her beatific smile still in place, "you want some more pancakes?"

"I couldn't eat another one if my life depended on it," he said. "Really, really good, Lillian. But now," he said as Lloyd stumbled sleepily into the room, "I better get over to the hospital and see how my family—the *rest* of my family—is getting along." He said the last with a wink at Lloyd. "You want to go with me?"

"Yes, sir, I do, but I'd just as soon not stay all day."

"I'm not planning to stay all day either," Mr. Pickens said. "As soon as the doctor comes in this morning, he's going to let your mother come home."

"This morning!" I said, surprised at such a short hospital stay. "Why, we better get ready for those babies."

As I started to spring from my chair, Etta Mae put her hand on my arm. "It'll probably be late morning before we can get them here. They have to wait till the doctor makes rounds."

As Sam and Mr. Pickens left the kitchen to prepare for the day and Lloyd stood by the stove with Lillian, Etta Mae leaned closer. "I want to talk to Dr. Hargrove about the babies before they come home. They're not nursing well, and I want to be sure he knows it."

Confused by this information, I asked, "Won't the nurses tell him?"

"I'm sure they will," Etta Mae said. "But Hazel Marie will be depending on me, and I want Dr. Hargrove to know who I am if I have to call him in the middle of the night sometime."

"Oh my goodness," I said, overwhelmed with one more thing to worry about. "You think something's wrong with them?"

"Oh no," she quickly said, "they're just small and they get tired before they've nursed long enough to get anything."

Mr. Pickens walked back in time to hear Etta Mae's last whispered comment.

Looking at him with concern, I asked, "Did you know about this?"

"That's why we stayed so late last night," he said, standing now by the table. "Hazel Marie was upset because she wants to nurse them, but they're not cooperating. She'll be okay with it if they have to be put on bottles, but she wants to keep trying for a while. Dr. Hargrove suggested leaving the babies in the hospital a few more days, but she didn't want to come home without them."

"I can't blame her for that," I said. "She's had those babies with her for nine months, so she sure wouldn't want to be without them now. I hope to goodness you're not planning to take off anywhere, Mr. Pickens. We're going to need all the help we can get."

He flashed me a quick smile. "I know my duty."

*And a good thing too,* I thought to myself, although I wondered what had happened to that Raleigh job he'd had to drop before even starting.

# Chapter 20

Sam left with Mr. Pickens because he wanted a ride to his house so he could check on the heat and water pipes. Lloyd decided to stay home and play with Latisha while awaiting his mother's arrival. Lillian and I went to Hazel Marie's room and changed the sheets on the bed, plumping up pillows and turning the covers down invitingly.

"They sure send them home early these days, don't they?" I commented while straightening a crooked lamp shade. Somebody, probably Mr. Pickens, was a restless sleeper.

"Yes'm, they sure do. An' I know she feel bad 'bout them babies not nursing too good, but if her milk don't come down, they need to get on bottles. They little enough already."

"We'd better send Mr. Pickens to the drugstore for bottles and formula, just in case. We need to be prepared and have every-thing here." I put an extra blanket across the foot of the bed, then switched to another subject of concern. "I hope James has Sam's house in good working order this morning. If he doesn't, Sam will be out there shoveling snow and no telling what could happen. Oh," I said as we heard the phone ring, "I hope that's not him now, saying he's broken something."

Hurrying into the living room, I picked up the phone to hear Mildred Allen's voice.

"Julia? Why haven't you let me know about Hazel Marie? I had to hear it from Emma Sue, who heard it from Pastor Ledbetter, who heard it from LuAnne, who called him in case he wanted to make a pastoral visit to the hospital."

"I'm sorry, Mildred," I said, easing into a chair for a long chat. "Things have been so hectic that I've not called anybody. I told LuAnne only because she called me. In fact, I was just getting ready to call you, but Hazel Marie will be coming home in a little while and we had to get her bed ready. Anyway," I said, pulling my sweater a little closer, "how are you faring in this weather? I guess you heard that we had the babies here while the power was out."

"I heard all about it, but I want to know every little detail from you. So let's hear it."

I told her, including all the details of that remarkable night and ending with the naming of the baby girls.

"Well," Mildred said, "I'm glad to hear how it really was because according to Emma Sue, it was you who delivered the babies." She sniffed. "That didn't sound right to me."

"It certainly wasn't. All I did was warm blankets and pray a lot."

"I'm glad to get that straight," Mildred said. "But while I have you, let me tell you that Emma Sue may be planning another baby shower for Hazel Marie. I thought you'd want to know, but don't tell her I told you."

"Oh my," I said, "I hope she won't do that. One shower's a gracious plenty, and LuAnne's already done that. Besides, the babies need time to settle in, and I'm not sure Hazel Marie will be in a party mood until they do. Or the rest of us either."

"I'll try to talk her out of it. But I want you to know that I am proud of you for not giving a shower yourself. Things have just gone to pot around here with so many people giving showers for family members. I know for a fact that the only reason Emma Sue hasn't already done something is because she kept expecting you to do it."

"She ought to know better. Giving a shower for a family member just isn't done. It's the tackiest thing in the world to ask for gifts for one of your own."

"That is the truth. Anyway, she can't do anything until some of this snow melts. But on to something else—I wanted to ask if you've heard anything more about that body they found."

"All I know," I said, "is what was in the paper, which was next to nothing. To tell the truth, I'd about forgotten about it with all that's going on here. What about you? Have you heard anything?"

"No, but I know who it was."

"You do? Who?"

"Well, think about it, Julia. You read the paper. Who do we know who was into real estate, then went into investment counseling? Remember we wondered at the time whether he knew what he was doing? And who was it who used to live here until he was sent to prison but not for as long as we thought he should've been?"

I gasped. "You don't mean...?"

"I certainly do. It has to be Richard Stroud. He's the only one who fits everything the paper said, and you know they have those early releases these days. It wouldn't surprise me a bit if Richard wasn't out roaming around as free as a bird."

"Oh my. I'd have to sit down if I weren't already doing so. Mildred, do you really think it might be Richard? Oh poor Helen—I wonder if she knows."

"I'm just wondering if I should call her, but I want to think about it for a while. I don't know whether she'd be considered next of kin, because she divorced him. Though, who knows? The divorce might not be final and you know how closemouthed she is. And if it's not final, she's still his kin. But listen, Julia, don't tell either LuAnne or Emma Sue yet. We need to be sure before it's spread all over town. In fact, don't mention it to anybody, although I'm just as sure it's Richard Stroud as I can be. I mean, who else could it be?"

Hanging up the phone after we'd assured each other that we both had plenty of milk and bread and that our furnaces were working, I sat for a while gazing into the fire, thinking of first one distressing thing after another. *Richard Stroud!* Could it have been he? And if so, what had he been doing in Miss Petty's toolshed? She wouldn't have been someone he'd known in the ordinary course of events. For one thing, she was of a younger generation, maybe about Hazel Marie's age. And before their passing, her parents had not been known for their social or community activities. In fact, I could recall her father only from seeing him occasionally in his hardware store, and I wasn't sure I'd ever known her mother. Nor could I believe that the Strouds, the Allens, the Conovers, or any of my friends had been close to the Pettys. So how would Richard Stroud have come to know their daughter?

It was the strangest set of circumstances I'd ever heard, and I couldn't make head nor tails of it. I knew Helen, at least as well as anybody knew Helen. She was the most capable woman in town, always organized and on top of whatever had been entrusted to her care. And we'd entrusted a lot to her. She either was or had been president or chairwoman or leader of any group she was part of. She was a small woman, neatly and classically dressed, hair, face, and nails perfectly groomed, warm without being effusive, and confident without arrogance.

Her home had reflected everything about her person, always neat, traditionally furnished, and well organized. I'd never seen it in disarray, probably because she and Richard had had no children. Though I expect if they had, their children would have been just as organzied as everything else about her.

I admired Helen, but I couldn't say I was close to her. I'm not sure anyone was, yet we all depended on her. As I sat thinking of Helen, a sense of shame swept over me. I'd done so little for her while she was going through such a trying time with Richard. The man had embezzled money—some of mine, in fact—and had gotten involved with an out-of-town developer's scheme to demolish the old courthouse and build luxury condominums in its place. Richard had been arrested, tried, and convicted, but he got off, according to some, with a slap on the wrist. Two years, as I remembered, was what he'd gotten, with, of course, the requirement of recompensing those he'd defrauded—at ten cents on the dollar, from what I'd heard. And let me say right here that in spite of the pittance required of him, he had not gotten around to recompensing me.

That was the reason I'd let my contact with Helen lapse. I knew she had been shamed and humiliated, and I had not wanted to add to her discomfort. And as I thought about it, I realized that I had not seen Helen in church for some time—an indication perhaps that she had other fish to fry.

As I was reminded of Richard's problems, a shudder ran through me at the thought of how the courts dealt with crimes involving money. They wouldn't put up with theft, embezzlement, or fraud, usually handing down heavy sentences, but as I've said, there had been many who'd thought Richard had gotten off lightly and I admit I'd thought the same at the time. In my present circumstances, however, having recently thought about jail time myself, I didn't find two years in prison all that light a sentence.

Helen ended up having to sell her lovely house so Richard could repay his losses, although as I've said, my loss had not been among them. Unlike Mildred, I was fairly sure that Helen had divorced him and that it was final, but that was only an assumption based on the fact that whatever Helen started, she generally finished. She'd moved into a small, not-so-upscale condominium and tried to carry on with her head held high. I admired that, but I'd felt no need to close any gaps in our friendship.

132 of Ann B. Ross

Now, however, I couldn't help but feel a deep concern for her. If that body was Richard's, would she be suffering silent recriminations or more shame and humiliation?

I've said it before and I'll say it again: whatever—good or bad—a husband does, his wife will get the brunt of it. She'll be credited or, more often, blamed for whatever he does. And from my experience, neither death nor divorce—unless accompanied by a move faraway and a completely new set of acquaintances— will keep his misdeeds from besmirching her. I know what I'm talking about because I was whispered about and blamed, ridiculed and slurred for all of Wesley Lloyd Springer's foibles, which had included everything from adultery to usury.

But I no longer cared what Wesley Lloyd had done. To be honest, I'd benefited from his underhanded manipulations, which certainly turned the tables on him. And I had no interest in Richard Stroud's sleight of hand with other people's money. In fact, I'd already written off my loss at his hands.

The truth was, I had more pressing money problems to deal with, the first of which was to set Sam onto the First National Bank of Abbotsville and teach it how to keep its accounts straight.

# Chapter 21

It wasn't until early afternoon that the contingent from the hospital arrived home, and right before they got there the power came on. What a relief it was to hear that generator chug down for the last time, filling the house with blessed silence.

I held the door, watching as they trooped in—Lillian holding on to Hazel Marie, who was wearing another workout outfit, which, apparently, was all she could get into given the fact that she wore her normal clothes so tight; Mr. Pickens looking dazed and distracted as he gingerly carried one swaddled infant in his arms; and Etta Mae balancing the other on her shoulder with one hand while managing Hazel Marie's makeup case with the other one.

It was all I could do not to snatch that child from her, using both my hands. But we all followed them to the bedroom, eager to see the babies unwrapped and settled into their new home.

I say we all followed them, but we were missing one. Sam had still not returned from his trip downtown to set the bank straight, and by this time I was convinced that he'd run into more problems than he'd expected. I decided, then and there, that if deputies showed up at my front door again, I was going to head out the back as fast as I could go.

But so much was going on in the bedroom that I hardly had time to think about going on the run. Etta Mae got the babies unwrapped—both of them had looked like pink sausages in their blankets—and settled side by side in the crib. Mr. Pickens insisted that Hazel Marie get in the bed and rest while he flopped down in the upholstered rocking chair. He kept taking deep breaths and blowing them out, as if everything had suddenly hit home and he didn't quite know what to make of it.

Lloyd and Latisha hung on the side of the crib, watching the babies as they slept, while Lillian told them not to breathe on them. Then she went to the kitchen and came back with a tall glass of milk, telling Hazel Marie, "You got to drink milk to make milk."

Apparently, that was the big problem, for Etta Mae asked Mr. Pickens to bring in the case of formula from the car. He quickly sprang up and headed out as if he'd been waiting to be told what to do. At the mention of formula, though, Hazel Marie's face fell. Etta Mae quickly assured her that they would continue to work on getting her milk to come down and that the formula was just a stopgap solution, in case it was needed.

I declare, all this talk of making milk and getting milk to come down and babies latching on just made me shiver. It was too much personal talk for me and, in my opinion, too close to home for any woman, whether she'd ever given birth or not. I crossed my arms over my chest and tried not to think about it.

Finally, we tiptoed out and left Hazel Marie to rest, which as Etta Mae said, "She better get while she can. Those babies will start tuning up before long."

And was she ever right. It wasn't long before first one started crying, and then the other, kicking and flailing about, getting louder and louder. Who would've thought that such tiny beings could make such a racket? As Lillian and Etta Mae changed them and put them to breast, I ushered Lloyd and Latisha into the living room.

"You two find something to do," I said. "But do it quietly, in case they get the babies asleep again."

Latisha looked up at me and in all seriousness said, "We oughta give 'em some of Great-Granny's biscuits and gravy. That'd put 'em to sleep. It always do me."

Well, I want you to know that those babies cried all afternoon, finally giving up and falling asleep about suppertime. From pure exhaustion, if you ask me. And Hazel Marie was in the same state. She'd fiddled with first one baby and then the next, then both at the same time, while they cried and she cried, and none of them got satisfied. Even Etta Mae was worn to a frazzle, pushing her hair out of her face as she dropped into a chair at the table. Mr. Pickens had gone in and out of the bedroom, trying to be of help by encouraging Hazel Marie, but he was equally worn out. A constant din will do that to you.

Lillian whispered to me as we took dishes to the table, "Them babies 'bout to starve, Miss Julia. That's a hungry cry if I ever heard it, an' Miss Hazel Marie might as well give up an' fix them bottles."

I agreed with her because the crying was getting on my nerves, but more than that, I couldn't stand the thought of anybody going hungry in my house. Sam finally came in, heard the noise, and pretended to turn around and go back out.

"They having a hard time?" he asked.

"Awful," I said, taking his coat. "What did you find out?"

"I'll tell you later, but you're all right, Julia. They know you didn't write those checks."

I pursed my lips, thinking that he could've let me know I was off the hook somewhat earlier, and saved me from worrying all day long. But he looked as tired as the rest of us, and I knew he'd spent the day on my behalf, so I unpursed my mouth and gave him a smile of thanks.

All evening those babies kept crying. They'd fall asleep occasionally when someone walked them or rocked them and then we'd get fifteen minutes or so of peace. Then they'd start in again.

Lloyd went upstairs early, closing his door to try to study

because we reckoned school would be open the next morning. "I didn't think I'd ever say this," he told me as he started up the stairs, "but it'll kinda be a relief to go to school. At least they make us be quiet."

I went in and out of Hazel Marie's room several times, wanting to be of help but hoping at the same time that they wouldn't need me. They never did. In fact, there was almost too much help, what with Lillian, Etta Mae, Mr. Pickens, and Hazel Marie, each with suggestions of what could be tried next to pacify them. Anything, however, except those rubber nipples expressly made for pacifying, which Etta Mae kept suggesting and Hazel Marie kept refusing to use on the grounds of their being unsanitary and likely to cause buck teeth.

It was a madhouse, so Sam and I went to bed. He gave me an update on his day's events, telling me that he'd spoken first to two of the bank's vice presidents.

"They realize that you didn't write those checks," he said. "But they weren't willing to speculate on who did. All they'd say was that it must've been somebody who had access to your signature so it could be copied."

"Forged," I said.

"Right, forged. The signatures were pretty good too, so whoever did it knew what he was doing. Anyway, your checking account is back where it was, and the bank and the stores will have to take the loss. Oughtta teach 'em a good lesson because the big check, the one for thirty-five hundred dollars, was cashed by one of their own tellers. She swears she asked for identification, and the man had it."

"The man?" I asked, turning on my back to stare at the ceiling. "What kind of identification of mine would some man have?"

"Beats me, and she claims she doesn't remember." Sam rolled on his side and put an arm around me. "I think she took one look at the check, saw your signature, maybe looked at your account, and just cashed the thing. You're fairly well known around town, Julia, and she probably didn't think twice about it."

"I expect she will from now on," I said with some satisfaction. Then remembering how I'd been accused and questioned, I asked, "But what about the deputies and the magistrate and Lieutenant Peavey? Are they going to drop the case against me? And apologize? Because they ought to."

"It's off the books, Julia. Don't worry about it. And," he said, yawning, "I'll tell you something if you won't pass it along."

I rolled my eyes but it was too dark for him to see. "I don't pass along rumor, gossip, or hearsay. Except to you and Lillian. And sometimes to Hazel Marie. So you can trust me to keep it to myself."

"Well, this is fact but the lieutenant wants to keep it quiet for now. They don't have a formal identification yet, but they're fairly certain they know who that body was. Peavey wouldn't say more, but he's confident that it was somebody who knew your signature well enough to forge it."

"I should say so," I said indignantly. "Richard Stroud would certainly know my signature."

Sam sat up in bed and looked down at me. "How do you know it was Stroud?"

"Mildred told me. She figured it out, except we weren't sure because we thought he was still in prison. I'm just wondering if Helen knew he was out. Maybe not, though, or he'd have died at home—unless Helen divorced him—instead of at Miss Petty's. Lie back down, Sam, we're both too tired to think straight." I rolled closer to him, feeling secure now that he had taken care of the bank and the sheriff's department and was safely home with me. "Thank you for all you did, you sweet thing, you."

He didn't answer, so I knew he'd dropped off. But as tired as I was, I couldn't do the same. Even with the door closed, I could still hear the caterwauling down below. I rolled and tumbled for some time, trying not to disturb Sam but worried sick about those babies. What if they were starving? Literally, I mean. Would Hazel Marie ever give in and produce some milk in some form or another? Preferably by way of a bottle? Should I call the doctor to talk some sense into her?

I heard whispering in the hall as Latisha knocked on Lloyd's door. "Lloyd," she said, her voice carrying as it always did, "them babies is keeping me awake, an' Great-Granny won't let me go downstairs. Can I come in?"

I heard Lloyd tell her they'd make a pallet on the floor for her, but that she was unlikely to get any rest because he could hear them too.

Lord, the crying was constant, and I was as bad off as Latisha about getting to sleep. Finally, a little after midnight, I slipped out of bed, put on a robe, and went downstairs.

It was bedlam in the bedroom, and I quickly stepped back out and went to the kitchen to fix a cup of tea. Just as I sat down at the table, Mr. Pickens came stumbling out. His hair was a tangled mess, his eyes red with dark circles underneath, and his face unshaved. He was in an undershirt with his pants zipped but his belt unbuckled.

He dropped into a chair across from me. "I didn't know it'd be like this," he said, running a hand down his face. "What in the world can we do?"

"You're asking the wrong person, Mr. Pickens, but Lillian thinks they're hungry."

"I know they are," he said, slumping in the chair as if he'd completely run down. "And Hazel Marie is beside herself because they won't nurse like they should. And I," he said with a sigh and a glance at me, "am obligated to go back to Raleigh and finish that job. I was going to do it while Etta Mae was still here, but..."

I stared at him for a full minute, guessing that he was asking my permission to go. "It would be easy enough to go, Mr. Pickens, and leave everything with Hazel Marie. A lot of men would, but I thought better of you than that." I am not above using a dose of guilt when it's called for.

Before he could answer, Lillian came stalking into the kitchen. "I don't care what anybody say, I'm fixin' them babies a bottle. They hungry an' that's all there is to it."

"Good!" I said, standing up. "I'll help you." Then, turning to Mr. Pickens, I said, "Mr. Pickens, take some responsibility and go in there and tell Hazel Marie that those babies are on formula as of now. That's what she wants you to do. She doesn't want to make that decision because, I expect, she'd feel like a failure. You just tell her that you're the daddy, and you're the one who's making the decison. She'll thank you for it."

Eventually, I thought, and after she cries for a while, which I didn't mention.

"Maybe I should," he said, but he didn't jump up to do it.

"No maybe about it," Lillian said, as she put together a bottle. "You better get on in there 'cause nobody gonna go hungry while I'm around."

I had never seen Lillian so determined and outspoken about anything, but I was thankful for it. She knew more about babies than anybody else in the house, so armed with her authority, Mr. Pickens got a second wind and headed for the bedroom armed with two warm bottles, with Lillian following him.

Within minutes, peace reigned throughout the house. On my way back upstairs, I glanced into the bedroom. Hazel Marie was sound asleep in the bed, Mr. Pickens was snoring away in the rocking chair, while Lillian and Etta Mae nodded over the two avidly sucking babies. I went to bed.

# Chapter 22

There was a steady stream of visitors over the next few days, all arriving with gifts and a desire to see the babies. Hazel Marie vacillated between pride in showing them off and worry about the germs they were being exposed to.

Lillian walked around with an air of justified competence now that she'd been proved right about what the babies needed. So when any question of child care came up, we deferred to her—not excluding her judgment concerning the type and frequency of infant excretory functions. It was a fact that as soon as the babies began to get adequate nourishment, they settled down to a fairly regular routine and the household gradually adjusted to it. Even Hazel Marie's spirits improved, in spite of her perceived failure, for she was up every morning, dressed and made up and waiting to show off the babies whenever the doorbell rang.

Mr. Pickens took longer to recover, unaccustomed as he was to getting up several times every night to hold a baby and a bottle. Lillian pointed out to Hazel Marie that bottle-fed babies got more of their daddies' attention because, she said, "The daddies don't have nothin' to do when the mamas is the onliest ones can feed 'em."

Etta Mae made herself useful in all kinds of ways: rocking babies, changing babies, feeding babies, and helping Lillian in the kitchen. I feared she would wear herself out, but since now the babies only woke up two or three times a night for a feeding,

Mr. Pickens told her to go ahead and sleep up in the sunroom, and for the time being, he'd handle the night shift.

So that was beginning to work out until the day Mr. Pickens came in with a fold-up cot and put it in his and Hazel Marie's room. "For Etta Mae," he said when I wondered if Hazel Marie had taken over the bed. "I want her sleeping down here while I'm in Raleigh finishing what I started."

Said like that, it didn't occur to me to argue, although I gave him one of my cold silent looks that Lloyd said could stop a train in its tracks, although I don't know why he'd know because I'd never aimed one at him. The look didn't stop Mr. Pickens either, for he had taken on a new air of authority ever since he'd laid down the law as to how those babies were to be fed. He was taking the role of fatherhood seriously, and as long as he didn't take matters too far, I was pleased to see it.

⁓⁓⁓

"Julia," Sam said, as he came into the house. "Get your coat. We need to go downtown." There wasn't a hint of a smile of greeting on his face or in his eyes. In fact, he was as serious as I'd ever seen him.

"Why?"

"I'll tell you in the car. Let's go."

Seated in the car beside him, I kept glancing his way but he was intent on driving. "Well?" I finally asked.

"Lieutenant Peavey wants to talk to you."

"*Again?* He's already talked to me, and you said he was satisfied that I didn't bounce those checks."

"I get the feeling that he's not so sure now." Sam still hadn't looked me full in the eye, concentrating as he was on driving.

"Well, what's changed his mind? Talk to me, Sam. What's going on?" By this time, I was clutching my pocketbook with one hand and the armrest with the other.

Sam pulled into a parking place beside the sheriff's office and turned off the ignition. He sighed and finally looked at me. "I don't know. The lieutenant called me a while ago while I was working at my house. Said something's come up and he wanted to know how much contact you've had over the past few weeks with Richard Stroud."

"*Richard Stroud!*" I almost screeched the name. "I've had *no* contact with him. The man's been in prison, as Lieutenant Peavey ought to know because he put him there. And as far as I know, he's still there, except..." I slumped back against the front seat of the car, recalling Mildred's guess as to the identity of the body in the toolshed. "They have a positive identification, don't they?"

Sam rested his hands on the steering wheel, gazing out the windshield between them as if the brick wall of the sheriff's office was a thing of intense interest. "How long have you known?"

"Known what?"

"That it was Stroud."

"I *haven't* known! It was Mildred who made a wild guess, which I have not repeated except to you, because I didn't know for sure and I didn't want to spread gossip. Besides, I've had my mind on a few other things here lately, if you haven't noticed, and simply have not had time for useless speculation." I turned sideways on the seat and glared at him. "Now look, Sam, if you have something to say, just say it."

"They found that fifth check of yours, folded up and stuck way down in the watch pocket of his pants. It's made out to Stroud and signed by you, but without an amount filled in. It all looks like your handwriting, Julia."

"Well, it *wasn't*! I've *never* written a check to him. I haven't laid eyes on that man since the day he was arrested, and it flies all over me that you think I have."

Sam hadn't looked at me for some little while, but at that moment, he did, his deep blue eyes filled with a ton of hurt.

"What about the little matter of a check for a hundred thousand dollars you gave him *before* he was arrested?"

"Oh. Well." I took a turn of looking at the sheriff's brick wall. "There is that. But I didn't want you to know about it."

"They found his records from back when he put himself up as an investment counselor, and there was your name." Sam's face was drawn and he looked tired, and the longer we talked, the sadder he looked. "Didn't you trust me, Julia? Or Binkie?"

"Of course I trusted you. I trusted both of you, and I still do. But let me explain, Sam. Please, let me explain because it's not as bad as it sounds. What happened was that a long-term certificate of deposit matured, one that Wesley Lloyd had in an out-of-town bank that nobody, including me, knew about. When the maturity notice came to the house, I intended to give it to Binkie and tell you about it. But, Sam, it was like found money because Richard had been pushing me to transfer the whole estate from Binkie to him, something I wasn't about to do. But because I admired Helen and wanted to help a friend, I *invested* that money with him. That's all that happened, and it happened years ago and I'd long since given up hope of seeing any of it again. And," I added, searching in my pocketbook for a Kleenex to wipe my eyes, "I didn't want you to know how foolish I'd been."

"He had it down as a payment."

"A *payment*! For *what*?" My eyes suddenly dried up as I stared at him with disbelief. "Why in the world would you ask such a thing? What would I be paying him *for*? I barely knew the man. I did it for *Helen's* sake, and for no other reason."

"Okay," he said, but there was no warmth in it.

"If you don't believe me, Sam, what do you believe?"

"I don't know, Julia. He had it down as payment for services rendered, and it just looks strange that he was getting money from you both before and after he was in prison . . ."

"He *stole* that money from me—both times. You yourself

showed me how somebody—and it had to have been Richard—
had ripped out those checks from my checkbook. He was a *crook,*
Sam, and I got taken in like a lot of others did." I reached out
and touched his arm. "I'm telling you the truth, which, I admit,
I should've done long ago. But believe me, I did not pay him for
any kind of services rendered. I invested with him, thinking I'd
learned enough to manage a little money on my own, and I got
burned. Binkie put it down as a loss on our tax returns and I
thought you'd ask about it, but you never did so I thought...Well,
I don't know what I thought."

"We better go in," he said, opening the car door.

"Sam, wait," I said, reaching for him again. "Please. I don't
want to go in there with you like this. I need you to understand
and not be hurt. I didn't mean to hurt you—I wouldn't hurt you
for the world. Just...let's just wait a few more minutes."

"He's waiting for us." Sam walked around the car and opened
my door. I climbed out, hoping that that gesture of courtesy por-
tended a change of attitude. It hadn't, for he took my arm without
a word and walked with me to see Lieutenant Peavey.

# Chapter 23

Who would've thought that Lieutenant Peavey would be more receptive to my explanations than Sam had been? Sam had sat beside me in front of the lieutenant's desk, acting more like my hired lawyer than my husband. In fact, there had been a decided chill radiating from him aimed in my direction.

In response to Lieutenant Peavey's questions, instead of "Mrs. Murdoch did not...," Sam would say, "Mrs. Murdoch *says* she did not...," and so forth. Finally, I decided to answer for myself, realizing that my attorney did not have his whole heart invested in the interview, and I told the lieutenant everything. And I mean everything: that I'd invested with Richard Stroud for charitable reasons, how I'd lost the money and never been repaid, why I had not sued to get it back, how checks had been stolen from the center of my checkbook because I stopped to get gas—he got a little confused at that, so I had to explain how I'd not been able to find the Texaco card and had dumped everything out, obviously failing to replace the checkbook, so that it had been left lying in plain sight on the car seat for Richard Stroud to come along and find. I told him that obviously Richard had copies of my signature on investment papers during our earlier dealings, so he had something to go by when he forged my checks more recently.

"And, Lieutenant Peavey," I summed up, "I assure you that I have not seen Richard Stroud since we were both at a certain party given by Mrs. Allen on the same day he was arrested some few years ago. And furthermore, I've had no contact with him at any point in time since then. I didn't know he was out of prison, I didn't know he was back in town, I don't know what he was doing in Miss Petty's toolshed, and I don't know why he died there." I gave a firm nod of summation, then added, "Or why he was killed there, as the case may be."

Sam gave me a sharp glance as Lieutenant Peavey asked, "Why do you say *killed*?"

The whole interview was beginning to get on my nerves. "Because," I said, "I don't know *how* he died, and because, as Lillian says, it's not exactly a natural death when you do it in a toolshed."

"Well," Lieutenant Peavey said, gathering up papers and stacking them neatly before putting them aside. "As it happens, it was a natural death in an unnatural place. The autopsy confirmed that he had a heart attack, which was probably intensified by hypothermia. That information is being released today."

I had the wild notion of nudging Sam and saying, "At least you can't lay that at my doorstep." But I didn't. I was afraid to touch him, for he was still engulfed in a coldness that kept him stiff and unsmiling.

After signing some papers that transcribed my answers to Lieutenant Peavey's questions, Sam and I walked out to the car. As gentlemanly as ever, he helped me into the front seat, then drove home in silence. And the longer it went on, the more anger I could feel welling up in me. I wanted to shout, "Lieutenant Peavey, who never believes *anybody,* believes me. Why can't you?"

But again, I didn't. Because the fact of the matter was, I couldn't figure out why Sam was so put out with me. So I had thrown away a hundred thousand dollars. I hadn't, by any means, done it intentionally, for it had been a goodwill gesture toward Helen, the kind of gesture I knew Sam had made to other people under different circumstances. He'd just been smart enough to distinguish well-intentioned people from crooks.

Or was he mad at me for not first discussing it with him? Or at least with Binkie? Yet he was always telling me that it was my money and that I had a say in how it was invested or spent. But when, on my own, I took a step—a wrong one, as it turned out—he closed up shop and would hardly look at me.

Or could it be, I suddenly thought as he turned the car into our driveway, that he suspected something had been going on between Richard and me? I almost laughed aloud—a decidedly unhelpful action, given his current state of mind if I'd actually done it.

Surely he couldn't think that. For one thing, Richard was, or had been, some few years younger than I was, and as far as I had known, he'd been happy with Helen and had never strayed—certainly not in my direction. There'd never been a smidgen of gossip about him. Well, except for his various business ventures, the last of which landed him in jail. There'd been plenty of gossip about that, nearly killing Helen with shame in the process.

No, I couldn't figure out why Sam was so distant and so silent and so hurt. I had wounded him deeply, that was plain, but I didn't even know what to apologize for. So I decided to issue a blanket apology and hope it would cover everything.

As he pulled out the keys and started to open the car door, I said, "Sam, I'm sorry. I am sorry for anything and everything I've done or said or even thought, if any of it hurt you. You know I'd never deliberately and with malice aforethought do anything to upset you, so I ask you to forgive me for whatever it is that has cut me off from you." I began to choke up, for he didn't immediately respond. "Please say you forgive me, or at least tell me what's wrong so I can correct it."

I didn't think he was going to answer, yet he stayed in the car and finally said, "You were awfully eager to go to Thurlow's the other night."

"Thurlow's?" I looked up with a frown. "When?"

"The night they found Stroud's body."

"Why, Sam, I was worried about Lloyd. I was going to look for him, but you went instead."

"Yes, but that didn't stop you. You went anyway, and what were you doing with Thurlow that kept you away for so long?"

"Wait a minute!" I said, thoroughly confused by this new tack and more than a little agitated by it. "Wait just a minute. Is this about Richard Stroud or Thurlow Jones?"

"Take your pick." He slid out of the car, stood by the door for a moment, then leaned down and said, "I think we need some thinking time. I'll be staying over at my house for a few days." And he closed the door and walked off through the backyard toward his house, leaving me sitting alone in the car, dazed by such an unexpected turn of events.

Stunned, I sat watching as he walked around patches of snow, going farther and farther away until he brushed past overgrown forsythia bushes to unlatch the gate that led out of the backyard onto the sidewalk. I watched his black overcoat grow smaller as he continued on his way until he turned a corner and was gone.

A wave of desolation filled the car, almost suffocating in its intensity. My head slumped down to my chest and a ringing in my head blocked out every thought except one: Sam had left me. I wanted to cry, but couldn't. I wanted to scream, but wouldn't—somebody might hear me. I wanted to run after him, beg him, plead with him, but I couldn't move.

And that reminded me of what I'd heard about Lois Iverson when her husband told her he wanted a divorce so he could marry his secretary. Everybody was talking about it—the word was that Lois cried and pleaded and begged him not to do it, finally falling to her knees and throwing her arms around his hairy legs—he'd been in tennis shorts when he made his announcement—and threatening suicide if he left.

Well, he went ahead and left, and she's still alive, but it was the consensus of both the book club and the garden club that none of us would degrade ourselves in such a shameful fashion, and that if she wanted to threaten anything, it should've been murder, not suicide, neither of which would've been carried out, but the threat of the former might've made him stop and think.

Mildred had leaned over to me and said, "There's not a man alive I'd kill myself over." Then she'd gotten up and given the report on our last flower show, while I thought admiringly of what Mildred had done when Horace had strayed—she'd given the biggest party the town had ever seen.

And still I sat, feeling the cold seeping in along with the desolation. I was about to freeze but was unable to move as I sat there like a statue in an unheated car. There was a hole in the center of my chest, and what had once been there seemed to be lodged now in my throat. I might never be able to speak again.

I saw Lillian look out the kitchen window, then in a few minutes she opened the door and came to the car, pulling a sweater on as she came. Frowning, she looked in the car window at me, then all around the yard. Finally, she opened the door and slid under the wheel in Sam's seat.

"What's the matter with you?" she demanded. "What you settin' out here freezin' to death for? Where's Mr. Sam?"

"Gone," I croaked, loosening whatever it was that had clogged up my throat. "Oh, Lillian, he's left me."

"Uh-uh, not Mr. Sam. Where'd he go, anyway?"

"His house. So he could think. For several days, he said. Oh, Lillian, he's so mad at me, and I don't know why. Not exactly, anyway. He may not ever be back."

Lillian didn't say a word, just sat there watching me sob and thinking over the situation.

Then out it came. "This is James's fault," she said, "and nobody else's."

"James? What's he got to do with it?"

"He always sayin' Mr. Sam b'long in his own house, always sayin' he miss cookin' for him, always tellin' him the house fallin' apart with nobody in it. An' all that sorry thing want is to keep his job, so he won't have to go lookin' for another one and have to do some work for a change."

"Why, Lillian, Sam has no plans to let him go. How in the world would what James thinks make Sam leave me?"

"'Cause he *there*! You think any man leave a good home if he don't have no place to go? No, ma'am, they always have somewhere to go 'fore they up and leave. An' that's what James been doin', always sayin' how he miss havin' *life* in the house. I bet he down there dancin' a jig right now 'cause Mr. Sam back where he b'long."

"Well, they Lord," I said, leaning my head back against the headrest. "You'd think Richard and Thurlow would be enough. Don't tell me I have to put up with James too."

# Chapter 24

Lillian walked me into the house, where we were met with a silence so unusual that I wondered if everybody else had left me too. I eased into a chair at the table. "It's so quiet."

"Yes'm, Mr. Pickens, he gone; the chil'ren still in school; an' the rest of 'em's in there sleepin'. An' 'bout time too—them babies been cryin' an' cryin'. I tell Miss Etta Mae they got the colic an' we oughta give 'em a sugar tit, but she say the doctor don't want 'em to have such as that. But a little sugar an' a drop of bourbon never hurt nobody."

I was too done in to worry about giving whiskey to a baby. In fact, if I'd been a drinking woman, I might've had a drop or two myself. As it was, I warmed my hands around a cup of hot chocolate that Lillian had set before me and tried to think what I could do to put things right.

"What am I going to tell Hazel Marie and Lloyd?" I whimpered as Lillian sat at the table, her arms propped in front of her. "To say nothing of everybody else. How does a woman explain being left high and dry?"

"You don't tell 'em nothin'. Mr. Sam, he always over at his house anyway, doin' whatever he do, an' everybody here so busy takin' care of babies, they won't even notice he gone. An' by the time they do, he be back home, an' James can moan an' groan all he want to."

"It's more than James, Lillian, although I understand what you're saying. Sam might've thought twice if he'd had only a motel room to go to." I rubbed my forehead and told her all the ins and outs of my dealings with Richard Stroud, his theft of both money and checks, my sworn statement to Lieutenant Peavey, which he believed but Sam didn't, and having Thurlow Jones thrown in my face as a final straw.

In fact, as I recounted the highlights of the day to her, I got so steamed up that the emptiness in my soul suddenly filled with outrage at the unfairness of it all. "He didn't even let me explain. I mean I did explain, because he was sitting right there listening to it, but it didn't mean a thing to him. He wouldn't even talk to me, Lillian. Just got out of the car and left." By that time I was so hot that I took off my coat and began to pace the kitchen floor. "Let me tell you something. Wesley Lloyd Springer thought he could treat me like a doormat and, well, actually he did. But I've turned the tables on him if he but knew it. When I look back, Lillian, I can hardly believe what I put up with with that man. I don't know another woman who would've tolerated being treated as if she weren't worth noticing, much less listened to or talked to or even looked at. And when I found out what he'd been doing all those years, I promised myself I'd never let a man treat me like that again."

I stopped and waited for her to respond, expecting to be told I should calm down and wait docilely until Sam worked out his problem and came home.

"Well," she finally said, heaving herself up from the table, "maybe it just as well Mr. Sam not here so he don't have to listen to all that. But I think it good you get it all out with jus' me to hear. Mr. Sam, he a fair man, so he'll think it over for a while, an' by that time you be missin' him an' he be missin' you, an' won't nobody be mad at nobody."

So I was right. She was telling me to just take it. Just wait and take it. Well, I could do that, but Sam had better not make me wait too long, because I was through being the last one in line.

～ ；～

I spent the rest of the afternoon stewing in our temporary bedroom upstairs while I cleaned out every drawer and shelf I could find. I had to stay busy in order to keep my anger level up, because if I ever sat down and thought about it, that awful desolate feeling would unwoman me again.

When Etta Mae asked at the supper table that evening where Sam was, I couldn't get out a word. But Lillian was quick with an answer. "That sorry James cook up some chicken an' dumplings 'cause he don't want to work outside in the cold, then he make Mr. Sam feel guilty if he don't stay an' eat it."

"Well, shoo," Hazel Marie said as she balanced a baby on her shoulder with one hand while eating with the other. "Looks like he could've invited us too and given Lillian a break."

"I'm glad he didn't," Lloyd said. "I'd rather have my chicken fried, and Lillian fries chicken better than anybody. And if somebody would pass it, I'd have another piece."

I'd thought we'd have little to say to one another without Sam there, but the babies and their needs took everybody's attention so that the empty place at the head of the table went almost unnoticed. Except by me, of course, but I was keeping myself at a slow simmer in order to get through the day.

When one baby started screaming—the one who was supposed to be sleeping—Etta Mae dropped a chicken leg on her plate and ran to pick her up. She came back with a red-faced, squalling infant whom Lillian immediately took from her.

"Finish yo' supper, Miss Etta Mae," she said. "This here's Lily Mae an' she need some lovin'." She wrapped the baby tightly, held it close to her ample bosom, and began walking around and through the house until blessed peace descended again.

"She's right, you know," Etta Mae said to Hazel Marie. "It's Lily Mae who's the loudest." She laughed. "You knew what you were doing when you named her after me and Lillian."

❧

Later when I was in bed, the anger at the way Sam had treated me began to seep away, and I was left in the loneliest state I'd ever been in. I couldn't get fixed. I couldn't find a comfortable place. I turned first one way, then the other, but the bed was too empty.

In my mental turmoil, I recalled a poem that Tonya Allen had shown me once when the book club met at Mildred's house. I'd thought at the time that it wasn't much of a poem, but Tonya told me that it was written by a Japanese lady a long time ago and wasn't supposed to be long and involved. I wished I could remember all of it, but the part I did kept running through my mind:

> *I sleep.... I wake....*
> *How wide*
> *The bed with none beside.*

It's a fact that some people can say a mouthful in only a few words, while others can talk all day and never say a thing. I knew many of the latter, but only a few of the former, Sam being the prime example. And did he ever pack a lot of pain and anguish and recrimination in the few words he spoke as he turned and walked off.

How in the world would I ever get through the next several days? Or would it be longer than that? Maybe Sam had come to the end of his rope and the few days would become forever. I couldn't bear the thought, and rolled and tumbled some more.

By the time the sun began to come up and I could rise along with it, I'd set myself a course of action. There was nothing for it but to find out all I could about Richard's postprison visit to town—a place you'd think he'd want to avoid, seeing that he'd flimflammed so many people here. Yet here he'd come, only to end up dead in the most unlikely place—in between Laverne Petty's house and Thurlow Jones's. Must be a reason he'd been there, and the more I thought about it, the more I realized that the toolshed was at the very back edge of Miss Petty's yard, which put it right next to the back boundary of Thurlow's yard.

We'd all assumed he'd been visiting Miss Petty, but maybe we'd all been wrong. Maybe it was Thurlow he'd been interested in. But why? As far as I knew, and I pretty well knew the facts, Thurlow hadn't been a part of the scheme cooked up by Richard and the New Jersey developer that had sent both of them to jail. Thurlow was about half crazy in some ways, but he was a wily character when it came to finances. That's why he had so much: he didn't fall for get-rich-quick schemes.

Still, the only thing I could think of to explain Richard's presence on a cold winter night in a toolshed that overlooked Thurlow's house was that he either had something on Thurlow or he wanted something from him.

But why was he in the toolshed? Why hadn't he been in Thurlow's house? Or in the front yard, even? Why in the toolshed as if he had been lurking and watching and waiting for something? Or somebody?

As I smoothed out the coverlet on the bed, I determined that the first thing I needed to do was check out that toolshed. Which house could be watched from it: Miss Petty's or Thurlow's? If, that is, either of them had been the focus of Richard's interest. I couldn't let myself overlook the possibility that the toolshed had simply been a place a sick man had chosen to wait out a sudden spasm that, unfortunately, led to a permanent wait.

But that didn't make sense. Why was he even in that part of town? Logically, Helen was the only one he had reason to want to see and she lived nowhere near his final resting place. And if he'd been walking on a cold night and suddenly become ill, why not knock on a door and get help?

Actually, none of it made sense, but that was because I didn't have all the facts. And now that the sheriff had determined Richard had died from natural causes, the case would be closed and I'd be free to look around for myself.

And that's exactly what I decided to do. If Sam was so concerned about Richard and me or Thurlow and me, it behooved me to straighten him out with the facts. And the first fact I had to make sure he grasped was that my being entangled with either one of those unsavory types—one about crazy and the other a felon—was laughable. Except Sam wasn't laughing, and neither was I.

I knew, of course, that it was currently trendy for older women to take up with younger men. I knew because Hazel Marie had pointed out several examples in the movie magazines she was constantly reading. But I'll tell you the truth: Richard Stroud had been too old to attract the interest of a mature woman looking for a young thing. Certainly not *this* mature woman, even if I'd had a yen for something fresh and green, which I most assuredly had not, and how Sam could've even considered such a thing was beyond me.

I went to the front windows to open the curtains, longing for a cup of coffee but knowing it was too early to disturb the rest of the house. Looking out the window onto Polk Street, I could see that fog from melting snow had almost hidden the church from view. The steeple, though, the one where pigeons roosted and littered the roof, rose up out of the fog, and I took it as a sign that I was on the right track.

Looking down at the street again, a pair of headlights pierced the fog as a white car eased to a stop in front of the house at the stop sign. An early riser, I thought, on the way to work—maybe to open a shop on Main Street—but as the car pulled silently past the stop sign, I almost lost my breath. If that wasn't Helen Stroud's car, I'd eat my hat.

# Chapter 25

My hat was safe. I could rarely distinguish one make from another when it came to cars, but Helen drove a Volvo, the rarest of cars in a town of American-made sedans and pickups, with more than a few Japanese models thrown in. The car suited Helen: neither was flashy and both were sedate and dependable.

So what was Helen doing riding around at daybreak, almost invisible in the fog? Where had she been and where was she going at such an unlikely hour? She had been headed toward town but was coming from the direction in which her husband, or ex-husband, had perished. But as I reminded myself, that didn't have to mean anything. Half the town's citizens resided in that direction. She could've been doing something entirely innocent, such as driving around because she couldn't sleep and just happened by my house at the same time I was up for the same reason.

There also could've been a dozen other reasons for Helen's early morning excursion, but the most likely ones were the few I wanted to look into. Number one, that toolshed: check out what might've drawn Richard to it. Number two, subtly and kindly interrogate Laverne Petty as to her connection, if any, to Richard. Number three, do the same with Thurlow, although not as subtly or as kindly.

I was going to need some help—two visitors with a casserole would be more welcome and less likely to inspire suspicion than one visitor with no legitimate reason for knocking on a door. Etta Mae came to mind—she'd have been perfect—but she had her hands full of babies, and Hazel Marie needed her. Lillian? Yes, maybe so, except I wasn't sure she'd do it. She, too, was too wrapped up tending babies to give me her full attention. Lloyd? I'd have to think about that. Miss Petty, after all, was his teacher and I didn't want to undermine his respect for her by prying into her personal life. In his presence, that is.

It struck me, then, that Helen might already be doing exactly what I was planning to do. If I'd been in her shoes, I'd want to know more than "natural causes in an unnatural place," especially because Lieutenant Peavey had left a lot of questions unanswered. But after thinking about it, I decided I didn't have the nerve to suggest that she join forces with me to find out what Richard had been up to. For all I knew, Helen could be grieving over her loss in spite of having divorced him, shocking most of us by her immediate cutting of the tie that binds. We'd all thought that she would stand by her man, at least until his prison sentence was up, for no other reason than to at least demonstrate her own fidelity. But she'd surprised us. The cell door had hardly slammed behind Richard before Helen instituted proceedings to cut him off entirely.

But who knows what goes on in the heart of a woman? Especially a woman like Helen, who, as far as I knew, had never hung out her dirty linen for all to see. The only one I could account for was myself, and the only reason to pry into other people's business was to prove to Sam beyond a shadow of a doubt that my life was an open book. Except for when I invested with Richard, which I would regret and atone for till my dying day.

As soon as I heard Lillian plod downstairs, I went around waking Lloyd and Latisha for school. By the time I got to the kitchen, one baby had tuned up from the back bedroom and the other quickly joined in.

"Morning, Lillian," I said, as I walked to the coffeepot to watch it finish perking. "I didn't sleep too well last night, but I didn't hear the babies. Did they sleep through?"

"Yes'm, pretty much. I hear Miss Etta Mae down here in the kitchen 'bout four o'clock, an' I start to get up to help her. But she poke them bottles in they mouths an' I didn't hear another peep."

"I didn't hear any of that," I said, wondering at how deeply I'd slept after such restlessness earlier. That, I assured myself, came from having made a decision and figured out a plan of action. I had determined sometime in the night that I would not sit around twiddling my thumbs while Sam pondered the state of our marriage. Who knew what conclusion he'd come to if he was left to ponder alone?

As soon as the pot stopped perking, I poured a cup of coffee for myself and one for Lillian before sitting at the table. She laid strips of bacon in a black iron skillet, then set it aside and joined me.

"I know why you not sleepin' so good," she said, cocking an eye at me. "You got yo' mind whirlin' 'round Mr. Sam an' what you can do to get him to come on back home. An' I hate to hear what you got cooked up. I know you got something goin' on, 'cause I see it in yo' eyes."

I heard little feet stomping around upstairs and knew that Latisha would be down soon. I had to talk and talk fast before the kitchen was full and the time for talk was past.

"I certainly do have something cooked up," I said, my face tightening as I leaned toward her. "You didn't think I'd take this lying down, did you? Just let my husband walk out without raising a hand to stop him? No, ma'am, he's got it all wrong, and I'm going to find out what's been going on and prove to him that I had absolutely nothing to do with it. Then he can beg for *my* forgiveness, instead of my begging for his."

"Oh, Law," Lillian said, raring back. "Now you on a rampage, and nothin' good gonna come of it." Then she hunched forward and looked me right in the eye. "You better think twicet 'fore you go messin' with Mr. Sam, gettin' him all riled up an' even madder than he already is. If he even mad at all. Sound to me like he got hurt feelin's more than anything else."

"Well," I said in my defense, "he hurt mine first—not believing me and walking off the way he did. Look, Lillian, the only thing I know to do is show him that I was not mixed up with Richard Stroud or Thurlow Jones, and the only way to do that is to find out what *they* were mixed up in. That makes sense, doesn't it?"

"Maybe to you it do, but maybe not to Mr. Sam. Maybe he want a helpmeet that stay home an' keep outta trouble."

"Then he married the wrong woman, and I don't believe that for a minute." I reached over and put my hand on her arm. "I need help, Lillian, somebody to go with me and be a witness. Will you do it?"

She jerked back in her chair. "How I'm gonna do that? Miss Hazel Marie need me, an' I got dinner to cook an' lunch to get ready jus' as soon as I get breakfast on the table. An' they's clothes to wash an' beds to change an' I don't know what all." Then she squinched up her eyes at me. "What you gonna do, anyway?"

"Just make a few visits, that's all. Maybe take a casserole or two with us. Or a cake, whatever's easiest, because I know you have lots to do. But I'll help you—I promise I will. I'll put the clothes in the washer and whatever else you need done."

"Who you gonna visit?"

"Miss Petty, for one, but we'll have to wait till this afternoon when school's out. But we can see Thurlow this morning..."

At her gasp, I hurried on. "It's important, Lillian, because LuAnne told me that Miss Petty stayed the whole night with him when we lost power. I haven't said anything about that because I didn't want to gossip, but we need to know what's going on with those two. Then the last, and maybe most important visit, will have to be to that toolshed."

"No, ma'am, no, ma'am," Lillian said, rising from her chair. "Neither you nor me is gonna go snoopin' where some ghost be hoverin' 'round."

"We have to, Lillian. We have to see if Mr. Stroud was in there because of Miss Petty or because of Thurlow, or just in there because he had no other place to go. And there won't be any ghosts. In fact, you won't even have to go inside. You can stand outside and be the lookout. Your eyesight's good at night, isn't it?"

"At *night*!" Lillian screeched so loud and jumped back so quick that I thought she'd bring everybody running to see what was wrong. "No, ma'am," she said firmly, closing her eyes and shaking her head. "No, ma'am, no, ma'am."

"Then I'll do it by myself. Tonight, after everybody's asleep, especially the babies. I'd like to have some company, but..." I shrugged my shoulders. "If that's the way it is, so be it. I'll do whatever it takes to bring my precious husband home where he belongs."

"What you think you gonna see in the dark anyway?" Lillian asked, giving me a hard look. "Why don't you go in the daytime like normal people?"

"That's just it, Lillian," I said excitedly because she was finally understanding what I was up against. "Richard wasn't acting like a normal person, and of course Thurlow never does. That's why we need to go at night so we can see what Richard saw. That's the whole point of it. And I promise, you won't have to put a foot inside. Just stand beside the door and let me know if anybody's coming."

"Well," Lillian said, somewhat grudgingly, "lemme think about it."

"Oh good! I'll wake you around two if, that is, the babies stay on schedule. If they don't, well, we'll have to see, but I'm going to do it, come what may."

"That's what I'm afraid of," Lillian said, as she put the skillet of bacon over a flame. "Whatever that 'come what may' might be, an' when it start comin' down on us."

# Chapter 26

Later in the morning, after the children were off to school and Etta Mae and Hazel Marie were washing babies, I sidled up to Lillian in the dining room. She was vigorously polishing the table with lemon oil and the scent nearly brought me to my knees because it reminded me so much of Sam. His aftershave had a much lighter aroma, of course, but still, everywhere I turned I was reminded of his absence.

Taking myself in hand, I whispered, "I've changed my mind about visiting anybody today. We need to see that toolshed first—tonight—then we'll know how to lead the conversation."

"I'm not leadin' nothin'," she said, rubbing the table harder than it needed. "I might go with you an' I might not, but everything else is your little red wagon."

"Oh, I know, I don't expect anything more. But to put off the visitations until tomorrow gives you time to fix something for us to take. Nothing fancy, Lillian, just something to get a foot in the door."

She grunted, mumbled something that sounded like, "My foot," and kept polishing what was already the shiniest table in town. I left her to it and went upstairs.

There I went through the closet and laid out the warmest clothes I could find to get me through a late-night reconnaissance: a woolen dress, two sweaters, heavy cotton stockings that Hazel

Marie called tights, a pair of cashmere socks, fur-lined gloves, galoshes to keep my feet dry, and a heavy coat. The weather had turned almost balmy for January in the last few days, but the temperature would be at its lowest in the dead of night.

Taking no chances on freezing, I slipped into Lloyd's room and snatched up two toboggan caps to keep our heads warm. Back in the pink bedroom, I laid everything out in a chair so they'd be ready to go when I was.

As I studied the layout, desolation swept over me again, and I had an urge to run to Sam and beg his forgiveness. Or call him, just to hear his voice. He might be just sitting at his desk waiting for me to make the first move. When the telephone rang at that moment, my heart lifted. I ran to the bedside table to answer it, then the little pride I had left made me hesitate as Lillian picked up downstairs.

She called me in a loud whisper from the foot of the stairs. "It's yo' pastor," she said when I leaned over the bannister. "An' we need to fix up something where I don't have to yell an' wake up them babies every time the phone ring."

The bottom dropped out when I heard that it wasn't Sam calling, and I sighed at the thought of what the pastor would want from me. If he'd somehow learned of the rift in our household, I hoped to goodness he didn't intend to suggest a counseling session. I knew too much about the state of the pastor's marriage to think he had anything to offer us.

When I answered the phone, Pastor Ledbetter said, "Miss Julia? I'm calling around to see if we'll have a good turnout today. Will you be there?"

"Be where, Pastor?" I didn't recall any meeting or service planned for the day and was momentarily disconcerted that something had slipped my mind. Surely he hadn't gotten together a *group* counseling session. That would be the last straw.

"The funeral. Or rather, the graveside service. I thought you would've received an invitation."

"An invitation to a funeral?" I was more than momentarily disconcerted at the idea of invitations being extended for a committal.

"Well, I don't mean an official invitation, exactly, although some people do it that way. I assumed that Helen would want you and a few others to be there."

"Helen? Oh, you mean *Richard's* funeral." Funny, I hadn't thought of the fact that Richard would need a burial, but of course he would. "I must say, Pastor, that I'm a little taken aback that Helen is arranging this. I thought they were divorced."

"Now, Miss Julia, you know I don't believe in divorce. I had a few counseling sessions with Helen and encouraged her not to go through with it. Once married, always married, I always say, and besides, there may have been some financial considerations for keeping the marriage intact, Social Security and so on—I'm not really sure. But there are all kinds of benefits, spiritual and otherwise, when you decide against seeking a divorce. So because Richard had no other family, she's assuming the responsibility. And under the circumstances, I commend her for selecting a graveside service and not a funeral in the sanctuary. Even so, I'm afraid that few people will be there, given his recent troubles, so I thought I'd call around with a reminder. Helen will certainly need the comfort of her friends during this trying time."

After getting the time, two o'clock, and the place, Good Shepherd Cemetery, of the service, I promised to do my best to be there. Hanging up the phone, I considered what I'd heard. So Helen had not followed through with the divorce—that was a surprise. But it was his words, "once married, always married," that rang in my head. I was well aware of the pastor's antipathy toward divorce, but hearing it again made me wonder if it would do any good for Sam to hear it, making me slightly more amenable to being counseled. But then I had to wonder if the pastor's belief in "once married, always married" meant that I was still married to Wesley Lloyd Springer, and if so, how things would work out in heaven if I had two husbands to contend with. And think of all the widows and widowers who'd also remarried. Why, when you consider all those once-and-future husbands and wives milling around, either trying to get back together or trying to avoid each other, heaven would be a place of complete turmoil.

Well, of course there'd be no marrying or giving in marriage in heaven, so I thought maybe when we all got there, the Lord would issue a Great and General Divorce Decree, in spite of the pastor's disbelief, and I wouldn't have to worry about it.

~⁓~

Hearing the commotion start up again downstairs, I went down to offer my help. Etta Mae was preparing bottles while the din got louder in the bedroom.

"Can I help?" I asked, but hesitantly because I'd pretty much stayed out of the way ever since the babies had taken up residence.

"You sure can," Etta Mae said. "You can feed one of them while I do the other one. Hazel Marie just washed her hair and she's dripping all over the place. We thought they'd sleep a little longer, but no such luck."

I followed her into the bedroom where she indicated the upholstered rocking chair. "Sit there, Miss Julia, and I'll give you one. Hazel Marie, go ahead and dry your hair, we'll take care of them." And before I knew it, I was given a very unhappy little girl.

"Here's the bottle," Etta Mae said. "Just put the nipple next to her mouth and she'll take it."

And did she ever! "This child acts like she's starved," I said, wondering at the intensity and strength of a pair of little working jaws.

Hazel Marie sat on the side of the bed, toweling her hair, and watched us. "I think the hair dryer woke them up, but they'll have to get used to that—I use it so much." She laughed, but I noticed that she kept her eye on me. And rightly so because I was feeding an infant for the first time in my life.

Hazel Marie let the towel drop as a dreamy expression crossed her face. "I can hardly wait for them to get a little older. I'm going to have so much fun fixing their hair and dressing them. I wish I knew how to smock, I'd make them little matching dresses and embroider some teddy bears or something across the smocking."

"You're already fixing their hair," Etta Mae said, holding up two tiny pink ribbons. "Miss Julia, you should've seen these bows in their hair. We'll put them back in, but they slide right back out when the babies start wiggling around."

After a while, I became accustomed to holding and feeding the baby and was able to relax and let the child eat without staring at her. Etta Mae sat across from me with the other baby, who took to the bottle with loud gulps, working away at it as if it were the last meal on earth.

"Pastor Ledbetter called a little while ago," I said, venturing a conversation while having the responsibility of such an important task as feeding a baby. "He's having services for Richard Stroud this afternoon, and he's afraid Helen will feel forsaken if no one comes. So he asked me to be there. And I'm just not sure I'm up to it."

"Why would she feel forsaken?" Hazel Marie asked, stopping to look out at me through strands of drying hair. "I thought she divorced him."

"I thought she had too," I said, moving my baby-holding arm the least little bit to avoid a cramp. "But apparently he, I mean the pastor, not Richard, talked her out of it at the last minute."

Etta Mae chimed in. "Preachers are always trying to talk somebody into or out of something."

"Well, it'd be the nice thing to do, I guess," Hazel Marie said. "To go, I mean, for Helen's sake. But I can't imagine the church will fill up, not for an ex-convict, anyway."

"I think they know that, because it's a graveside service," I said.

"Oh my goodness," Etta Mae said. "I bet that means they're burying just his cremains."

"Cremains?" Hazel Marie asked. "What's that?"

"His ashes," Etta Mae told her. "What's left after being cremated."

"Yuck, as Lloyd says," Hazel Marie said. "I wouldn't want to be cremated, would you?"

"I doubt you'd know it at the time," I said.

"Well, but still," Hazel Marie responded, scrunching up her shoulders, "the thought of it makes me shiver. I'm going to write that down somewhere: don't cremate me. And, Miss Julia, don't let J.D. do that to me. I want to rise up on the last day all put together, not scattered to the four winds."

"I expect," I said, somewhat dryly, "that the Lord is able to manage whatever is called for. But I admit I feel pretty much the same way. I'd prefer a burial rather than a cremation, and come to think of it, I'd better write that down too in case Sam has other ideas." If he was even around at the time, I thought but didn't say. A shiver ran across my own shoulders.

"Well," Etta Mae pronounced, "I know a lot of people who've had their loved ones cremated, then gotten them back again."

"How in the world?" Hazel Marie asked as she started combing through her still-damp hair.

"Well, see," Etta Mae said, "there's this company that'll take the loved one's cremains and make a diamond out of it and put it in a ring or a pendant or whatever you want. So you can have your loved one always with you."

"I never heard of such a thing," I said, as Hazel Marie's mouth gaped open. "Etta Mae, is this baby all right? Her face is so red and she's sweating all through her hair."

Etta Mae laughed. "She's fine. They get hot and sweaty when they're nursing. Takes a lot of energy, I guess. But I'm telling the truth. About this company, I mean. It's called something like Forever Together Gems. They take the ashes, which are mostly carbon, just like diamonds, and put them under a lot of pressure and out pops a diamond. The only thing I can't figure out is how they can make the different colors. Or maybe," she said, musingly, "the colors depend on what kind of ashes they are. I mean, maybe men have a different color than women do, or children are different from adults. I don't know. I do know, though, that you can get blue, red, yellow, and colorless diamonds, so maybe they just add dye."

"Etta Mae," Hazel Marie said, "you're making that up."

"No, I'm not. I had a patient one time—Mr. Buck Hanson—and he had two diamond rings made from his first and second wives. Wore one on each hand. His first wife was the red diamond and his second was the yellow, but I never did ask him how he'd gotten those colors—whether that's just the way they turned out or whether he'd had a choice. If he did, maybe he picked them because of their temperaments. His third wife wasn't too happy about them because she said his two ring fingers were all taken up and she didn't want to be a pinkie ring."

"You *are* making that up!" Hazel Marie said, and I was inclined to agree with her, although it was awfully entertaining in spite of the subject matter.

Etta Mae giggled. "I'm not, I promise you. And as it turned out, Mr. Hanson died before his third wife did. I ran into her on the street one day and she was wearing what looked like a big sparkly diamond on a chain, you know, like a pendant? And I'll just bet you that was Mr. Hanson himself, hanging around her neck."

"Well," Hazel Marie said, looking off in the distance as she cogitated about it, "I guess I wouldn't mind being cremated if J.D. wanted to make a diamond out of me. But if he does, he better wear me and not leave me in a jewelry box somewhere."

"Oh for goodness sakes, you two," I said, "let's get off this morbid subject. Etta Mae, I think this child's had enough." The baby was slack in my arms, sound asleep, the nipple loosened from that strong vacuum as milk drooled from her mouth.

Etta Mae showed me how to hold the baby on my shoulder and pat her back, which I did until air bubbles erupted with a loud clap and spit-up flowed down my back. Eau de baby, Etta Mae called it.

# Chapter 27

I went to the Stroud funeral, or rather, the graveside service, hating every minute of it because I felt hypocritical appearing to honor a man who'd stolen from me left and right. Of course, few knew how he'd about picked me clean because I'd hidden the fact that I'd invested with him, and I hadn't had time to tell anybody about the stolen checks.

But having good manners means doing the right thing even when you don't want to. I do my best to do what is correct in all circumstances, although the Lord knows, sometimes it almost kills me to do it. Take standing around in cold, blustery weather waiting to inter a man for whom I had not the slightest bit of respect. But services for the dead, as this Presbyterian understands them, are really for the comfort of the living—in this case, Helen, although I wondered at how much comfort she actually needed—and not for the glorification of the one who's passed on.

And to be perfectly honest, I thought that Sam would be there. We could've at least stood together and maybe he would've reached for my hand. Instead, I was one of only eight or nine others gazing down at the casket resting on straps over an open grave, listening to Pastor Ledbetter read from the Scriptures. Most of the mourners were men who, most likely, had had business dealings with Richard. I recognized two bank vice presidents who probably were there to make sure they couldn't sue him for unpaid loans.

And of course there was old man Randall, who never passed up a funeral whether he knew the deceased or not. I'd once heard him say that he'd lived so long he knew everybody in town even if he couldn't remember who they were. He never missed a postfuneral reception either, making full use of the buffet table.

Then there was Stuart Hardin, a local restaurant owner, who may or may not have known Richard but who made it a practice to attend any community gathering, usually holding forth vigorously on some issue he was interested in. I squinted as I tried to read what was on the big round pin on the lapel of his overcoat, but he was across the grave from me and it was hard to see. But when Stuart adjusted his position, stepping closer to the gaping hole, I silently gasped. The man was running for county commissioner, and even though it was months before the primary, there he was, sporting a campaign pin advertising himself. Of all the tasteless things I'd ever seen, using a funeral service as a campaign event was among the worst. If I were Helen, I'd snub him good.

Holding my coat together against a cold blast of wind, I glanced at Helen, not wanting to stare at her. She was dressed fittingly in black but was dry-eyed and without expression so that I couldn't help but wonder what she was thinking and feeling. Maybe she'd loved Richard deeply—after all, they'd been a couple for years and seemingly had been content and well suited. It had only been Richard's fairly recent foray into investments and developments that had started him on his downhill slide.

Actually, I figured that any grief Helen had experienced had come when Richard was in the process of sliding, not now when he'd finally hit bottom. The shame and humiliation he'd heaped on her head must have been worse for her than losing him entirely.

All unbidden, a line from something I'd read or heard suddenly flitted through my mind: *I'm glad you're gone, you rascal, you,* and I had to stifle myself.

Funny, isn't it? How in the most somber and inopportune of

circumstances, the mind will play such a trick on you. I had to think of Sam and the pain in my heart to keep myself from laughing out loud.

The service was short, as it was designed to be, and no one, other than the pastor, was given the opportunity to say a few words. I declare, I've been to funerals that went on and on as one person after another praised and eulogized the deceased until he was unrecognizable. I've even on occasion wondered if I'd gotten the time wrong and ended up at the wrong funeral.

I well remember just such an amazing two-hour lovefest, during which the deceased had been praised to the skies for his humility, his commitment to the Lord, his kindness, honesty, compassion, and generosity to Christian causes, specifically those operated by the eulogizers. I'd walked out of the church behind the man's sister and heard her whisper to her husband, "I wish I'd known the man they were talking about."

That was the saddest commentary on a life I'd ever heard. When you treat others better than the ones closest to you, something is wrong with your priorities.

When the pastor finished the last prayer, he walked over to Helen and took her hand, murmuring a few comforting words. The rest of us swayed from foot to foot, eager to leave but waiting for a signal of some kind. It came when Helen turned away, head lowered, and walked toward the funeral home's limousine. Ordinarily, family members would linger to receive condolences, hugs, and shoulder pats from those attending the service, but understandably Helen wanted to leave. As she passed, she caught my eye and nodded an acknowledgement of my presence. I think she appreciated it, because not another single, solitary person in our social circle had come.

As I trudged down the hill toward my car, avoiding tombstones and grave sites, it struck me that Richard had probably perpetrated his investment schemes on every one of our friends.

That was why none of them had shown up. And in a way, it made me feel less foolish for having invested with him myself.

"So, Lillian," I said as I walked in the door, "that was my good deed for the day, although how much good it did I don't know. Probably gave me pneumonia from standing out in the cold, but Helen saw me there and that was the whole purpose."

Lillian turned around, her eyebrows raised. "You didn't go to the house?"

I stopped with my coat halfway off. "Why, I didn't even think of it. But you're right, I should've gone on to Helen's for the reception. But everybody was getting into cars and leaving, and nothing was said about any kind of gathering." I studied the situation for a minute. "Maybe I should run over to her place and see if anybody's there. Attending the service was only half a good deed."

"Don't stay too long, 'cause we gonna eat early. If I got to wander all over creation in the middle of the night, I got to get to bed."

I smiled with relief. She would be going with me when the time came.

I drove to the area Helen had moved to when she'd had to give up her home to help pay the restitution demanded of Richard by the court. That would've been a bitter pill to swallow, right at the time of life when a woman would expect financial demands to ease off. I knew how she must've felt because there'd been a time when it seemed that Wesley Lloyd Springer had sent me to the poorhouse, and I still had the occasional nightmare of being homeless and penniless in my old age.

Coming up to the Laurel View condos, I turned into a paved parking area and studied the four two-story buildings to find Helen's address. It was in the fourth building, the one at the back, and as I parked at the curb, I made note of the many empty spaces. If Helen was having a postfuneral reception, not many mourners had shown up.

Standing on the small stoop, I rang her doorbell, waiting and hoping that at least one or two people would be there. I had no desire to be the only comforter. Shivering as the wind gusted around the corner, I checked the address I'd written down against the number on the door. I was at the right place, but nobody else was. Ringing the bell again, I looked around to see if any others were coming to comfort the widow. There wasn't another soul anywhere.

Turning away, I thought that maybe Helen had had all she could stand and didn't want to see anyone. I could understand that. She was probably in bed with the covers over her head, as I would be—and often was after discovering Wesley Lloyd's perfidy. I slipped a calling card behind the brass house numbers so she'd know I'd been there and walked to the car.

Interesting, though, that Helen's white Volvo was nowhere to be seen. There were no garages or carports for the residents of Laurel View, only assigned parking spaces for each unit. Maybe the reception was being held at the church in the Fellowship Hall. But no, from my house across the street, I would've seen people going and coming.

There was only one conclusion: Helen's grief, if any, was being assuaged somewhere else. But I couldn't think of anyone close enough to her who would provide it. Maybe she was at her attorney's office, seeing to last-minute legal issues. That was the most likely explanation.

On the way home I thought of swinging by Sam's house, just stop, go in, and have it out with him. In a sweet way, of course. But not begging either. There was no reason in the world why two mature individuals who loved each other couldn't sit down and work out their problems without one walking off and taking up residence in his own house. The thought of it still frosted me, and as I approached his house, I could feel the resentment building up. There it was, with the yellow glow of lamps in the windows, smoke curling from the chimney, all looking so warm and homey that it about tore me up. And to top it off, I could see James inside the hall, busily Windexing the windows in the front door—something he probably hadn't done in weeks. I had no doubt that there would be a meal in the oven, filling the house with the aromatic promise of good things to come.

I sped on past, fuming as I realized that the rival for my husband's attention had turned out to be none other than that sorry James.

# Chapter 28

"Lillian," I whispered, as I leaned over the bed in the dead of night to put my hand on her shoulder.

She didn't move, but Latisha groaned, turned over, and flapped her arm across Lillian's head. I carefully moved the arm and gave Lillian a gentle shake. "Lillian!" I whispered a little louder. "Wake up. It's time to go."

Lillian's eyes popped open, or at least I think they did, because I was stumbling around in the dark for fear of waking everybody. I felt her staring up at me, then she carefully slipped out of bed, adjusted the covers over Latisha, and reeled out of the room behind me.

"My clothes in the bathroom," she mumbled. "I gotta get 'em on."

"I'll be in the kitchen," I said, and felt my way downstairs, thankful for the meager glow from the streetlight on the corner.

Dressed in all the layers of clothing I'd earlier laid out, I waited by the back door, holding two of the large flashlights we'd used when the power was out. Lillian shuffled in, looking twice her size from all the sweaters under her coat. She didn't look at me, just went through the door I held open, grumbling with every step. I ignored her and stepped outside, pulling the back door shut as firmly and quietly as I could, and stumbled down the steps behind Lillian. And ran into her as she came to a dead stop in the yard.

"You got yo' car keys?" she whispered.

"We're not taking the car. I don't want to wake anybody."

"Yes'm, but if you have yo' car keys, that mean you have yo' door key too."

Oh, Lord, locked out! It took me a minute to come to grips with my lack of foresight, but there was nothing to do but plunge ahead. Clasping Lillian's arm and urging her onward, I said, "Let's worry about it when we get back."

"I can't see a thing," she said, bumping up against me.

"Well, I can't turn on a flashlight yet. Hold on, Lillian, and we'll be on the sidewalk soon. Careful," I said, steering her to the right. "Don't run into the car."

When we gained the sidewalk, the walking was easier, lit by pools of light from the streetlamps on each corner. I could see one circle of light after the other stretching out before us in the still, cold air. Worried that some insomniac neighbor would glance out a window and see us, I walked as if I had a purpose for being out at such an ungodly hour. I had discarded the idea of slipping from bush to bush through backyards to avoid being seen. It was too cold and too dark and too treacherous underfoot for such evasive action when all we had to do was act as if it were normal to take a walk at two-thirty in the morning with the temperature hovering around eighteen degrees.

As we passed through a circle of light a block from the house, our shadows stretching out behind, then in front of us, I looked at Lillian, whose breath was steaming out of her mouth in puffs.

"Here," I said, pulling Lloyd's hats from my pocket. "We better put these on to keep from losing heat. That's what they say, anyway."

We each pulled a toboggan cap over our heads and down across our ears and foreheads. I looked at the light blue cap with a Tarheels basketball logo on her head and had to laugh until I saw she was doing the same at me. And no wonder, for the one I put on was a garish mixture of red, olive green, and orange with a yellow tassel on the top. It was too cold for humor, though, so we hurried on, Lillian pulling a scarf over her mouth and nose leaving only her eyes showing, while I did the same with my coat collar.

"Come on," I said, urging her on. Then glancing down, I almost tripped. "Why, you're wearing pants! I've never seen you wear pants before. Where'd you get them?"

"You never seen me walking 'round when it so cold before either," she said. "I get them at Walmart when I know you gonna go through with this. They got flannel on the inside."

"Well, you were smart. I wish I still had those green polyester ones I threw away. Let's step it up. I'm about to freeze."

Six blocks is a long way to walk when you're trying to blend into the shadows and keep blood circulating in your feet. And as it turned out, the walk was longer than six blocks because I realized that we'd be better off approaching the toolshed through Miss Petty's yard rather than through Thurlow's. So we had another block to go around before stopping at the edge of her yard. Her house was dark, and I pictured her lying asleep, dreaming of raucous middle schoolers and how she could tame them. At least I hoped she was asleep. I didn't care what she was dreaming of.

The streetlights at each corner of the block gave us enough diffused light to see a thick hedge along what seemed to be Miss Petty's property line.

"Let's scoot along the hedge," I whispered. "We'll follow it to the backyard and find the toolshed."

Lillian didn't move. "I don't know, Miss Julia. Scootin' don't suit me, an' it too dark to see anything, much less no toolshed."

"We can't stop here, Lillian. There's nothing to see. We might as well go home."

"That's what I think," she said, turning away. "Le's us go."

"No, wait, don't leave me now. We're almost there."

"What if she got a dog?"

"I already thought of that," I said, pulling a wad of tinfoil from my pocket. "I brought a chunk of meat, just in case."

"That from the roast I cook for supper?" Lillian's voice edged up in disbelief.

"It's in a good cause, Lillian. Now, come on. We could've been halfway there."

I eased into the shadow of the hedge, and after a brief hesitation, she followed me, her hand gripping the back of my coat. I couldn't tell what kind of hedge it was, maybe laurel or rhododendron or, more likely, as I felt needles swish across my face, hemlock.

Lord, it was dark. No moon or stars visible in the cloudy sky and too scared of discovery to turn on a flashlight, we stumbled along, stepping in and out of dips in the uneven ground, and slipping on frozen patches of snow. Passing the house, I could barely make out a smaller building, or rather a darker, uneven blob, a little farther back. Surprised at the size of Miss Petty's lot, I mentally figured it to match Thurlow's, which was one-fourth of the block, facing the opposite street.

I took Lillian's arm and stepped out of the cover of the hedge, moving across the yard toward the darker shadow at the back of the lot. I almost stumbled as my foot stepped off the uneven ground onto a gravel drive. We followed it to the black shape that indicated a building of some kind, and feeling around on the weathered and splintered boards, I was able to make out a pair of large doors.

"It's a garage," I whispered. "The toolshed must be on the side."

Lillian was breathing heavily by then, not from exertion but from anxiety, maybe from pure fear. She was walking so close to me that she was almost on my heels. I felt my way past the garage, heading for what appeared to be an appendage on the side. Tall weeds beside the wall hindered our way, and Lillian almost fell as she sidestepped what turned out to be a discarded bucket.

"A little way more," I whispered. "I can't find the door."

As I turned the corner, a long moaning sound floated through the night. Lillian stopped, stiff as a board, just as my hand found a tattered strip of slick weatherproof tape. Torn crime-scene tape, I figured because I watch television.

"This is it," I whispered, relieved that we were on the spot. "The door will be here somewhere."

She didn't move. "You hear that?"

Another moan, ending in a muffled bark, stiffened me beside her. I stood stock-still, staring at Miss Petty's dark house.

"That's *Ronnie!*" Lillian said, panic edging her voice.

"Who?"

"Mr. Thurlow's ole dog. We got to go 'fore he get here." She started to turn away, but I grabbed her.

"Wait, don't leave. He's in the house, Lillian, and Thurlow won't let him out. It's too cold, and that dog's as old as the hills. Please wait—it'll only take me a minute to look inside." Even as I reassured her, I pictured Thurlow's huge, slavering Great Dane bounding across the yard, intent on launching himself through the air and onto our backs. My hands trembling and my heart banging in my chest, I kept scrambling along the wall, hoping to finish up and be gone.

"Gimme that chunk of meat," Lillian said, her voice quavering. "Maybe it hold him off if he come."

I pushed the foil-wrapped meat into her hand, and hurriedly feeling my way, I found the door to the toolshed and pushed it open. Now was the time for the flashlight. I clicked it on and swept it around the dirt-floored room. Shelves filled with old pots and various hand tools lined the back wall, while rakes and shovels leaned against a side wall. An old power mower stood in a corner, and half-empty bags of fertilizer and potting soil rested haphazardly under the shelves.

But not entirely haphazardly, for as I played the light around the room, I saw that two full fertilizer bags—one stacked on the other—had been placed a suggestive length from the side wall— the wall at the very back of Miss Petty's property.

"*Miss Julia!*" Lillian hissed, as she stuck her head in the door. "Hurry up, that dog still cuttin' up."

"Just one more minute." As I recalled Thurlow's dog, I remembered it as being stiff and grizzled, much like Thurlow himself, and unlikely to be allowed to roam free. I was sure the dog would be kept inside on such a cold night. The truth of the matter was that after my first flash of fear, I was now too intent on what I was doing to pay attention to the sound of long-distance barking. Thurlow would think a cat was roaming around.

Carefully guarding the beam of the flashlight, I walked over to the two stacked bags and played the light over the cleared space around them. Large footprints were visible in the soft dirt, which could've been Richard's or, most likely, those of investigating deputies. I shivered, picturing Richard's final moments in this lonely shed, the pungent smell of mower gas and fertilizer filling his last conscious sense. At the thought of his dying moments, I swung the light beam around in case his ghost was hovering in a corner. I had to grit my teeth to keep from running out the door, screaming.

Making a mighty effort to be sensible and do what I needed to do, I turned the light back onto the stacked bags. There'd be no clues, I was sure, for the shed would've been thoroughly searched. Still, those bags put me in mind of something, and positioning myself to face the wall, I gingerly sat down on them, figuring that the indentation would perfectly fit somebody's rump. It did, for it fit mine fairly well.

I sat for a minute looking at the blank wall, then moved the flashlight beam so that it threw a shadow against the wall. Right at eye level I saw a knothole in a board. Easing up close, I looked to see what I could see.

Well, of course it was black as pitch outside so who knew what Richard had been able to see. I couldn't see a thing, but it was a hole to the outside because I could stick my fingers through it.

Pressing my eye to the knothole again, I suddenly gasped, "Oh, Lord!" I sprang up and headed for the door. A kitchen light in Thurlow's house had come on, his back door swinging open as a huge, four-legged shadow came leaping out.

"*Run, Lillian!*" I grabbed her and took off, that dog baying behind us.

"Oh, Jesus!" Lillian gasped, making tracks as fast as she could. In fact, she passed me, holding out a hand that I grabbed and was dragged along with her.

Just as we reached the hedge, I felt something nudge up against me—from the back and unnervingly close to a personal place. I yelped and Lillian turned around, waving her arms.

"Get away! Shoo, dog!" she hissed, but the dog turned its attention to her, its tail flapping against my side hard enough to give me a whipping. "Get, dog! Get from here!"

After recovering from the first shock, I realized that Ronnie wasn't barking and that Great Danes are generally a friendly breed. I began to breathe again. Lillian, who generally steered clear of all breeds, was bravely pushing me behind her and trying to hold off the dog.

"He's friendly, Lillian," I whispered. "He's not going to hurt us. Let's just go and he'll go home."

That's all we could do, so we did it, retracing our steps beside the hedge until we reached the sidewalk, our new addition dogging every step we made, his inquisitive nose all over us. We scurried along with backward glances at Miss Petty's house, hoping it would stay dark. Ronnie kept right behind us, nudging Lillian now and then as she jumped and gave out a muffled shriek with each nudge.

"Go home, Ronnie!" I said as we hurried along the sidewalk, the dog bounding along with us. "The meat, Lillian! It's the meat he smells. Give it to him and let's get away from here."

"Oh, Law, I forget." She took the chunk of roast beef from her pocket and unwrapped it. Then she threw it behind us, and Ronnie jumped for joy, taking off to gobble it up when it landed.

We hurried along, practically running, especially after faintly hearing Thurlow calling and whistling for Ronnie. Expecting more than a snack, though, Ronnie wasn't interested in going home. I looked over my shoulder as we neared Mildred's house and saw the ungainly dog loping up behind us, his rear end slightly out of line, his tongue hanging out and a toothy grin on his face. He followed us every step of the way home.

# Chapter 29

"How we gonna get in?" Lillian asked, as we turned into our yard. "And what we gonna do 'bout *him*?" She pushed Ronnie's big head away, but he kept stepping on her feet and snuffling around her pocket.

"Look." I pointed toward the back of our house where yellow light spilled from the kitchen windows. "Somebody's up."

As we approached the back stoop, I could see Etta Mae at the counter, preparing bottles. I tapped on the door, saw her head jerk up and her eyes widen in fright.

I pressed my face against the window in the door so she could see who it was. She took one look at my absurdly capped head, let out a shriek that would wake the dead, and hightailed it out of the kitchen.

Lillian rattled the doorknob, calling, "Miss Etta Mae! It's us—let us in!"

I kept tapping smartly on the glass, but Etta Mae disappeared down the back hall, yelling, "Hazel Marie! Call the cops, they're breaking in!"

Babies started screaming and so did Hazel Marie.

"Oh, Lord Jesus, what we gonna do?" Lillian moaned. "They gonna put us in jail."

"*Ronnie!*" I yelled, turning on the dog, which had pushed his head under my arm. "Get away from me. Go home!" The dog apparently had had enough of night roaming and wanted inside, where it was warm. He shouldered his way between Lillian and me, stood on his hind legs, and looked through the window. Throwing his head back, he started baying.

At my wit's end by this time, what with the racket inside and out, I thought of running over to Mildred's and using her phone just to get into my own house.

Just then, the swinging door from the dining room pushed open and Lloyd stumbled into the kitchen. Still in his pajamas, his hair standing on end and without his glasses, he peered short-sightedly around, looking for the source of the din.

Lillian and I tapped and rattled harder to get his attention. He looked our way, his eyes squinched up, trying to make out who was there.

"Lloyd, it's us!" I shouted. "Let us in."

Recognition partially dawned, and he crept closer to the door to be sure. Just as he put his face against the window on the other side, Ronnie leaped up again, looking at him eye to eye.

"Whoa!" Lloyd said, springing back. Then I heard him yell toward his mother's room. "It's all right, Mama! It's just a dog."

Then, thankfully, he turned the knob, unlocking it, and the three of us—Lillian, Ronnie, and me—fell forward into the kitchen. Ronnie was delighted. His tail wagging with joy as it thumped against everything within reach, he licked Lloyd's face with abandon.

"Who is it?" Lloyd yelled, pushing the dog away and scrambling away from us. "What d'you want?"

"Lloyd," I cried, "it's us! It's us!" Realizing that the world was fuzzy to him without his glasses, I snatched off the cap, feeling the static electricity crackle in my hair.

He jumped back another step at the sight and screamed, *"Mama!"*

Hazel Marie came running from the back hall, swinging a

lamp with the cord trailing behind her. Babies cried. Ronnie barked, and Lillian took off her coat and closed the door.

"Everybody jus' hush up," she said, having reached the end of her rope. "Nobody be breakin' in. We jus' let the door lock behind us, that's all."

"Oh, Lordy," Lloyd said, patting his chest. "You scared the daylights out of me."

Hazel Marie lowered the lamp—it was the one shaped like a rabbit that she'd bought for the nursery they didn't yet have.

"What in the world?" she asked, looking around, trying to figure out what was going on.

"Miss Julia an' me," Lillian said without turning a hair, "we hear something outside an' we go see what it was. That's when the door locked up on us, but it was jus' this ole dog an' we all get locked out."

Every one of us turned to look at Ronnie, who'd found a heat vent. He circled it a couple of times, then flopped down across it with a great sigh. Putting his head on his front paws, he looked up at us with his great, mournful eyes.

"Well, for goodness sakes," Hazel Marie said, as Etta Mae eased up behind her, holding both squalling babies. "I thought something awful was happening. Etta Mae was about to run out the front door with the babies." She took one of the babies and jounced it a little, with no effect. "Let's get them fed, Etta Mae. Lloyd, you all right?"

"Yes'm, I think so. I didn't know who it was. All I saw was that dog." We all turned to look at Ronnie again, asleep now on the heat vent. "He sure does smell bad," Lloyd said, as the sour odor of old dog permeated the kitchen.

"Jus' wait," Lillian said darkly, remembering our first meeting with Ronnie a few years back when the activity of his digestive system nearly ran us out of the room. "He gonna smell worse'n that 'fore long."

⚬⦂⚬

I could hardly wait to get in bed, so drained from trekking around in the cold and from the spurts of adrenaline brought on by fright that I was asleep by the time my head hit the pillow. Lillian and I had been gone only a little more than an hour, although it felt like a good bit more than that, so there was time for a few more hours of sleep.

We'd not lingered in the kitchen, even though everybody but Latisha had been up. The babies had soon quieted and gone back to sleep, as had Hazel Marie and Etta Mae. Lloyd, still in his flannel pajamas, had squatted beside Ronnie for a few minutes, crooning and petting him.

Lillian, who could hardly keep her eyes open, edged up to me. "What you gonna do with that dog? He need to go home."

"Well, I'm not about to take him home now or call Thurlow to come get him either. I'll call him first thing in the morning."

"It already mornin'," she grumbled, "an' none of us have a lick of sleep."

"Let's go back to bed," I said, heading out of the kitchen. "There's time for a good long nap. Come on, Lloyd. That dog will be here when you get up."

Lillian looked at me with disbelief. "You jus' gonna leave him here in my kitchen?"

"He'll be fine, Lillian. We'll close all the doors so he can't wander around. Besides," I said, gazing at the slumbering dog spread out now over the vent and half the kitchen, "who'd be able to move him?"

So the house fell quiet as we went to our separate rooms and crawled back into bed. I'd intended to spend a few waking minutes going over the significance of Richard's watching not Miss Petty's house but Thurlow's, but as I've said, I went immediately to sleep.

So deeply did I fall into sleep that I could not rouse myself when I heard Sam come in downstairs and push through the swinging door to the dining room. Instead, as my heart leaped with joy, the peace of having him home, regardless of the time of night, spread contentment and satisfaction throughout my limbs, dropping me further into sleep. He was home where he belonged, and I dreamed of the many ways I could welcome him back. I wanted to tell him how happy I was, and I wanted to hold him close, yet I couldn't bestir myself enough to hold out my arms when he crawled into bed.

"Sam," I mumbled, snuggling up against his back, "I'm so glad you're home." I felt his warmth enfold me, letting me know that whatever had come between us was now resolved. It was over and done with. I think I smiled the rest of the night.

❧

Waking in the gray light of dawn, I found one arm and one leg hanging off the side of the bed as I clung to the edge of the mattress. Whatever resolution Sam had come to, he certainly had missed me. He was a deadweight against my back and had crept closer and closer to me during the night until he'd almost pushed me out of the bed. Being periously close to tumbling to the floor, happiness nonetheless flooded my soul. He was home! He could have the whole bed if he wanted it—I didn't care.

Grabbing the corner of the nightstand, I pushed back to give myself room to turn over. "Sam, honey, move over. I need some room."

Sam sighed deeply but he didn't budge. I pushed harder, trying with one foot on the floor to get some leverage. Finally I was able to flip over, wrapping my arm around Sam and holding on to keep from falling off the narrow strip of bed.

Sam suddenly stirred, then sat up in bed, turning so that he was staring directly into my eyes. Then his tongue slid out and he licked my face.

*I was in bed with Ronnie.*

# Chapter 30

"Thurlow!" I said through gritted teeth as I stood in the kitchen, gripping the telephone so hard my knuckles had turned white. Ronnie, the big sneak, was dancing around Lillian as she prepared breakfast. "Come get your dog!"

"Is that where he is? What's he doing over there?"

"Don't ask me, but it's a pretty come-off when people let their dogs wander all over creation and wake people up and disturb a whole household and eat them out of house and home."

I hadn't told a soul where Ronnie's wandering had taken him during the night, and I certainly hadn't said who I'd thought he was. I'd never hear the end of it if I had. And I was still so low and blue at discovering it wasn't Sam in my bed that I wasn't in the mood to be laughed at for having thought it was.

Saying that he'd be right over, Thurlow hung up and I turned to Lillian. "Does that dog need to go out? I don't want him ruining my rugs."

"Big as he is, he ruin more than rugs, he take a mind to. But I already let him out, hopin' he'd go home. Then here he come, jumpin' on the door an' whinin' like he freezin' to death. He been under my feet ever since. *Move*, dog!" She gave Ronnie a shove with her hip as he gazed from his great height at the eggs she was scrambling.

Thurlow appeared at our door within minutes, coming in and

greeting Ronnie affectionately. "You been a good boy? Huh, have you, have you?" he said, petting him up, then turning to me. "I hope he's behaved himself."

"He's been fine," I said, although I nearly choked getting the words out. I would never in my life get over the shock of finding a Great Dane in my bed. I must admit, though, that other than taking up the whole bed, Ronnie had been a perfect gentleman.

After explaining that Ronnie had awakened us in the middle of the night, demanding admittance, Lillian and I glanced at each other, waiting to see if Thurlow believed us. Seemingly, he did, for he told Ronnie he'd have to do his business early from now on because he wasn't getting out at night again.

Although I wasn't yet ready to visit with Thurlow, I invited him to have breakfast with us and he accepted. Actually, I thought later that he'd been hoping to be asked. Lillian had to scramble more eggs and, when the biscuits ran out, put bread in the toaster. The man ate as if he were starved. I was just as glad that Mr. Pickens and Sam weren't with us—somebody would've had to make a grocery run.

Hazel Marie and Etta Mae came to the table, each with a baby in her arms, and a fussy baby, at that. They squirmed and cried, and Lillian pronounced *colic* again, while Thurlow cast glowering eyes at the two little noisemakers. The ruction didn't curb his appetite, however, or if it did, I'd hate to see him eat in peace. Latisha and Lloyd, preparing for school, only added to the uproar, while Thurlow heaved exasperated sighs at the goings-on. But not one word or one disparaging glance did he aim toward Ronnie, who was in everybody's way as he lumbered around, hoping for a handout. I could've slapped his face—Thurlow's I mean, not Ronnie's, although having a dog as big as a horse in your kitchen can unsettle the most genteel of us.

But while I had Thurlow, I decided to save myself a trip to his house, which I had not been looking forward to, and subject him to an interview. Pursuant to that, I suggested that he and I take our coffee to the living room. He thought that was a fine idea, especially because Latisha was making known her unhappiness with the lunch Lillian had packed for her.

Thurlow took a seat on my sofa and I sat on one of the wing chairs by the fireplace. Before I could even begin to guide the conversation, Ronnie pushed through the swinging door in the dining room and bounded over to Thurlow. Pushing himself between his master and the coffee table, tail thumping against everything he passed, he collapsed on Thurlow's feet. As the coffee table teetered, I had to spring forward to rescue my Steuben swan before it fell.

"Good dog," Thurlow said, ignoring the near tragedy.

With Ronnie finally settled, I wracked my brain for a subtle way to broach the uppermost subject on my mind. After thinking up and discarding several roundabout feelers, I couldn't for the life of me think of a subtle way, so I just came out with it.

"So, Thurlow, what do you think Richard Stroud was doing in that toolshed?"

"Dying. Or haven't you heard?"

"Oh for goodness sakes," I said, exasperated with him, "that's not what I mean. I'm sure he didn't *go* there to die, and that's what interests me: What was he doing there all by himself in the first place?"

"Maybe he wasn't by himself. Have you thought of that?"

"Who would've been with him? Nobody killed him. He died of natural causes, or haven't you heard?"

That impish, almost malevolent, glint glittered in Thurlow's eyes, and with a smirk he said, "Stroud wasn't a young man, and any unusual exertion in an older man can bring on a heart attack. So," he went on as if he'd figured it all out, "it stands to reason that whoever was with him hightailed it out of there when he keeled over. Let that be a lesson to you: as old as Murdoch is, don't be making too many demands on him."

It took me a minute to understand what he was talking about, then I really could've slapped his face. I felt my own face redden, as I gripped the arms of my chair, infuriated that he would make such a personal remark. "I'll tell Sam that you're worried about him," I said with as much sarcasm as I could muster. "I'm sure he'll appreciate it, seeing that you're such an expert, as old as you are."

His smirk grew into a grin, pleased that he'd gotten to me. "Yep, that's why I know a man has to pace himself. But you're right. Stroud was in that toolshed for a reason, and although I don't want to start any false rumors, think whose toolshed it was. Maybe that's who was with him."

"*Miss Petty?* Why in the world would she meet him in a cold, dark toolshed when she has an entire house to entertain in? That's ridiculous, Thurlow."

"Well, I'm just saying. Don't ask me what a frivolous woman would do. You'd know better'n me."

That just tore me up, and I fumed for a few seconds, trying to think of a comeback that would settle him good. Then I realized how neatly he kept getting to me, distracting me from any sensible discussion. And with that realization, I knew that was exactly what Thurlow intended to do: put me on the defensive and put me off anything of substance. Still, I longed to turn the tables on him and tell him that I knew what Richard Stroud had been doing, and it hadn't been having a tryst in a toolshed.

But with effort, I managed to keep my own counsel because I didn't yet know why Richard had sat on two bags full of fertilizer gazing at the back of Thurlow's house through a knothole on a cold night that ended up being his last night on earth. And if Thurlow knew the why of it, I knew that as contrary as he was, he would not enlighten me.

Then it struck me as plain as day: there was no *if* about it. Thurlow knew.

So maybe I'd been wrong about Thurlow's having too much

sense to get embroiled in Richard's moneymaking schemes. If the two of them had been involved, and it turned out that Richard had been caught, whereas Thurlow hadn't, how would Richard feel? Richard had suffered considerable public shame—his arrest, trial, and conviction had been in the newspapers for weeks—and he'd spent time in jail, while Thurlow stayed as free as a bird. I could just picture Richard steaming and stewing behind bars, then as soon as he was released, coming back to settle a few scores. I could imagine Richard watching Thurlow's house, knowing Thurlow to be as guilty as he was and plotting some kind of revenge.

Of course, a toolshed was a poor place to be plotting anything, but what did I know?

"Well," Thurlow said, slapping his hands on his thighs, preparing, I hoped, to leave. "Be that as it may, me and Ronnie better get on home. 'Preciate you looking out for him, although I can't figure out why he ended up here. He's never left the yard before." He stared at me as he got to his feet. "I hope nobody *enticed* him. I wouldn't like that a-tall, no sir, I wouldn't."

I rose to see him out, carefully avoiding his eyes in case he could see my uneasiness. "I can't imagine anyone enticing a dog that size. But to be on the safe side, if I were you, I'd keep him inside from now on." In case, I thought but didn't say, another visit to the toolshed was required.

After seeing Thurlow and Ronnie out, I stood by the door and watched as they walked away, Thurlow in his worn coat and baggy pants, and Ronnie shambling along beside him. Two old men, I thought, who, if you didn't know better, could arouse pity in a tender heart.

But I knew better and hurried to the kitchen to tell Lillian what I'd figured out and to discuss with her the significance of a particular knothole. In fact, I'd tell her everything except whom I'd slept with the night before.

# Chapter 31

"We need to talk," I whispered, sidling up to Lillian as she loaded the dishwasher. "Come to the living room, so the girls won't walk in on us."

"I be there in a minute," she said, but she didn't sound all that eager to do it. "I got to get this done first."

I waited in the living room, pacing a little as various thoughts and plans flitted through my mind.

Finally Lillian came in drying her hands on a dish towel. "What we got to talk about?"

"Well, first I want to thank you for your quick thinking last night when they asked what we were doing outside. What you said was perfect and nobody questioned it."

She just grunted because she was as staunchly against the telling of stories as I was, but also like me, she understood that you don't have to tell all you know when the circumstances are such that the better part of discretion is to say as little as possible.

"But listen, Lillian, I found out what Richard Stroud was doing in the toolshed, which was what we wanted to do and therefore worth everything we went through. There were two bags full of fertilizer on top of each other that made a seat, like a chair, and they were placed right in front of a knothole. And when I sat down and looked through that hole, I could see right down on Thurlow's backyard and the back of his house. That's what I was doing when I saw his lights come on and the door open to let Ronnie out. So you see?"

"No'm."

"Why, Lillian, it's plain as day. Richard was watching Thurlow. Miss Petty didn't have a thing to do with it, although Thurlow's been implying all along that she did."

"That what Mr. Thurlow say?"

"He didn't say anything this morning, because I didn't tell him I'd figured it out. There's only one reason Richard would've been spying on Thurlow, and I'm just as sure as I'm standing here that Thurlow was in on Richard's fradulent investment schemes. But somebody outsmarted somebody and Richard ended up in jail for it. And you know as well as I do that a lot of money was never accounted for, and I think Richard thought that Thurlow has it. And Richard must've needed money or he wouldn't have stolen checks from me." I waited for her to say something, but she didn't. "So what do you think?"

"I'm jus' wonderin'," she said, frowning, "what all that have to do with you and Mr. Sam."

"Why," I said, flinging out my arms, "it doesn't have anything to do with us, but that's just the thing. Don't you see, Lillian, if I can prove to Sam that I had nothing to do with any of it, he'll be satisfied and come on home."

"Why don't you jus' go over there an' tell him all that an' ast him real nice to come home? Then you won't need to go about provin' nothing."

"I already explained and apologized to him until I was blue in the face, and it didn't do any good. And I'm not going to demean myself by groveling at his feet. Look, Lillian, I know Sam, and an emotional scene would do nothing but embarrass him. He has a logical, analytical mind, which means he'll respond to sane and reasonable arguments. And that's what I'm looking to present to him." Full of self-righteous determination, I ignored her skeptical look. "So now we know what Richard was doing, but we don't yet know exactly why he was doing it. But a money connection is the logical conclusion, don't you think?"

"Maybe so, 'cept what you gonna do about it if it is?"

"That's where I'm stuck," I admitted, sitting down abruptly. "I can't think what the next step should be. I was going to see Miss Petty this afternoon, but I'm convinced that she has nothing to do with it. It's just her misfortune to live behind Thurlow."

After Lillian returned to the kitchen, I stayed in the living room thinking up and discarding ideas of how I could convince Sam that I was not involved with either Richard or Thurlow. It was still beyond me how Sam could think I was personally interested in either one of them. Then it hit me.

That wasn't it at all. Sam was smart enough to have come to a money connection long before I had. After all, I did invest with Richard Stroud and had kept it from Sam. *That* was what had hurt him so badly: he thought I didn't trust him with my finances and had gone behind his back to take up with Richard. And *then* it suddenly struck me: it would seem to Sam that I—who was never careless with money—had left a checkbook in an unlocked car for somebody to steal a few checks, leaving me seemingly innocent of aiding and abetting. It was an easy jump to assume that somebody had been Richard Stroud. Once Sam came to such a conclusion, one thing had led to another until now he no longer trusted me.

There was only one thing to do: follow the money. Easier said than done, though, because I didn't know where to start. The courts had taken everything Richard had to recompense those he'd cheated—everything they could find, that is. There sure hadn't been anything left for Helen to live on. She'd had to give up her home and, as I'd recently heard, take a part-time paid job at some nonprofit agency. I didn't think she would've done either one if there'd been money stashed away somewhere.

So maybe Thurlow had it, and Richard had wanted it back.

Lord, it was too much for me to figure out. Sitting there study-ing on it until my brain was half addled, I became aware of the noise from Hazel Marie's room. The babies had revved up again, and she and Etta Mae were bustling around changing diapers and fixing bottles, slamming doors, and talking over the din, with Lil-lian chiming in from the kitchen. I thought of going back there to see what I could do, but they had a baby apiece and could surely manage without my help. I wondered how long Lillian would be willing to stay day and night without a break. I thought I might suggest that she and Latisha take the weekend off so they could go home and rest. Lillian's house would certainly be quieter than mine.

Every time the phone rang, as it just did, my heart jumped, imag-ining that it was Sam calling to apologize. That was ridiculous of me to even think of, because he wouldn't call. He would just come walking in, as I'd thought he'd done last night. But I didn't want to dwell on that little mix-up, so when I answered the phone, I still hoped it would be Sam.

"Julia?" Mildred Allen spoke with a catch in her voice, almost as if she weren't sure she wanted to say anything. "I am so very sorry. Are you all right? Can I do anything to help?"

"I'm fine, Mildred, and I don't need any help, although Hazel Marie and Etta Mae might. Why do you ask?"

"Why, honey, I thought you'd be devastated. I mean, *I* was. In fact, I still can't believe it."

"Believe what? What're you talking about?"

"I understand if you don't want to talk about it. I wouldn't want to either. But the word is getting around, and I thought you needed to be prepared."

"Mildred, I'm not following you at all." All I could think of were the various kinds of word that might be getting around. Images kept flashing through my mind: Lillian and I sneaking around in the dead of night, Ronnie following us home and ending up in my bed, Thurlow insinuating something unwholesome about me, as he'd tried to do about Miss Petty. "Tell me what you're talking about."

"Oh, Julia," Mildred sighed, "I know this is going to do you in, but I heard that you and Sam have separated."

*"Who told you that?"*

"Oh good. I knew it wasn't true, and I'll just tell the one who told me that it's not, and the talk will soon die down."

"No, now I want to know who told you such a thing."

"Well, I guess she won't mind my saying who it was, because she didn't believe it either. In fact, she was indignant toward the one who told her."

*"Who,* Mildred?"

"Ida Lee, and you know she's not a gossip. If she was, I'd have to move out of town." Mildred giggled as much as a large woman can giggle. "But seriously, she's most concerned about you, and she'll be relieved when I tell her it's not so."

Ida Lee, I thought, and immediately calmed down. Mildred was right about Ida Lee, who was the most reserved, elegant, and closemouthed housekeeper of all. Well, Lillian was her equal in keeping what she knew to herself, but I'd have to pass on the elegant part.

"She may be relieved," I said, "but I'm not. Where did she hear it? Who told her?"

"James came by last night—I think he may be courting her, but he's barking up the wrong tree if he thinks Ida Lee would be interested in him. Anyway, he told her that Sam has moved back into his house, and James thinks it's for good."

"That sorry James," I said, so perturbed I could've gone to Sam's house and wrung his neck—James's, not Sam's. I blew out my breath and went on. "Mildred, Sam is staying at his house, but it's entirely temporary. He's staying there because he's at a tedious place in that book he's been writing for ages, and there's so much noise and activity here that he can't think straight. James doesn't know what he's talking about."

"Well, that certainly explains it, and I can just imagine how hectic it must be with two babies and all the extra help you have and everybody milling around. It's a wonder you haven't moved out too."

"I admit I've been tempted," I said, thankful that she fell in so easily with my explanation. "But you know I just can't leave Hazel Marie and those babies."

"You are so good, Julia. You put me to shame. Well, anyway, I was thinking that you might want to get out for a while and I'm asking a few people over for tea tomorrow morning. Very casual because it's so last-minute, but Ida Lee is making real spiced tea, the kind with all the fruit juices, not that instant Tang and Red-Hot candy concoction. And," she went on, "the weather's been so bad, I'm about to get cabin fever, so I thought a little social get-together would do us all good."

"Why, I'd be delighted," I said, and I was because it would be a chance to face down any tendril of gossip that James had started in any other quarter.

"Oh," Mildred said, "and it's going to be slightly ecumenical because I'm asking that new lady preacher the Methodists have. I've heard that she is charming, but that's because she comes from a good family and went to Duke. It has Methodist ties, you know. And she made her debut at the Terpsichorean Ball in Raleigh and I heard she had a real rush by all the escorts. It's a wonder she's not married, but I guess she had a call to the ministry instead."

"I hope so," I said, "given that's where she is. But how did you meet her?"

"Oh, I haven't, but Tonya has and she just thinks the world of her. I wanted to wait till Tonya got back from St. Thomas, but I'm about to go crazy closed up in this house."

Tonya, I thought, who was born and raised as Anthony or Tony until he went up north as a young man and been transformed by surgery and hormones. Living next door as he grew up, I'd watched as he became more and more theatrical in his mannerisms and dress, displaying dramatic tendencies like wearing capes and twirling walking sticks. None of it had bothered Mildred—she doted on the boy and figured he'd outgrow his peculiarities.

But he hadn't, and something happened after his transformation, for now Tonya was a serene and sensible young woman whom you wouldn't hesitate to ask to pour at the head of your table.

"Well, if Tonya likes her, she must be nice," I told Mildred. "I look forward to meeting her. What's her name?"

"Poppy Patterson. I don't know her real name, because she says to just call her Poppy." Mildred laughed. "You can tell she was a popular girl with a nickname like that."

Poppy? I thought. Pastor Poppy? This should be interesting.

# Chapter 32

After asking if Hazel Marie would be able to come and being assured that it was still too soon after childbirth for her to be out, Mildred ended her call. She had also included "that baby nurse Hazel Marie hired," for which I mentally commended Mildred for her comprehensive invitation list. But to leave Lillian alone with both babies? No, that was too much to ask. Of course I did tell Hazel Marie and Etta Mae that they'd been invited and that I had refused for them. Hazel Marie said, "Good, because I'm not going anywhere until these babies are old enough to go with me."

I couldn't help it. I rolled my eyes because don't you just hate it when a mother brings along an uninvited child? I mean, what are babysitters for, anyway?

So I had no qualms about having spoken for them. Besides, I was more than ready to be out on my own and away from the havoc the babies were creating in the house.

It would be such a change, don't you know, to hear about something other than the number and color of infant evacuations, which baby slept the longest, which one nursed the best, which garments they would wear, how long their nightly colic would last, and on and on. Hazel Marie and Etta Mae discussed nothing but the care and feeding of babies, and Lillian was almost as bad. In fact, she constantly marveled at the number of diapers those two babies used, repeatedly expressing gratitude to whoever had invented the disposable kind.

"Jus' think," she said to Etta Mae, "if we usin' the cloth kind, that washin' machine be goin' all day every day, an' we be thankin' the Lord for 'lectricity 'stead of throwin' away them Pampers."

"Yes," Etta Mae said, "and that reminds me of my granny telling about when she didn't even have electricity, much less a washing machine. She had to scrub diapers in a tub with a washboard. Imagine doing that. She used Octagon soap and still had to boil the diapers to get them clean."

"My mama did the same thing," Lillian said, settling down at the table to reminisce about the old days. "I 'member helpin' her hang 'em out on a clothesline when I was jus' a girl, an' on the cold days they'd freeze stiff as a board."

"Well," Hazel Marie said, coming into the kitchen in time to hear part of the conversation. "I'm glad we don't have to do that, but we're going to break the bank keeping those little girls in Pampers. Etta Mae, I just opened the last pack. Do you mind running to the store?" Then with just a tinge of exasperation, she said, "That's going to be J.D.'s job if he ever gets back here to do it."

⌇

That was the sort of thing they talked about all day long, although this conversation had been a little more interesting than the ones about diaper rashes. So I was looking forward to being among adults who had more than one interest. It would be a welcome change for me.

And come to think of it, I'd not been out of the house since those babies were born. Except, of course, for Richard's funeral and that night stroll to Miss Petty's toolshed, neither of which I counted as a social excursion.

Still, the thought of socializing while my heart was so heavy over Sam's absence brought on a renewed wave of desolation. If it was all I could do to keep up a good front for Hazel Marie and Etta Mae, how in the world would I be able to conduct myself normally with a roomful of watchful and suspicious women? They would be avidly interested in Pastor Poppy, I was sure of that, and if I was lucky, she'd be the center of their attention. But James was known to be a source of gossip and the grocery aisles were his venue. He only needed to tell one shopper at the meat counter that Sam had moved out for half the town to be pitying me and adding my name to their prayer lists.

Well, I could use their prayers, and even if the prayers were somewhat skewed, the Lord would know the truth of it. So I would go to Mildred's and steel myself to ignore the whispers and the glances. Heaven knows I'd had enough experience in the past of holding my head high as rumors and speculations swirled around me.

I dressed carefully the following morning, putting on a gray wool dress and the matching gray pumps with the Ferragamo old-lady heels that Hazel Marie said would complete my outfit. Then I added my pearls and, after a slight hesitation, pinned on the diamond brooch that I'd rewarded myself with after learning the extent of Wesley Lloyd Springer's folly, as well as that of the estate he'd left. I took my winter-white cashmere coat from the closet and, from a drawer, the beautiful pink and gray plaid scarf that Lloyd, on his mother's advice, had given me for Christmas. I put them both on and stood before the mirror.

Not bad, I thought. Not outstanding—only an airbrush on my face could accomplish that—but not bad. And right here I'll give some advice to whoever happens to need it. When you're suffering from some emotional devastation that you don't want to advertise around town, you should go the extra mile with your appearance.

Dress up, put on makeup, have your hair done—and your nails too if you can afford it—and plaster a smile on your face. You'll not only make them think twice about any gossip going around, you'll feel better too.

When I went into the kitchen to get my purse and gloves, Lillian gave me an approving nod. "You lookin' real nice, Miss Julia," she said. "I got the car all warmed up for you."

"Why, Lillian, I'm just going next door. I'll walk."

"No'm, it twelve degrees out there an' risin' slow. You don't need to be walkin' in it." Then she leaned toward me and lowered her voice. "It's a wonder you an' me both don't have pneumonia from all that walkin' we already done."

So I drove to Mildred's, backing the car out onto Polk Street, putting it in forward gear, then easing the half block to her driveway. I pulled in onto the brick-paved U-shaped drive and parked beside several other cars in what Mildred called her motor court. I nearly froze in the walk to her front door, dreading the drive back home when there'd be nobody to warm the car for me.

Inside, it was a different story. Mildred greeted me warmly with a hug, even though she knew full well that I prefer a handshake. Still, her house was bright and welcoming with huge fires in the drawing room fireplace and in the one in the dining room. As Ida Lee took my coat, I saw fifteen or so women milling around, drinking tea from Mildred's Spode—her second- or maybe third-best china because it was a casual affair—and talking with one another.

Everybody seemed to have had the same idea I'd had: they were all dressed well with plenty of pearls or gold jewelry. Made me wonder if they, too, were dealing with some emotional distress. Then Emma Sue Ledbetter came in, took one look, and almost walked back out. She was wearing a pair of plaid wool slacks and a turtleneck sweater—perfectly fine for the weather but not for the company.

She sidled up to me as I stood in the foyer, waiting for the line at the dining table to thin out.

"Oh, Julia," she whispered, her face red and her eyes moist. "I never can get it right and I'm so embarrassed. You know it took me the longest to buy even a pair of pants, much less wear them in public, and Larry still gets tight-lipped when I do, and I got it wrong again. I thought, as cold as it is and Mildred saying it would just be a few friends for a cup of tea, that it would be *casual*. And it's not!"

"Don't worry about it, Emma Sue," I said, trying to reassure her. "I expect several are going on to lunch afterward. That's probably why they're dressed the way they are."

She looked at me with accusing eyes. "Are *you* going on to lunch?"

"Well, no, but you know I never wear pants, so I didn't have a decision to make. There have been times, though, when I have wished with all my heart that I had a pair." The night before last, to be exact, but I didn't mention that. "Hold your head up, Emma Sue, and don't give it another thought."

"Well, you're right," Emma Sue said, taking a deep breath. "Nobody cares what I have on, except they'll probably talk about me. But the Bible tells us to take no thought for what we wear or for what we eat." She dabbed at her eyes with a Kleenex, then took my arm. "Let's go see what Mildred's serving."

# Chapter 33

A little surprised that Mildred had not asked Emma Sue to pour, I walked with her to the dining room and saw the reason why. Instead of a tea tray at the head of the table, she had placed her embossed sterling urn on the sideboard for guests to serve themselves—Mildred's idea of casual. So we helped ourselves, filling our cups, then our plates with cheese straws, ham biscuits, nuts, and small skewers of fruit.

Then we wandered across the foyer to the drawing room, where a group surrounded the new Methodist woman minister. We eased closer in order to introduce ourselves.

Emma Sue whispered to me, "Larry's trying his best to come to terms with this. She was at the last meeting of the County Ministerial Association, and when he got home, he had to spend an hour in prayer just to get over having a woman there. You know how he feels about that."

Did I ever. Pastor Ledbetter was of the old school and felt that women should cover their heads and keep their mouths shut when it came to church services. I wouldn't go quite that far, although I had to admit that I would find it unsettling to have a black-robed woman half my age explaining, expounding, and explicating Scripture, as well as excoriating us, from the pulpit. And when it came to a Communion service, I would never be sure that a woman was suited for a sacramental role. But maybe I've just lived too long to embrace change for its own sake.

And another thing: with a woman minister, you get into the complications of how to address her. I well recall the problem the Episcopalians had when they had their first woman assistant priest. Her official address, would you believe, was *Mother* Melanie, and she was less than half the age of the majority of the parishioners. Frankly, I would find it intolerable to call a snip of a girl *Mother*.

Well, of course, no one had a problem with referring to a young man as *Father*—I mean, if you were an Episcopalian or a Catholic to begin with because that's what they call their ministers. Besides, the title is hallowed by centuries-long usage, and nobody thinks a thing about it.

I don't know the answer, but then I don't have to. We Presbyterians frown on anything that smacks of Romanism—in spite of the ecumenical efforts of some—so we'll stick with *Pastor,* which can go either way. Although as long as Pastor Ledbetter's around, we won't have the problem.

Intellectually, I am all for women doing whatever they want to do and going as far as they can with it. It's the emotional, almost the instinctual, reaction to women in the pulpit that makes me hesitant to accept them without question. I guess I'm of the old school too, which isn't always bad except when it lines me up with Pastor Ledbetter.

I declare, though, as I stood sipping tea and getting my first glimpse of Pastor Poppy, I didn't know what to think. Mildred was right: she was lovely. One of those young women you wouldn't call overweight but who had all the womanly curves anyone could want, and then some. She had her auburn hair in a French twist with little tendrils around her face, which took your eye with its smooth and glowing complexion—aided and abetted by expertly applied makeup. Eyeliner and lip gloss, even! Her brown eyes sparkled as she chatted, managing her teacup with the ease of someone long accustomed to dealing with slippery china. And every time she moved, I got a whiff of Shalimar, another plus in her favor.

Her red wool dress was tightly belted, emphasizing the roundness above and below. The dress was well fitted, almost too much so, as the neckline tended toward a fashionable cleavage, saved by a little strategically placed lace. Sheer black stockings and the highest of heels and—I almost gasped, considering the weather— open toed to reveal bright red polish on her toenails, matching that on her fingernails. Velma was going to love this woman, to say nothing of Hazel Marie.

Pastor Poppy had a bubbly laugh she freely used, drawing others to her. There was an easy social air about her, and nothing at all of an obvious piety that so often puts people off. If I hadn't known beforehand, I never would've picked her out of a crowd to be a minister of the Gospel. Whatever possessed her to become one, I didn't know, but she was as removed from John Wesley and his brother as a preacher could get.

I couldn't help but wonder what the men at First Methodist thought of her. The older men, I mean. I had no doubt that the younger ones would be dancing attendance.

Pastor Poppy greeted Emma Sue and me, turning her sweet and open smile on us. I could feel the tightness in Emma Sue, because even though she railed against some of Pastor Ledbetter's strictures on her as his wife, she had a high view of Scripture, particularly of anything Paul had written about how a church should be run.

"So," Emma Sue said, "you're the new youth minister at the Methodist church? Or is it minister of music?" Trying to fit this young woman into an acceptable slot.

"No," Pastor Poppy said with a pleasant smile. "I'm full-fledged. I'm the assistant pastor, which I'll be for a few years until the bishop assigns me to my own congregation."

"Oh," Emma Sue said, swallowing hard. "Well, we don't, ah, have bishops so I don't know how that works."

"I hardly do either," Pastor Poppy said, laughing. "I just do what I'm told and try to stay out of trouble."

I immediately warmed to her for the ease she had displayed toward Emma Sue, who could so quickly be hurt and offended. And who could also do some hurting and offending herself.

"And," Pastor Poppy went on, "you're the Reverend Ledbetter's wife, aren't you? I've been wanting to meet you. I've heard such wonderful things about all the work you do in your church and in the community—especially the Homeless Walk you've organized. I'm planning to be there, and maybe we could have lunch afterward. I'd love to know I could turn to you if I need to."

Well, that just melted Emma Sue right there. "Oh yes," she gushed. "Anytime. Anytime at all."

Before I had time to engage Pastor Poppy in conversation, LuAnne Conover bustled over, put her hand on my arm, and whispered, "I have to talk to you. Let's go to the morning room."

Mildred's cherry-paneled morning room, which I would've termed the library and Hazel Marie would've called the den, was behind the central staircase, and LuAnne tugged me into it and closed the door.

"Julia, I can't believe this. *What* is going on with you and Sam?"

I sighed and sat down in a leather wing chair. "What've you heard, LuAnne?"

"Well," LuAnne said, blowing out a breath of air as she launched into her tale. "I had to run to the drugstore this morning—that's why I was late getting here—to pick up some Pepto-Bismol for Leonard. He just suffers with his stomach, and anyway, I saw Velma there—she was getting a refill of her blood pressure medication, and I didn't even know she had blood pressure. But who wouldn't, fixing hair all day like she does? Anyway, she asked me what in the world you were thinking of to get involved with Thurlow Jones so soon after Sam moved out. Well! You could've knocked me over with a feather when I heard that—you can imagine. So …" LuAnne collapsed in a chair, her eyes filling with tearful concern. "I am just devastated for you. Is it true, Julia? Is your marriage on the rocks? I'm not even going to ask about Thurlow—I know that couldn't be true, although Velma said one of her clients told her she saw Thurlow leaving your house with that old dog of his early yesterday morning."

With an act of will I calmed myself, although if the word was out in Velma's Hair Salon, I might as well pack up and move out of town. But not before beating that sorry James half to death.

There was nothing for it but to repeat the story I'd given Mildred: Sam needed uninterrupted time to work on his book, which he couldn't get at home. And then repeat the story that Lillian had given Hazel Marie and Etta Mae: Thurlow's dog had gotten out, showing up at our house in the middle of the night, and Thurlow was simply retrieving him.

"That's all there is to it," I said. "And it is just pitiful the way rumors get started and people believe them. But one thing is certain, LuAnne: our marriage is not on the rocks, and people ought to understand what a household is like with two infants and somebody trying to write a factual history. It just beats all I've ever heard the way everybody is so quick to believe the worst."

LuAnne blotted her eyes. "I am so glad to hear that, Julia. I didn't believe it in the first place, but to hear you say it relieves my heart. I was hurting for you."

I believed her, for as often as LuAnne exasperated me, she had also been a dear friend for years.

"Well," I said, standing up because I was so on edge and it was taking all I had to keep my nerves from completely fraying. "I'm glad you told me. There's not a thing I can do to stop the talk but live through it and hope it'll die out."

"There is something else, Julia," LuAnne murmured, twisting her hands in her lap. "But it's so far-fetched that I hate to bring it up."

"No need to stop now. What is it?"

"Well, I heard last week, and don't ask me who told me, because I can't remember, that you had some money invested with Richard Stroud and—now don't get upset, but there was some speculation that when he ended up dead in Miss Petty's toolshed, he thought he was at your house, trying to get more money."

"At *my* house! LuAnne, that's the most ridiculous thing I ever heard. How could anybody—even in the throes of a heart attack—mistake a toolshed for my house?"

"Well, I know, I know. That's why I didn't say a word to you. But that just goes to show how people can misinterpret the simplest things." LuAnne glanced at me, then away. "Of course, they're wondering how he was cashing your checks around town too."

"He *stole* them! That's how he was doing it. At least, that's what Lieutenant Peavey thinks, because my signature was forged. And I am going to sue somebody at that bank for telling it, and whoever it was ought to be arrested because the forgery is still being looked into, and that constitutes interference with an active investigation if you ask me."

"LuAnne," I went on, rubbing my forehead where a stabbing pain had started, "I can't take much more of this. Talk, talk, talk, that's all anybody does, and why they're so interested in me, I don't know."

"Oh, that's easy enough. It's because so many odd things happen to you. Just look at what you did after Wesley Lloyd died and left you with Hazel Marie and Lloyd. You came out of that mess smelling like a rose, or rather, with more money than you know what to do with, to say nothing of snaring the most eligible widower in town. And you are outspoken, Julia, so you can't blame people for wanting to know what'll happen to you next."

"They Lord," I said and opened my pocketbook to look for some aspirin.

# Chapter 34

I wanted to go home, but it was too soon to take my leave. They'd surely wonder why I was being so unsociable. Then if they heard any of James's tales, they'd believe them. So I stayed, finding a chair in a corner of the drawing room to wait until I wouldn't be the first to go.

The guests began to break up into groups of two or three for more personal chats. And a few found chairs, as I had, no longer able to stand for long. Mingling was a thing of the past for me, although at one time I could mingle with the best of them, never getting tired or running out of chitchat.

Now, though, it all seemed so futile, although I appreciated Mildred's efforts to relieve the winter doldrums.

Sitting there, hoping to be left alone, the conversation with LuAnne kept running through my mind. It had put me so much on edge that it was all I could do to maintain a calm exterior. She would be the first to notice if I became agitated. But agitated I was, and I could only hope and pray that I had put LuAnne's suspicions to rest.

"Mrs. Murdoch?"

I looked up to see Pastor Poppy standing hesitantly before me. "Yes? But please call me Julia. Everybody does." Except store clerks and bank tellers, which I immediately corrected if they did.

"Thank you. May I talk with you a minute?"

"Why, certainly. Sit here beside me." I indicated an empty chair that she drew close.

Having settled herself and pulled down that short red dress as far as it would go, she smiled and said, "I hope you won't think I'm being intrusive, but somebody mentioned that you know Mr. Thurlow Jones."

"Everybody knows him," I said, hoping the tightness in my voice wasn't giving me away. Why in the world would this woman approach me with a question like that? "Yet nobody really knows him. I, least of all."

"I'm hoping you know him well enough to give me some advice. I've discussed this with my senior pastor but, frankly, he was little help. You see, Mr. Jones has started coming to services at First Methodist, and of course we're all pleased to have him. I understand that he's never been a regular churchgoer, but he's been coming every Sunday for a few weeks now. But this past Sunday, something happened that really distresses me and I'd like to put it right."

Well, this intrigued me because I'd never known Thurlow to darken the door of any church, and although I'd not noticed any change lately in his demeanor or in his actions, going to church might eventually result in changes to both. At least we're told it will have that effect.

"What happened last Sunday?" I asked.

She sighed, looked down at her hands, and said, "I had the sermon, only my second since I've been here, and I guess I upset him. We'd just finished the presermon hymn and as the congregation sat down, I went up into the pulpit and announced a prayer. Just as I started, Mr. Jones closed his hymnal shut with a loud bang, shocking everybody because it was so quiet. Then he stood up and made his way to the center aisle and walked out, slamming the door behind him."

"My word," I said, picturing what that would've looked and

sounded like in a church where the congregation was on its best behavior. There'd been plenty of times I would have liked to have walked out on Pastor Ledbetter, but good manners and fear of a spectacle had kept me in my seat. "That would be upsetting, but maybe you veered from the usual service in some way? You know how people get so accustomed to doing things a certain way that they can't adjust if you add a hymn or move anything around."

"No, ma'am, everything was just the same. But I'm pretty sure it was the prayer I started to read. I thought it was beautiful and inspiring, but I guess he didn't." She sighed again. "I was just wondering, because you know him so well, if you would intercede for me. I'd love to talk with him, but when I called to see if I could visit, he told me he'd had a bellyful of women in the pulpit who didn't know what they were talking about. Of course," she went on, frowning, "there's nothing I can do about being a woman. But I thought if he got to know me, he might be more amenable to putting up with my preaching once a month or so. It's still hard to believe that I could've run somebody out of church."

"Well, Pastor, uh, Poppy, it doesn't surprise me that he walked out. What surprises me is that he was there in the first place. But let's think about this. You say you hadn't gotten into your sermon. So you weren't actually preaching, just starting with a prayer, which is certainly appropriate and shouldn't have offended him. But Thurlow doesn't mind making a scene, so maybe it was something in your prayer that upset him."

"I really don't see how. It was beautiful, if he'd only stayed long enough to hear it all. It started out, 'Oh, Father, forgive us; Oh, Mother, nurture us,' and went on from there. I found it on the Internet."

I just stared at her. As lovely as she was in the face, I couldn't help but wonder what was in her head. "Well, there's your problem," I said, thinking that I might've been tempted to walk out too if I'd had such as that prayed over me.

"What? You mean because it came off the Internet?"

"No, I mean because of the *Mother* business. God the Father is male, not a female and therefore not a mother. Although," I added hastily, "he certainly has some female attributes—he would have to because he created them in women. I'm talking about his kindness, compassion, mercy, and, yes, nurturing and caring, all of which women have in abundance but are rarely observed in men. I guess, though, that Thurlow was outraged to have the idea sprung on him like that."

"You think that was it? That I referred to God as Mother?"

"Oh yes, I'd say so. And what really surprises me is that he was the only one to walk out." I touched her arm in sympathy because she looked so distressed. "Look, new ideas have to be introduced slowly in a town like this. Maybe give some Scriptural background first—if you can find any." I patted her arm in an encouraging manner. "I'm sure you'll do fine, just stay away from family members for a while." I smiled at her, and she managed a weak one back at me.

"I'll try, though I just hate the thought of running somebody off. If you get a chance, would you ask him to talk to me about it?"

"If I get a chance, but I assure you that I am not close to Thurlow and usually avoid any contact with him." And she'd do well to do the same, but I didn't suggest that. Who knew, she could be the agent of change for him, although I'd believe it when I saw it.

When Mildred came by to ask if we wanted more tea, she stayed to chat awhile. While she and Pastor Poppy talked, I got a glimpse past Mildred of Madge Harris putting on her coat, and across the room I saw Miss Mattie Freeman with a hand clasping each arm of her chair, rocking back and forth to build up enough spring to get her to her feet. That was my cue for leave-taking, so I rose from the chair and made my courtesies.

Shivering all the way home in a frigid car, I was also trembling inside from what I had heard. My name was certainly being linked to

Thurlow's, first by LuAnne, who'd heard it from Velma, who'd heard it from a client, which meant everybody who'd had a hair appointment had probably heard it too. And all because Thurlow and his smelly dog had been seen leaving my house early one morning. And come to think of it, which I did, the same thing had been implied about Miss Petty's leaving Thurlow's house early one morning.

I declare, for a confirmed bachelor Thurlow Jones was really making a name for himself by being out so early on two mornings, and if my name hadn't been involved, I could've laughed about it. But I wasn't laughing, because if Sam heard the latest, his suspicions would be confirmed.

And then there'd been Pastor Poppy, who'd been told that I was close enough to Thurlow to intercede for her. That just frosted me good, and I wished I knew who'd told her that. I couldn't blame her, for she was so new in town that she couldn't know the ins and outs of who knew whom, and why and how little they knew them. Or something like that.

As I pulled into the drive at home and crawled out of the car, practically frozen, I decided that something had to be done. It simply wasn't like me to let rumor and gossip run rampant. It was one thing to ignore the talk if Sam and I could laugh about it together. It was another to allow it to further alienate us. And I'd bet my bottom dollar, if I'd been a betting woman, that if James heard any of it, Sam would soon know it too.

"Lillian," I said as soon as I walked in the door, "you have to help me."

"Yes'm, that's what I always do."

"Yes, I know you do, but I'm really depending on you now. Where are the girls?"

"They all nappin' 'cause the babies is sleepin'. They have to get it when they can."

"Well, come sit down and let me tell you what happened. I am just sick about it and something has to be done."

So I told her all the implications I'd heard at the tea about a special relationship between me and Thurlow Jones, getting more and more agitated as I spoke.

She wasn't particularly impressed, saying, "That don't sound like much to me. You ought not let it bother you."

"You don't know the women in this town the way I do," I said, frowning. "Although it was James who started the whole thing by telling about Sam's being gone. And see, that just opened the door. Because it's human nature to figure that if a husband is out of the picture, another man must be in it. But who would've ever believed that they'd put Thurlow Jones in a picture with me?"

"Well, look like to me you jus' have to raise yo'self above it an' make out like none of it have anything to do with you."

"No, Lillian," I said, laying my head on my arm as it rested on the table. "What I have to do is get Sam back home."

I stayed that way for a minute or so, as a wave of despondency swept over me. Then something else swept over me and I raised my head to look at Lillian. "I just realized something, which I should've done a long time ago. I really don't give a rip what they say about me. I am past caring if they think I'm involved with that lunatic Thurlow Jones or that I was financing Richard Stroud or that my hair's a mess or my silver's tarnished or I'm crazy for being Hazel Marie's friend or I have too much money." I sat up and straightened my shoulders. "I don't care if they laugh at me for being a fool over that boy of Wesley Lloyd's or for disapproving of women who wear dresses so short you can see Christmas. Lillian," I went on, as my eyes filled as full as Emma Sue's ever had, "all I care about is having Sam home again, and I'm going to do whatever it takes to convince him of that."

"Now that's the Miss Julia I know," Lillian said with a nod of approval. "You got to put first things first an' let the rest of it jus' pass you on by."

I stood up, feeling renewed and rejuvenated. A spate of talk by the uninformed, no matter how widespread, was not going to get *me* down. "I'm going to see Sam."

"Good! That's what you shoulda already done, but 'fore you go," Lillian said, "I got to tell you they's not a spot of tarnish on any silver in this house. It all polished within a inch of its life."

# Chapter 35

After assuring Lillian—several times—that I had meant no offense, that my reference to tarnished silver had been merely a figure of speech, an example of the less-than-monumental worries that often cluttered my mind.

My explanations didn't do much to reassure her, because she went to the pantry and brought out a bottle of Wright's silver polish. Setting it on the kitchen counter, she mumbled, "I look at it all again, soon's I get time."

Hurriedly putting on my coat before I lost heart, I said, "I wish you wouldn't worry about it. Right now I wouldn't care if every piece of it was black with tarnish. I'm going to see Sam and get this mess straightened out." Just as I opened the door to leave, I turned back. "I just thought of something, Lillian. One thing that'll surely bring Sam home is for Mr. Pickens to get back here."

Lillian looked up from the sandwiches she was making for lunch. "That jus' add to who all's already here. How you figure Mr. Sam wanta be here with a house full?"

"No, I mean it'll be Mr. Pickens who'll want his family in their own house—*Sam's* house. At least that's the arrangement they've made, which means that Sam will have to vacate his house, and where else will he go except back here?"

Lillian screwed the lid back on the mayonnaise jar, saying

nothing until she'd put the jar back in the refrigerator. Then she turned to me and said, "That mean Lloyd goin' with 'em too, don't it?"

Oh, Lord, a pain in my heart stopped me in my tracks and I put a hand on the door to steady myself. "I guess it does," I managed to say. How had it come to this—that I'd have to lose one to regain the other?

⤙ ; ⤚

Sitting in the car, shivering while it warmed up, I had to resolutely put out of my mind the thought of losing Lloyd. Oh, I knew I wouldn't be *losing* him—he'd be only four blocks away, but I liked having him around, liked sharing a secret smile with him, liked watching him grow into the fine and decent young man I knew he would be.

But, I sighed, first things first, as Lillian had said, and the first thing was to put my marriage in order. And I was ready to do whatever it took to accomplish that. If it took groveling, then I'd grovel. Somewhere along the way, I'd lost my pride and the high horse I'd been riding on.

Then, as the heater began to put out a little warmth, I felt the onset of a better idea. If there was one thing Sam enjoyed, it was analyzing and solving a problem. He was good at it too. And didn't I have a problem? I certainly did, and what better way to engage his interest than to ask his help in solving it.

That's what I'd do. I'd lay everything on the table—no holding back on anything, even the fact that I'd invested with Richard Stroud, which he already knew anyway. I'd tell him about slipping out at night with Lillian and finding that knothole in the toolshed—figuring out what Richard had been doing would be a fine problem for Sam to solve. I certainly hadn't been able to.

And if things went according to plan and Sam began to mellow, I might tell him about Ronnie's night wandering and where he'd ended up. Sam would have a good laugh over that, although he might wonder how I could mix Ronnie up with him.

Yes, I thought to myself as I put the car in reverse and backed out of the drive, I wouldn't hold back anything. I'd let him see that I was being open and honest, freely admitting any missteps I might've made, even when they reflected badly on me.

That was the way, perhaps the only way, to break through the wall between us. He wouldn't be able to resist untangling a knotty problem, and while he was doing it, maybe he'd smile at me again. And maybe he'd reach for my hand, and maybe . . .

Oh, I could see it all: Sam and I would be a couple again, laughing and talking together, whispering in the night and being close to each other.

I stepped on the gas and headed for his house, my heart pounding with eagerness to get there. But, I cautioned myself, I couldn't go in expecting great and wonderful things immediately. I'd have to approach him as someone in need, someone asking for his advice calmly and rationally because he was the best one to give it. I'd have to be a petitioner, like a client seeking an attorney's help. Then, well, if in giving the help, his heart began to melt, then one thing could possibly lead to another.

As I pulled to the curb at Sam's house, I was surprised to see James picking up fallen limbs and litter that the wind had strewn across the yard. He was wearing a heavy coat and an aviator cap with dangling earflaps against the cold. I was pleased to think Sam was giving him enough jobs to keep him busy and out of the grocery stores. But at the thought of the tales he'd spread around town, I could feel my mouth tighten. Taking a deep breath, though, I calmed myself down and focused on what I'd come for. James could be taken care of later.

"Hello, James," I said as I stepped out of the car and approached him. "It's a cold day to be out, isn't it?"

"Yes, ma'am, it is," he said, his eyes blinking furiously. "How you doin', Miss Julia?"

"Why, I'm fine, and hope you are too." I started to walk around him because he was standing in the middle of Sam's walk. "I've come to see Sam. Is he busy?"

"Um, yes, ma'am. He, ah, he real busy. You might wanta come back a little later. That be better, Miss Julia."

I stopped, realizing that James was blocking my way and still not moving aside. "Well, I certainly don't want to interrupt his work, but I've come on a matter of some urgency. Unless," I said, looking toward the house, "there's some reason he's unavailable."

"That's it," James said, nodding as if he'd found the right answer. "Mr. Sam, he's not 'vailable right this minute. He havin' his lunch, an' he havin' a guest eat it with him."

"Oh, I see," I said, stepping back. "Well, he's probably interviewing someone for his book or somebody wanting him to run for the town council. Or maybe from the church."

"Yes, ma'am, uh-huh," James said, bobbing his head in agreement. "That's mos' likely it. Yes'm, I'd say that's what it is."

"Then I'll have to come back another time." I turned to leave, deeply disappointed, but knowing that I needed to see Sam when he didn't have a luncheon guest. I'd simply chosen an inopportune time.

Back in the car, I leaned forward to turn on the ignition, noticing as I did that James was still standing in the middle of the walk, watching me. He'd acted strangely from the moment I'd driven up, but I assumed it was because he knew he'd talked out of school and was worried about what I'd do. I smiled to myself: let him worry.

As my eyes swept the yard to see how well he'd cleaned it of debris, I caught sight of the back end of a car that was parked behind Sam's house, almost but not quite hidden.

Something dropped in the pit of my stomach, leaving a hollow and aching place. The breath caught in my throat when I recognized what I was seeing.

If that wasn't a white Volvo between the house and the garage, I'd eat my hat.

~ · ~

I arrived home a changed and chastened woman, so undone by Helen Stroud's being Sam's luncheon guest that I wasn't sure I'd ever draw a painless breath again.

Lillian looked up from the counter where she was working. "What he say?"

"Nothing," I said, removing my coat as I walked through the room. "He was unavailable. I'm going upstairs for a while. I need to rest."

"Well, you need to eat something first. Everybody else already had they lunch, so set on down an' I fix you something."

"It's all right, Lillian. I had plenty at Mildred's." I pushed through the door into the dining room. "I think I may be coming down with something."

She kept talking, but I kept walking through the dining room and the hall and up the stairs where I could close the bedroom door and let the blackness descend.

I thought of crawling into bed with the hope that sleep would stop the pain, but I didn't make it that far. I collapsed in one of Hazel Marie's pink velvet chairs by the window and thought I might never get up again. *Helen!* Helen, *again*.

Right after everything began to come out about Richard's fraudulent investment schemes, Helen had leaned on Sam. How well I remembered seeing Sam's car at her house—and right when I'd intended to visit and offer my support as a compassionate friend. Needless to say, I'd whizzed on by without stopping, even though I'd had one of Lillian's pound cakes to give her. I'd been shaken to my core to learn that Sam had been the one—the *only* one—she'd turned to in her distress, and Sam himself had not been all that eager to share that information with me. She'd wanted legal advice, he finally said, and according to him, the little he could do for her hadn't been worth mentioning to me.

A likely story is all I could say, especially now that he was entertaining her, sending James outside so they could have an intimate lunch. More legal advice? Another likely story because her legal problems, in the form of her crooked husband, had just been committed six feet under.

As I sat there with images of Sam and Helen flickering through my mind, the hollow place inside of me began to fill up with something hard and cold. And gradually I began to count the blessings I still had: Lloyd and Lillian and Latisha and Hazel Marie. And Etta Mae was a faithful friend, as was Mr. Pickens when you really needed him.

If Helen ended up with Sam, I could give my house to Hazel Marie and Mr. Pickens, while I moved to a condominium. Wouldn't that be a pretty come-off? Me, changing places with Helen.

*No,* I said aloud and stood up. I was not going to let my imagination run wild, dreaming up unlikely events that only made the pain worse.

I went downstairs determined to rise above it all and hold my head up high. "Lillian, I've changed my mind. I believe I would like a snack. Just a small one because it's late."

"They's some cheese and fruit in the 'frigerator," she said, on her way out of the kitchen. "I got to help get them babies ready for the doctor."

I stopped cold, my own problems sinking to the bottom. "What's wrong? Are they sick?"

"No'm, they goin' for they first checkup, an' every time we get one ready, the other'n need changin'. I bring the clean one out here to you while they mamas get ready."

And she did, putting little Julie, snugly wrapped in a blanket, in my arms. I sat at the table, holding the baby close, and marveled at the perfection of her tiny features. I smoothed the soft hair on her head, and suddenly two dark eyes blinked open and looked right at me.

I didn't know if she could see anything. She was, after all, barely a week old, but in that moment, as we gazed at each other eye to eye, I realized how rich and full my life could be, even if it didn't work out the way I wanted it to.

# Chapter 36

The "mamas," as Lillian called both Hazel Marie and Etta Mae, had finally gotten the babies cleaned, dressed, and bundled up for the trip to the doctor's office. Hazel Marie was beside herself because the hair ribbons kept sliding out, especially after Etta Mae put caps on the babies' heads. Then they had a difficult time getting them strapped into the car seats, Etta Mae leaning into the backseat from one side and Hazel Marie from the other. Etta Mae couldn't get the strap buckled and Lillian tried to help her but the two of them wouldn't fit through the door. Then Hazel Marie bumped her head on the car frame when she straightened up too soon.

"Dang it!" she said, wincing and holding her head. "If J.D. doesn't soon get back here, I don't know what I'm going to do."

Etta Mae started laughing because she and Lillian got wedged into the door, and the baby they were trying to buckle in suddenly spit up, soiling the beautiful little outfit that Hazel Marie wanted the doctor to see.

"Well, I kinda want him to get back too," Etta Mae said. "But I don't think you can blame hitting your head on him. On second thought, though," she went on as she got behind the wheel, "buckling in squirming babies is a daddy job and he can take it over from now on."

They waved to Lillian and me, as we turned back to the house.

"I hope they get a good report from the doctor," I said as we went inside.

"Yes'm, me too. But I 'spect they will. Them babies is puttin' on weight an' sleepin' good for they age." She opened the refrigerator door. "You ever get that snack you wanted?"

"No, but it's so close to dinner, I think I'll wait. Lloyd and Latisha will be home pretty soon, so maybe I'll have something with them."

"You still feelin' poorly?"

"No, just a little under the weather. Probably just tired, so I think I'll go to the living room and look at the paper for a while."

It was a sign of how done in I was over seeing Helen's car at Sam's that I didn't unload part of the pain onto Lillian. But I couldn't talk about it—I was still too shocked and, yes, too mortified after learning that the husband I thought so sweet and loving and faithful could so quickly begin to trifle with another woman.

I had barely gotten settled good—hadn't even opened the newspaper, although I didn't want to read it, just hide my face behind it—before the front doorbell rang, and LuAnne Conover came barreling in.

"Julia," she said, shedding her coat, gloves, and scarf on her way to the living room sofa, "if you're busy, just say so. But I had to be down this way and thought I'd stop in and see what you thought of Preacher Poppy."

"I think she prefers Pastor Poppy, or maybe just Poppy in a social setting. But she seemed nice enough, pleasant and friendly. Why? What did you think?"

Frankly, I didn't care what LuAnne or anybody else thought about the new lady minister. My heart was so heavy that I just wanted to curl up somewhere in the dark. But I rallied what few resources I had left to visit with LuAnne, while hiding the misery I was feeling.

"Oh, I thought she was nice enough," LuAnne said, settling

in for a long chat. "But have you ever noticed how many women preachers the Methodists have?"

"Well, no, I haven't. Never even thought about it."

"Then think about it, Julia. I've heard of two in Asheville and there's one I know of in Greenville and now one here." ,

"That's not so many."

"It's more than *we* have," LuAnne said, and right tartly too. "Wonder why that is."

"I expect it's because Methodist ministers are sent. Their bishops assign them to churches, then rotate them around. As far as I know, the local churches have no say in who fills their pulpits. They take what they're sent. We Presbyterians, on the other hand, go through a long rigamarole of interviews, trial sermons, and voting on whom we want to call. How many female candidates do you think would survive such a process in a church like ours?"

LuAnne giggled. "Not many. Can you imagine Leonard voting to call one? Or old Mr. Leland or, my goodness, any of the session? And come to think of it, I doubt many of the women would want a woman preacher, especially one as luscious looking as Pastor Poppy."

"She is nice looking, and she seems very sweet. I declare, though, she looks like a well-to-do postdeb just dabbling in a ministerial career until the right man comes along. But who knows? She might do some good, although she's certainly not your typical pious recent seminary graduate."

"Oh, don't mention pious seminarians! You remember that young assistant Pastor Ledbetter had for a while? Butter wouldn't melt in his mouth, he was so above it all. Miss Mattie Freeman said his shorts were too tight." LuAnne laughed and I smiled at the memory. "Anyway," she went on, "I like a preacher who looks like a preacher, which a woman doesn't, and I'm so pleased that Pastor Ledbetter has taken to wearing a black robe in the pulpit. It gives him so much more authority, don't you think?"

I rolled my eyes the least little bit, because Pastor Ledbetter didn't need to assume any more authority than he already had. "Let's just say that the robes are easier on the eyes than some of his ties. But I'll tell you this, LuAnne, if he starts wearing those clerical collars, I'm going to move my letter to the Episcopal church."

"Oh, you're always saying that. Besides, that's what their preachers or priests or rectors or whatever they're called wear all the time. You never see one without a white turned-around collar and a black whatever-it-is attached to it."

"It's a dickey, I think, although a dickey is something women wear under a low-cut dress, except most of them don't these days. Poppy had one on at Mildred's, but it wouldn't qualify as anything clerical, being lace and all. Anyway, I could put up with it at the Episcopal church because they've always done it. It's just when Presbyterian ministers start *adding* things they've never done before that I draw the line."

"You wouldn't be happy in the Episcopal church, Julia, and I wish you'd quit threatening to move your letter. Besides, they're getting as bad as the Methodists with all their women priests." LuAnne stopped and thought for a minute. "Wonder if they *are* priests? Wouldn't they be priestesses? Although that has a pagan sound to me."

"I tell you, LuAnne, good solid churches are getting hard to find these days. So many changes, so many so-called mega-churches and television churches—just sit in your living room and send in your money—online even. I don't know what the world is coming to. I used to look down on people who said they could worship just as well on a golf course as in a church, but I'm about ready to take a few golf lessons. At least there wouldn't be any deviations from the rules of the game."

"Oh, Julia, you're just talking. You wouldn't ever leave First Presby, and I can just see you out swinging a golf club." Then

LuAnne looked around and asked, "Are the babies asleep? I'd love to see them."

"They've gone for their first visit to the doctor. I hope he can do something about their colic—they cry for about two hours every evening. Oh, and, LuAnne, that twin stroller is just wonderful. Hazel Marie just cried when she saw it. You were very generous, and I know she's going to get a lot of use out of it."

"Well, you know Emma Sue wanted to give her another baby shower, but the babies came so fast, and in a snowstorm too, that she hasn't been able to get her ducks in a row. Besides," LuAnne sniffed, "I think the one I gave her is more than sufficient, even for twins. Hazel Marie got some nice things."

"She certainly did, and you're right. One shower is enough for anybody. We've been so consumed by all the care that two infants require that we wouldn't have time for another party anyway. I hope Emma Sue will let it slide."

"Well, good," she said, and with that, I knew she hadn't been paying attention to half I'd said. It was confirmed when she went on: "What does Sam think about woman preachers? Of course I expect every man in town will be all for them, once they get a look at Pastor Poppy."

Not wanting to get her on the subject of Sam, I delicately changed tacks. "Sam is the most tolerant of men, so he wouldn't have a problem. But let me tell you who does." And I went on to tell her what Pastor Poppy had told me about Thurlow Jones walking out of First Methodist in a huff.

"No!" LuAnne said with a wide smile. "Did he, really? Oh, I'd loved to have been there to see that. I expect every church member everywhere has wanted to do the same thing at one time or another and just didn't have the nerve. But I didn't know he even went to church. When did that start?"

"Poppy said in the last few weeks or so—fairly recently. And it surprised me too. Anyway, she asked me to intercede for her, as if I knew him well enough to talk him into doing anything he doesn't want to do." I frowned at the thought. "I plan to stay as far away from Thurlow as I can."

"Oh, Julia, I think you should try to get those two together. Why, you might be able to bring him into the fold for good. Only," she stopped and giggled again, "be sure to aim him toward the Methodists, not us."

The back door slammed open and a burst of talk erupted in the kitchen, Latisha's piercing voice overriding the others.

"That's Lloyd and Latisha home from school," I said. "Lillian will be making hot chocolate or something. Would you like a cup?"

"No, thanks, I have to be going. I just dropped by to see what you thought about Poppy. It's a nice change to have somebody new to talk about."

I smiled in response and said, "She seems very sincere and truly concerned about upsetting Thurlow. But I give her credit: She's the only person I know who's managed to offend him. It's usually the other way around."

# Chapter 37

After seeing LuAnne out, I went back to the chair in the living room and waited for the blackness to descend again. But before it could fully engulf me, Lloyd pushed through the swinging door and came over to my chair. Instead of hanging on the arm of the chair as he used to do, he sat on the ottoman and stretched out his legs. The boy was getting tall, I noticed. Well, not exactly tall, because I doubted he'd ever be that, but taller.

"Miss Julia," he said in his usual serious manner, "Miss Petty gave us a real talking-to today. You won't believe what all she told us."

"What did she say?"

"She told us that somebody has been messing around her toolshed—you know, *since* that body was found, and she was real serious about it too. She said it happened either while she was at school in the daytime or most likely at night, and she's not going to put up with it." Lloyd frowned, squinching up his eyes. "Who in the world would plunder around at *night* where somebody had died?"

"I can't imagine," I said, trying to keep my voice on an even keel. "Does she have any idea who it was?"

"No'm. She said she called the deputies and showed them where a bucket had been moved and the crime-scene tape had been pulled off, and maybe a few more footprints, but they didn't give her much satisfaction. Said it was probably kids wanting to scare themselves. Or something."

"That's probably who it was."

"Well, I don't know. I sure wouldn't be hanging around that place, especially at night. Anyway, she said if we knew anybody who'd done it or who wanted to do it, we better tell them that she was on the lookout. And she said she's making arrangements to catch whoever it was if they come back. And then she said, 'You have been warned!' Like she just knew it was some of us. I tell you, it gave me the shivers, and I haven't been anywhere near that place."

"You can't blame her for being concerned, I suppose," I said, trying to downplay what he was telling me. "I wouldn't be too happy if somebody was fiddling around in our yard either. Especially at night."

"No'm, me either. But what worries me is who it could be that was doing it. Miss Petty and the cops, too, are wrong if they think it was kids. We'd be too scared. So I'm thinking it was somebody else, somebody with a reason to be there. Maybe for the same reason Mr. Stroud had."

I'd always known that Lloyd was smart, but this just iced the cake. Of course he was correct—that's exactly what Lillian and I had been doing—not that we'd known Richard Stroud's reason, but to discover what it had been.

"Lloyd!" Latisha yelled. "You better get on in here if you want a brownie. I'm about to eat 'em all up."

Lloyd grinned and got up from the ottoman. "She means it too. Anyway, I thought you'd want to know that something's still going on at that toolshed."

"It's a mystery, though, isn't it?" I said, dismissively, and picked up the newspaper as if I had some interest in it. But underneath I was squirming at the thought that we'd left a trail at the toolshed. It was comforting to know, though, that no one seemed to be following it to the real culprits.

Hearing more commotion in the kitchen than the usual, I threw aside the paper and went to see what was causing it.

"Why, Mr. Pickens," I said, surprised to see him standing there with a pleased smile on his face and his suitcase at his feet. Lillian was delighted to see him, as always, and Lloyd had just released himself from a big hug, while Latisha stood back, eyeing the new arrival with curiosity.

"I'm home!" he said, spreading his arms as if he expected us to cheer. "Where's Hazel Marie? Where're my babies?"

It took a while to explain the visit to the doctor and to assure him that it was a routine visit and that all was well.

"'Cept they got the colic," Lillian said. "So you better get ready to do some floor walkin'."

"I can do that," Mr. Pickens said, somewhat smugly, although I doubted he knew what he was talking about. He'd had plenty of experience with wives, but none that I knew of with infants.

"J.D., guess what!" Lloyd said, excitement catching in his voice. "Something's still going on at Miss Petty's toolshed. She told us somebody has been messing around in it, probably at night, and I think she's scared to death. She didn't say she was, but she called the deputies about it because she says she's not going to put up with it. Can you believe that?"

"Whoa, slow down," Mr. Pickens said. "Come help me unpack and tell me all about it."

As they headed for the bedroom, Latisha tagging along behind, Lillian looked at me, her eyes big with concern.

"What we gonna do, Miss Julia?" she whispered, her voice quavering.

"They don't have a thing on us, Lillian. They think it was children, and they'll go on thinking that. Nobody saw us, well, except Ronnie and he's not talking. We don't have anything to worry about."

"I hope you right." Lillian turned back to the stove and stirred something in a pot. Then abruptly she stopped and said, "What if somebody else 'sides us been in there? What if they lookin' for the same thing we was lookin' for? What if that somebody else saw us there an' was hidin' in a bush, watchin' everything we did?"

"Lillian, Lillian," I soothed, "you're just thinking up things to worry about. There was nobody else there when we were, and there won't be if we have to go back."

"No, ma'am, uh-uh. You not gonna catch me goin' back there. I already have my fill of it."

"Well, I'm not planning a return trip, believe me. I'm just saying that we have nothing to be concerned about."

Just then Hazel Marie and Etta Mae, each carrying a baby, rushed in, along with a gust of cold air.

"Where is he?" Hazel Marie asked, her eyes shining. "His car's outside, so I know he's home."

"Right in yonder," I said, pointing toward the bedroom. "He's unpacking."

"Here, Miss Julia," she said, plopping a baby in my arms. "Hold Lily Mae for me. I'll be right back." She dashed for the back hall, but she didn't get very far. Mr. Pickens met her, and there was a warm and to those who were in the line of sight a somewhat embarrassing reunion. Hazel Marie smothered his face with kisses until she got to his mouth where he stopped her for a good long while.

Latisha, standing right next to them and watching intently, said, "My goodness, that look jus' like teevee."

Etta Mae laughed as she began to unwrap Baby Julie, shedding blanket, cap, and sweater, one after the other. "Looks like I'll be heading back to the sunroom. Here, Miss Julia," she said, exchanging babies with me, "let me swap with you and get that one unwrapped."

"At least in the sunroom you'll get a full night's sleep for a change," I said. "And we'll see how Mr. Pickens likes changing and feeding every two hours or so."

"It'll be interesting, won't it?" Etta Mae laughed, then expertly took both babies to their crib, sidling past their parents who were still making a spectacle of themselves.

After that, there was a constant coming and going with Lloyd going out to Mr. Pickens's car to retrieve his hanging bag and Mr. Pickens folding up the cot that Etta Mae had been sleeping on and Hazel Marie putting away his clothes and Latisha following two steps behind Mr. Pickens everywhere he turned, and one baby after another announcing dinnertime.

I was finally able to catch Mr. Pickens alone in the back hall. "Mr. Pickens," I whispered, "I would deeply appreciate it if you wouldn't ask about Sam in front of the others. He's working on his book and won't be here for dinner, so if you wouldn't mention it, I'd be grateful."

Those black eyes bored into mine as he studied me, quickly recognizing a deeper concern in what I'd said. "Want to tell me a little more? Maybe I can help."

"No, not at this time, I don't think. I just don't want to discuss it in front of the children, and Hazel Marie has enough on her mind without adding anything. But," I went on, not wanting to close any door that might shed some light on my predicament, "maybe later we can talk."

"Anytime," he said, and put a comforting hand on my arm. "I'm always ready to listen."

I nodded and moved away as Hazel Marie called to him. I was left thinking that I might indeed talk to him in his capacity as an investigator about a certain knothole in a toolshed, but as an adviser on marital problems? With his credentials, I hardly thought so.

# Chapter 38

"Lillian," I said as soon as we'd finished breakfast the next morning, "I want you and Latisha to take a break. You've been working night and day ever since those babies have been here."

"No'm, Miss Etta Mae been the one gettin' up at night. I been sleepin' most of the time."

"Still, you need some time off. Take the weekend off and rest up."

"I guess I will, then, but who gonna do the cookin' 'round here?"

"I expect we'll manage all right." Although, frankly, I wasn't sure how well we would.

Lillian had been running by her house occasionally to check on water pipes and so forth, but it had been some time since she'd spent a night there. I thought she and Latisha both would be pleased to be going back, but Latisha pitched a fit.

"I thought we was *livin'* here," she wailed. "What Lloyd gonna do without me around? An' them babies *need* me!"

It took awhile for Lillian to calm her and to assure her that she'd be back after school every weekday. "We got to see 'bout our house," Lillian told her. "And think of all the play-pretties you got waitin' for you."

"Well, I don't know, Great-Granny," she said, wiping her eyes with the hem of her dress. "Look like every time that big ole black-eyed man come, we have to leave. An' that's just a pure-tee shame."

My heart went out to her because she had truly latched on to Mr. Pickens, following him around throughout the house and gazing at him in awe. That's what happens when a child grows up without a father—Lloyd was doing the same thing. Mr. Pickens had a huge gap to fill in the lives of those two fatherless children, and I had to admit, so far he was doing fairly well at it.

And why wasn't Sam here helping him? I wasn't the only one who needed him, and he should've thought of all he meant to these children before he took off and took up with Helen Stroud.

And just as I began to build up another head of steam over Sam's lack of consideration, he called.

"Julia?" he said, as the sound of his voice weakened my knees. "James said you came by yesterday. Is there anything I can do for you?"

*Yes, yes, you can come home!* The words flashed through my mind, but I bit them back.

"Well," I said instead, "I did have a matter to discuss with you, but James said you were unavailable so I left."

Sam laughed under his breath. "That James. He's worse than a nursemaid. You should've come on in, Julia, I would've stopped whatever I was doing."

Uh-huh, I thought, you would've gotten up from the table and left your guest stranded just to talk with me? Not likely. Then I realized that James hadn't told Sam exactly when I'd come by. He didn't know that I'd been there when he was fully engaged with somebody else.

"It doesn't matter," I said stiffly. "It really wasn't all that important."

"Well," he said and let a few moments pass. "I'm always available to you, and you're always welcome at my house."

*And so are you at mine,* I thought, *so why don't you get yourself back here?* Instead of saying it, though, I told him of Mr. Pickens's return, then brought the unsatisfactory conversation to a close.

Then, before I could fall into the depths again, the phone rang under my hand. Hoping that Sam was as unhappy with the previous call as I had been, I snatched up the receiver only to hear an unexpected voice.

"Miss Julia? It's Poppy Patterson. I hope I haven't caught you at a bad time."

"Why, no, I was just, uh, standing here. How are you, Poppy?"

"Actually, not so good. I'm still upset over what happened with Mr. Jones last Sunday. It's keeping me awake at night, trying to think of what I can do to make it right. I'll just be done in if he's not in church tomorrow, knowing it's my fault he's not there."

"Oh, Poppy, you shouldn't feel that way. Thurlow Jones is one of those people you can never please. If it hadn't been what you said last Sunday, it would be something else."

"Yes, ma'am, maybe so, but it *was* something I said, and I was wondering if you'd go with me to call on him."

"Well..."

"Please, Miss Julia. He won't talk to me on the phone—he just hung up on me—so he'd probably close the door in my face if I go by myself. I thought, because you know him so well, that he'd at least let us in and I'd have a chance to explain."

I was silent for a few minutes, thinking over the ramifications. How and from whom had she gotten the impression that I knew Thurlow so well? *Nobody* knew him, and that was a fact. He had such an erratic personality that no one could predict what he would do or say next.

Still, this would give me a perfect excuse to visit Thurlow and maybe get a reverse view of Miss Petty's toolshed, and maybe that would reveal why Richard Stroud had been interested enough to spend a cold January night spying on Thurlow's house.

"All right, Poppy," I said, "I'll go with you, but you have to understand that I make no promises. Thurlow's just as likely to close the door in my face as he is to anybody. We may not get in at all, but I do commend you for wanting to try. When do you want to go?"

"This afternoon? I can pick you up about two. And thank you so much. If this doesn't work, at least I'll have tried everything I know to do."

❧⸱⸲

I was just as glad to be leaving when Pastor Poppy rang my doorbell at one-forty-five that afternoon, although I had a few qualms about doing so. Lillian and Latisha had left, and Etta Mae had taken the afternoon off to check on her single-wide and to get, I supposed, an uninterrupted nap. That left Hazel Marie and Mr. Pickens alone to care for both babies, something they were going to have to get used to, although Hazel Marie looked a little wild-eyed at having to do it so soon.

Mr. Pickens was being his usual cocky self, saying, "Don't worry, honey. What can be so hard? We're bigger than they are."

Etta Mae had just laughed and told Hazel Marie that she'd be back by suppertime. "I'll bring us some barbecue from The Smokehouse in Delmont. Lillian's not here, so that'll make a good supper."

Indeed it would, because not one of us was much of a cook. I slipped Etta Mae some money for the takeout, then met Pastor Poppy at the door for our joint church visitation. She was a fashion picture in a long, black double-breasted coat and black patent-leather boots with stilletto heels, making me feel quite dowdy beside her.

We left together in her vehicle, which was neither car nor truck. Or maybe it was both, but whatever it was, I almost needed a step stool to get up into it. As Poppy stepped on the gas, my head was jerked backward as the tires, gathering speed, chirped on the pavement.

"Sorry," Poppy said, laughing. "This thing gets away from me every now and then."

I gripped the armrest with one hand and my pocketbook with the other, thankful for the safety harness and praying for air bags. We flew down Polk Street, turned left onto Thurlow's street, and pulled up in front of his house with the tires scraping the curb.

"Well," I said, letting out the breath I'd been holding, "that was . . . exhilarating. Now, Poppy, let me warn you before we go in. Mr. Jones can be rude, crude, insensitive, insulting, and on occasion, indecent. You mustn't take it personally, because that's the way he is with everyone. I've certainly had my share of verbal abuse from him. So if you have a thin skin, I'd recommend we crank up and forget about seeing him."

"No," she said, taking her lip in her teeth and gazing out the window at Thurlow's two-story brick, vaguely Georgian house, its high gabled roof overlooking the brick wall around the property. "No, I have to try to make amends. I can't let something I said be the reason he rejects our church. And I do appreciate your coming with me, Miss Julia. Maybe," she said with a charming smile, "if the Methodists can't get him, the Presbyterians can."

*No, thank you,* I thought, then felt a stab of guilt. If I could think of Thurlow as a little lost lamb, as Poppy apparently did, I might've felt differently. But to my mind and on the basis of past experience with him, he was more like a ravening wolf.

We got out of the car and walked through the gate in the brick wall onto the brick walkway that led to the front door. I stopped just past the gate and took it all in. The winter storms had left hardly a mark on the lawn—no litter, no debris from the bushes and trees that enclosed the spacious yard. Even with the patches of unmelted snow in the shaded areas, the landscape looked tended and pruned. Looking up at the house, I saw all the shutters in neat array, none hanging askew as they'd once done. And looking down at the walkway, I saw not one blade of grass or weed between the bricks, whereas the last time I'd walked it, the weeds had been up to my knees.

"My land," I said in awe, "there have certainly been some changes here. You wouldn't believe how he usually keeps it. Maybe Thurlow really has had a change of heart." Then I told Poppy how Thurlow had always had the most disreputable property within the town limits, making himself an affront to all his neighbors. "Look," I said, as we approached the front door, "even the brass is bright and shiny. Well, let's see if his manners have been polished as well."

I rang the doorbell as Poppy and I stood shivering in our coats. I rang it again and waited, but nobody came. Just as I started to turn away, Poppy reached around me for the brass lion's head knocker and thunked it roundly several times.

"My word," I said under my breath, then quickly drew back as the door was flung open.

My first thought on seeing Thurlow was that whoever had spruced up his house and yard had bypassed him. He stood there glowering at us, his hair in an absolute mess, his plaid shirt stained, and his loose trousers gathered by a belt with a flapping tongue. His eyes glittered behind smudged glasses and his unshaven face had a scowl on it that would have discouraged a less determined woman than Pastor Poppy Patterson. Me, for example.

"What the Sam Hill is goin' on?" he demanded. "Can't a man get any rest without a bevy of women banging on his door? And if you're selling or begging, you can just take it on down the road. I ain't in the market."

He stepped back to close the door just as Poppy, with a bright smile on her face, stepped forward to enter. He could do nothing but move aside and I could do nothing but follow.

As she started unbuttoning her coat, Poppy looked around the entrance hall. "My, what a lovely home you have, Mr. Jones," she said, favoring him with a guileless smile. "This paneling is beautiful, so rich and warm. It's similar to what I've seen in the governor's mansion in Raleigh. How old is your house?"

"Built in 1892," Thurlow said, taken aback by her ease after his less-than-welcoming greeting. "One of the oldest in town. Still standing, that is."

"I love old houses," Poppy said. "I expect it's been in your family for a long time. Would you mind showing us around? I'd love to see it."

Thurlow immediately led her, as I tagged along, to the room on the left. He threw back the door to a small formal room I'd never seen before and began pointing out the old portraits on the wall.

I stayed in the background for fear of disrupting the rapport that Poppy had established with her interest in old things. Maybe he felt that included him as well. But whatever it was, Pastor Poppy had gained us admittance and, so far, Thurlow seemed thoroughly taken in by her admiration of his home.

Who would've thought that was all it would take?

# Chapter 39

After showing us the dining room, Thurlow led us back to the big front room on the right of the hall. This was the room Lillian and I had once visited and the room that appeared to be the most used. All through the guided tour, I had been struck by the neatness and cleanliness of the floors and furniture—there'd been no dust or stacks of books and newspapers left where they'd fallen. This was all in stark contrast to what I'd seen in my previous visit.

The library, as he now called it, and where he offered us chairs, was equally clean, but bore evidence of Thurlow's daily use. There was the same old recliner by the fireplace, the same pile of old papers beside it, and the same old Ronnie splayed out in front of the fireplace so that you could hardly pick your way past him.

I took a seat on the end of the sofa farthest from Ronnie, while Poppy sat in a chair next to Thurlow's recliner. She shrugged out of her coat, then crossed her legs, leaving a black-stockinged gap between the hem of her skirt and the top of her boots.

"So," Thurlow said, plopping himself down in the form-fitting recliner, "I've already told you I'm not buying anything or donating anything; let's get that straight right now. So why am I being blessed or harassed with a visit from two such elegant ladies?"

I wanted to tell him that sarcasm was unbecoming, but he wouldn't care. Poppy laughed her bubbly laugh, but I felt a shiver across my shoulders, fearing that Thurlow was just revving up for some of his usual hurtful bluster. I didn't want Poppy to have her feelings hurt or be humiliated when he began to rant and rave.

"Oh," she said in a merry fashion, "we don't want a thing from you. I asked Miss Julia to come with me because you're a hard man to catch, and I am fishing for men."

"Ha!" Thurlow said and pulled the lever that reclined him a few degrees. Ronnie lifted his head, then plopped it down again. "I bet you think I don't know the double meaning of that. Well, I do, and I didn't have to go to a seminary to know it."

"Then you know why I'm here," Poppy said, a little teasing in her voice. "I am sorry if I offended you last Sunday—"

"*If! If* you offended me!" Thurlow shouted, and straight up came the recliner. "You offended every right-thinking man there. Listen to me, young lady, God is not a mother and I can prove it. Let me get my Bible."

He sprang out of the chair, looked around the room, then sat back down. "Well, I can't put my hands on it right now, but," and he lifted a finger to her, "it says *he, he, he* all the way through. And it's a crying shame that we have to put up with women up there trying to preach without them poking some heathen message down our throats. You're a fine-lookin' woman—you ought to be fishin' for a husband. You ought to be married. You ought to be raisin' children, not up there usurpin' a man's place."

I stiffened as he built up a head of steam as fierce and as outrageous as I'd feared. Poor little Poppy, she'd be outtalked and outwitted, and most likely reduced to tears before he was done.

Instead, though, she leaned over and gave him a light tap on the arm with the back of her hand. With a delighted smile on her face, she said, "Why, you old misogynist!"

Up came the recliner again, almost catapulting Thurlow out of it. "Miss-*what*?"

"You heard me, and you don't fool me. You're trying to make

me feel bad because I made you rethink some of your ingrained beliefs. I gave you something new to think about. Now you can reject the new..."

"I did! Or didn't you see me walk out?"

"*Or,*" Poppy went on, her eyes twinkling as she challenged him, "you can broaden your understanding of God and deepen your faith."

"I'm gonna prove you wrong!" And he was on his feet again. "Let me get my Bible. And by the way, I've never yet seen a preacher come visitin' without his own Bible."

"Well," Poppy said, with another bubbly laugh, "you've just seen one. Besides, I'm pretty much up on Scripture and don't need to point out chapter and verse every time I turn around."

Thurlow plopped back in the chair, seemingly outdone by her claim. "Arrogance!" he yelled, disturbing Ronnie so that he stood up and shook himself. "Scriptural arrogance, that's what it is. That's what happens when women get above themselves. Madam Murdoch, why're you just sitting there without saying a word? What do you think of women getting too big for their britches and climbing up in a pulpit? Let's hear from you for a change."

"I think," I said, choosing my words carefully, "that I wouldn't want to get between God and whomever he's called to preach, regardless of what kind of britches they wear."

Thurlow's eyes bugged out at me, while Poppy threw back her head and laughed. "She's got you there, Mr. Jones. Now listen, we could go round and round about this and never come to a meeting of the minds. I think you're just a big ole teddy bear that just likes to argue and get the best of whomever you're arguing with. And I expect, deep down, you don't really care who's in the pulpit and that half the time you don't even pay attention to what they say. Well, I want to change that. I want you to give me another chance and come back to church. You can walk out again if you want to and I'll come visit you again, and next time, you can bet

I'll bring my Bible." Then she laughed her merry laugh. "I know where mine is."

I had never in my life seen Thurlow without a word to say. He stared at her, his mouth half open, then he stared some more. It seemed a good time to absent myself, so I stood up.

"Excuse me," I said to Thurlow. "I'd like a glass of water. Do you mind if I go to the kitchen?"

He flapped his hand at me. "Go, go." Then to Poppy, "Now you listen to me, young lady."

"Don't you 'young lady' me," Poppy said, giggling, "you ole sweet thing, you."

*Lord, help us,* I thought, as I hightailed it through the dining room and into Thurlow's kitchen. Never in my life had I witnessed such a pastoral visit as this one had turned out to be. What were they teaching seminary students at Duke? Or maybe at any seminary?

Well, whatever it was, Poppy, with her smiles and giggles and laughs, along with her refusal to let Thurlow outtalk her, was more than holding her own.

I hurried to the window over the sink, the one that looked out over the backyard and the one, I quickly confirmed, that was in a direct line with Miss Petty's toolshed. I couldn't see the knothole, of course—it was too far away and there were too many tree limbs in between—but I knew where it was, and I came to the firm conclusion then and there that it had been the back of Thurlow's house—which meant Thurlow himself—that Richard Stroud had been watching.

Leaning over the sink to scan the yard, I saw a dilapidated building that might once have been a stable and was now a remodeled garage. To assure myself that Richard would have had a wide-angle view, I leaned farther over the sink, then almost levitated to the ceiling when I felt a nudge in a most sensitive area.

"*Ronnie!*" I said in a harsh whisper as I whipped around. "Don't sneak up on me like that."

I swished past him, trying to pull myself together after such a fright. Just because we'd shared a bed didn't mean he was free to take liberties.

Breathing rapidly, I hurried out into the hall, where I found Poppy and Thurlow. She was buttoning her coat, readying herself to leave, but the two of them were still going at it.

"Well, you can't just sit at home and criticize," Poppy was saying. "For all you know, there'd be some of the finest preaching around, and you'd miss it all."

"Ha! I'd like to hear some of that fine preaching," Thurlow said, his eyes glittering at her. "Lord knows I've not heard any lately."

"You can't hear it if you're not there."

"I'll be there," Thurlow said, leering at her in open challenge. "You can bet your sweet patootie I'll be there."

With Poppy laughing her head off, I murmured our farewells, and pushed her out the door before Thurlow could close it on us.

We were halfway down the walk when he opened the door and stuck his head out. "Yeah, and I'll be taking notes too!"

# Chapter 40

"And probably kickin' you-know-what too," Poppy said, laughing as she turned on the ignition.

I latched on to the armrest as she took off. "I'll tell you," I said, as I caught my breath, "I have never in my life witnessed a pastoral visitation like that one. How did you know to stand up to him like that?"

"Oh, my daddy's pretty much like him," Poppy said, as if handling Thurlow had been all in a day's work. "I did like Mr. Jones's house, though. Except, funny thing, it didn't seem to go with him. Or he with it."

"I noticed that too. But it's his house that's different, not him, because it used to be as unkempt as he is. Why, the last time I was in it, which has been some while ago, it was dark and dusty and cluttered. I could hardly believe what I saw today. Maybe," I mused, "he finally broke down and hired some household help."

"Well," Poppy said, "he needs to hire a personal trainer or valet or something too. I have to tell you, I kept picking up a rank, musty odor."

"That was Ronnie, but," I corrected myself, "it could've been either or both."

As we parked in front of my house, I invited Poppy to come in and meet Hazel Marie and Etta Mae. "You can see the babies too."

"I'd love to," she said, "but I have a bunch of teenagers meeting at the church at four. I better come back another time."

"Drop by tomorrow afternoon," I said, my hand on the door handle. "I think Hazel Marie's planning to have the babies on display. We'd love to have you. And, Poppy, I have to tell you that I am in awe at what you accomplished with Thurlow. I think you should have a seminar or something for preachers in this town to teach them how to conduct pastoral calls."

She laughed. "Well, we Methodists have to deal with backsliders all the time, so we have a number of tricks up our sleeves."

Actually, I didn't know that Thurlow had ever been anywhere to backslide from, but I wasn't in the mood for theological quibbling. I had something else on my mind, so taking my leave, I walked toward the house thinking of the transformation in Thurlow's house. Why, even the draperies had been cleaned and freshened. Some even, I suddenly realized, replaced. Who in the world could've done that—not him, that was certain. Yet I couldn't imagine Thurlow engaging an interior designer. For one thing, he wouldn't want to spend the money, and for another, he'd never before cared what his house looked like.

Some kind of change had come over him, although it hadn't quite made it to his personal grooming. And going to church! That was the most amazing thing of all. As long as I'd known him, or rather, known *of* him, which had been years, he had not been a churchgoing man. Oh, every once in a while I'd heard of some preacher of one persuasion or another going to visit him, hoping to entice him into the fold. They'd all been run off either by his nasty disposition or by his open contempt for what he perceived as unctuous moneygrubbing.

Someone had said that years ago, a Pentecostal Holiness pastor told Thurlow how welcome he'd be in his church. Thurlow had said, "Yeah, and the next thing, you'd be wanting me to tithe.

Well, I'll give you a tenth—a tenth of nothing, and we'll see how welcome I'd be then."

I walked up onto the porch, still marveling at Pastor Poppy's skill with the crankiest man in town. Just as I pulled my keys from my pocketbook to open the door, a sudden thought stopped me. I had a fairly cranky man on *my* hands too.

Could I take a lesson from Poppy's handling of Thurlow? Maybe I could, except Sam was nothing at all like Thurlow, being sane, for one thing. Still, they were both men, and men respond to laughter and teasing, with a little flirting thrown in for good measure.

❧

I stood there, jiggling the keys in my hand, wondering if I could manage a little flirting. I was out of practice, you know, having done so little of it in my life. I simply wasn't the flirty type, but Poppy had shown me how to do it. She'd even done it during a theological discussion with Thurlow of all people, and she wasn't even married to him. How much easier it should be for me to do the same, and more, in another kind of discussion with a man I was married to.

I turned on my heel, went down the steps, and crossed the front yard to the car before I could talk myself out of it. Nothing ventured, nothing gained, as they say, and if James tried to keep me out, I venture to say he would regret it.

As it happened, James was nowhere to be seen when I arrived at Sam's house. Hesitant to just barge in, although it just killed me to behave like a visitor to my own husband's house, I rang the doorbell.

"Why, Julia," Sam said as he opened the door. "Come in."

I plastered what I hoped was a beguiling smile on my face. "Are you very busy this afternoon? I don't want to disturb you if you're working."

"Not at all. Come on in and sit down. I'm glad to see you." He was saying all the right things as he led me into his office but no more than what he'd say to any visitor.

Instead of taking a seat on the leather sofa where we'd often sat together, I went to one of the chairs facing it. Books and papers were piled on his desk behind the sofa, so I knew I'd interrupted his work. But, I comforted myself, it was late in the day and time for him to stop.

He hadn't taken my coat, which gave me a hint that my welcome would soon be worn out. So following Poppy's lead, I shrugged my coat back, then crossed my legs, leaving a gap of a few inches from the hem of my skirt to the top of my Naturalizer pumps—providing not quite the same view as Poppy had, but I could only work with what I had.

I cocked my head at Sam and smiled. "How're you doing, you ole sweet thing, you?"

His head snapped around and his eyes bugged out. "What?"

I laughed, trying for bubbly but not quite making it. "I'm just letting you know that I'm tired of sleeping alone."

He came over and sat in the chair next to me. "I didn't think you'd mind that at all."

Batting my eyelashes, I reached over and gave him a light tap on the arm with the back of my hand. "Where did you get that idea? I keep dreaming of you and searching for you in my sleep. I think you ought to come back home and get some lovin'."

He started laughing, almost putting me off, and said, "Are you feeling all right? What is this?"

"It's your lonely wife, sweetheart, here to tell you that I can't go on like this." Then, fearing that I'd gotten too serious too quickly, I ran my hand down his arm and said, "You always smell so good, and you're so big and strong, you just make me weak in the knees."

Well, that put a twinkle in his eyes, so I lowered my voice to a husky whisper and asked, "Where's James?"

His voice was even huskier. "At the store, but who cares?"

As I reached for him, he suddenly stood up. "Wait, Julia, there're too many things that need to be worked out."

"That's why I'm here," I said, coming to myself. And I went on and confessed everything I'd ever done that he hadn't known about, from investing with Richard Stroud to throwing away his old fishing hat. "And on top of that," I went on, "I went with Pastor Poppy Patterson, the new woman minister at First Methodist, to call on Thurlow Jones. Now, I assure you, it was not a personal visit so don't jump to any conclusions. I simply accompanied her because she asked me to and, Sam, I watched as she led that crabby old man back to the church." I lifted my head and closed my eyes. "It was the Lord's work, if I've ever seen it."

Sam walked a few paces, then turned to me. "Is that everything?"

I nodded, then cringed. "Except, maybe you don't know that Lillian and I visited Miss Petty's toolshed."

"When did you do that?"

"The other evening," I said, dismissively. "Long after the deputies were through with it. And we went to see if we could find out why Richard had been in it, so I could show you I had nothing to do with his being in town." Then I added, "Lillian thought we should."

He didn't say anything for a while, then he said, "Lillian, huh?"

"Well, maybe it was my idea first, but, Sam, all I had in mind was to prove I have no interest in Richard or Thurlow. It was all for you, and, well, I miss you so much." I started crying then, which tore my flirting plan all to pieces. "And I love you, and I wouldn't hurt you for anything in the world."

He came over and pulled me to my feet, but not to him. "Julia, listen to me. I love you and I miss you too, but you keep too much to yourself. It's as if I'm not part of your life, and that hurts. I sometimes feel that Lillian knows more about you than I do. You leave me out of what you're doing, as if I'm not important enough to be a part of it."

"Oh, Sam," I said, leaning my head against him in despair. "I didn't know you felt that way. I know I'm inclined to go my own way, but it's not because I want to keep things from you." I wiped my eyes against his sweater. "Well, maybe I do, but it's because I'm afraid you'll think the less of me if you know what I'm doing."

"It's for my own good, huh?"

"Well, yes, but now I see I was wrong. I promise, from now on I'll tell you everything, everything, everything. You'll get so tired of hearing me that you'll be pulling your hair out. Or mine, one."

I felt him laugh deep in his chest. "If you'll call me ole sweet thing again, I promise there'll be no hair pulling."

So I did, and did again, until the back door crashed open and James called, "It's me, Mr. Sam. I'm back with the groceries."

# Chapter 41

We quickly separated as we heard James coming down the hall, telling Sam he'd found the Granny Smith apples he wanted.

"An' I got a ham an' some catfish an'..." He stopped dead in the middle of the hall as Sam and I walked out and he saw me. "Why, Miss Julia, how you doin'? I didn't know we had comp'ny."

"Hardly company, James," I said, pulling on my gloves. "We were just speaking of you. I expect you should run on and get those groceries put up, don't you?"

He gave me a shaky grin and fled to the kitchen.

"Sam," I said, "we really haven't resolved anything, have we?" Meaning, of course, *when are you coming home*?

"Oh, I think we have. It's just a matter of timing now. With Pickens back, I'll talk to him tomorrow and see when they'll be able to move in here. In the meanwhile, I'll get my notes and things packed up to take over to your house—*our* house. I'll do my writing over there from now on."

"That would be wonderful. We can move back into the big room downstairs where they are now and fix up Hazel Marie's old room as an office for you. That way you'll be where it's quiet and away from household noise." I smiled at him. "How do you feel about a pink office?"

He laughed, gave me a very nice kiss, and walked out onto the porch with me. After a few more comments from him, I went on my way, feeling immeasurably better. His last words were, "I'll see you in church tomorrow," and I knew we'd be sitting together like always.

Getting in the car and driving back to the house, I came to the conclusion that I had overlooked, or perhaps, never realized, the fact that my husband had tender feelings—feelings that were near the surface and easily bruised. All of this, I thought, because I had done a few trivial things without sharing them with him!

And what were they? Like anybody with sensitive feelings, Sam had built up a stack of them, not saying anything at the time but allowing them to pile up. But how could I have consulted him about going to Florida on the track of jewel thieves with Lloyd and Etta Mae when he was in Russia at the time? And had he wanted me to wake him up that stormy night when Poochie Dunn took Etta Mae and me up on the courthouse dome and we got shot at? And what about the time that Lillian and I, well, we weren't even married then, so that wouldn't count.

Still, I'd learned that I'd better start asking him to accompany me whenever I needed to get something done. The only problem with that, and the reason I'd not shared any of my plans with him before this, is he'd try to talk me out of them or put his foot down.

Well, at least Lillian and Etta Mae would be relieved not to be aiding and abetting anymore.

Then I realized something else. Right before I left, Sam had mentioned that he'd spoken to James about staying on to cook for the Pickens family and James had agreed.

I pulled into the driveway at home so fast that I almost crashed into the garage. Slamming on the brakes, the car jerked to a stop, my head wobbling back and forth in the momentum. *That Sam!* He had already been planning to come home even before I made a flirting fool of myself.

I sat for a minute, thinking it over. Was I mad at him for tricking me? Well, no, I was too happy about being back in his good graces. Actually, I kind of admired him for giving me a taste of my own medicine. And, the thought suddenly occurred to me, his trickery could make null and void my promise to consult him about every little thing I did.

Feeling even better than I had when I left Sam's house, I waltzed into my own, only to find utter chaos. Both babies were screaming, Hazel Marie was jouncing one in her arms as tears streamed down her face, Etta Mae was hurriedly placing the takeout barbecue on the table, and Mr. Pickens, walking the other baby, looked as if he'd been wrung through the wringer.

"Here, Etta Mae," I said, taking off my coat, "let me do that while you help with the babies."

She gave me a grateful glance and handed me a styrofoam container of cole slaw. "Lillian's right about the colic. Every evening about this time, they cut loose."

Etta Mae took the baby from Mr. Pickens, telling him to go ahead and eat while he could. Instead of sitting at the table, he leaned against a counter, his head bowed, as if he were worn to the bone.

"Are you all right?" I asked.

He shook his head. "One afternoon," he said, running his hand across his face. "And they've cried evey minute of it. Is it like this every day?"

"Pretty much," I said complacently as I emptied the cole slaw into a china bowl. "But, see, we've built up a tolerance for it, while you're coming in cold. You'll get used to it."

He just stared at me, a harried look on his face.

"Sit down, Mr. Pickens," I said, turning him toward the table. "Go ahead and eat. It may be a long night."

I couldn't help but ride him a little because he'd been mostly absent during these first hectic days.

As the crying suddenly decreased by half, Hazel Marie stumbled out and collapsed in a chair at the table. Her makeup had long worn off and her hair needed a comb, and she looked in no mood to repair either.

"I've given up," she said, tears welling up-again. "We can't just let them cry their little hearts out."

"That's right, honey," Mr. Pickens said, putting a hand on her shoulder. "If it'll help, let's just do it."

"Do what?" I asked, spooning baked beans onto Hazel Marie's plate. Then I lifted my head as the other half of the crying abruptly stopped. "What's Etta Mae doing to them?"

I saw what she'd done when she came walking out, a silent baby in each arm.

"Here," she said, handing one baby to Hazel Marie and the other to Mr. Pickens. Each one was tightly swaddled and sucking peacefully away on a pacifier. "I don't want to put them down until we're sure they're asleep."

Hazel Marie gazed mournfully down on the daughter in her arms. "I didn't want them to have pacifiers. Everybody says it's so hard to break the habit once they start."

Mr. Pickens grinned, put down his fork, and reached for her hand. He was getting quite adept at doing everything one-handedly. "So what, if they take 'em to kindergarten? Who cares, as long as they're happy now?"

"I guess so," Hazel Marie said, cuddling the swaddled baby closer. "I just don't want their teeth to come in crooked."

"That's an old wives' tale," Etta Mae said with some authority. She dried her hands after washing them and came to the table. "You and J.D. have good straight teeth, so they will too. I wouldn't worry about it."

Good advice, I thought. Besides, crooked teeth could be fixed—a small future price to pay for a little peace and quiet tonight.

Later in the evening, as I climbed the stairs to my lonely temporary bedroom, I wondered how much longer I'd have to wait before my husband was with me. I was more than ready to move back into the spacious room that Sam and I had vacated in favor of Hazel Marie and Mr. Pickens when they were first married and Hazel Marie, heavy with child, had been forbidden the stairs. But when would they be ready to move to Sam's house and be on their own?

Not until those babies were on some sort of schedule and Hazel Marie no longer needed Etta Mae's help, I realized. That could be awhile. Actually, it would be when, if ever, Hazel Marie could manage by herself. Lord goodness, that being the case, I thought as I closed the bedroom door behind me, Sam might never be back.

Hazel Marie was the dearest person you'd ever want to know—sweet and thoughtful, and always eager to learn and do the right thing. She had been a comfort to me in the years between Wesley Lloyd Springer's demise and Sam's advent in my life, and she continued to be a loyal friend and companion. I wouldn't say a thing against her for the world.

But let's face it, Hazel Marie wasn't a take-charge person with the ability to manage two things at once, and why the Lord saw fit to give her two babies at once was beyond me to understand. Of course it was reassuring to know that James would stay on to cook and clean for the Pickens family, but child care? No, I didn't think so. Hazel Marie was going to need a nanny or an au pair or somebody to help her until those babies were old enough to go to school.

James himself created another problem. I kept telling Sam that he was letting James get by with too much, or rather, with doing too little. I could just envision James intimidating Hazel

Marie and running the house the way he wanted to. Hazel Marie would never be able to put her foot down and straighten him out.

Then I smiled to myself. Mr. Pickens could. James would meet his match, and then some, when Mr. Pickens moved into Sam's house. That would fix James and maybe pay him back for gossiping and trying every way he could to keep Sam and me apart.

With that comforting thought, I began to undress for bed. I put on a long flannel gown and pulled socks onto my feet, all necessary because I would be sleeping alone. My warm husband was still four blocks away and not in my bed, heating it up.

Going to the front windows to open the curtains so the streetlight would cast a glow after the lamps were off, I noticed that the wind had picked up. I shivered, wondering how low the temperature had dropped. Tree branches were tossing and scraping against the house. A paper bag tumbled down the empty street, and the traffic light on the corner swayed on its cable. Just as I adjusted the curtain, a white car eased through the green light, headed on Polk Street away from town.

My mouth opened in a gasp as I recognized the car as the same one that had been going *toward* town in the early morning hours only days before. Somebody was spending Saturday nights with somebody, and I didn't have to eat my hat to know who one of those somebodies was.

# Chapter 42

*Wrong, wrong, wrong,* I said to myself as I came out of my flannel gown and started dressing. Don't even *think* that Helen Stroud is on her way to Sam's house. He would not do that to me, not at any time, but certainly not now after assuring me he's coming home.

But even as all that was running through my mind, I was snatching up underclothes, thick stockings, or tights, as Hazel Marie called them, searching through the closet for the heavy wool dress I'd worn on another cold night, my breath rattling in my throat as I tried to hurry without making noise and fumbling to put on enough warm clothes at the same time. The weather had begun to warm up, melting the last of the snow and making the ground soggy. But cold temperatures at night put a layer of ice over every watery place, so I got out my rubber galoshes too.

My hands were shaking so much that I pulled on the tights inside out, twisting them around in such a way that I could hardly take a normal step. Stepping into low-heeled shoes, then the galoshes, and grabbing a heavy coat, I sneaked out into the dark hall, noting with relief that Lloyd's door was closed with no light showing under it. Then, remembering what I'd forgotten, I turned around and went back to my room for gloves and Lloyd's multicolored cap that I'd failed to return to his closet.

As I slipped down the staircase in the dark house, my nerves stretched to the snapping point, I prayed that nobody would be up tending babies. *Thank you, Etta Mae,* I thought, *for the peace that pacifiers had wrought.*

Then I sat down on the bottom step of the stairs and thought through what I was about to do. I didn't want to go out in the cold night by myself, but I certainly couldn't just go to bed and let nature take its course. I had to find out where Helen was going and what she would do when she got there.

If I hadn't given Lillian the weekend off, she'd go with me. She wouldn't like it, but she'd do it. And Etta Mae was right at the end of the upstairs hall in the sunroom. Maybe I could wake her and she'd go. But no, she'd be afraid the babies would wake up, and Hazel Marie and Mr. Pickens would need her. And they would, because Mr. Pickens hadn't quite gotten the hang of changing diapers, even disposable ones. In fact, he became nauseated every time he discovered more than he expected.

Hazel Marie would go up to wake Etta Mae, and when she found an empty bed, she'd be dialing 911, thinking Etta Mae had been kidnapped. I could do without having every deputy in the county on the prowl.

Briefly I thought of Lloyd but quickly discarded that idea. He'd be grand company and up for anything, but with the frigid weather he might catch a cold. Besides, if—and I really mean *if*—I found Helen's car at Sam's, which I didn't believe for a minute, I didn't want Lloyd to know about it.

That left me to go it alone. I started to rise, then sank back down, recalling the promise I'd made to Sam just that afternoon.

"Now, Julia," he'd said, "anytime you get an urge to take matters into your own hands and go off on some wild-goose chase, stop and think."

Well, that's what I was doing, wasn't I? Why else would I be sitting on a stair step in the middle of the night, gathering my nerve to brave the wintry blasts?

Of course, he'd said something else too: "And come talk to me about it. If it's worth doing, I'll do it with you, and we'll leave your partners in crime out of it."

Yes, well, I could see me asking Sam to help me discover where Helen was spending the night. I didn't think he'd be amenable to casing his own house.

Determined to do what had to be done, I got up and slipped through the rooms into the kitchen, where the hood light over the stove had been left on for visual aid in preparing bottles when needed. I stood and waited for a bit to be sure no one else was stirring, then, congratulating myself on having a little foresight this time, I found my keys and put them deep in a pocket. I didn't intend to get locked out again.

And I didn't intend to walk all over creation, freezing to death either. This time I was going to take a chance and take the car, counting on the baby tenders to be dead to the world from lack of sleep. My plan was to drive straight to Sam's, check for a white car, and return home before anybody missed me.

As I carefully closed the kitchen door behind me, I stood on the back stoop waiting for my eyes to adjust. Just as I stepped out onto the yard, the overhead light in the kitchen came on.

*Somebody was up.* Plunging between two huge boxwoods, I crouched down behind them and peeked through the windows to see who it was. Oh, Lord, it was Mr. Pickens, the last person I wanted to see or wanted to see me. He was stumbling between refrigerator and sink, yawning and scratching himself. But even half asleep, his detecting antenna would pick up the least little thing, so the car would be staying right where it was. Which meant I'd have to walk.

The nearest way to Sam's was to go through my backyard and out the back gate. Popping up, then back down, I watched Mr. Pickens move back and forth in the kitchen, preparing baby formula. Then he parked himself in front of the sink, right in front of the window that overlooked the backyard, and stood there and stood there—doing who-knows-what while I waited and waited. For all I knew, he'd fallen asleep.

Crouched down as I was, my knees started aching and I knew I had to move even if it meant going the long way. So I melted into the row of boxwoods that lined the driveway and, staying close, crawled on my hands and knees to the sidewalk. Then I had the devil's own time getting to my feet with nothing to leverage myself with but limber boxwood twigs. I not only scratched my hand, but also left a gaping hole in the big bush on the corner.

Scurrying along the sidewalk, I didn't feel safe from curious eyes until I was well past Mildred Allen's yard and in the dark spot between streetlights. I stopped and pulled on Lloyd's cap, feeling the bite of the wind for the first time after the surge of adrenaline.

I waited a few minutes under the branches of Mildred's forsythia, which hung over the sidewalk, to consider a plan of action. I was way off the shortest course to Sam's house, which would add a couple more blocks to the four that it normally was.

Well, it couldn't be helped, and longing for the car heater that would just about be revving up by now, I started walking, thinking and planning as I went. To tell the truth, I didn't know what I'd do if I found Helen's car at Sam's—just knock on the door and invite myself in? I cringed at the thought. I'd spent my life avoiding making a spectacle of myself—even when I had every right to make one—and I wasn't going to start now.

No, I'd simply confirm my suspicions and go back home to bed. That's where I'd decide what to do next. I had to stop and lean against the low stone wall that bordered the Whitakers' yard as pure misery overtook me. I *didn't* suspect Sam of two-timing me with Helen. I really didn't, yet here I was sneaking around to check on him even after he'd made it clear only hours ago that he was eager to come home.

What was the matter with me? Why couldn't I trust the most honest, open, and decent man I'd ever known?

Well, of course anybody who knew me could answer that. Wesley Lloyd Springer, my first and long-departed husband, engaged in a secret liaison that lasted a decade while I blithely and blindly lived a life of unquestioning trust, unable to imagine that he was capable of such treacherous behavior.

But Sam wasn't anything like Wesley Lloyd. I kept telling myself that but wondered why I wasn't able to stay home in bed, secure in that knowledge. Just because one husband had been unfaithful didn't mean the next one would be. I knew that, but like any Presbyterian, I was a staunch believer in the doctrine of original sin, a preexisting condition with the potential for additional sin. I wouldn't be able to sleep until I found out whether Sam had allowed the potential to become the actual.

When I knew that, *then* I'd go to bed.

By the time I got to Sam's house, having walked the extra blocks because of how I'd started out, I was breathing hard and my chest was burning from the cold and from my dashes into the shadows when two cars passed by on the street. Because Mr. Pickens had lingered so long at the sink, causing me to reconfigure my route, I was approaching the back of Sam's house. Slipping under the low branches of an ancient hemlock on the edge of his yard, I had a clear view of the back porch and the garage on the far side. No lights were on in the house, but one burned at the top of the stairs that led to the small apartment above the garage. *James,* I thought, and hoped he was a sound sleeper.

That one burning bulb cast enough light for me to see that there was only Sam's old—and I mean *old*—red pickup parked in front of the garage. There were no other vehicles parked behind the house, not even where I'd seen Helen's car once before. Avoiding the yard entirely, I walked along the sidewalk to the front of Sam's house and saw that the driveway was clear. Then I walked the length of the sidewalk in front of the house to make sure that a certain white car had not been sneakily parked where it would draw no attention.

Feeling more and more confident that I was on a fool's errand, I decided to continue on to my house and go to bed. Whoever Helen had been going to see, it had not been my faithful Sam. Getting a second wind, I stepped out smartly, taking the short way home because surely by that time Mr. Pickens was no longer hanging over the sink.

Then I stopped, turned around, and hurried back the way I'd come, anxiety burning a streak through my chest. Sam's garage had been closed. Sam had only one car. Sam's pickup was in the driveway. It was a two-car garage.

# Chapter 43

Looking up and down the sidewalk, then scanning the house and the garage, I saw nothing to deter me. No new lights were on, and everything was quiet except for the rattling of tree branches in the occasional gust of wind. Avoiding the driveway, I scooted across the grass toward Sam's pickup, then edged along it until I reached the double garage doors.

Bending over beside a front tire, I studied the matter, then sat down and studied some more. Whoever had last driven the pickup—James, most likely—had left the truck parked right between the two doors and so close that there was no way to lift a door and swing it up. No need to even try—even if I had the strength, it would be blocked by the truck.

As the cold from the concrete driveway began to seep through all the layers of wool I had on, I came to the conclusion that getting in the garage through those doors was out of the question. My next thought was to try to peep through the small windows along the top of the doors, but when I tried that, I wasn't tall enough to see more than the garage ceiling.

So, carefully holding on to the hood of the pickup, I hoisted one foot onto the front fender, and straining to get the other one off the ground, I almost made it. The fender creaked and groaned with my weight and shifted downward, one end falling to the pavement as my feet slid to the ground. Losing my balance, I banged against the garage doors, making enough noise to wake the dead and breaking Sam's truck at the same time.

Flying to the far side of the garage, I squatted in a clump of weeds that James hadn't cut, terrified that the whole neighborhood would be up in arms. I don't know how long I stayed there, watching for lights to come on and doors to open. Gradually, as nothing happened, my heart rate slowed and I began to consider what to do next.

Knowing that James was sleeping, or maybe lying half awake right above my head, I began to creep along the far side of the garage. I hugged the side of the garage, turning the corner to go along the back, fighting weeds and straggly bushes every step of the way. All I wanted was one good look inside, but there were no windows anywhere.

But as I got around to the side with the stairs—and the burning light above them—I found a door under the stairs, a normal door that led into the garage. Praying that it wouldn't be locked, I crept to it and turned the knob. With a sigh of relief, I pushed it open and sidled inside, closing it quickly behind me in case James came out onto the stairs and saw it open.

Easing along and feeling my way in the dark, I groped across the concrete floor to the car parked inside—*one* car! And it was Sam's car. I touched it, patted it, and blessed the fact that it was all alone.

I knew it—of course I knew it. I'd known it all along—Sam was as true as true could be, and I could've floated on air with the relief that came from finding an empty space where Helen's car could've been but wasn't.

In fact, I was so overcome with relief that I whirled around in that empty space like a crazy woman, tripped over my own feet, and fell against the workbench. Grabbing the edge of the workbench to stay upright, I knocked over a tin can full of nails or screws or something metallic that men save and never use.

The tin can hit the concrete floor with a clatter, spewing nails or whatever they were all over the place, and the thump of feet—big feet—hit the floor above me. James was on his way.

I flew to the door, almost skidding on a million screws scattered everywhere, but not stopping until I was out the door and curled up under a clump of some kind of bushes in the Masons' backyard next door.

I heard the door of the apartment above the garage open and waited to hear the sound of James's feet running down the stairs. It was quiet for the longest time until I heard James whisper, "Who's there?" All was quiet until he whispered again, "Anybody out there?"

Bless his heart, he was as scared as I was, and not about to come down to investigate. All I had to do was wait until he went back to bed, then I could leave.

I waited and waited, and almost waited too long. Two car doors slammed somewhere in the front of Sam's house, then two strong flashlight beams began to crisscross the yard. That sorry James had called the cops.

Then lights began to come on in the house, which meant that Sam was up.

I had to get out of there before the deputies started looking around the garage. Backing out of the bushes and staying low, I scurried from one shadow to the next, intent on crossing the next street and melting into one yard after the other until I was out of the vicinity. Getting picked up by the deputies was unthinkable. They wouldn't put me in jail, but they'd put me in the paper. I could see the headlines: LOCAL WOMAN CAUGHT TRESPASSING. No, it would be worse: ELDERLY WOMAN CAUGHT TRESPASSING.

As soon as I deemed it safe, I dashed across the street, making tracks for dark places wherever I could find them. Thank goodness, the people in the houses I passed were all decently in bed and no one challenged me. I stumbled through one yard after another, praying that all dogs were safely inside, then groped my way across an empty lot, stopping only when my breath gave out, which was when I fell flat on the ground after breaking through an ice-covered puddle. More worried about breaking a hip than muddying my coat, I stumbled on to a group of pine trees. And all the time I was going farther away from Sam's house and, even worse, farther away from mine. I was intent on getting far enough from Sam's to be able to cut sideways, then pick up a straight track toward home.

But every time I thought it was safe enough to cut across, I'd see car lights coming slowly toward me as a sheriff's cruiser patrolled the streets. And on top of that, spotlights were being played across the sidewalks and yards, which just did me in. You'd think they were after a common criminal.

After slogging through backyards and side yards and across empty lots full of briars and thorny bushes, I was exhausted and about ready to sit on a curb until a deputy picked me up. I could hardly catch my breath, my knees ached, and it was all I could do to put one foot in front of the other. Sitting on the cold ground behind an oak tree, I decided to just head home. If a deputy stopped me, quite possibly I could talk my way out of it. I mean, a lot of insomniacs take walks in the middle of the night, don't they?

But no, I couldn't bear the embarrassment of being questioned and, more than likely, disbelieved. And I couldn't bear the thought of facing Lieutenant Peavey's skeptical frown and Sam's disappointment when they called him. So after resting for a while and hearing no cruisers pass by, I peeked around the tree to get my bearings, just sure that I'd traversed a mile or more—all out of the way and getting farther from home with every step. I could've cried because I was so tired and fed up with being on the run.

My only hope of getting out of this mess with my pride and reputation intact was to get home and pretend none of it had ever happened. So before my nerve gave out, I stood up and ran—if you can call my shuffling steps running—into the street. Just as I got midway, I heard the heavy motor of a cop car, almost idling as it turned the corner, the probing beam of a spotlight sweeping both sides of the street.

I flew the rest of the way and flung myself through a thick hemlock hedge, the branches snagging Lloyd's cap from my head. With no time to retrieve it, I rolled away, hugging the ground as the car eased closer. Why didn't those deputies go home? Or go get a doughnut?

When the car finally passed, it was all I could do to get to my feet in the darkest yard I'd yet encountered. There was a distant glow from a house in the next lot to my right, but the light wasn't strong enough to do me much good. But at least somebody was up, and I wondered if I dared knock on the door and ask for help. Then, as I realized I'd only come six blocks and was still within the search area, I recognized Thurlow's house. Which meant that I was in Miss Petty's backyard.

Maybe that wasn't so bad. I leaned against a tree, catching my breath and considering my options. Would Thurlow give me temporary refuge until the deputies got tired of cruising? Yes, he probably would, but I'd never hear the end of it and neither would anybody else in town, including Sam.

And here came that patrol car again, and more than that, another cruiser came from the opposite direction. They stopped right in the middle of the street, their cars idling side by side and front to back as deputies are wont to do when they want to socialize. Stooping down and duckwalking until I came to another tree, I waited, listening to the static of their radios and the mumble of words as they chatted with each other.

Then the spotlights on both cars flared on and their beams began a slow sweep of Miss Petty's yard starting at the front and moving toward the back.

I ran. I ran in spite of aching knees and panting breath and bone tiredness. If I'd run into a tree, I'd have killed myself. There was one place left, one place they were unlikely to search, given the outcome of the last person hiding in it: Miss Petty's toolshed.

# Chapter 44

I slammed against the toolshed, frantically searching for the door as the bright beams penetrated Miss Petty's huge yard and swept closer. I pushed open the door a mere crack, slipped in sideways, and closed it, hoping that the movement had attracted no attention.

Scuttling to the two fertilizer bags, still exactly where I, and Richard before me, had left them, I sank down and bent over, pulling my coattail over my head to make the smallest target I could. As I sat there trembling, the spotlight beams crossed the toolshed back and forth, lighting up the interior through the cracks in the walls.

Carefully, I peeked up from my coat and glanced around to make sure I was alone. You can never tell these days who or what you'll find in out-of-the-way places. Everything was as I remembered it: tools hanging from the wall and standing in the corner, an oil-streaked power mower that reeked to high heaven, bags of potting soil, and the two bags of fertilizer I was sitting on. Nothing looked changed or disturbed since I'd last been in it, a most reassuring assessment because now I didn't have Lillian for company, and even though I felt reasonably safe from discovery—those deputies would rather play with their spotlights than beat the bushes—I had a tingling feeling about being alone in the place where Richard had passed.

There was nothing for it, but to wait it out, and after a while, the deputies got tired of their light display and I heard the cars begin to move off.

Safe at last, I thought, at least for the moment. I sat up straight and heaved a deep sigh, then began brushing the mud from my coat and picking leaves and twigs out of my hair. On my way out, I'd have to look for Lloyd's cap in case it became evidence that would lead to me. It was one of a kind, so who else in town would be caught dead in such a fool's cap? Lloyd certainly wouldn't. He'd never worn it.

In the meantime, I would stay where I was long enough to rest from my exertions and long enough for the deputies to find something else to do. But the longer I sat, the darker and colder it got as the wind sliced between the aging wallboards.

Feeling my limbs stiffening up, I pushed myself to a standing position and began to walk around the small space to loosen them up. I still had several blocks to travel before reaching home, and I couldn't afford to be half crippled from sitting too long.

After circling the dirt floor a couple of times while keeping far away from anything that could be knocked over, I soon got tired of it. Needing something to relieve the boredom while I waited for a safe time to leave, I sat down on the bags again, this time facing the knothole in the back wall. Thurlow's lights were on, so I thought I'd watch him for a while and maybe learn what Richard had found so engrossing. That, after all, had been my intention all along—until, that is, Helen's night moves distracted me.

What I couldn't understand was why Richard had only watched Thurlow. If he was in such dire need of money that he had to steal and forge my checks, why hadn't he accosted Thurlow and demanded his share of their ill-gotten gains? That's what accomplices usually did, wasn't it?

Pressing my face against the cold boards, I looked one eyed through the knothole, centering on the bright window in Thurlow's kitchen. All I could see were appliances and kitchen counters, and those not so clearly—Thurlow had a deep backyard and it was like looking at a tiny picture on Lloyd's pocket phone. Nothing was going on, so I soon tired of staring at what wasn't there. Just as I started to pull back, a woman, wearing something red and filmy, walked in front of the window, then turned as if speaking to someone else. Undeterred by shame at spying on unsuspecting people—they could've closed the curtains—I pressed my eye closer, my mouth gaping in disbelief.

If that wasn't who I thought it was, then I wasn't half freezing on two bags of fertilizer in a toolshed.

And she had been speaking to someone, because that someone walked up to her, put his arms around her, nuzzled her neck, and slipped the red filmy material from her shoulders.

*No!* I whispered, but it was. Neat, clean, fastidious Helen Stroud and grizzled, old *Thurlow!* No wonder Richard had had a heart attack. I almost had one myself.

Glued to that hole, I couldn't believe what was right before my eye. It was Thurlow whom Helen had been coming to and going from the times I'd seen her. And that was the reason Richard ended up dead on a dirt floor—he'd been spying on them until his heart gave out.

But which one had he specifically been spying on: Thurlow, because Thurlow might've ended up with the scammed money? Or Helen, because who wouldn't want to know what a spouse was doing? As far as I knew, Helen was still Richard's wife—at that time, that is, because she was now his widow—so maybe he'd wanted to get the goods on her as well. It must've torn him up to discover the two of them together. Poor Richard. I could almost feel sorry for him, bereft of both wife and funds by one ragtag manipulator.

But my sudden spurt of pity did nothing to release Richard from his most recent crime against me. I was going to make sure that everybody knew that INSUFFICIENT FUNDS stamped on a returned check was not my fault, even if I had to take out an ad in *The Abbotsville Times*. And never show my face in the Sav-Mor drugstore, the Jiffy Lube car service, or Ingles grocery store ever again, which wouldn't bother me because I didn't go to any of them anyway.

But whatever Richard's motives had been, not one side of such an unlikely triangle had anything to do with me—so there, Sam. As the lovers moved out of my sight, I pulled back and sat for a minute, thinking. I didn't need to see any more. I had enough to convince Sam that I'd been not only an innocent bystander but an unknowing one, and to convince Lieutenant Peavey and the bank as well.

I might just go wake Sam up and tell him so. Smiling to myself as I thought about the improbable couple I'd just seen, I wondered how in the world Helen could stand being around Thurlow, much less submit to his nuzzling. Of course, there was no accounting for taste, but I'd thought Helen had better than that.

It was time to go. Surely the deputies had had other calls and I could get home without interference from them. Besides, I could hardly wait to tell not only Sam but Hazel Marie and Lillian too. And wouldn't LuAnne and Mildred be shocked and amazed to hear about Helen and Thurlow?

I muffled a laugh, then jerked upright as a cold prickling sensation spread along the back of my neck and across my shoulders. Listening intently, my heart pounding, the rakes in the corner rattled again. A streak of fright coursed through every stiff muscle in my body. Up like a flash, I ran to the door. Throwing it wide, I heard a snap and a ghost dropped down in front of me. Too shocked to scream, though I tried, and crazed with fright, I ran right through it, heading for the hedge and the safety of the street.

I don't know how I got through the hedge. I pushed and shoved aside branches as hemlock needles pulled and scratched my clothes, my face, and my hair. Dashing out into the street, looking neither to the right nor the left in my terror, I was suddenly pinned in the glare of headlights as a car came to a screeching halt.

Leaning piteously on the hood, wanting only the company of something human, I heard the car door open and footsteps coming toward me.

"Ma'am? You almost ran into me. Are you all right?"

I looked up, saw a deputy's uniform, and almost fainted with relief. Still gasping with fright and unmindful of having spent hours hiding from his ilk, I clung to him.

"A ghost," I sobbed. "I went right through it, like . . . like nothing was there. But I saw it. Hanging there, a ghost."

"Ma'am, ma'am, hold on. What are you doing out here? You know what time it is?"

"I don't . . . let's go. I have to get away. It could be coming." Wanting only to get in his car and leave, I turned toward it and stumbled over his feet.

He caught my arm and leaned toward me. "Hey, careful there. You have a little too much to drink?"

"*No*. And if you'd seen what I saw, you wouldn't be asking such a question. I'm telling you, we better get out of here before it comes after us."

"Okay, okay, but where do you live? Tell me," the deputy said, turning me toward the headlights to get a good look, "where do you live?"

I pointed in a vague direction. "Over there."

"Let's get you in the car," the deputy said, walking me toward the back door.

"Good, that's good. Ghosts can't . . . Lock the door."

"Don't worry, I will." The deputy was grinning as he closed the door, then he crawled into the driver's seat and started mumbling and talking in numbers on his radio.

Trembling, I crouched in the corner of the backseat, as far from Miss Petty's toolshed as I could get, watching fearfully for any signs of the ghost's materializing out of the hedge.

The deputy turned with his arm along the top of the front seat, looking at me through the mesh screen. "You wander around much at night, ma'am?"

*Did he know something?* "Hardly ever," I temporized.

"Well, we've been searching for a prowler in the area. Where all have you been tonight?"

"Minding my own business, young man, and I'm telling you there's a ghost in that yard, or outside it, or somewhere around here—no telling where it is now, and I don't even believe in ghosts. But I saw it even though I'm a Presbyterian, and I ran right through it like, like it didn't have a body, and Pastor Ledbetter won't believe me, but I know what I saw."

"Uh, ma'am, you take any medications? You know, to help you remember things?"

*He thought I was demented.* "I certainly do not," I snapped, then reconsidered. Maybe I should let him think I'd wandered from home and couldn't find my way back. There'd be no question about trespassing at Sam's house or spying on Thurlow if he thought I'd had memory loss, although I was far from senile, as anybody who knew me could verify.

"Well," I said, "maybe an aspirin now and then, and a laxative when I need it. But I don't need either one to know what I saw, and I saw a ghost and it was right where somebody died, and Lillian says that spirits hover around for a while when somebody dies. I want to go home now."

"How 'bout I take you to the emergency room? You might need to be looked over."

"No, thank you. All I need is for you to put this car in gear and take me home. I'll show you where I live when we get there. Turn left at the corner."

"Can you tell me your name now?"

"I could, but I prefer not to. Besides, you haven't introduced yourself either."

He laughed, put the car in gear, and we moved away, leaving, I fervently hoped, Richard's ghost in Miss Petty's toolshed, where it belonged.

# Chapter 45

"You sure you live here?" the deputy said as he pulled to the curb.

"I certainly am. Do you think I'd direct you to somebody else's house?"

"Well, you never know." He still had that amused smile on his face, humoring me as if I didn't know who or where I was. He leaned over to look out the side window at the dark house. "Nobody's up. Guess they haven't missed you yet."

"Let's hope not." I groped for a door handle. "How do I get out of here? I can't get it open."

"I'll come around and let you out." He did, and as I climbed out onto the sidewalk in front of my house, he said, "We'll knock on the door and be sure it's the right place."

"There's no need for that." I pulled the keys out of my pocket and dangled them in front of him. "I can manage by myself. Besides, they've probably been up half the night. Wall-to-wall babies, you know."

That set him off again. In the gray light of predawn, I saw a worried look come over his face. "Ma'am," he said, frowning, "I think I know who lives here, and I'm not sure you do."

I jangled the keys again. "Come watch me open the back door." I had the urge to tell him I'd lived here for more than forty years, not all of them good ones either.

He peered at me so long that I felt compelled to smoothe the hair out of my face and to stand a little taller. Frowning, he asked, "You wouldn't be Mrs. Sam Murdoch, would you?"

I turned so he couldn't look too closely and started walking toward the back door. He followed, holding my arm. "A friend of hers," I said. "Just visiting, and this will teach me not to take a walk in a strange town. I'll be leaving in the morning, well, *this* morning now that it's already here." I inserted the key, turned it, and opened the door. "See? They gave me a key because they know I'm prone to long walks. You can run along now. Thank you for your help." I closed the door in his face and hurried through the kitchen and up the stairs to the safety of the bedroom.

As I closed the door and turned the lock, I flipped on the chandelier and nearly screamed at the apparition in front of me.

"Oh, Lord," I gasped as I recognized myself in Hazel Marie's full-length mirror. Twigs and hemlock needles and leaves sprouted from my head to my toes; my coat was smeared with mud, my face scratched, tights torn, shoes clumped with mud, and my hair was straggling all over my head and in my face. I looked like a wild woman and I was shivering like one too. No wonder the deputy wanted to take me to the emergency room.

And it was Sunday morning. Sam would be expecting me in church.

As tired as I was, the excitement of seeing him, sitting with him and holding his hand, gave me a spurt of energy. And assuring myself that no ghost would dare darken the door of the First Presbyterian Church, I began to get out of my torn and muddied clothes, figuring they were all destined for the trash. Normally I preferred a bath to a shower, but that morning I took both: a shower first to wash my hair and a bath to soak out the soreness that was sure to come.

Dressing carefully in my most elegant outfit—a lavender wool skirt and a matching jacket with braid on the placket and the cuffs—I prepared to meet my returning husband, all the while hearing the sounds of early risers downstairs. Babies were crying, the refrigerator door was opening and closing, water was running, and Mr. Pickens's heavy footsteps were tromping back and forth between the kitchen and bedroom.

Deliberately putting aside all thoughts of the strange occurrences of the previous night, I concentrated on making the most of the next hour or so with Sam. Taking a last look in the mirror, I almost gave up. I'd had to wash my hair—a part of my toilette that I'd given over to Velma years before—and I couldn't do a thing with it. There it lay on my head, flat and unstyled. I needed Hazel Marie and her curling iron.

So down to the kitchen I went, yawning and creaking as my aching body protested each step. If you want to know the truth, I could hardly straighten up, and soaking in a tub hadn't helped.

"Why, Miss Julia," Etta Mae said, working away at something by the counter. "You're up early." She was in her usual jeans and sweater, which meant that she didn't have going to church in mind.

"I couldn't sleep for some reason," I said and opened the freezer and looked in. "Lillian left some blueberry muffins. How does that sound for breakfast?"

"Sounds good to me. Soon as I plug a couple of little mouths, I'll fry up some bacon." She started out of the kitchen, turned around, and said, "You look real nice this morning."

"Thank you, but my hair's a mess," I said, touching it self-consciously. "I hope Hazel Marie has time to work on it for me."

She did: after the babies were changed and fed, Mr. Pickens was out of the bathroom, Lloyd had been sent back upstairs to dress for church, and we'd all eaten, she sat me down in front of a dresser and heated the curling iron.

"What did you do to this?" Hazel Marie asked as she ran a comb through my lank hair. "It looked so good yesterday."

"Slept wrong on it, I guess. It was standing up on one side, so I washed it."

"Well, don't do it again." Hazel Marie picked up the curling iron and went on. "I don't want to burn you, so stay real still."

That was hard to do, for I was so full of what I'd discovered during the night that it was all I could do to stay quiet, much less stay still. I had a great urge to tell her about Helen and Thurlow, but restrained myself because I couldn't figure out how to tell it without telling how I'd found it out. And I wanted to tell Sam first. Not that he'd be awed by such an unlikely coupling—as Hazel Marie would be—but because I wanted him to understand that I was not the woman involved with either Richard or Thurlow, thereby bringing our estrangement to a conclusive end.

Busily curling and back combing, Hazel Marie said, "Your hair's gotten so long, I think I'll do it up in a chignon."

"Whatever works," I murmured, half asleep from being up all night.

"There," Hazel Marie said, waking me with a hand on my shoulder. "How do you like it?"

I blinked and gazed bleary eyed but pleased in the mirror. "Why, Hazel Marie, it's beautiful."

"Whoo," Etta Mae said, coming into the room. "That bun on the back of your head is what I call glamorous. You're really stylin' now, Miss Julia."

Taking a hand mirror, I looked at my hair from all sides, becoming more and more pleased with what I saw. I was now as far from the apparition I'd seen in another mirror as I could be. You'd think I was an entirely different woman, which was just fine with me. I didn't want anybody putting two and two together and coming up with Mrs. Sam Murdoch.

Just as Lloyd and I were leaving for the service, having bypassed Sunday school on the grounds of needing my hair fixed, Lillian called. "Latisha 'bout to have a fit to come see the babies.

So, 'less somebody already cooked something, I'll fix us all some dinner."

"Nobody's cooked a thing, Lillian," I said, laughing at the thought. "I was just going to make sandwiches, so you come right on. We'll be happy to have you."

～⁖～

Lloyd and I slipped into our usual pew, where Sam was waiting for us. He smiled at me, patted my hand, and leaned close to whisper what I expected to be a loving compliment on my elegant appearance.

Instead, just as the processional started and we began to rise, he said, "Had a little excitement at my house last night. I'll tell you about it later."

Well, that took my mind off the service. Did he suspect that *I* had been the excitement? Surely not, I reassured myself—he wouldn't have welcomed me so warmly. Still, it worried me, which was about the only thing that kept me from falling asleep.

And a good thing it was, because Pastor Ledbetter's sermon topic didn't bode well for keeping me awake. He prided himself on being up to date—au courant, as Emma Sue called it—on what was going on in the world, especially in Abbotsville and, more particularly, in his congregation. And he could find Scripture verses to back up whatever stance he wanted to take on any given topic.

I was sure that the pastor would preach on the place of women in the Church, which, according to him, was not up behind the pulpit. About once or so a year, he felt compelled to preach a sermon having to do with women, and each time he did I wondered whom he was aiming at: Emma Sue or me. And with Emma Sue coming home from Mildred's impromptu tea, rhapsodizing about Pastor Poppy Patterson, I thought he'd figure it was time for another dose of straight talk so we wouldn't get any feminist ideas.

That would be fine with me—I'd heard it all before and I could catnap without missing a thing. The only reason I was there that morning was to be with Sam, anyway.

So when the pastor announced that his text was from the book of First Samuel, specifically King Saul's consultation with the witch of Endor, I wondered what had set him off. It never took much—reading or hearing of spiritualism, Ouija boards, children dressed as ghosts and goblins on Halloween, even Halloween itself. But this time it had been an article in the Asheville paper about a coven of witches dancing around a tree.

I began to nod off as he droned on about Saul's fear of the Philistine host and how the Lord's help was no longer forthcoming. Going to the witch of Endor, Saul begged her to call on the deceased prophet, Samuel, to give him military advice.

"And when," Pastor Ledbetter went on, "against her better judgment, she called forth Samuel out of the earth, Samuel said to Saul, 'Why hast thou disquieted me to bring me up?'"

That woke me up. *Had I disquieted Richard in the toolshed?* Heaven knows I hadn't meant to.

But no, in the light of day and sitting in church, I could discount to some extent what I'd seen and heard the night before. I mean, I didn't believe in ghosts, yet here was my own pastor speaking of them as if they were actual beings. He didn't say that the shade of Samuel was imaginary or that Saul was mentally ill or that the witch of Endor used a magic trick. He was saying that the ghost of Samuel was real and *reachable*.

For the rest of the sermon my eyebrows stayed up as far as they would go. It was the only way I could keep my eyes open as I waited to hear what could be done once a dead person was disquieted.

Not much, as Saul learned. I comforted myself by recalling that, unlike Saul, I'd visited no witch and done no calling forth. If there'd been any disquieting of Richard's rest, it'd been done by Helen, not me.

With that reassuring thought, I dozed off during the collection, only to be startled awake when the pastor announced the closing hymn. I came to enough to catch Sam and Lloyd grinning at each other.

"Tired, honey?" Sam whispered.

I nodded as we stood. "Babies cried half the night," I murmured, and hoped he believed me.

After filing out of the church as slowly as I could manage so everyone who'd heard James's grocery aisle news could see that Sam and I were together, I asked him to have Sunday dinner with us.

"I can't, sweetheart," Sam said. "Pickens is coming over to discuss moving arrangements—he's still not comfortable about taking over my house. So man to man, I'm going to convince him that it's the best plan for all of us. And," he went on, smiling, "James has been cooking all morning."

James, *again*!

So Lloyd and I left the church, my mood lighthearted because Sam was making plans to return to the head of my table, where he belonged.

As we waited for passing traffic before crossing the street, what I saw parked in front of my house made me want to turn around and go back. Maybe I could tell Lloyd that I needed a private word with Pastor Ledbetter or that I'd left something in the pew or that I had to ask LuAnne about the Cirle meeting. But we were too close and I wasn't quick enough to come up with a single valid excuse to avoid what was waiting for me.

# Chapter 46

"Wonder what that patrol car's doing at our house," Lloyd said.

"Probably looking for Sam," I said, as dismissively as I could. "They may have arrested an old client of his. Latisha's waiting for you, so you run along and I'll see what he wants." By this time a vaguely familiar deputy had crawled out of his car and was waiting for us on the sidewalk. "Watch the traffic, Lloyd," I went on, "and tell Lillian I'll be there in a few minutes."

Lloyd scampered across the street, gave a friendly wave to the deputy as he went by, and disappeared into the house. I walked sedately up to the officer, keeping a serene but slightly questioning expression on my face, as if willing, but not necessarily eager, to help our local law enforcement personnel.

"Mrs. Murdoch?" he asked, seemingly hesitant to question me. In the daylight, I saw how young he was and how unsure he was in dealing with influential and law-abiding citizens.

"Yes?" I observed him coolly, noting his name tag—Deputy Will Powers—and met his eyes as if I had nothing to hide.

"I'm, uh, well, I was on duty last night and I picked up a woman, a lady, who seemed to be lost and, well, a good bit confused. She told me she was visiting you and directed me here, although I wanted to take her to be checked out at the emergency room. She looked pretty messed up. Well, not really *messed up*, ma'am, I mean, more like she'd had a rough time." He stopped and I waited, giving him no help at all. "Well, anyway, I got to worrying about her, thinking I might shoulda taken her to the hospital anyway. And, uh, I just wanted to make sure she's all right."

"How very thoughtful of you, Deputy Powers," I said in a distant manner. "I'll be sure to commend you to Lieutenant Peavey. Your concern is well placed. We'd noticed a real deterioration of my friend's cognitive functions since her visit last year, so we put her on a bus home this morning. Her daughter is, as we speak, making arrangements for full-time care."

"Then that's a relief," Deputy Powers said. "I sure didn't want to miss something on my first week of patrol duty. But, Mrs. Murdoch, I don't want to offend you or anything, but up close, the two of you could be sisters. Not," he hastily added, his face suddenly tinged with red, "that you look anything like she did last night, but I mean, up close. Kinda."

I permitted a condescending smile to tighten my mouth. "She was once a beautiful woman, so I'll take that as a compliment. Now, they're waiting Sunday dinner for me, so I must go in. Thank you again, Deputy, for your commitment to duty."

I offered my hand in a queenly manner and he hesitantly shook it. Then I turned and walked toward the house without glancing back, but listening as he got into his car and drove away. Gaining the living room, I closed the front door and leaned against it, drained from withstanding his dutiful follow-up on a possibly vagrant woman.

If that close call hadn't taught me the value of good grooming, nothing would.

After we'd finished lunch, which we called dinner on Sundays, I longed for a good long nap. I stayed awake, though, because I half expected Sam to show up with Mr. Pickens after they'd concluded their negotiations as to who was going to live where. It was a settled fact that Lloyd's inheritance could buy almost any house that Hazel Marie and Mr. Pickens wanted, on the grounds that the child needed a place to live. But Mr. Pickens was the last person on earth who would accept such a handout. Yet he was also about the last person on earth who could afford the kind of house Hazel Marie would want. I'd done my job of instructing her in the finer things of life almost too well. Not that she was demanding the best, not that at all. In fact, I think she'd live in a tent if Mr. Pickens was in it with her, but with a family of five, a little more than a tarpaulin was clearly called for.

Sam's solution was for them to move into his house, although the problem of financing their stay remained. Could Mr. Pickens buy it with no help from Lloyd's estate, which he wouldn't accept anyway? Would they rent it? Rent to own? Or as Sam had suggested, live rent-free and take care of it?

There was no easy answer, considering Mr. Pickens's commendable yet obstinate determination to take care of his own family, as well as his lack of funds. I didn't care how they worked it out, for I had already decided to suggest that Lloyd remain with me until Hazel Marie felt comfortable managing a house and those twin babies on her own. Which, if my luck held, would be about the time Lloyd went off to college.

As it turned out, both Sam and Mr. Pickens lingered and lingered as the afternoon wore on. So I helped feed the babies, feeling almost like an old hand at it by now. As I held a bottle and rocked one of them, unsure who it was, I almost nodded off until I began to wonder what was delaying the men.

Of course! What would be more natural than that Sam would ask Mr. Pickens's opinion about the prowler they'd had the night before? I could just picture the two of them, with James adding his two cents, reconstructing the crime. But, I reassured myself, I'd worn gloves, leaving no fingerprints, indeed leaving nothing but an overturned tin can and a million screws scattered across the garage floor.

*And footprints!* I realized. Footprints in the muddy ground around the garage, across the yard, and into the Masons' yard, and if Mr. Pickens was bound and determined to stay on the trail, across the street and on and on right straight to a certain toolshed.

"This baby's asleep, Hazel Marie," I said, too edgy to keep sitting there. "Shall I put her down?"

Etta Mae stopped folding baby garments and walked over. "I'll take her. I need to put her in her little Sunday outfit."

Hazel Marie put the one she was holding on her shoulder and patted its back. "Thanks, Miss Julia, for helping out. We're trying to straighten up in here before people start dropping in. Binkie called and asked to come by to see the babies, and LuAnne wants to come, and no telling who else. And I don't know what I'm going to wear. I can't get into anything."

"Give it time," Etta Mae said. "You'll lose that baby weight soon enough. You already are, it looks to me. Just put on something loose and you'll look fine."

"Well," Hazel Marie said, "I had to wear safety-pinned skirts early on, so I guess I can do it again. Oh, and Miss Julia, Helen Stroud called too. She wants to come by, and I'm so glad. I haven't seen her in ages."

"Me either," I mumbled, although it hadn't been all that long since I'd seen more of Helen than I'd wanted to.

"Oh, and something else," Hazel Marie said, "we ought to be thinking about christening these babies pretty soon, don't you think? I don't know what the right age is to do it, though I've seen Pastor Ledbetter christen toddlers and on up. I don't want to wait that long. I want my little girls christened as soon as possible. I think I'll sleep better when they are."

Etta Mae laughed. "You'll sleep better when they stop waking up every two hours. But I know what you mean. I like the idea of christening infants, although the church I grew up in didn't believe in it. You had to be old enough to know what you were doing, and we got baptized in a river instead of sprinkled on the head."

"Christening, baptizing," I said, "I'm not sure I know the difference, if there is any. Although I don't think you'd christen an adult. That'd surely be a baptism. Let's talk to Pastor Ledbetter, Hazel Marie, and see what he says."

"Yes, I thought I would." Hazel Marie gazed off at the ceiling for a while—a sure sign of some deep thinking. "You know how the pastor, after he christens a baby, always carries it up and down the aisle so everybody in the church can see it? I just worry that if he tries to carry two, he might let one slip."

"I don't think he'd do that, Hazel Marie," I said, wondering about the things she came up with to worry about. "You know he'd be careful. Or he might ask one of the godparents to carry one, or maybe both godparents could each carry a baby while he stayed out of it. And on that subject, have you decided whom you'll ask to be godparents?"

"No'm," she said, sighing and lowering her eyes, "I haven't. There're so many people I'd like to ask, I just can't decide."

"Well, let me put your mind at ease about one thing. You shouldn't ask Sam or me, and our feelings won't be hurt if you don't. You should ask somebody young, somebody who'll be around as these babies grow up and, of course, somebody who'll watch over their spiritual growth if you and Mr. Pickens aren't around to do it. So if we're on your list, you can scratch us off. Besides," I went on with a satisfied smile, "I figure Sam and I are already Lloyd's godparents, or as good as, even though we're slightly beyond the ideal age limit."

Hazel Marie's eyes suddenly filled up as if a spring had broken loose somewhere, and before I knew it, she was in full weeping mode.

"Oh, Hazel Marie, what is it?" I asked, immediately concerned that I'd said something to hurt her. Either that or she still had hormones close to the surface. "Did I say something wrong?"

"No'm," she sobbed, her hands over her face. "Not that. It's all my fault because I didn't want him dunked in that filthy river and I've never done anything about it, and he's already half grown."

Etta Mae and I looked at each other, trying to understand what she was talking about.

"Who, Hazel Marie?" I asked. "And what haven't you done?"

She took her hands down and looked up at us, her face red and blotched from crying. "Lloyd, my precious Lloyd. I've never had him baptized, *or* christened, and I'll probably go to hell for it too."

"My goodness," I said, sinking down on the side of the bed, the wind suddenly taken out of my sails. "Well, Hazel Marie, I'm just as much at fault as you, and maybe more, because I just assumed..." I stood up, patted her shoulder, and said, "Stop crying now. We'll take care of it. Nobody's going to hell in this house—not if I have anything to do with it."

# Chapter 47

As Hazel Marie dried her tears and began to dress for our Sunday afternoon visitors, I left her to it and went to the living room to think over what could be done. Maybe we could have Lloyd christened at the same time the babies were, or if the rites were the same, we could baptize all three at once. Thank goodness we Presbyterians believe in baptism by anointing—or sprinkling, as some call it—which can be done on infants without fear of damage. If we'd belonged to a church that believed in total immersion—or dunking, as some less-than-pious folks called it—we'd have drowning to worry about. In that case, we'd be forced to wait until the babies were old enough to hold their breath.

Sitting there thinking it over, I felt done in by my own slackness in not seeing to Lloyd's eternal welfare before this. To have assumed that he had had the benefit of baptism in or out of the cradle was to have assumed more than I should have. Hazel Marie had been a single mother, and a kept woman at that, so it made perfect sense that she would've been less than eager to stand before a congregation and present her misbegotten infant for the sacrament of baptism.

There was only one thing to do. Well, two things. The first was to make arrangements with Pastor Ledbetter to have Lloyd baptized as soon as possible, although I knew it couldn't be right away. The pastor would require Lloyd to attend a catechism class and then pass an oral test concerning his beliefs and understanding of the faith—all of which would take time. The second thing to do was to cover the gap between then and now, and I intended to take care of that.

With that decided, I turned to the other matters that were crowding my mind. Walking into the kitchen, I found Lillian alone at last as she finished cleaning up from dinner.

"Lillian, I want to tell you something, but you have to keep it quiet. I have at last found out what Richard was doing in Miss Petty's toolshed and it will be the talk of the town as soon as I can tell it. The problem is, I can't tell it without admitting how I discovered it, and how I discovered it doesn't make me look very good."

"Then," she said, "if I was you, I wouldn't tell it."

"Well, but I have to, at least to Sam, so he'll know that none of it had anything to do with me. Once he hears what I saw last night, he'll understand that."

"Last night!" She put the last pan in the dishwasher and looked at me in amazement. "You mean to stand there an' tell me you went out to that toolshed *again*? By *yourself*?"

"I didn't intend to, Lillian. I just ended up there to keep from getting picked up by a deputy, and you were right to be afraid of it. That place *is* haunted. You won't believe this, but I actually saw Richard Stroud's ghost. And I am still a bundle of nerves, because you know I don't believe in ghosts. But I saw the thing and I ran right through it as if nothing were there."

"Oh, Law," Lillian said, her eyes wide. "What you do then?"

"Well, I got picked up by a deputy after all and was glad of it. The only problem with that was he thought I was deranged and out wandering around because I was lost, and I had to pretend to be my friend who really was senile."

She squinched up her eyes at me. "What?"

"It doesn't matter," I said, waving my hand. "What does matter is this: Richard was spying on either Helen or Thurlow—I haven't figured out which one yet. Could've been both, I guess, and found out that they're seeing each other—and I mean *seeing* each other—and it shocked him so bad that he had a heart attack. Can you believe that?"

She shook her head. "No'm."

"Well, me either, except I saw them with my own eyes. *Eye,* I mean, through that knothole and through Thurlow's kitchen window. And there's no mistake—they are an item. And Sam needs to know that, but how can I tell him without admitting I was looking for Helen's car in his garage? Which means that I was the one who was his prowler. You know, the one that James called the deputies about."

Her frown got deeper as a look of concern swept over her face. "You feelin' all right, Miss Julia?"

"I'm feeling fine, Lillian, better than fine since I learned what's really going on." I turned as the front doorbell rang. "That's our company. The first of it, anyway. Lillian, if you'll put out some pound cake slices and fill the coffee urn—oh, and maybe put a pot of spiced tea on the dining room table—we'll let everybody help themselves. Then I want you to go upstairs and stretch out on the bed and rest. Or just go on home whenever Latisha will let you."

She rolled her eyes. "That might be never. She think she got to watch them babies."

By the time I got to the living room, Etta Mae had already welcomed LuAnne in and was taking her coat, If Etta Mae hadn't caught the coat, I think LuAnne would've let it fall to the floor, she was so thrilled to see the babies. And they were a sight to see: both babies were dressed in long pink dresses and little white socks with lace on them; they wore pink ribbons in their hair. Hazel Marie sat in a wing chair, holding them and smiling proudly as if she were holding an audience.

A fire was burning brightly in the fireplace, all the lamps were on, and someone had picked up the Sunday papers. The room was beautiful, but Hazel Marie and her lapful made it even more so.

LuAnne went into raptures, talking a mile a minute and exclaiming over the wonders of twin babies. Of course she wanted to hold one, so as soon as she arranged herself on the sofa, Etta Mae handed one to her. Hazel Marie watched every move, eager enough to show off her offspring but not all that happy about having them passed around.

I sat beside LuAnne, guiding her hand behind the baby's head, hoping that my proximity would ease Hazel Marie's fears. Though she might have appreciated my help, LuAnne didn't.

"You don't have to show me, Julia," she said. "I know how to hold a baby. I had two of my own, you know."

Before I could respond, the doorbell rang again and Etta Mae answered it. She ushered in Helen Stroud, looking as neat and tidy and composed as she always did. We all greeted her, although it was all I could do to reconcile her present appearance with what I'd seen the night before. Her classic suit and sensible heels just did not compute with that filmy red negligee. As she oohed and aahed over the baby in Hazel Marie's lap, I kept seeing her in Thurlow's arms and wondering again what she saw in him.

"Could I hold her?" Helen asked, as she sat in a chair next to Hazel Marie. "Just for a minute?"

Etta Mae handed the baby to Helen and arranged it in her lap. A glow came over Helen's face as she looked down at the baby. Like me, Helen had never had children, but unlike me, she'd never had anyone like Lloyd to fill that empty space. Unless it was now filled by Thurlow, who certainly needed better raising than he'd had.

With her arms empty, Hazel Marie sat back in her chair, her eyes going from one child to the other, always watchful.

"Here, Hazel Marie," Etta Mae said, putting a cup and a dessert plate on the table beside her. "Have some tea and cake. Oops, there's the doorbell again."

And in came Binkie and Coleman, Coleman holding little Gracie. All three were smiling and talking, as Gracie squirmed to be put down. I stood to greet them, as Binkie threw her arms around Etta Mae, then hurried to Hazel Marie to do the same.

As pleased as she was to see them, Hazel Marie became even more alert, concerned, I knew, about Gracie having a cold or some other infectious disease. But Gracie wasn't interested in the babies. As soon as she saw Lloyd, she toddled straight to him, everybody else, including her parents, forgotten.

"Come on, Gracie," Lloyd said, "want to go play in Mama's room?"

And down the hall they went, Lloyd leading the way, Gracie following, and Latisha right behind her, trying to pick her up.

Binkie sat on the other side of LuAnne on the sofa, and LuAnne reluctantly gave the baby to her. Then they both began to examine the baby's little feet and hands, exclaiming over the tiny gold bracelet that Hazel Marie had put on the baby's arm.

"Which one is this, Hazel Marie?" LuAnne asked.

"That's Lily Mae and Helen has Julie."

"I don't know how you tell them apart," LuAnne said. "They look just alike."

Hazel Marie just smiled, content in a mother's knowledge of her own babies.

Binkie said, "Look, Coleman, see how darling this little precious thing is?"

"I see it," Coleman said, "and I see you lookin' real natural, holding it."

"Don't get any ideas," Binkie said, laughing.

Coleman looked at me. "Sam around?"

"He should be home any minute," I said, hoping that was true. "He and Mr. Pickens are looking over Sam's house." Then, hearing the sounds of entry from the kitchen, I went on. "That may be them now."

And it was. Sam and Mr. Pickens came in, and Coleman stood up to shake hands. Etta Mae, ever helpful, brought in some dining room chairs. Sam, in his usual genial way, walked around the room, speaking to Binkie, LuAnne, and Helen. When Sam got to Helen, I watched carefully for any silent communication as he greeted her. I couldn't help being suspicious because, notwithstanding his stated intent to return home or her nightly visits to Thurlow, I couldn't forget the private luncheon they'd had.

Mr. Pickens followed Sam's lead, though not with the same social ease that came so naturally to my husband. But if the setting had been a bar or a juke joint instead of my living room, it would've been a different story.

But Mr. Pickens handled himself ably enough, considering the disreputable elements he associated with in his line of work. In fact, he gazed proudly at his daughters and accepted with grace the praise that was heaped on him. He leaned down and kissed Hazel Marie, then drew a chair next to her and sat down. I was increasingly pleased with how well he was fitting into his fourth marriage and first fatherhood.

Still watchful for any surreptitious communication between Sam and Helen, a few questions came to mind. Could Helen be playing Sam off Thurlow? Or vice versa? Could Sam still have some interest in her, and if so, what did men see in her, anyway? Surely Sam didn't know that Helen was seeing Thurlow and that Thurlow was seeing a great deal more of Helen than anyone suspected.

Should I tell him? And if so, how could I tell him what I'd seen last night? He needed to know what she was up to, but I couldn't tell him without revealing what I'd been up to, prying into other people's business and taking all kinds of chances with my own life and limb—the very kind of thing that ran Sam up a wall.

It was a quandary, all right, and if not for that constant worry, I would've enjoyed the afternoon: the talk and the laughter as people went to and from the table, the sound of the children laughing and playing, the babies passed from arm to arm, the fire warming the room, and Mr. Pickens lighting up Hazel Marie's face as he whispered to her.

When the doorbell rang again, Etta Mae was right there to answer it, making me wonder how we ever would have managed without her. She never seemed to tire, never held back from whatever was needed, whether it was caring for the babies or pitching in with kitchen work. And above all, I would never forget how she'd helped with the snowbound delivery of the babies.

At the sound of her voice and that of someone else at the front door, I rose to see who it was.

"Hey there, Miss Julia," Pastor Poppy Patterson said, a big smile on her face as she handed her coat to Etta Mae. "I'm dropping in like you asked me to, and I've just met Etta Mae, here. Etta Mae, we ought to go out for coffee one of these days real soon and have a good long talk."

Etta Mae beamed, immediately taken by the lovely young woman, who apparently made friends upon first sight. I took Poppy around and introduced her, stopping for her to coo over each baby and for her to heap compliments on Hazel Marie for her accomplishment.

As we walked toward the dining room table, where Coleman and Helen were filling their coffee cups, Pastor Poppy pulled me aside.

"I just have to tell you," she said with a mischievous smile, "Mr. Jones was in church this morning, and he did exactly what he said he'd do—took notes all through my sermon. I expect I'll hear from him sooner or later, but I wanted you to know that our visit worked. So thank you again for going with me and getting me in the door. It was all your doing."

"Oh, not at all, Poppy. Anyway, I was glad to do it. I expect, though, that he was secretly glad to see you just to have a chance to take you to task. That's the way he is. Now let me get you some coffee or would you prefer spiced tea?"

We turned toward the table and came face to face with Helen. "Helen," I said, "I'd like you to meet Pastor Poppy Patterson from First Methodist. Poppy, this is Helen Stroud."

Searching for some way to characterize Helen, as I tried to do whenever I made introductions, I almost added, "She's one of our most faithful Presbyterians," even though I had not seen her in church since long before Richard's demise. I had assumed that shame over his fraudulent activities had kept her away, and I had admired her for it.

Then I was glad I'd held my tongue, for Poppy laughed and said, "Oh, I know Helen. She's one of our regular visitors—so regular, in fact, that we might be about to make a Methodist of her."

# Chapter 48

Well, *that* set me back on my heels. And the first thing that came to mind was this: Did Helen and Thurlow sit together at the Methodist church? But no, they must not, or Poppy would've mentioned it, or more likely, she'd have asked Helen to go with her to visit Thurlow. I was willing to bet, although I wasn't in the habit of betting, that Poppy knew nothing of their unlikely, and to me unseemly, liaison.

So, I mused, as I excused myself to replenish the cake tray and fled to the kitchen, Thurlow, who had never darkened a church door before, and Helen, a lifelong Presbyterian, were both showing up—apparently separately—at the Methodist church. What did that say about their intentions?

I didn't know, but I did know that Pastor Ledbetter would accept in a dignified, yet sorrowful, way the loss of a faithful member to another church, while Emma Sue would be hurt to her soul. All I could think was that if Helen had indeed been the reason that Thurlow was going to church, then she was doing what no one else had been able to do. And maybe, I suddenly thought, she'd done some other things that no one else had been able to do: things like clean and refurbish Thurlow's house and yard.

Now if she'd just turn her hands to *him,* I'd give her all the credit in the world. Provided that she stayed away from Sam at the same time.

I heard the doorbell ring again and hurriedly finished slicing another pound cake. Wondering who else had come in, I started through the swinging door into the dining room. Then hearing an unexpected voice, I slid the tray on the table and slipped back into the kitchen before anybody saw me.

My heart pounded away, as "Be sure your sins will find you out" ran through my mind. The last person in the world that I expected or wanted to see was standing in the hall talking to Sam. And why did *he* have to answer the door? Easing the swinging door open just a tiny bit, I listened.

"Come on in, Deputy," Sam was saying. "I expect you know Coleman, don't you?"

"Yes, sir. Sergeant Bates, good to see you," Deputy Will Powers said. "Sorry to barge in like this. I just wanted to bring this by, in case anybody here lost it."

And would you believe he pulled out Lloyd's many-colored cap and held it out toward Sam?

"No," Sam said, "no, I don't think it's ours."

"Well, it's lookin' a little worse for the wear. The wind was blowing it around, right near where I picked up Mrs. Murdoch's friend this morning, and I thought it might be hers."

I gasped and let the door close. Leaning against the wall, I was suffering pure mortification. Sam was going to find out what I'd done and where I'd been, and for all I knew he'd stay at his house, living with Hazel Marie and Mr. Pickens forever.

Then, unable to keep from listening, I eased the door open a bare inch, just in time to hear Lloyd say, "Why, that looks like *mine*. Where'd it come from?"

"Found it in the street, next to Miss Laverne Petty's house. You been visitin' over there lately?"

"No, sir," Lloyd said firmly. "I know better than to go over there. She told us she was going to fix anybody who snooped around her toolshed."

Deputy Powers laughed. "She sure did that, all right. She rigged up a sheet over the shed door so it would flop down when the door was swung open. And," he said, still laughing, "I didn't believe Mrs. Murdoch's friend when she said she'd seen a ghost— thought she was confused or something. That was my mistake, so I hope you'll pass along my apologies."

I couldn't listen to any more. Sam was going to want some answers and some explanations, and I declare, I'd about run out of both. I had the urge to get my coat and just leave—and would've if I'd had anywhere to go. So who came pushing through the door? The very one I wasn't ready to face.

"Julia?" Sam said, coming into the kitchen. "You need any help?"

"I'm just putting on another pot of coffee." Busying myself at the counter, I turned away from him. "They're having a good time in there, aren't they?"

"It's like ole home week." Sam got a bag of coffee out of the refrigerator and handed it to me. "A deputy stopped by a minute ago to show us a cap he'd found. Lloyd said it looked like one of his, but the deputy thinks a friend of yours lost it. Which was a little odd, because I didn't know you'd had a houseguest."

"Well, how could you? You haven't been around. Besides, it was just someone I used to know. She won't be coming back." I turned the faucet on full blast, noisily filling the coffeepot, hoping to cut off any further discussion on that subject. "Did you and Mr. Pickens come to a decision?"

Sam grinned, a sure sign that he was pleased with himself. "Yep, but I had a hard time convincing him. You know how he feels about supporting his family on his own. So I went into this long song and dance about how I'd been all but destitute when I first hung out my shingle and how clients were paying me with chickens and hams and so forth, none of which would pay the electric bill. And how when I wanted to get married, an uncle helped me, practically gave me the house because he was going into a nursing home. I told Pickens that I was simply passing along the help that somebody had given me, as if, you know, it was a moral obligation for me to do the same."

"My goodness," I said, touched by his story of how he'd gotten through hard times. "I didn't know all that."

"No reason for you to," Sam said, his deep blue eyes twinkling. "It wasn't exactly true, but a little white lie in a good cause never hurt anybody."

My heart lifted as I looked him straight in the eye, sharing a conspiratory smile. "I couldn't agree more." And at that instant, I felt a sense of redemptiom for all the little white lies I'd told, as well as those I had on reserve in case I ever needed to tell them.

"Anyway," Sam went on, "we got that settled and they'll move in as soon as Hazel Marie feels up to it. We were about ready to join the party here when James came in and started telling Pickens about the prowler we had last night."

"Prowler? My goodness, did you catch him?"

"No," Sam said, laughing. "It was probably an animal looking for a warm place. But James wanted Pickens to investigate, because he'd never heard of an animal that could unlock a door."

I almost said, "That door wasn't locked," but caught myself in time. I let it pass, realizing that James had been covering himself for forgetting to lock it, and that Sam understood that. As far as I was concerned, an animal looking for a warm place was the perfect explanation, door locked or not.

"Now, listen, Julia," Sam said in a more serious tone, "I've been wanting to tell you something, but I was asked not to tell anybody. Except now, with Richard out of the picture, I've been released to tell you, and only you. Can you keep a secret? I mean, a deep, dark secret?" Sam was smiling as he edged closer to me and lowered his voice.

"Why, you know I can. You wouldn't believe the secrets I've kept, and I've never revealed a one of them."

"Well," he said, taking a deep breath, "Helen came over to see me the other day—I gave her lunch because she had so much to talk about. Anyway, here's the big secret: she's going to marry Thurlow."

"No!" I widened my eyes as far as they would go. "I can't believe that."

"Well, believe it, because it's true. Her problem, however, was that Thurlow wanted her to sign a prenuptial agreement. That's what she wanted to talk to me about. I looked it over and told her she absolutely could not sign such an unfair document. It would've given her no security at all, which, frankly, I think is basically what she's looking for. That, and a free hand in fixing up that old house of his. Maybe him too. Anyway, I showed her how she could turn the tables on him."

"How? You know Thurlow likes to get the best of any deal he's involved in."

"Exactly, but I also know that Thurlow respects anyone who can get the best of him. He admires cleverness, so that's what we gave him. I worked up a prenuptial agreement for *him* to sign and, believe me, it secures her future and it covers everything she wants from him and then some, including joining a church. They've been visiting several churches to see which one would suit them both when the time comes." Sam stopped and laughed under his breath. "Helen told me a minute ago that Thurlow scanned the agreement, then grabbed a pen and said, 'Where's the dotted line?' Apparently, he is totally smitten and delighted with his savvy future bride."

"My goodness," I said. "I don't know which floors me more: Helen marrying Thurlow or Thurlow going to church."

"Well, it won't be the First Presbyterian. Helen said it reminded her too much of Richard, and besides, Ledbetter really turned her off when he lit into her about divorcing Richard. Told her it was cruel and inhumane to hit a man when he was down and in prison. So she waited, expecting an amiable divorce when Richard got out, which he'd apparently agreed to.

"Instead, though," Sam went on with a frown, "Richard got both early release and religion at the same time. Absolutely no divorce. He intended to oppose it every step of the way, including a public recounting of her infidelity while he was, as he said, rotting in jail. She would've gotten her divorce, of course, but it would've been a three-ring circus."

"Oh my," I said, "and Helen hates public spectacles."

Sam smiled ruefully and shook his head. "It was already getting to be a mess with Richard pestering her all the time and her having to sneak around to see Thurlow."

"Well, have you ever," I mumbled; then, thinking that this was the opportune time to cover myself, I went on. "Do you suppose Richard knew about her and Thurlow? I mean, he died so close to Thurlow's house."

"Without a doubt, he knew. Ever since his release, Richard had been begging her to get back together, then he started following her. Stalking her was more like it. So he knew, and I'll tell you something else. I checked out Miss Petty's toolshed right after the deputies removed his body, and there was evidence that he had been watching Thurlow's house through a knothole in the wall." Sam leaned against the counter, watching me ladle out scoops of coffee. "I guess he saw more than he could handle."

"That is just amazing," I said, looking up at him with an expression of wonder. "And you were brilliant to figure that out when even the deputies missed it. I'm so proud of you."

I stepped away as a few more thoughts sprang to mind. "I guess Richard should be commended for making Helen a widow instead of a divorcée. He certainly passed on in the nick of time." I smiled, switched on the coffeepot, and went on. "And you know something else, Sam? Now I understand why Thurlow kept bringing up Miss Petty's name, implying that she was seeing Richard and might've instigated his heart attack. It was his way of steering suspicion away from Helen." I just shook my head at the ins and outs of it all. "But I will never understand how Helen could fall for him—they are such opposites in every way you can think of."

"Well," Sam said, somewhat wryly, "let's just say that she sees the potential in him."

"Why, Sam," I said, looking at him with a teasing smile, "you don't mean to imply that Helen is materialistic, do you?" Before he could respond, I thought of something else. "I've often wondered whether Thurlow had a hand in Richard's investment scheme and maybe ended up with all that missing money everybody talks about. That could've been part of what Richard was doing sneaking around Thurlow's house—he wanted his wife and his money. Or rather, everybody else's money, which he stole from them. From us, I mean."

"Could be," Sam said, as his arm slid around my shoulders, "but I expect we'll never know, and to tell the truth, I don't especially care."

As a burst of laughter rang out from the living room, Sam's arm tightened around me. He pulled me closer. "They're having such a good time in there, they won't miss us. Let's go to my house. Just you and me."

I melted into him. "Right now?"

"Right now." Sam began to nuzzle my neck, and frankly, it was a whole lot better than watching somebody else's neck get nuzzled.

My breath quickened. "Where's James?"

"Off courtin' somewhere, which is exactly what I have in mind."

⌒᛫⌒

Later that night, after Sam had brought me home, supper had been cleared away, and everybody was deep in sleep, I filled a toothbrush glass in the bathroom. Then carefully tiptoeing across the hall, carrying the glass and a flashlight, I slipped into Lloyd's room.

Placing the flashlight on Lloyd's desk so that the beam cast a dim glow in the room without shining directly on him, I walked over to his bed. Standing there and looking down at that boy, my heart filled with love, and, I admit, some sadness too. Sadness because he'd been hidden from me for the first nine years of his life. I'd missed seeing him in his cradle, holding and rocking him as an infant, as I was getting to do with his sisters. I'd missed seeing him take his first steps, teaching him to read, and watching him grow during those years when I'd had no knowledge of his existence.

I sighed because, considering who his father had been, it was just as well I hadn't known. I probably wouldn't have appreciated anything about the child.

As I stood watching, I saw how Lloyd was snuggled down under the covers against the night chill—it's not healthy to sleep in a hot room, you know. His fine hair was splayed out on the pillow, and all I could see was the top of his head. That was all right. It was all I needed.

I knelt down beside him, then hesitated. Being neither an ordained minister nor a priest, I'd not been instructed in the various sacramental methods. Should I pour water on his head or just drip it on? Either way, he'd end up sleeping on a wet pillow.

So, ever mindful of Lloyd's health and comfort, I compromised. Dipping my fingers in the glass, I flicked a few drops of water on his head. "I baptize you," I whispered, "in the name of the Father and of the Son and of the Holy Spirit. Amen."

If I'd known how to make the sign of the cross, I'd have done that too. But I didn't, so not wanting to mess up a sacred rite, I left it off. Then, rising with difficulty—I spilled water all down my gown as I stood up—I asked the Lord to bless my pitiful and

310 ~ Ann B. Ross

unofficial ceremony as a stopgap until a better one could be arranged. Then, with my wet gown clinging to me, I went on to ask the Lord to accept my private effort in the spirit in which it was offered and to protect this child throughout his life, which I fervently hoped would be long and blessed with health and prosperity.

Then I hurryied back to my room, changed my gown, and went to bed, relieved that there were no more misunderstandings, no more secrets to hide, and no more toolsheds to be visited. I could sleep, secure in the knowledge that Sam would soon be with me, the Pickenses would be well settled not too far away, and Lloyd was fully, if somewhat unconventionally, baptized.

Sighing with satisfaction, I pulled up the covers and closed my eyes—everyone in my family was safe, except . . . my eyes popped open—Mr. Pickens!

Well, I thought, I'll have to think of something else to put him right. There was no way in the world I was going to approach that man in the dead of night with a glass of water in hand.